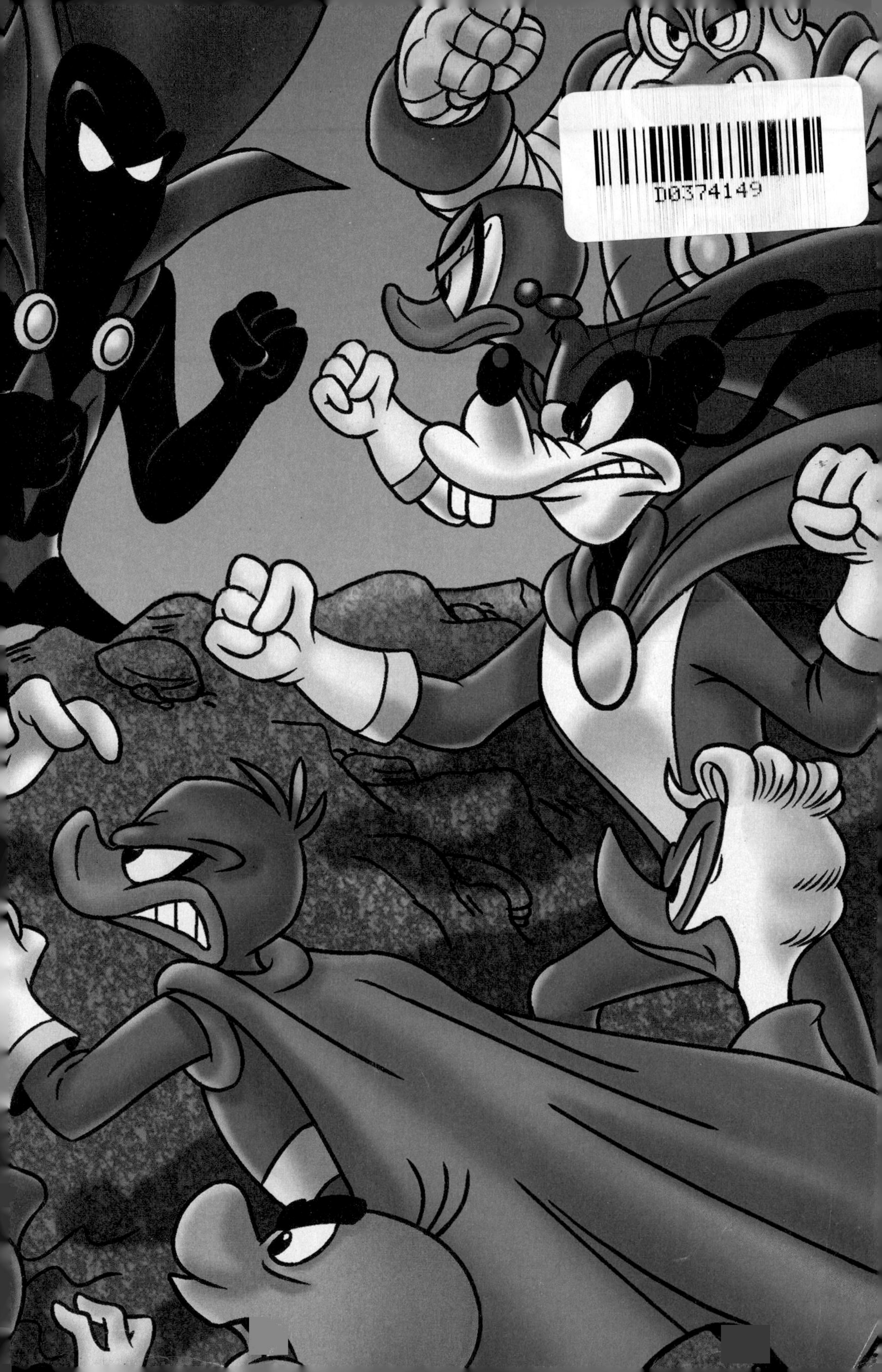

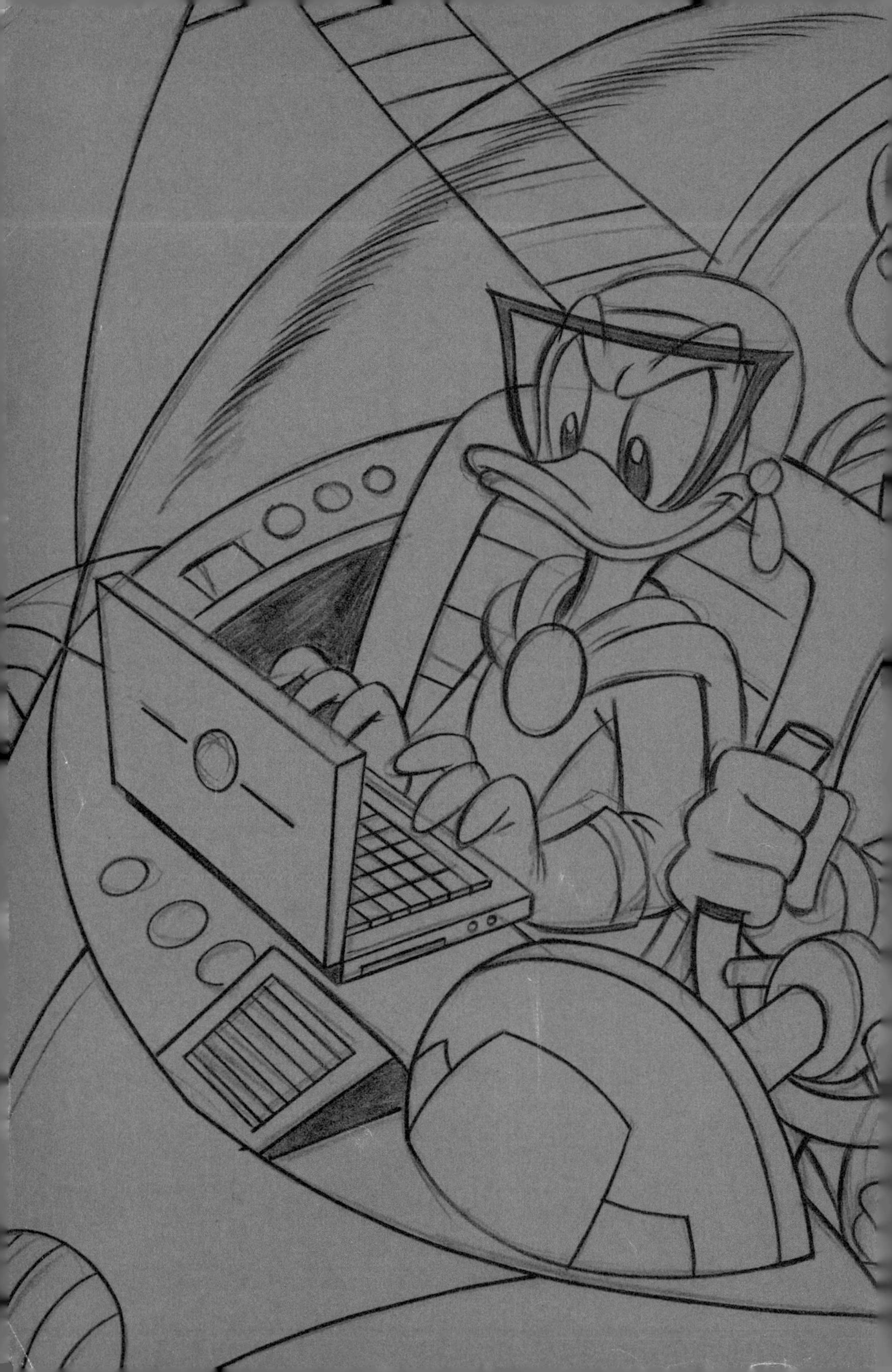

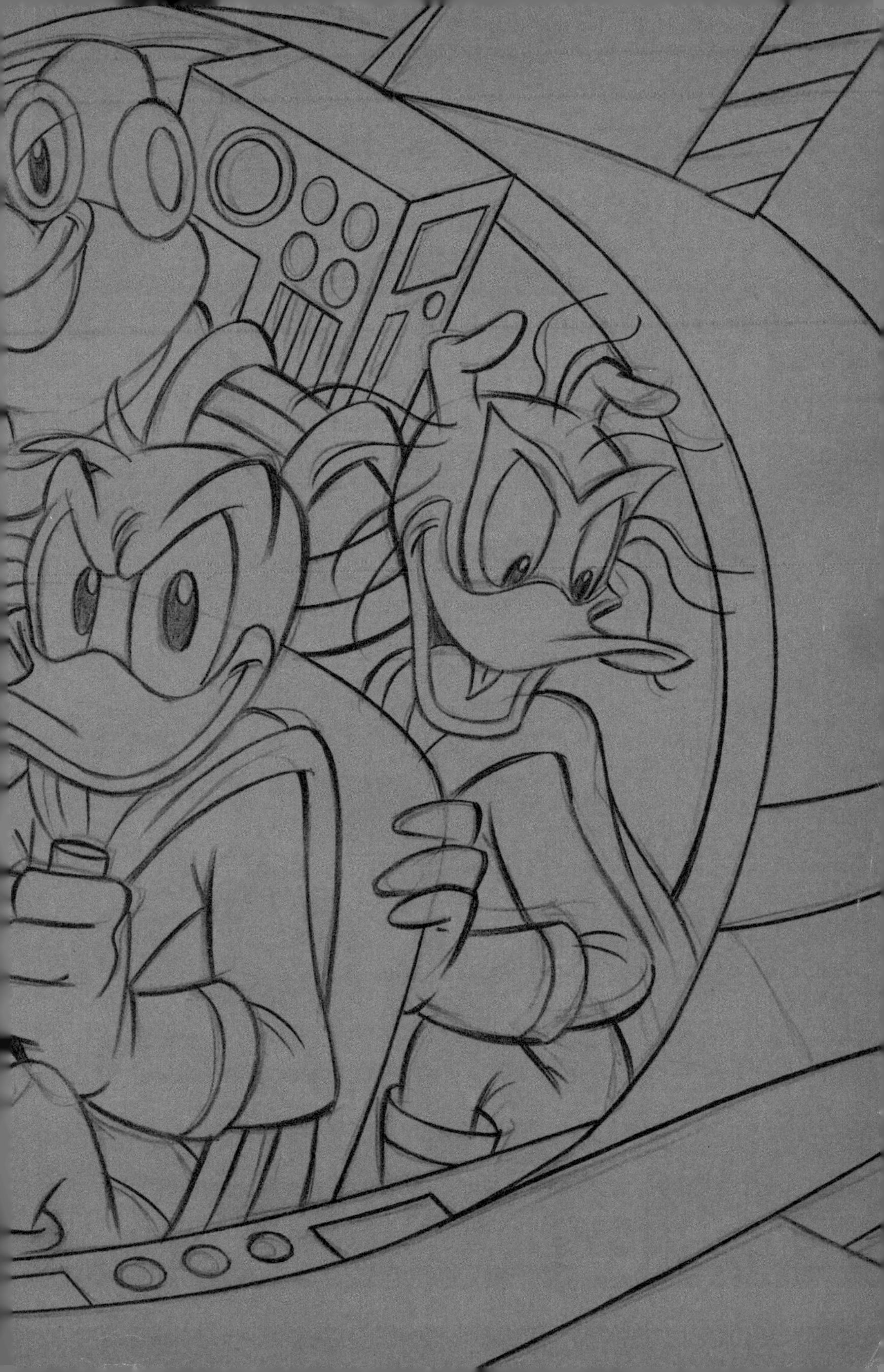

DISNEY'S
HERO SQUAD
ULTRAHEROES

ROSS RICHIE
chief executive officer

MARK WAID
editor-in-chief

ADAM FORTIER
vice president,
publishing

CHIP MOSHER
marketing director

MATT GAGNON
managing editor

JENNY CHRISTOPHER
sales director

FIRST EDITION: JANUARY 2010

10 9 8 7 6 5 4 3 2 1
PRINTED BY WORLD COLOR PRESS, INC.
ST-ROMUALD, QC, CANADA.

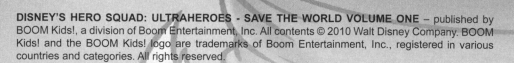

DISNEY'S HERO SQUAD: ULTRAHEROES - SAVE THE WORLD VOLUME ONE – published by
BOOM Kids!, a division of Boom Entertainment, Inc. All contents © 2010 Walt Disney Company. BOOM
Kids! and the BOOM Kids! logo are trademarks of Boom Entertainment, Inc., registered in various
countries and categories. All rights reserved.

Office of publication: 6310 San Vicente Blvd Ste 404, Los Angeles, CA 90048-5457.

A catalog record for this book is available from OCLC and on our website www.boom-kids.com on the
Librarians page.

WRITERS:
RICCARDO SECCHI, ALESSANDRO FERRARI & GIORGIO SALATI

ARTISTS:
STEFANO TURCONI, ANTONELLO DALENA, ETTORE GULA & EMILIO URBANO

EDITOR:
AARON SPARROW

COVER:
STEFANO TURCONI

HARDCOVER CASE WRAP:
MAGIC EYE STUDIOS

TRANSLATOR:
SAIDA TEMOFONTE

LETTERER:
DERON BENNETT

SPECIAL THANKS:
JESSE POST, LAUREN KRESSEL & ELENA GARBO

ASSISTANT EDITOR:
CHRISTOPHER BURNS

WITHDRAWN

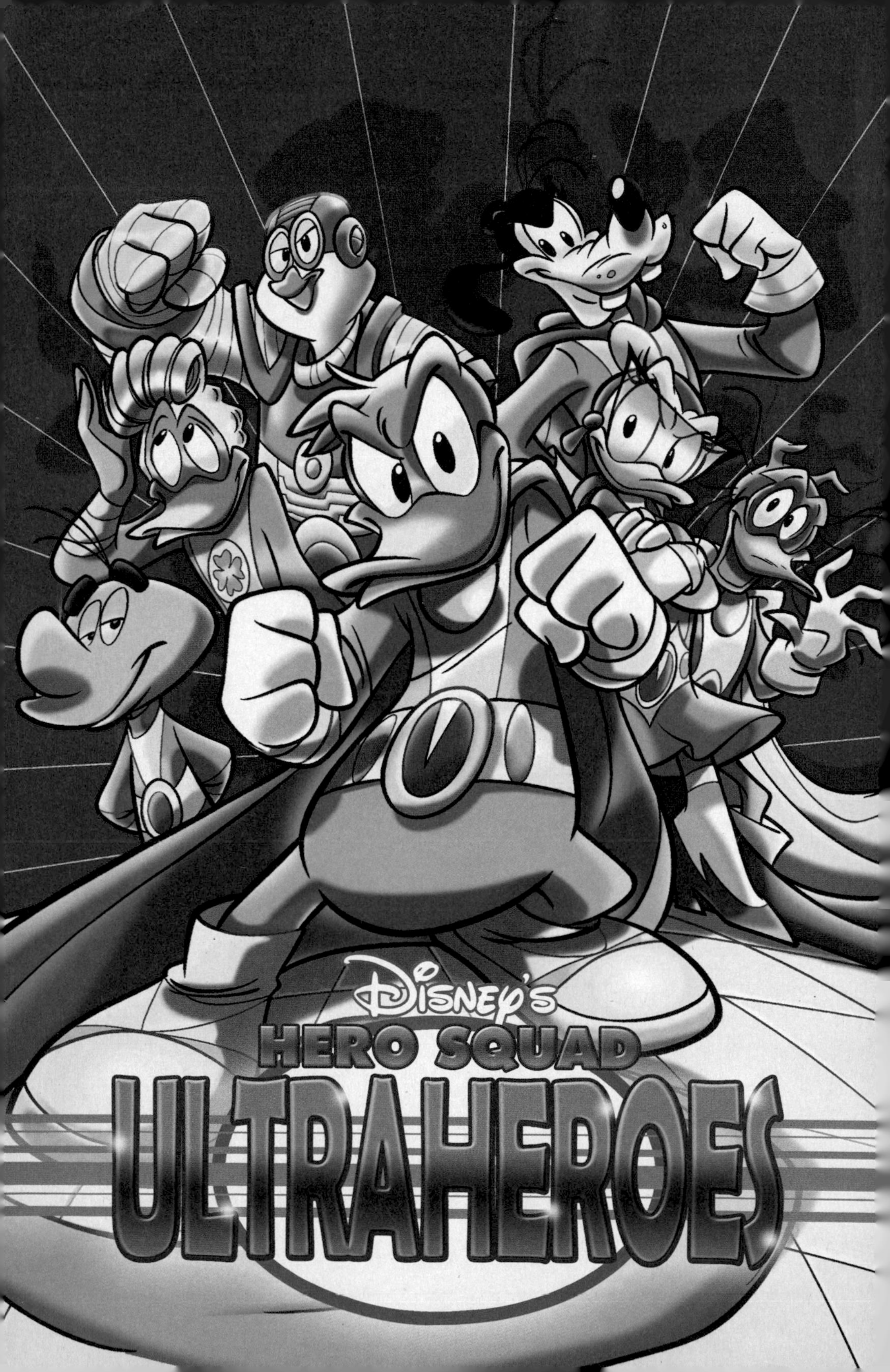
DISNEY'S
HERO SQUAD
ULTRAHEROES

QUICK, BEFORE HE HEARS US!

ON A QUIET NIGHT IN DUCKBURG, SCROOGE MCDUCK WAS ABOUT TO GET SOME UNEXPECTED VISITORS...

GO!

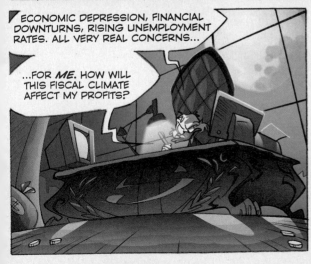

ECONOMIC DEPRESSION, FINANCIAL DOWNTURNS, RISING UNEMPLOYMENT RATES. ALL VERY REAL CONCERNS...

...FOR *ME*. HOW WILL THIS FISCAL CLIMATE AFFECT MY PROFITS?

?

≑CLICK≑ IN SPORTS TODAY, DUCKBURG VERSUS REAL DUCK AND REAL DUCK ≑CLICK≑

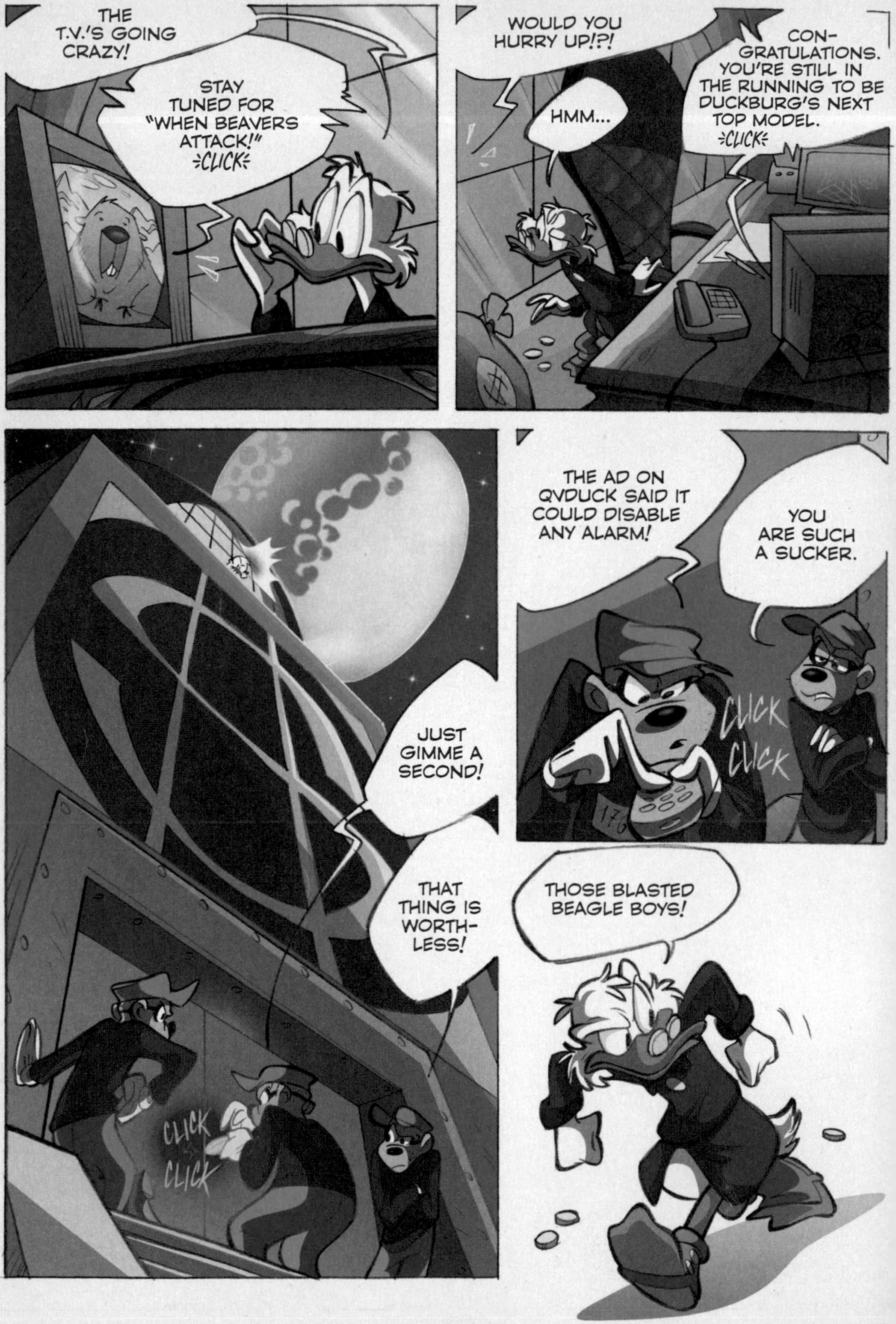
THE T.V.'S GOING CRAZY!
STAY TUNED FOR "WHEN BEAVERS ATTACK!" CLICK
WOULD YOU HURRY UP!?!
HMM...
CON-GRATULATIONS. YOU'RE STILL IN THE RUNNING TO BE DUCKBURG'S NEXT TOP MODEL. CLICK
JUST GIMME A SECOND!
THAT THING IS WORTH-LESS!
CLICK CLICK
THE AD ON QVDUCK SAID IT COULD DISABLE ANY ALARM!
YOU ARE SUCH A SUCKER.
CLICK CLICK
THOSE BLASTED BEAGLE BOYS!

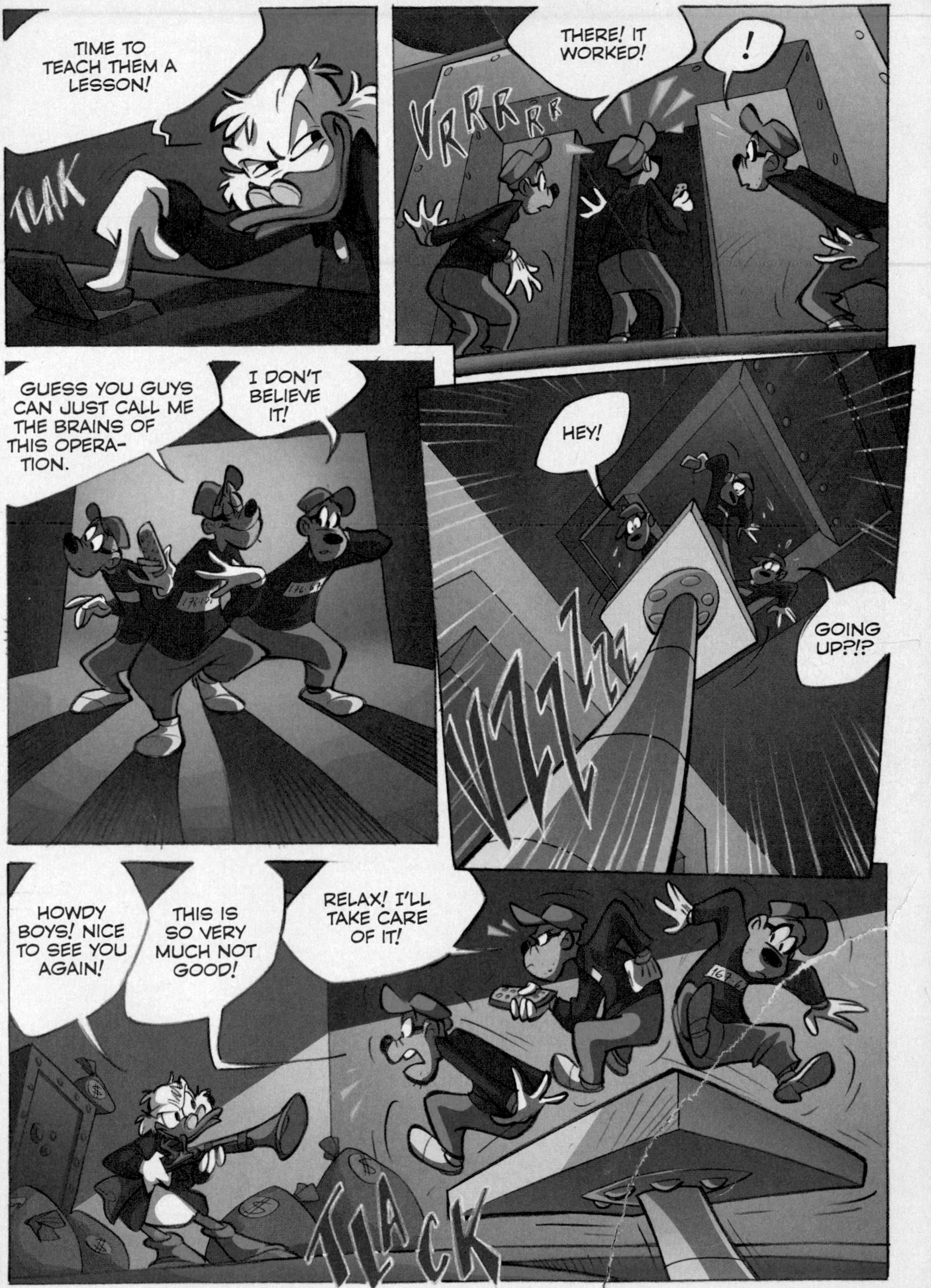
TIME TO TEACH THEM A LESSON!
TLAK
THERE! IT WORKED!
!
VRRRRR
GUESS YOU GUYS CAN JUST CALL ME THE BRAINS OF THIS OPERA-TION.
I DON'T BELIEVE IT!
HEY!
VZZZZZZ
GOING UP?!?
HOWDY BOYS! NICE TO SEE YOU AGAIN!
THIS IS SO VERY MUCH NOT GOOD!
RELAX! I'LL TAKE CARE OF IT!
TLACK

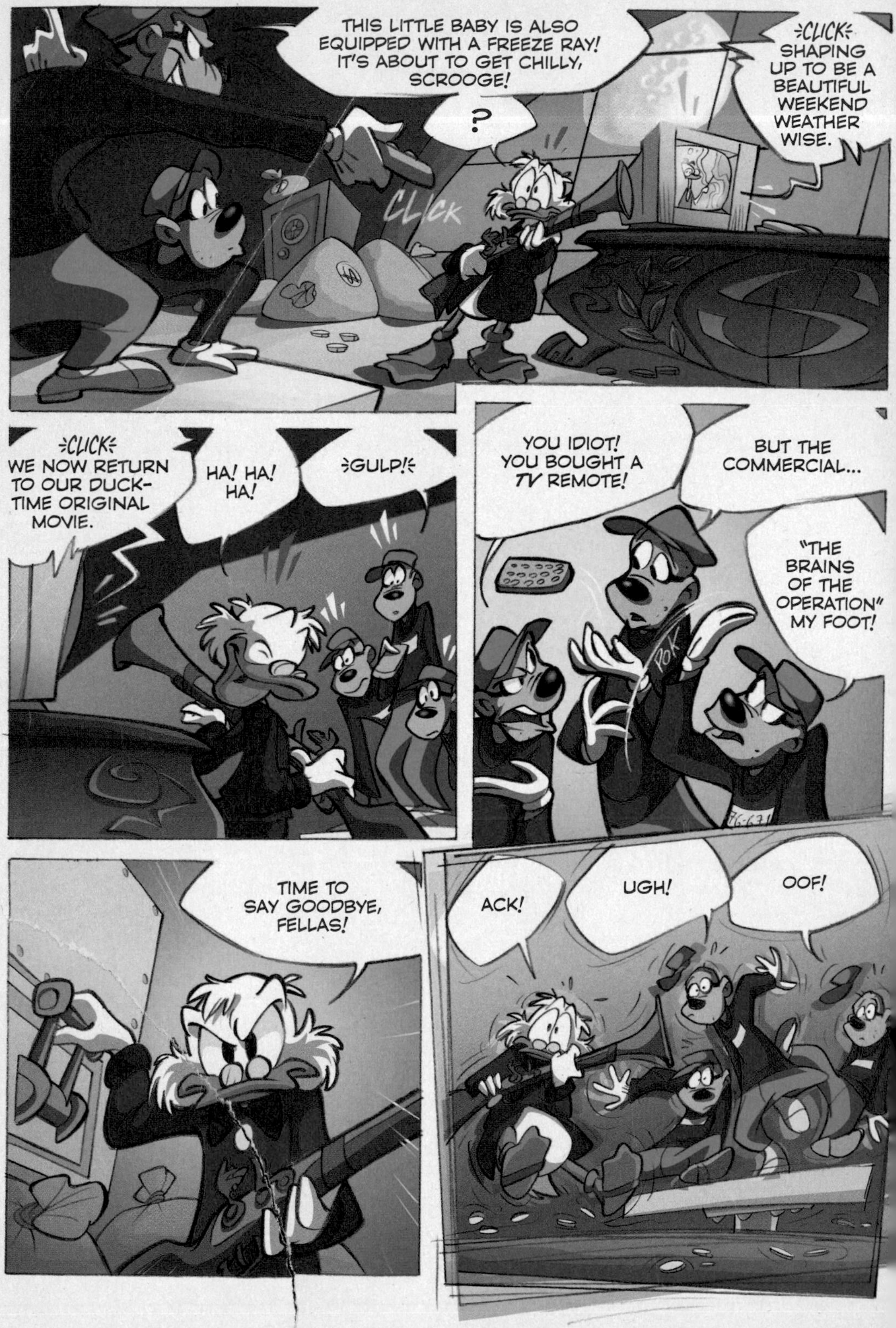
THIS LITTLE BABY IS ALSO EQUIPPED WITH A FREEZE RAY! IT'S ABOUT TO GET CHILLY, SCROOGE!
?
CLICK
CLICK SHAPING UP TO BE A BEAUTIFUL WEEKEND WEATHER WISE.
CLICK WE NOW RETURN TO OUR DUCK-TIME ORIGINAL MOVIE.
HA! HA! HA!
GULP!
YOU IDIOT! YOU BOUGHT A TV REMOTE!
BUT THE COMMERCIAL...
"THE BRAINS OF THE OPERATION" MY FOOT!
POK
TIME TO SAY GOODBYE, FELLAS!
ACK!
UGH!
OOF!

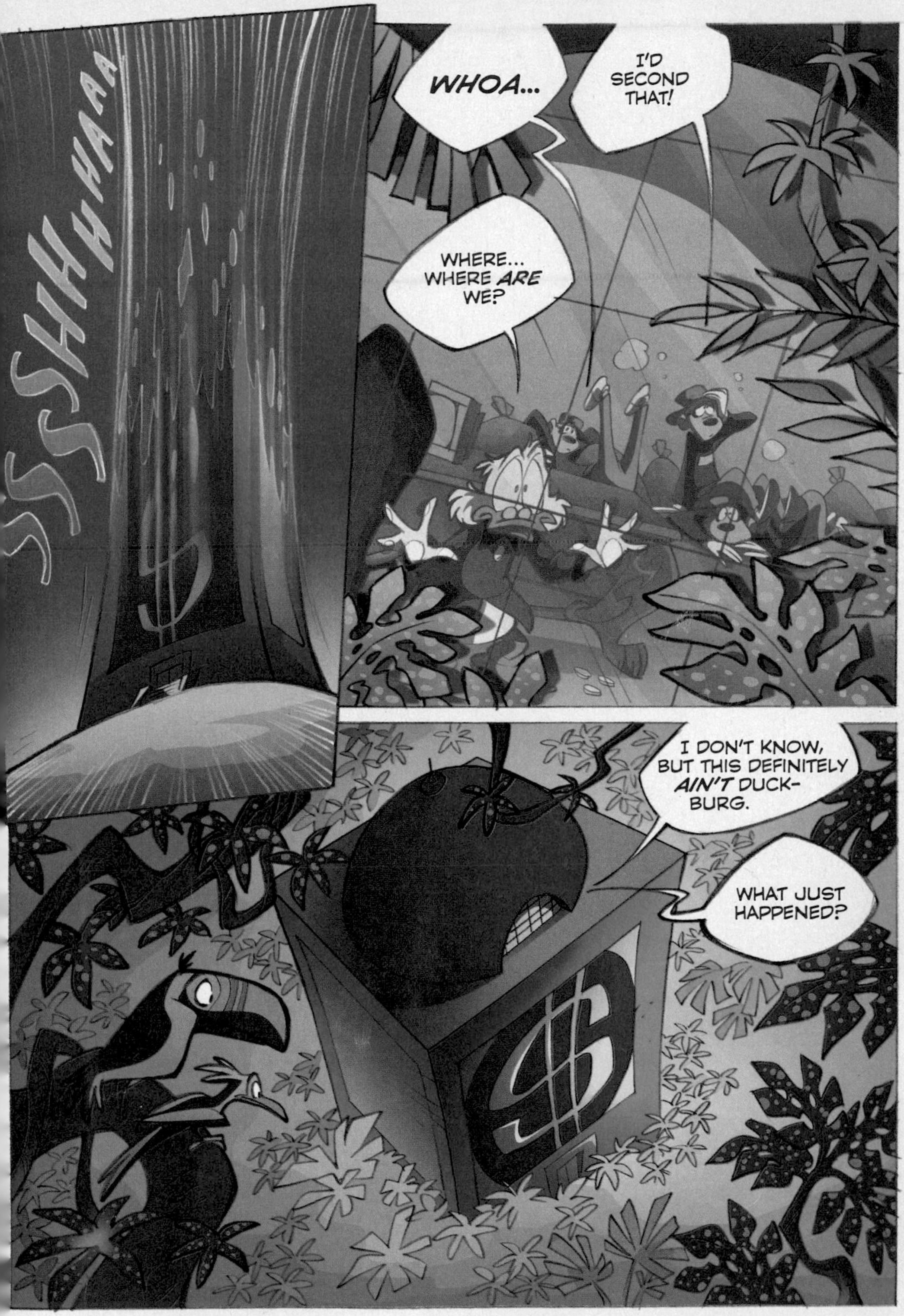
SSSHHHHHAAA
WHOA...
I'D SECOND THAT!
WHERE... WHERE *ARE* WE?
I DON'T KNOW, BUT THIS DEFINITELY *AIN'T* DUCK-BURG.
WHAT JUST HAPPENED?

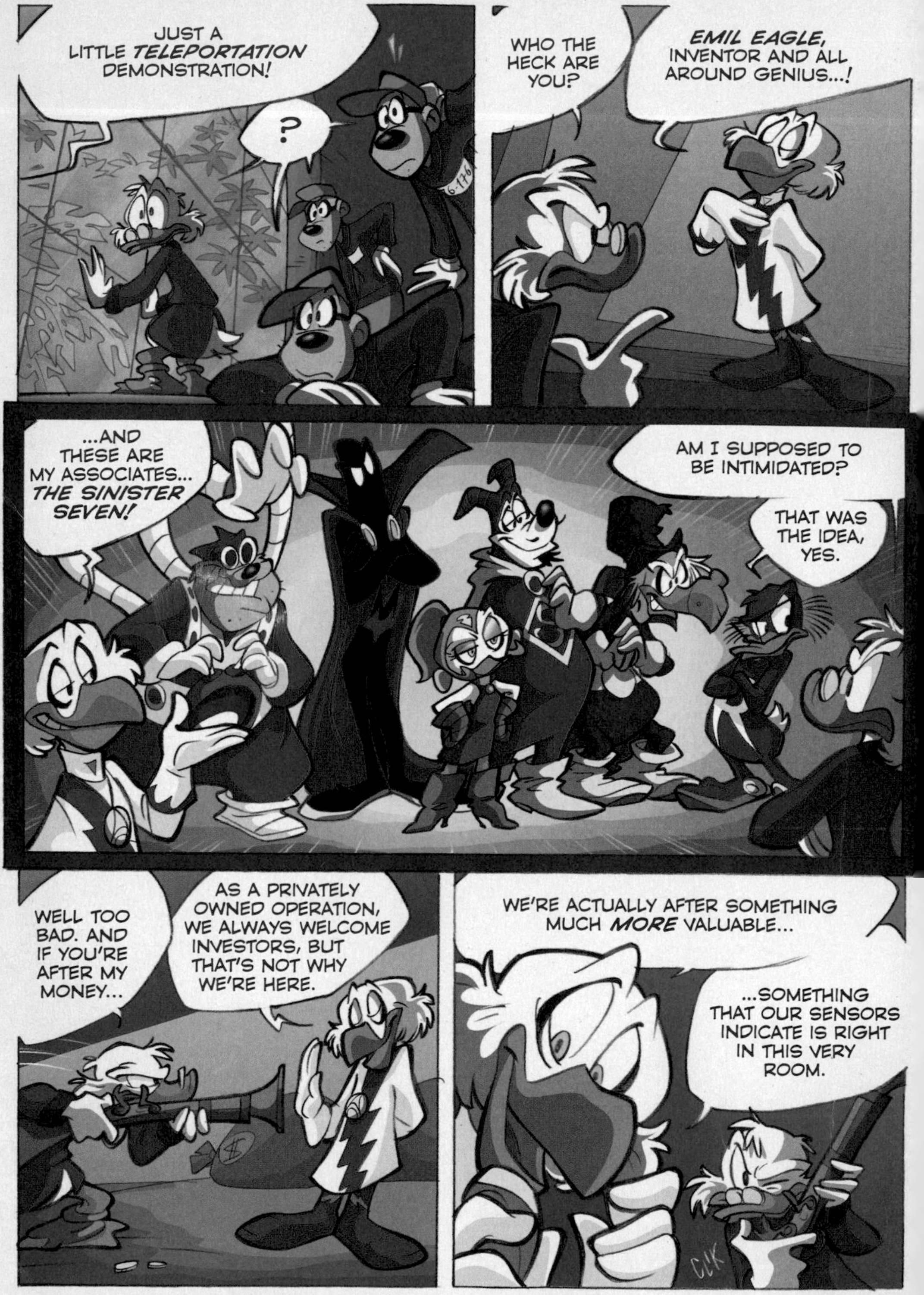
JUST A LITTLE TELEPORTATION DEMONSTRATION!
?
WHO THE HECK ARE YOU?
EMIL EAGLE, INVENTOR AND ALL AROUND GENIUS...!
...AND THESE ARE MY ASSOCIATES... THE SINISTER SEVEN!
AM I SUPPOSED TO BE INTIMIDATED?
THAT WAS THE IDEA, YES.
WELL TOO BAD. AND IF YOU'RE AFTER MY MONEY...
AS A PRIVATELY OWNED OPERATION, WE ALWAYS WELCOME INVESTORS, BUT THAT'S NOT WHY WE'RE HERE.
WE'RE ACTUALLY AFTER SOMETHING MUCH MORE VALUABLE...
...SOMETHING THAT OUR SENSORS INDICATE IS RIGHT IN THIS VERY ROOM.
CLK

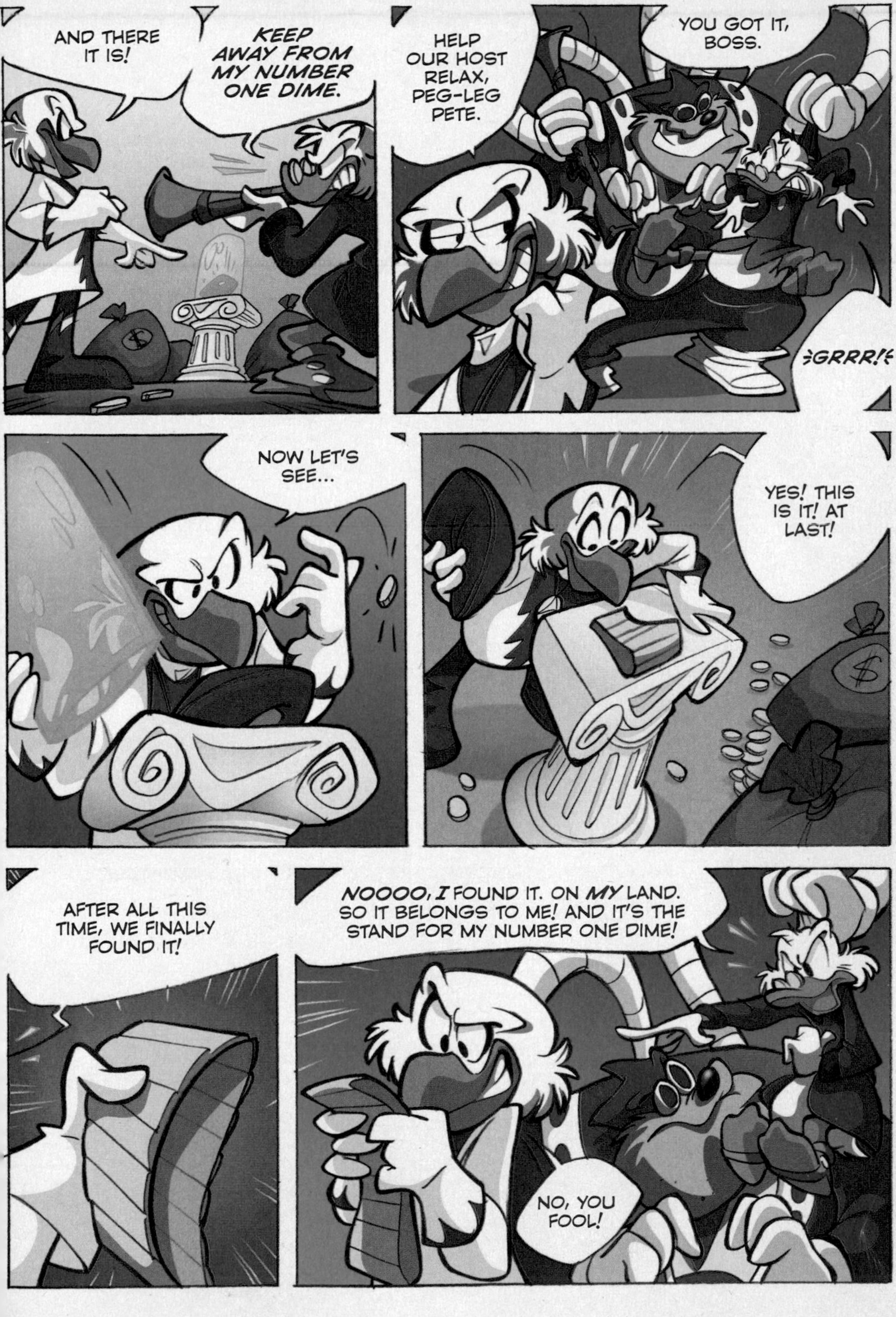
AND THERE IT IS!
KEEP AWAY FROM MY NUMBER ONE DIME.
HELP OUR HOST RELAX, PEG-LEG PETE.
YOU GOT IT, BOSS.
GRRR!
NOW LET'S SEE...
YES! THIS IS IT! AT LAST!
AFTER ALL THIS TIME, WE FINALLY FOUND IT!
NOOOO, I FOUND IT. ON MY LAND. SO IT BELONGS TO ME! AND IT'S THE STAND FOR MY NUMBER ONE DIME!
NO, YOU FOOL!

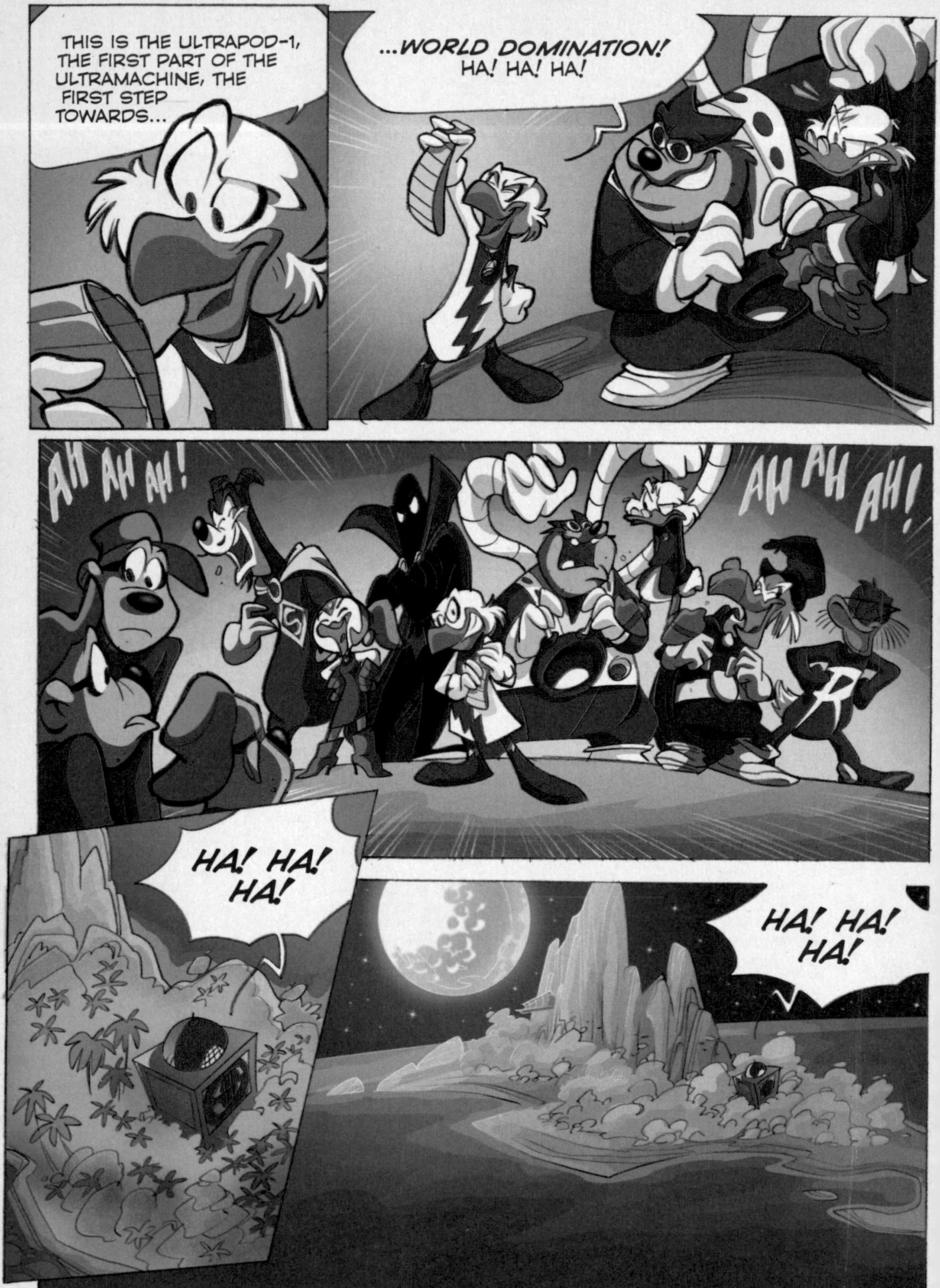
THIS IS THE ULTRAPOD-1, THE FIRST PART OF THE ULTRAMACHINE, THE FIRST STEP TOWARDS...
...WORLD DOMINATION! HA! HA! HA!
AH AH AH!
AH AH AH AH!
HA! HA! HA!
HA! HA! HA!

CHAPTER ONE

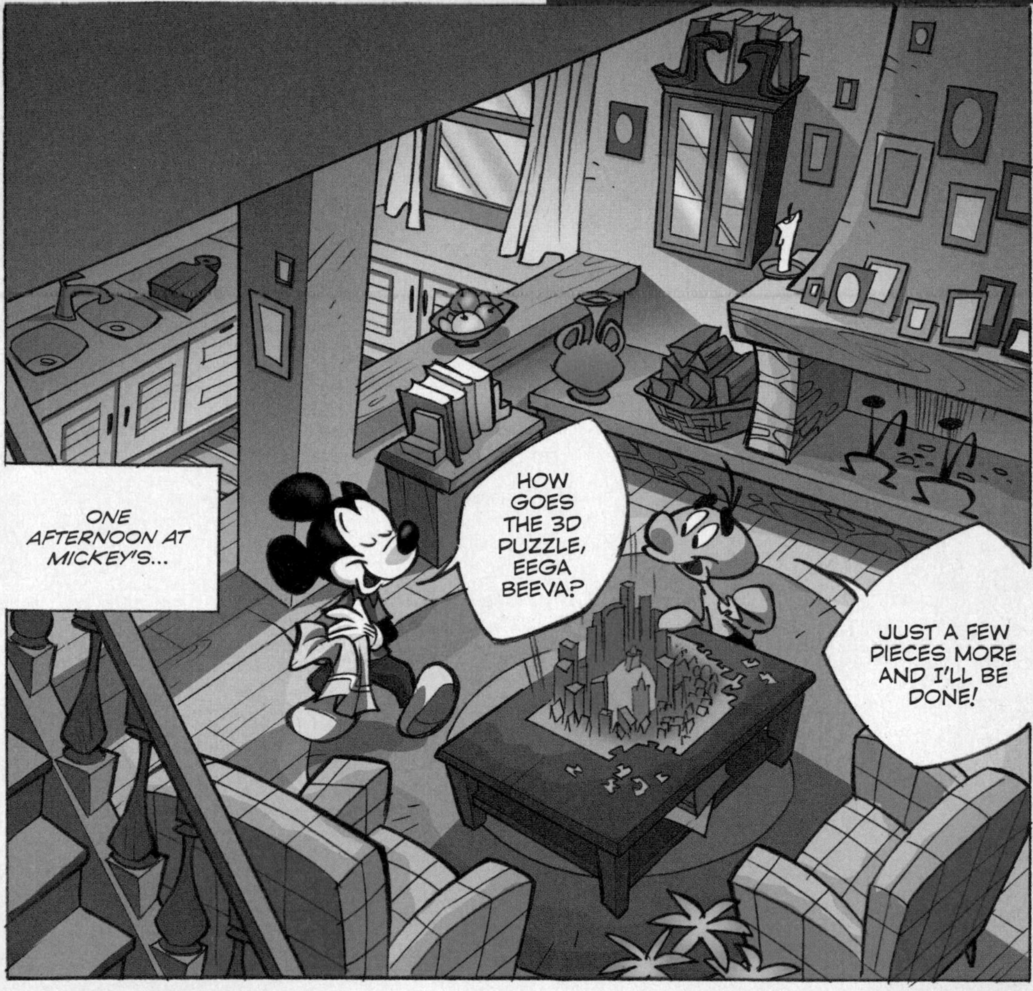
ONE AFTERNOON AT MICKEY'S...
HOW GOES THE 3D PUZZLE, EEGA BEEVA?
JUST A FEW PIECES MORE AND I'LL BE DONE!

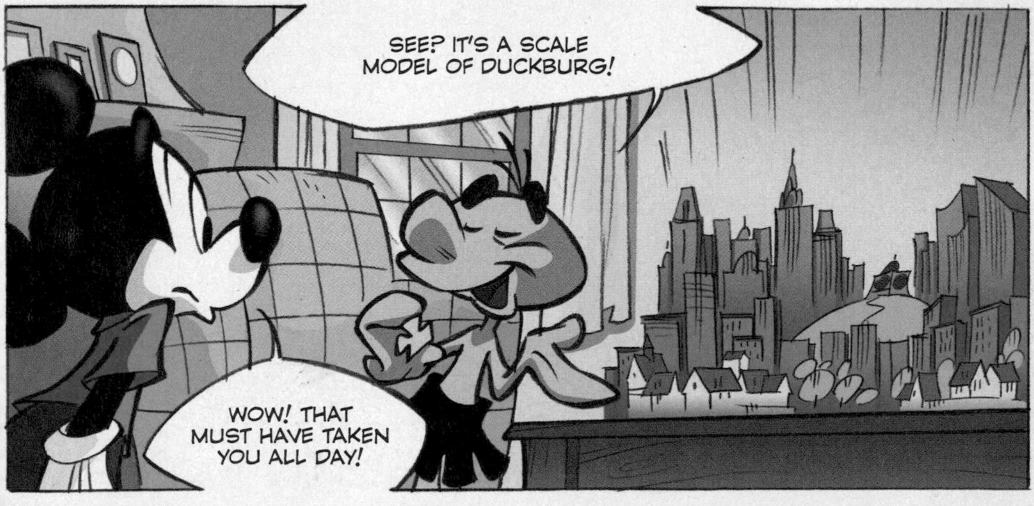
SEE? IT'S A SCALE MODEL OF DUCKBURG!
WOW! THAT MUST HAVE TAKEN YOU ALL DAY!

NO. JUST AN HOUR.

IMPRESSIVE!

AFTER DUCKBURG, I THINK I'LL DO ANOTHER CITY, LIKE ST. CANARD, IF YOU WANT TO HELP!

SOUNDS FUN!

SPEAKING OF DUCKBURG...HAVE YOU HEARD ABOUT THE DISAPPEARANCE OF SCROOGE MCDUCK AND HIS MONEY BIN?

OF COURSE!

YOU COME FROM THE FUTURE*, DO YOU HAVE ANY IDEA HOW... HUH?!

SCROOGE MCDUCK VANISHES

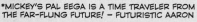

*MICKEY'S PAL EEGA IS A TIME TRAVELER FROM THE FAR-FLUNG FUTURE! – FUTURISTIC AARON

DRIIIIN

DRIIIIN

DRIIIIN

DR

DRIII

ALL RIGHT, ALREADY! I'M COMING!

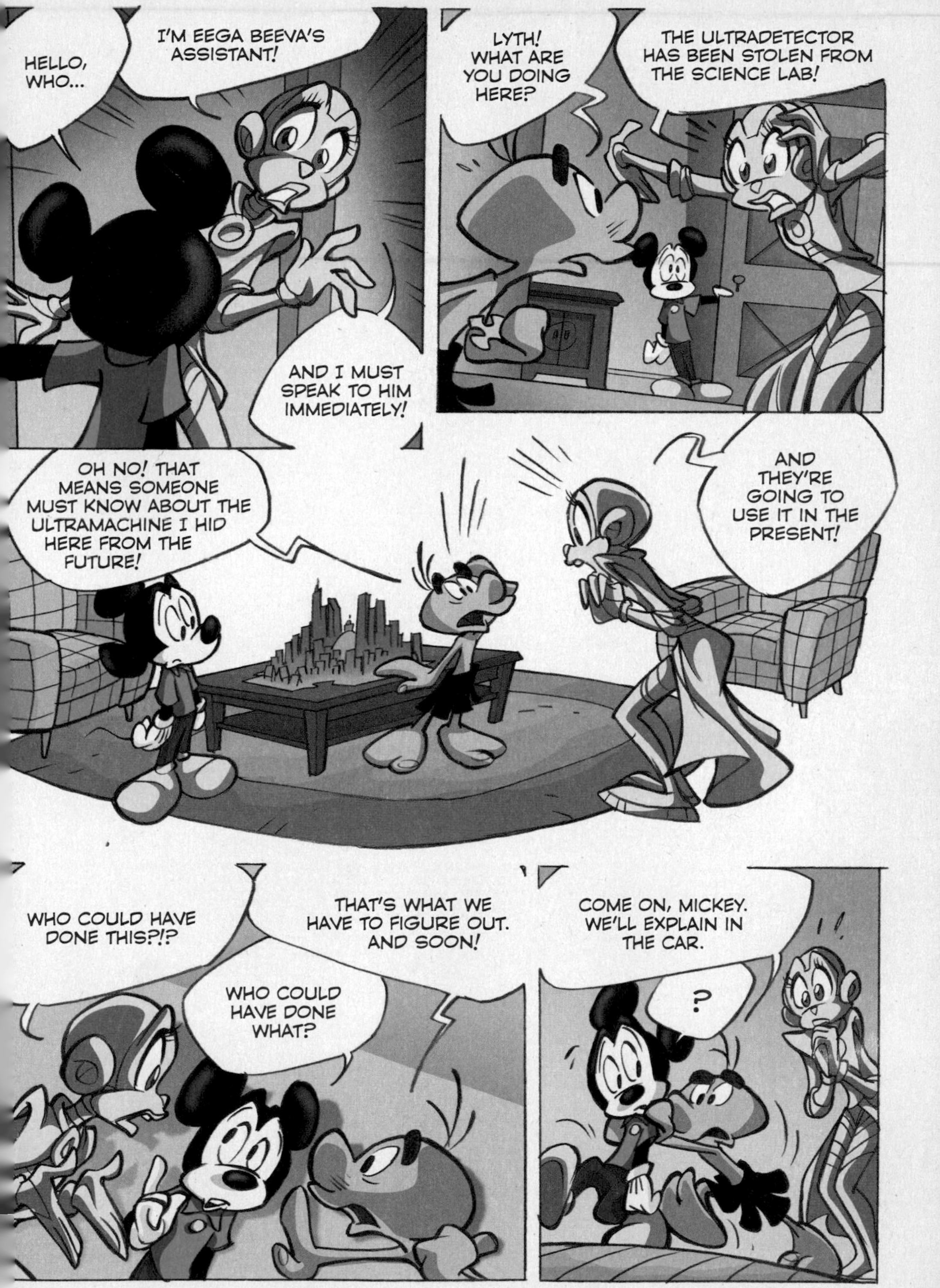
HELLO, WHO...
I'M EEGA BEEVA'S ASSISTANT!
AND I MUST SPEAK TO HIM IMMEDIATELY!
LYTH! WHAT ARE YOU DOING HERE?
THE ULTRADETECTOR HAS BEEN STOLEN FROM THE SCIENCE LAB!
OH NO! THAT MEANS SOMEONE MUST KNOW ABOUT THE ULTRAMACHINE I HID HERE FROM THE FUTURE!
AND THEY'RE GOING TO USE IT IN THE PRESENT!
WHO COULD HAVE DONE THIS?!?
THAT'S WHAT WE HAVE TO FIGURE OUT. AND SOON!
WHO COULD HAVE DONE WHAT?
COME ON, MICKEY. WE'LL EXPLAIN IN THE CAR.
?

OKAY. WE'RE IN THE CAR...

THEN GET US TO DUCKBURG!

EMERGENCY PROCEDURES HAVE ALREADY BEEN ACTIVATED!

THEN IT WON'T BE LONG...

?

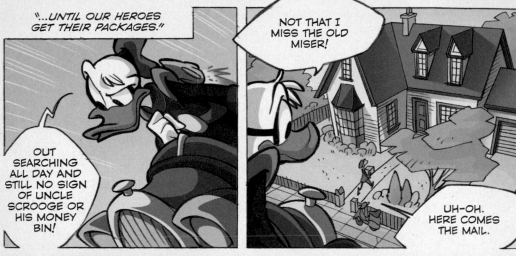

"...UNTIL OUR HEROES GET THEIR PACKAGES."

OUT SEARCHING ALL DAY AND STILL NO SIGN OF UNCLE SCROOGE OR HIS MONEY BIN!

NOT THAT I MISS THE OLD MISER!

UH-OH. HERE COMES THE MAIL.

DING DONG

*DONALD DONS A CAPE + TIGHTS TO DEFEND DUCKBURG AS THE DUCK AVENGER! – AVERAGE AARON

TIME FOR THE DUCK AVENGER TO TURN BACK INTO DONALD DUCK!*

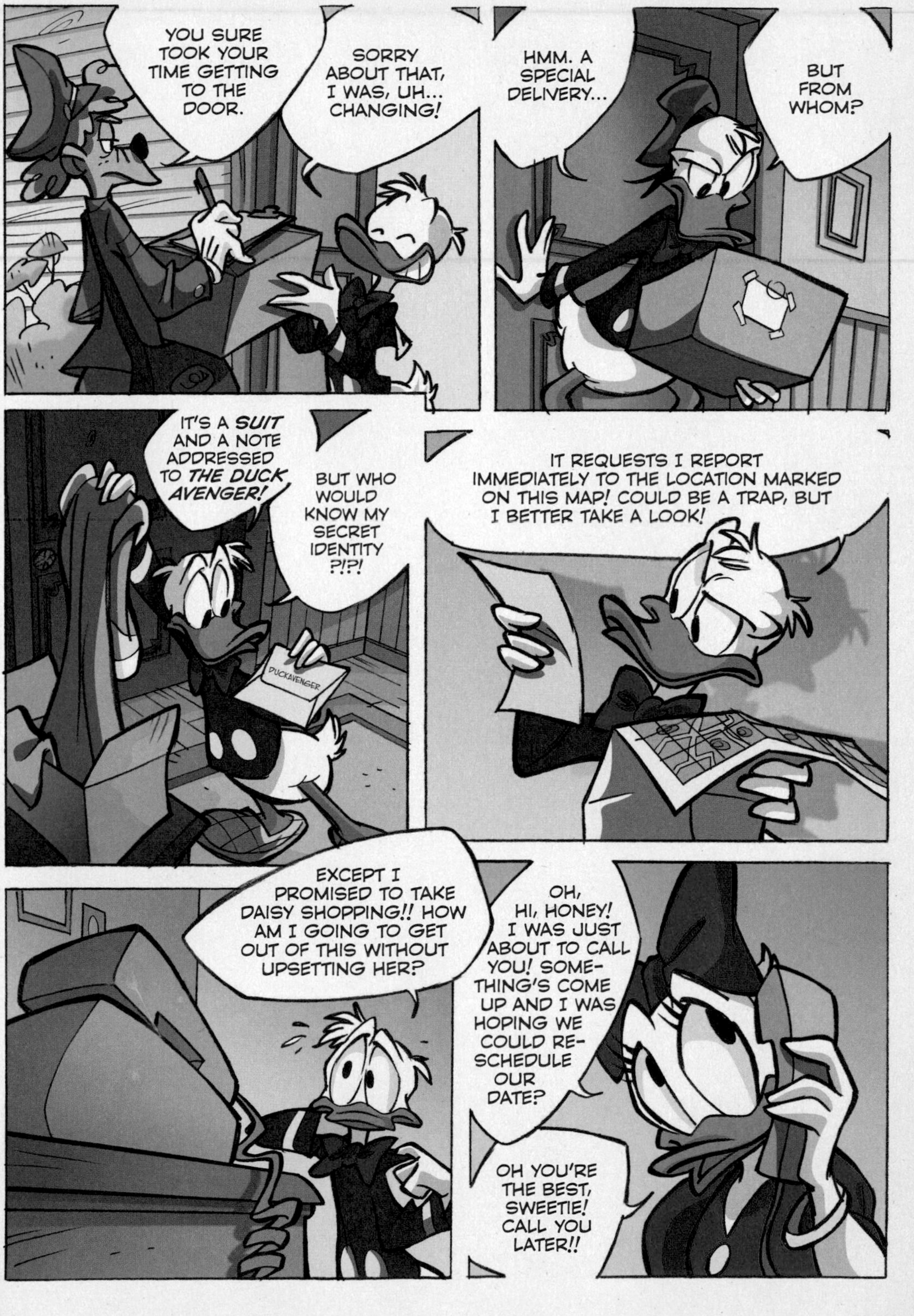

YOU SURE TOOK YOUR TIME GETTING TO THE DOOR.
SORRY ABOUT THAT, I WAS, UH... CHANGING!
HMM. A SPECIAL DELIVERY...
BUT FROM WHOM?
IT'S A SUIT AND A NOTE ADDRESSED TO THE DUCK AVENGER!
DUCKAVENGER
BUT WHO WOULD KNOW MY SECRET IDENTITY ?!?!
IT REQUESTS I REPORT IMMEDIATELY TO THE LOCATION MARKED ON THIS MAP! COULD BE A TRAP, BUT I BETTER TAKE A LOOK!
EXCEPT I PROMISED TO TAKE DAISY SHOPPING!! HOW AM I GOING TO GET OUT OF THIS WITHOUT UPSETTING HER?
OH, HI, HONEY! I WAS JUST ABOUT TO CALL YOU! SOMETHING'S COME UP AND I WAS HOPING WE COULD RESCHEDULE OUR DATE?
OH YOU'RE THE BEST, SWEETIE! CALL YOU LATER!!

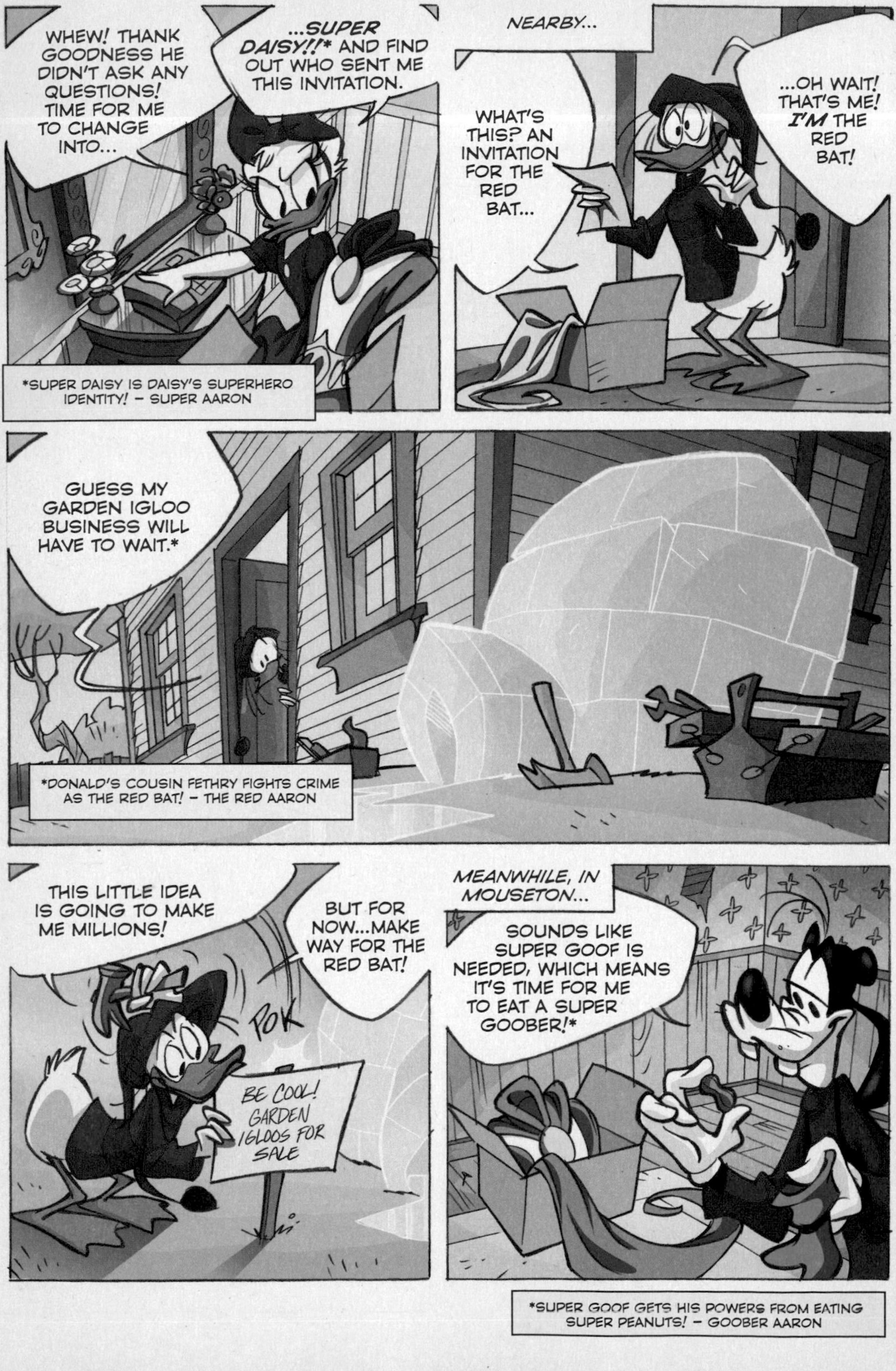
WHEW! THANK GOODNESS HE DIDN'T ASK ANY QUESTIONS! TIME FOR ME TO CHANGE INTO...
...SUPER DAISY!!* AND FIND OUT WHO SENT ME THIS INVITATION.
*SUPER DAISY IS DAISY'S SUPERHERO IDENTITY! – SUPER AARON
NEARBY...
WHAT'S THIS? AN INVITATION FOR THE RED BAT...
...OH WAIT! THAT'S ME! I'M THE RED BAT!
GUESS MY GARDEN IGLOO BUSINESS WILL HAVE TO WAIT.*
*DONALD'S COUSIN FETHRY FIGHTS CRIME AS THE RED BAT! – THE RED AARON
THIS LITTLE IDEA IS GOING TO MAKE ME MILLIONS!
BUT FOR NOW...MAKE WAY FOR THE RED BAT!
POK
BE COOL! GARDEN IGLOOS FOR SALE
MEANWHILE, IN MOUSETON...
SOUNDS LIKE SUPER GOOF IS NEEDED, WHICH MEANS IT'S TIME FOR ME TO EAT A SUPER GOOBER!*
*SUPER GOOF GETS HIS POWERS FROM EATING SUPER PEANUTS! – GOOBER AARON

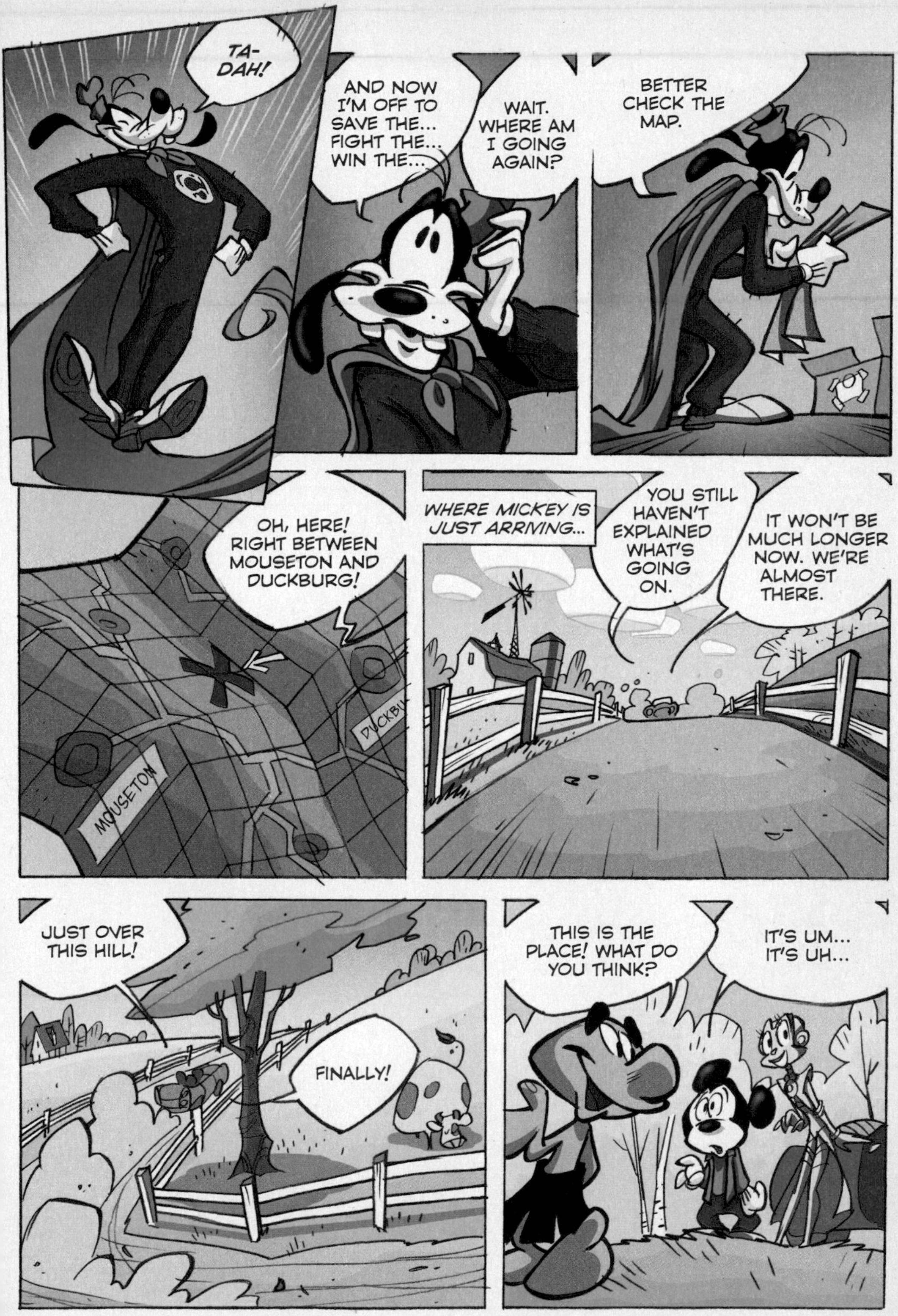
TA-DAH!
AND NOW I'M OFF TO SAVE THE... FIGHT THE... WIN THE...
WAIT. WHERE AM I GOING AGAIN?
BETTER CHECK THE MAP.
OH, HERE! RIGHT BETWEEN MOUSETON AND DUCKBURG!
MOUSETON
WHERE MICKEY IS JUST ARRIVING...
YOU STILL HAVEN'T EXPLAINED WHAT'S GOING ON.
IT WON'T BE MUCH LONGER NOW. WE'RE ALMOST THERE.
JUST OVER THIS HILL!
FINALLY!
THIS IS THE PLACE! WHAT DO YOU THINK?
IT'S UM... IT'S UH...

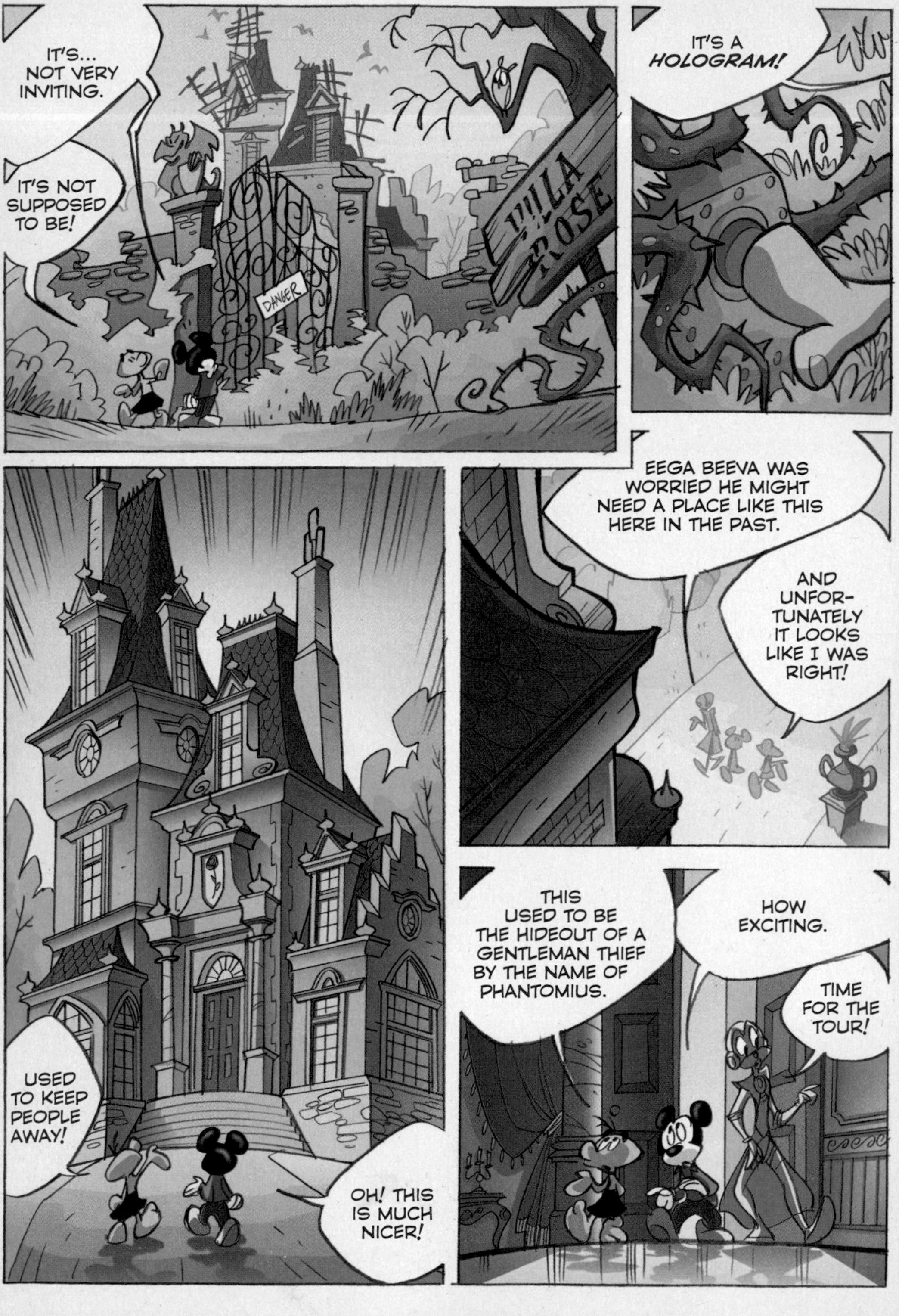
IT'S... NOT VERY INVITING.
IT'S NOT SUPPOSED TO BE!
DANGER
VILLA ROSE
IT'S A HOLOGRAM!
USED TO KEEP PEOPLE AWAY!
OH! THIS IS MUCH NICER!
EEGA BEEVA WAS WORRIED HE MIGHT NEED A PLACE LIKE THIS HERE IN THE PAST.
AND UNFORTUNATELY IT LOOKS LIKE I WAS RIGHT!
THIS USED TO BE THE HIDEOUT OF A GENTLEMAN THIEF BY THE NAME OF PHANTOMIUS.
HOW EXCITING.
TIME FOR THE TOUR!

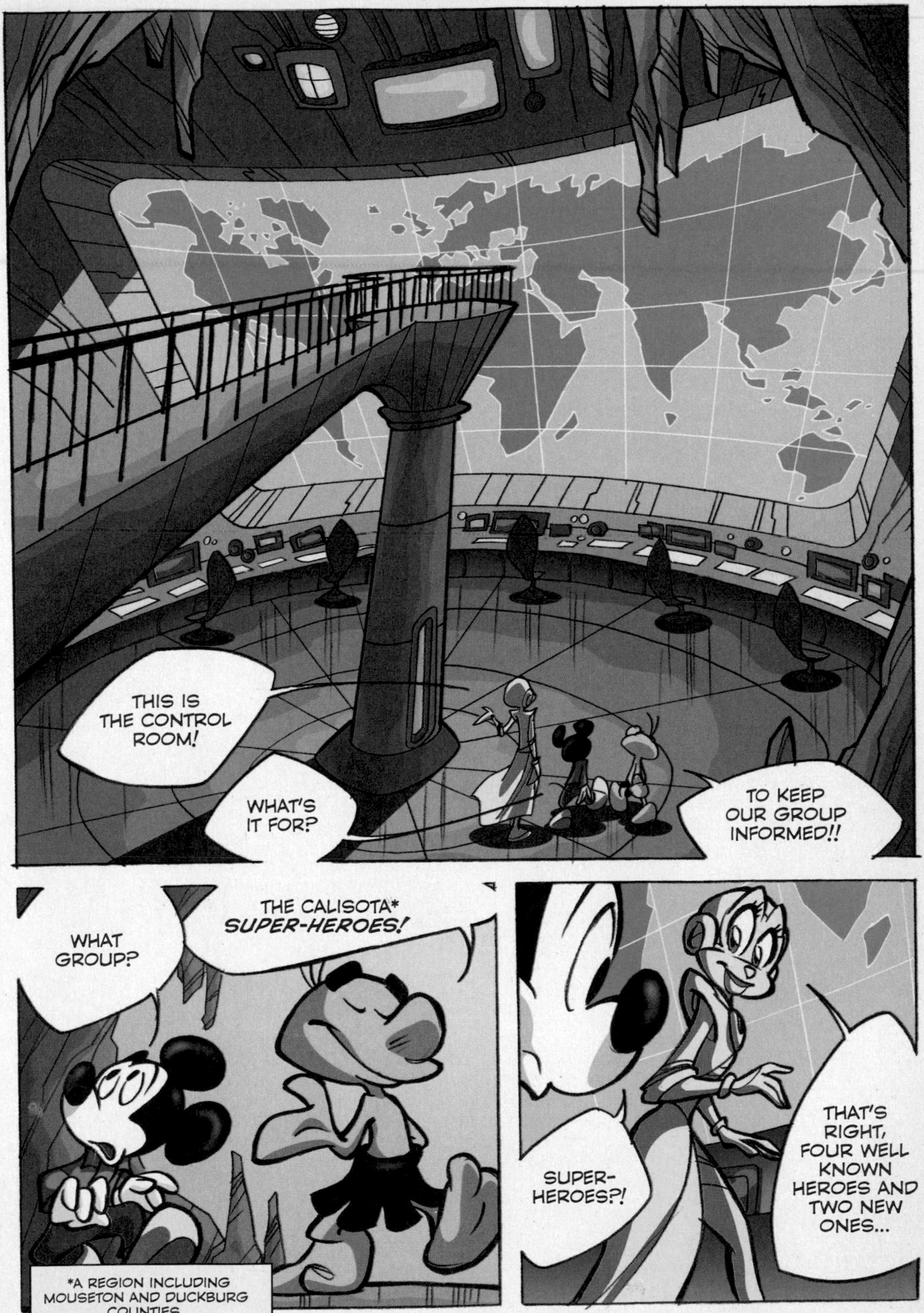
THIS IS THE CONTROL ROOM!
WHAT'S IT FOR?
TO KEEP OUR GROUP INFORMED!!
WHAT GROUP?
THE CALISOTA* SUPER-HEROES!
*A REGION INCLUDING MOUSETON AND DUCKBURG COUNTIES.
SUPER-HEROES?!
THAT'S RIGHT, FOUR WELL KNOWN HEROES AND TWO NEW ONES...

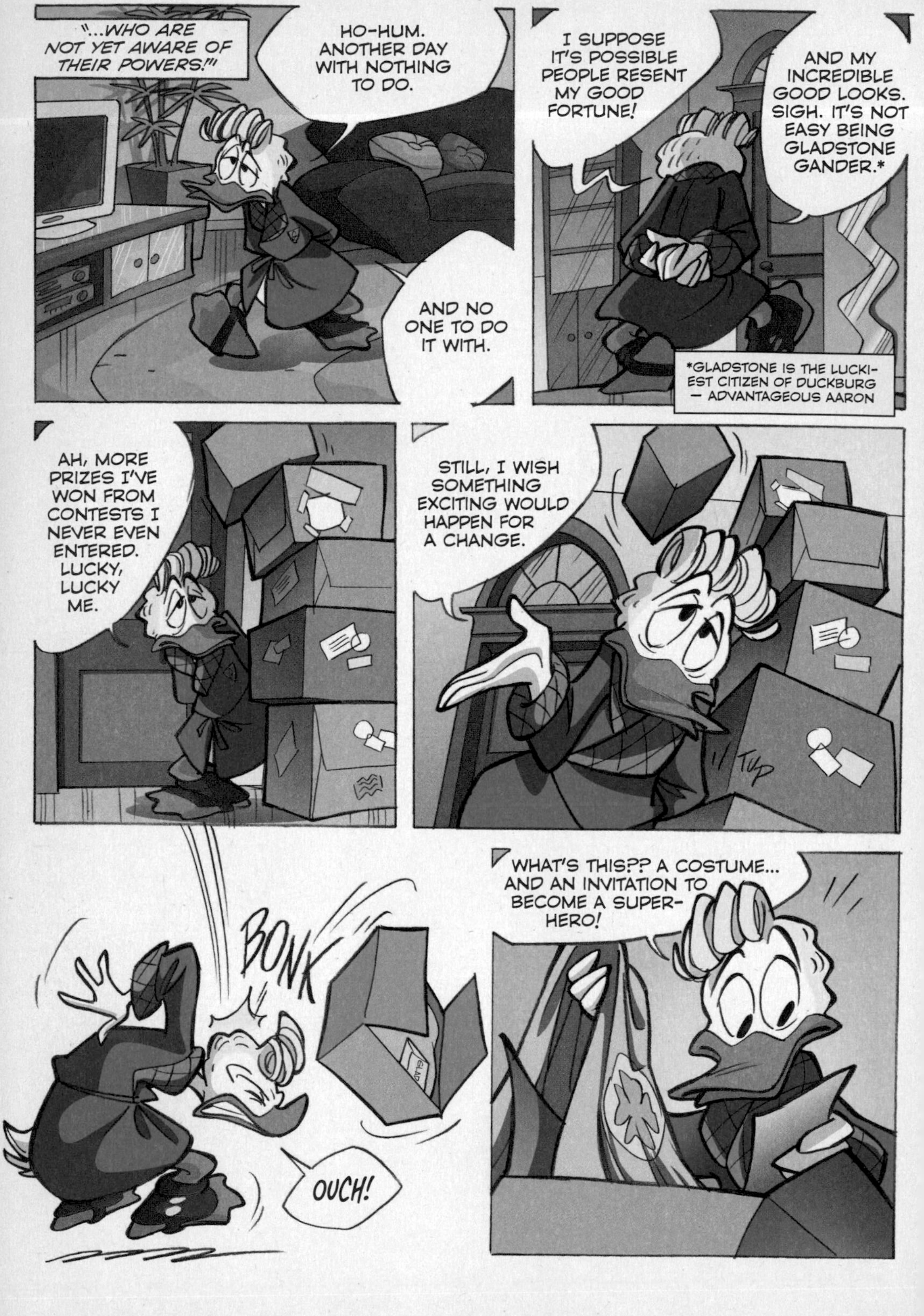
"...WHO ARE NOT YET AWARE OF THEIR POWERS!"'
HO-HUM. ANOTHER DAY WITH NOTHING TO DO.
AND NO ONE TO DO IT WITH.
I SUPPOSE IT'S POSSIBLE PEOPLE RESENT MY GOOD FORTUNE!
AND MY INCREDIBLE GOOD LOOKS. SIGH. IT'S NOT EASY BEING GLADSTONE GANDER.*
*GLADSTONE IS THE LUCKIEST CITIZEN OF DUCKBURG — ADVANTAGEOUS AARON
AH, MORE PRIZES I'VE WON FROM CONTESTS I NEVER EVEN ENTERED. LUCKY, LUCKY ME.
STILL, I WISH SOMETHING EXCITING WOULD HAPPEN FOR A CHANGE.
TUP
BONK
OUCH!
WHAT'S THIS?? A COSTUME... AND AN INVITATION TO BECOME A SUPER-HERO!

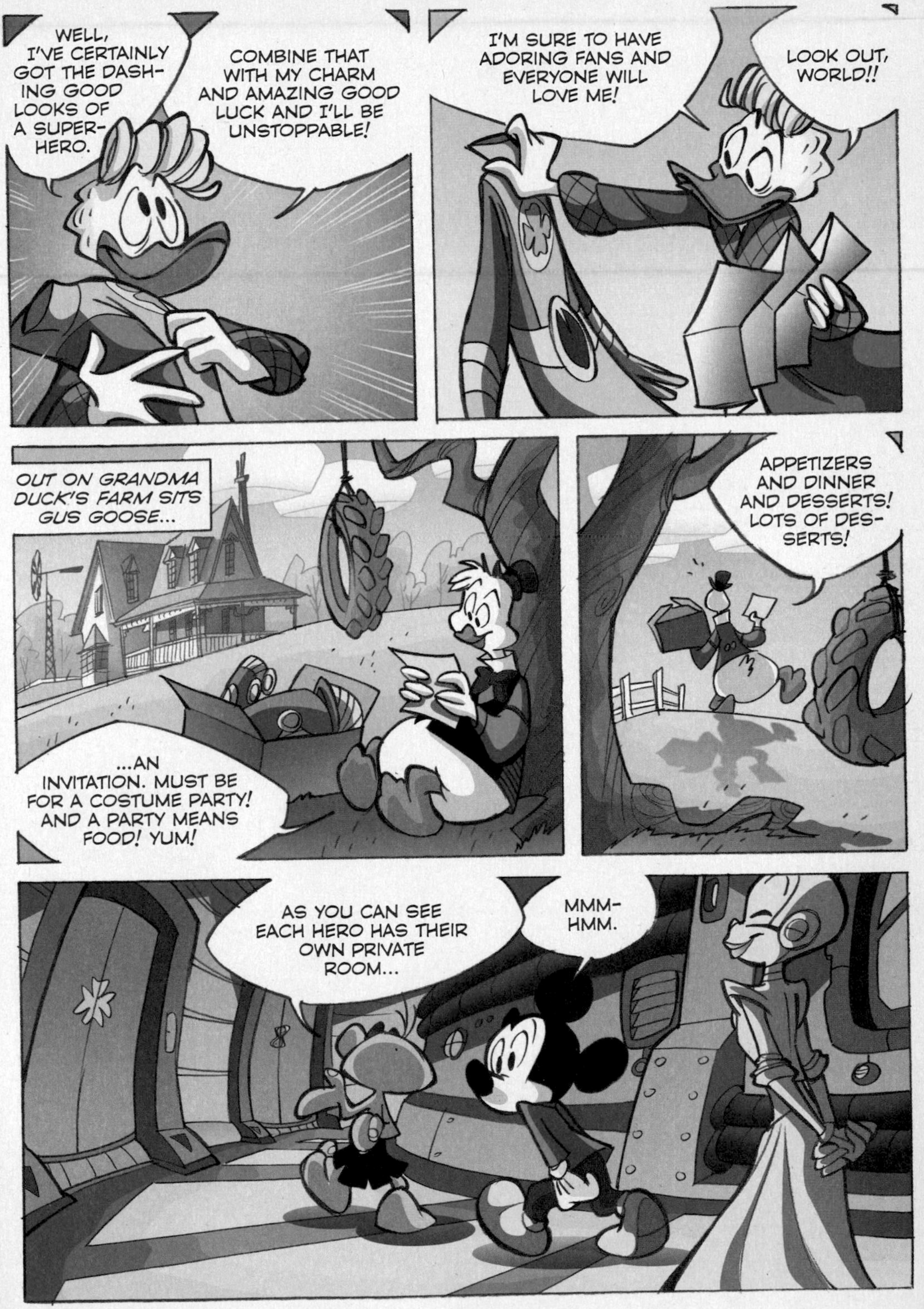
WELL, I'VE CERTAINLY GOT THE DASHING GOOD LOOKS OF A SUPERHERO.
COMBINE THAT WITH MY CHARM AND AMAZING GOOD LUCK AND I'LL BE UNSTOPPABLE!
I'M SURE TO HAVE ADORING FANS AND EVERYONE WILL LOVE ME!
LOOK OUT, WORLD!!
OUT ON GRANDMA DUCK'S FARM SITS GUS GOOSE...
...AN INVITATION. MUST BE FOR A COSTUME PARTY! AND A PARTY MEANS FOOD! YUM!
APPETIZERS AND DINNER AND DESSERTS! LOTS OF DESSERTS!
AS YOU CAN SEE EACH HERO HAS THEIR OWN PRIVATE ROOM...
MMM-HMM.

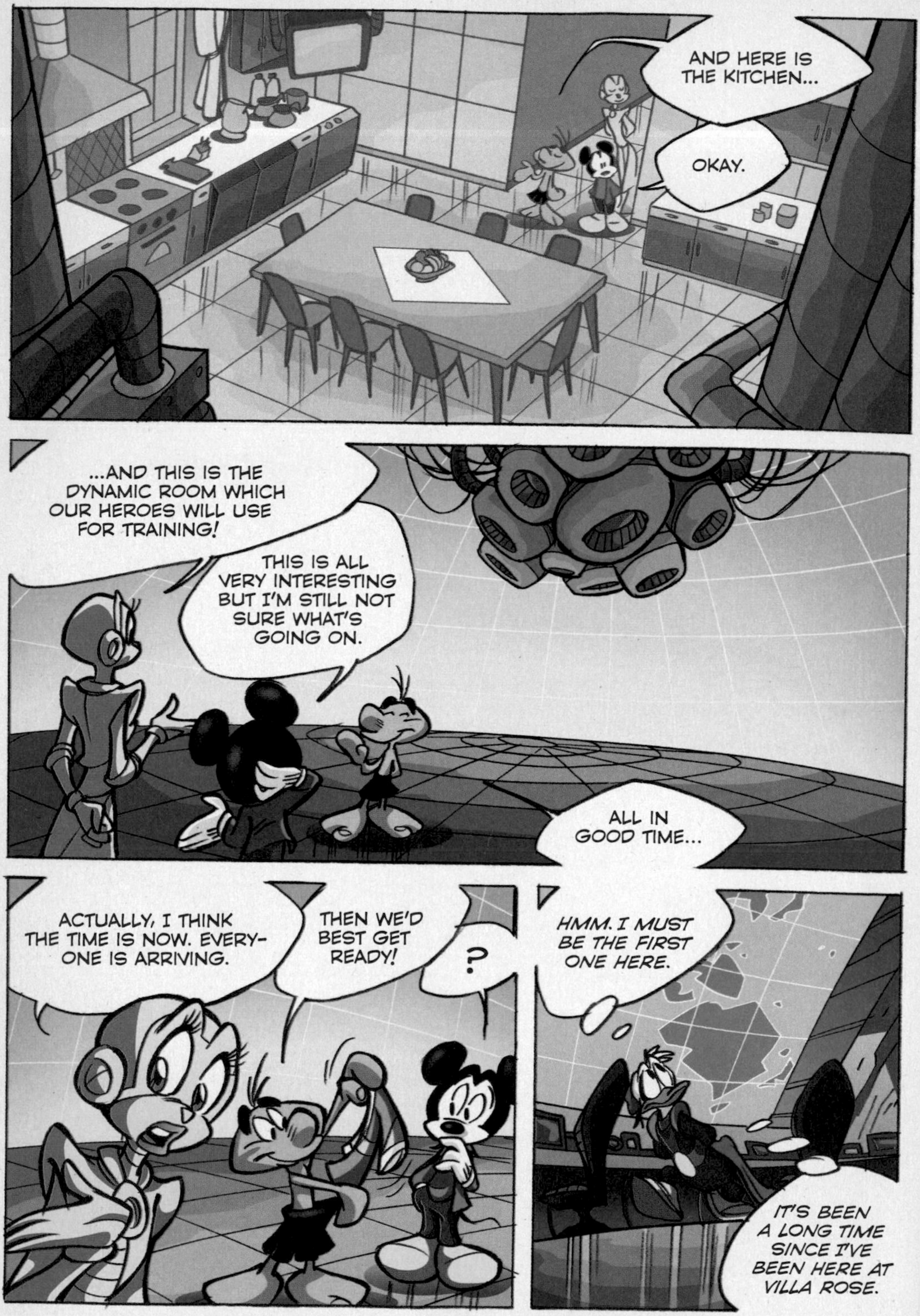
AND HERE IS THE KITCHEN...
OKAY.
...AND THIS IS THE DYNAMIC ROOM WHICH OUR HEROES WILL USE FOR TRAINING!
THIS IS ALL VERY INTERESTING BUT I'M STILL NOT SURE WHAT'S GOING ON.
ALL IN GOOD TIME...
ACTUALLY, I THINK THE TIME IS NOW. EVERY-ONE IS ARRIVING.
THEN WE'D BEST GET READY!
?
HMM. I MUST BE THE FIRST ONE HERE.
IT'S BEEN A LONG TIME SINCE I'VE BEEN HERE AT VILLA ROSE.

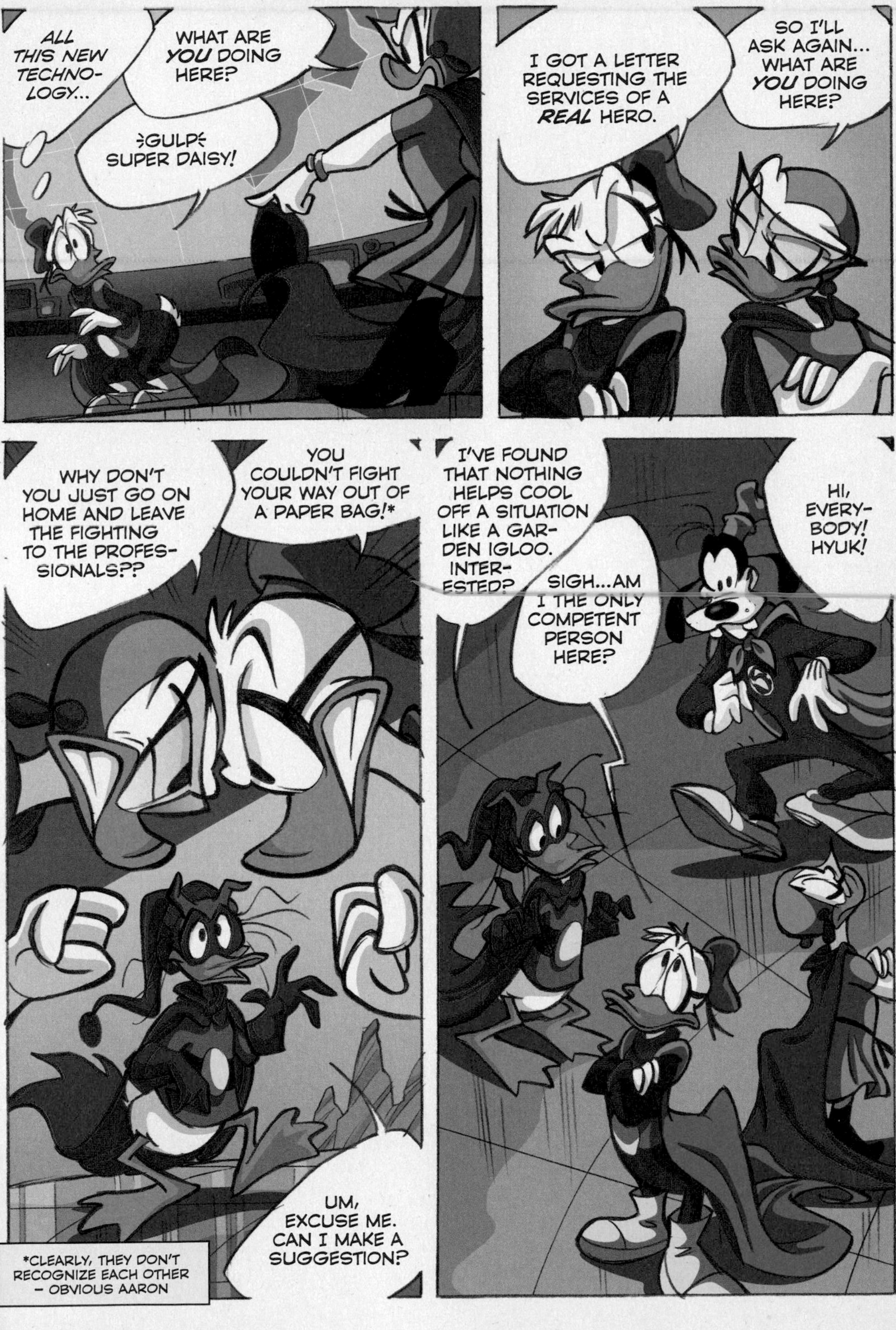
ALL THIS NEW TECHNO-LOGY...
WHAT ARE YOU DOING HERE?
GULP SUPER DAISY!
I GOT A LETTER REQUESTING THE SERVICES OF A REAL HERO.
SO I'LL ASK AGAIN... WHAT ARE YOU DOING HERE?
WHY DON'T YOU JUST GO ON HOME AND LEAVE THE FIGHTING TO THE PROFES-SIONALS??
YOU COULDN'T FIGHT YOUR WAY OUT OF A PAPER BAG!*
UM, EXCUSE ME. CAN I MAKE A SUGGESTION?
*CLEARLY, THEY DON'T RECOGNIZE EACH OTHER – OBVIOUS AARON
I'VE FOUND THAT NOTHING HELPS COOL OFF A SITUATION LIKE A GAR-DEN IGLOO. INTER-ESTED?
HI, EVERY-BODY! HYUK!
SIGH...AM I THE ONLY COMPETENT PERSON HERE?

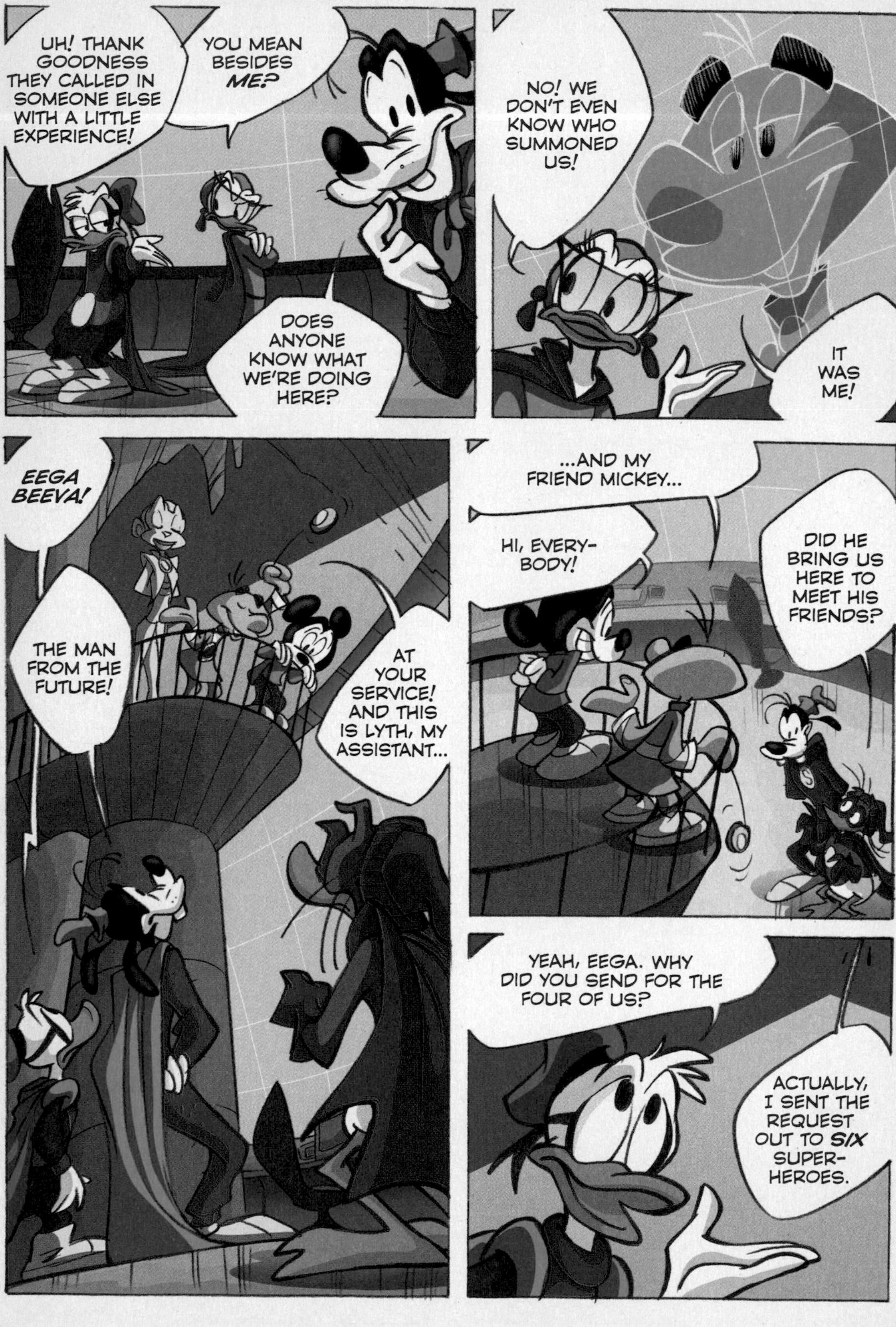
UH! THANK GOODNESS THEY CALLED IN SOMEONE ELSE WITH A LITTLE EXPERIENCE!
YOU MEAN BESIDES *ME?*
DOES ANYONE KNOW WHAT WE'RE DOING HERE?
NO! WE DON'T EVEN KNOW WHO SUMMONED US!
IT WAS ME!
EEGA BEEVA!
THE MAN FROM THE FUTURE!
AT YOUR SERVICE! AND THIS IS LYTH, MY ASSISTANT...
...AND MY FRIEND MICKEY...
HI, EVERY-BODY!
DID HE BRING US HERE TO MEET HIS FRIENDS?
YEAH, EEGA. WHY DID YOU SEND FOR THE FOUR OF US?
ACTUALLY, I SENT THE REQUEST OUT TO *SIX* SUPER-HEROES.

CHAPTER TWO

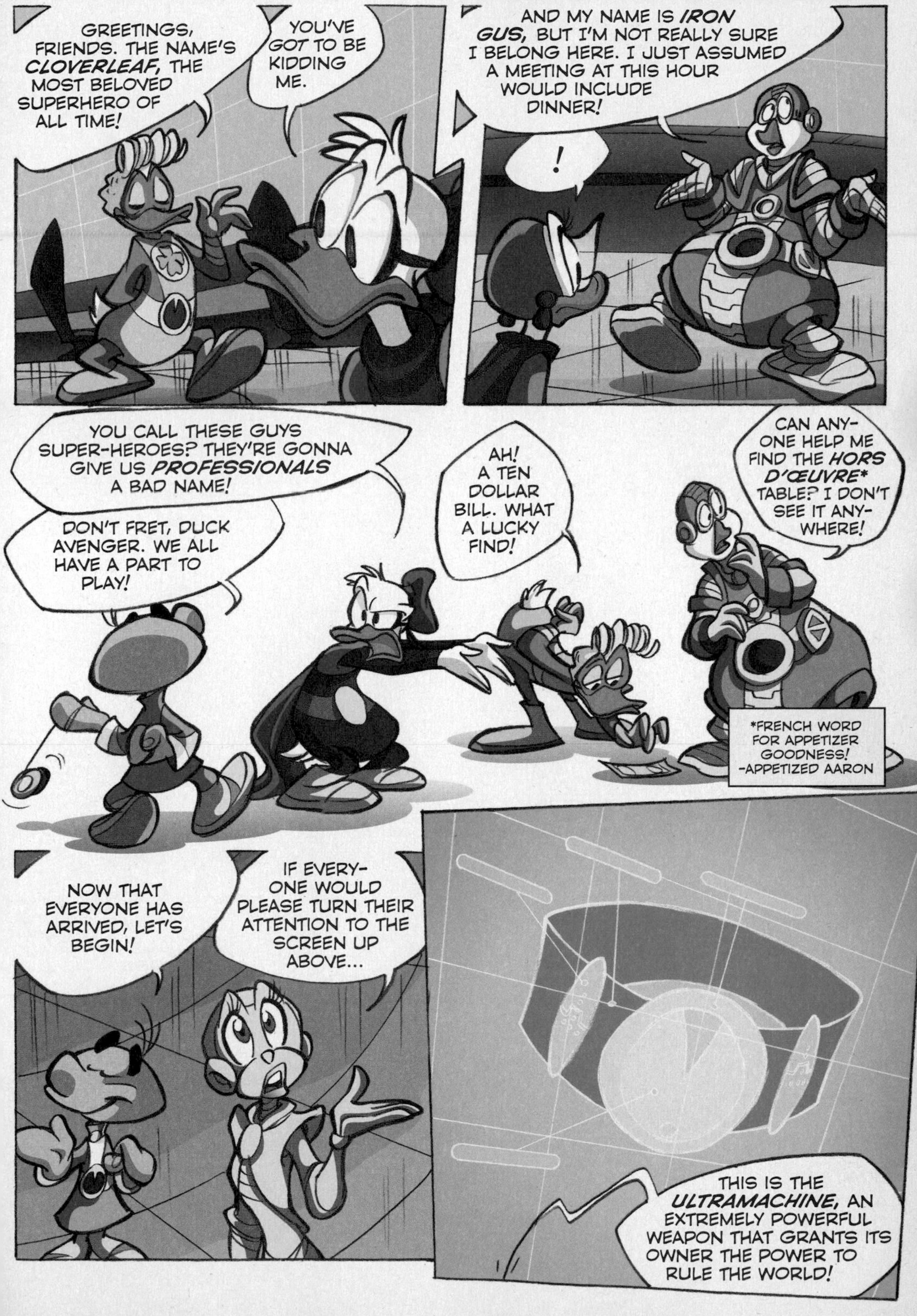
GREETINGS, FRIENDS. THE NAME'S CLOVERLEAF, THE MOST BELOVED SUPERHERO OF ALL TIME!
YOU'VE GOT TO BE KIDDING ME.
AND MY NAME IS IRON GUS, BUT I'M NOT REALLY SURE I BELONG HERE. I JUST ASSUMED A MEETING AT THIS HOUR WOULD INCLUDE DINNER!
!
YOU CALL THESE GUYS SUPER-HEROES? THEY'RE GONNA GIVE US PROFESSIONALS A BAD NAME!
DON'T FRET, DUCK AVENGER. WE ALL HAVE A PART TO PLAY!
AH! A TEN DOLLAR BILL. WHAT A LUCKY FIND!
CAN ANYONE HELP ME FIND THE HORS D'ŒUVRE* TABLE? I DON'T SEE IT ANYWHERE!
*FRENCH WORD FOR APPETIZER GOODNESS! -APPETIZED AARON
NOW THAT EVERYONE HAS ARRIVED, LET'S BEGIN!
IF EVERYONE WOULD PLEASE TURN THEIR ATTENTION TO THE SCREEN UP ABOVE...
THIS IS THE ULTRAMACHINE, AN EXTREMELY POWERFUL WEAPON THAT GRANTS ITS OWNER THE POWER TO RULE THE WORLD!

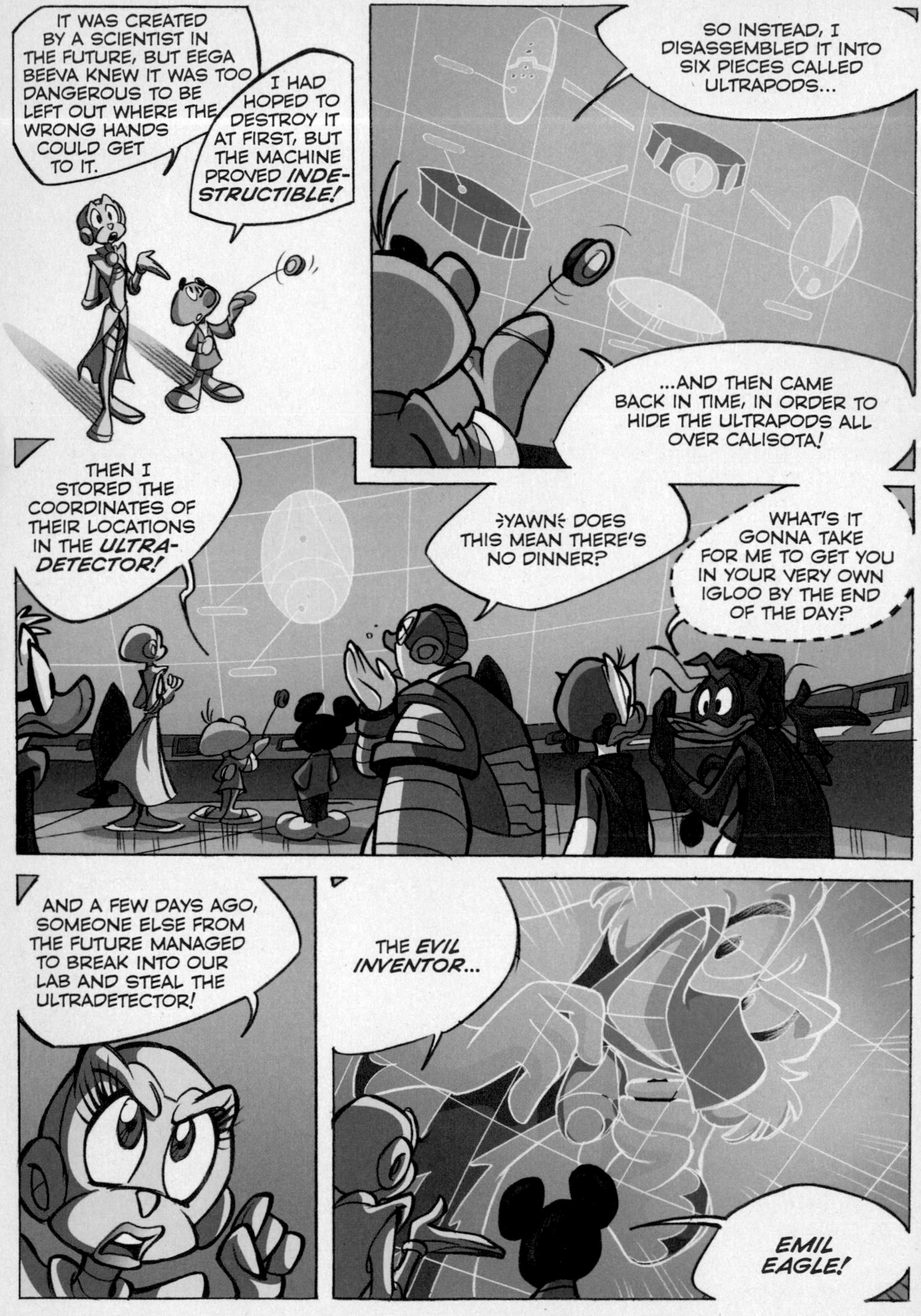
IT WAS CREATED BY A SCIENTIST IN THE FUTURE, BUT EEGA BEEVA KNEW IT WAS TOO DANGEROUS TO BE LEFT OUT WHERE THE WRONG HANDS COULD GET TO IT.
I HAD HOPED TO DESTROY IT AT FIRST, BUT THE MACHINE PROVED *INDESTRUCTIBLE!*
SO INSTEAD, I DISASSEMBLED IT INTO SIX PIECES CALLED ULTRAPODS...
...AND THEN CAME BACK IN TIME, IN ORDER TO HIDE THE ULTRAPODS ALL OVER CALISOTA!
THEN I STORED THE COORDINATES OF THEIR LOCATIONS IN THE *ULTRA-DETECTOR!*
YAWN DOES THIS MEAN THERE'S NO DINNER?
WHAT'S IT GONNA TAKE FOR ME TO GET YOU IN YOUR VERY OWN IGLOO BY THE END OF THE DAY?
AND A FEW DAYS AGO, SOMEONE ELSE FROM THE FUTURE MANAGED TO BREAK INTO OUR LAB AND STEAL THE ULTRADETECTOR!
THE *EVIL INVENTOR...*
EMIL EAGLE!

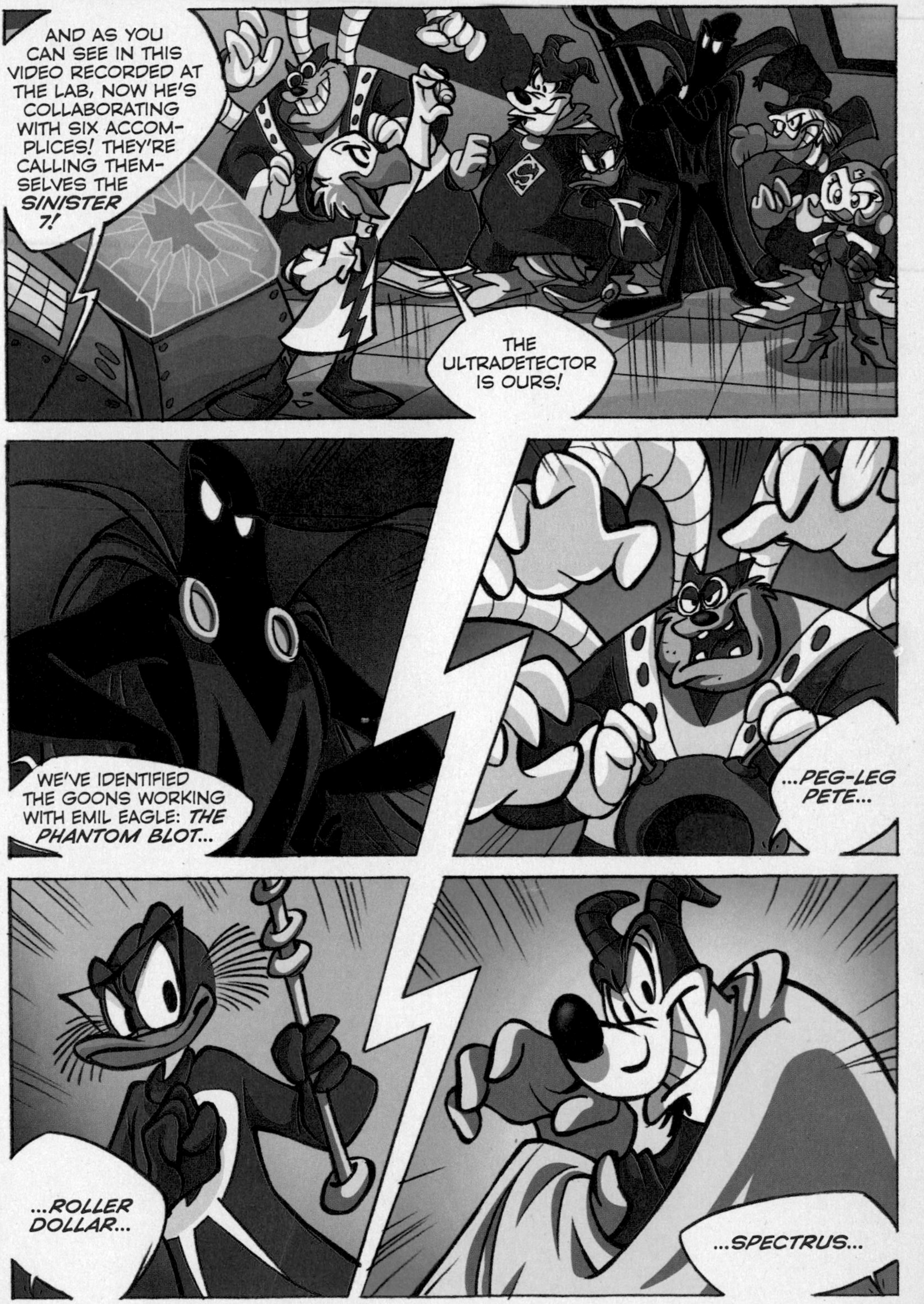
AND AS YOU CAN SEE IN THIS VIDEO RECORDED AT THE LAB, NOW HE'S COLLABORATING WITH SIX ACCOMPLICES! THEY'RE CALLING THEMSELVES THE *SINISTER 7!*
THE ULTRADETECTOR IS OURS!
WE'VE IDENTIFIED THE GOONS WORKING WITH EMIL EAGLE: *THE PHANTOM BLOT...*
...*PEG-LEG PETE...*
...*ROLLER DOLLAR...*
...*SPECTRUS...*

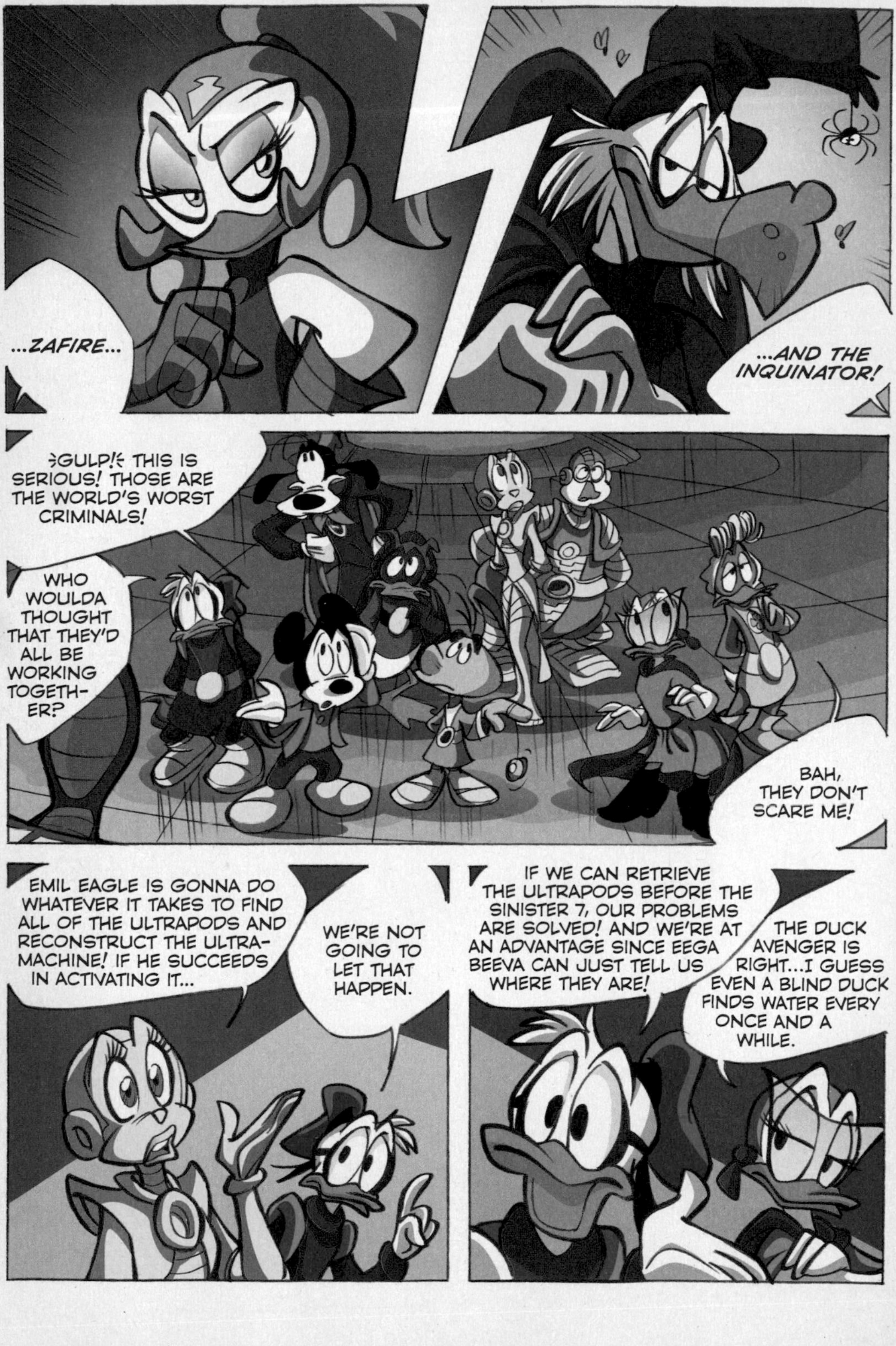
...ZAFIRE...
...AND THE INQUINATOR!
GULP! THIS IS SERIOUS! THOSE ARE THE WORLD'S WORST CRIMINALS!
WHO WOULDA THOUGHT THAT THEY'D ALL BE WORKING TOGETH-ER?
BAH, THEY DON'T SCARE ME!
EMIL EAGLE IS GONNA DO WHATEVER IT TAKES TO FIND ALL OF THE ULTRAPODS AND RECONSTRUCT THE ULTRA-MACHINE! IF HE SUCCEEDS IN ACTIVATING IT...
WE'RE NOT GOING TO LET THAT HAPPEN.
IF WE CAN RETRIEVE THE ULTRAPODS BEFORE THE SINISTER 7, OUR PROBLEMS ARE SOLVED! AND WE'RE AT AN ADVANTAGE SINCE EEGA BEEVA CAN JUST TELL US WHERE THEY ARE!
THE DUCK AVENGER IS RIGHT...I GUESS EVEN A BLIND DUCK FINDS WATER EVERY ONCE AND A WHILE.

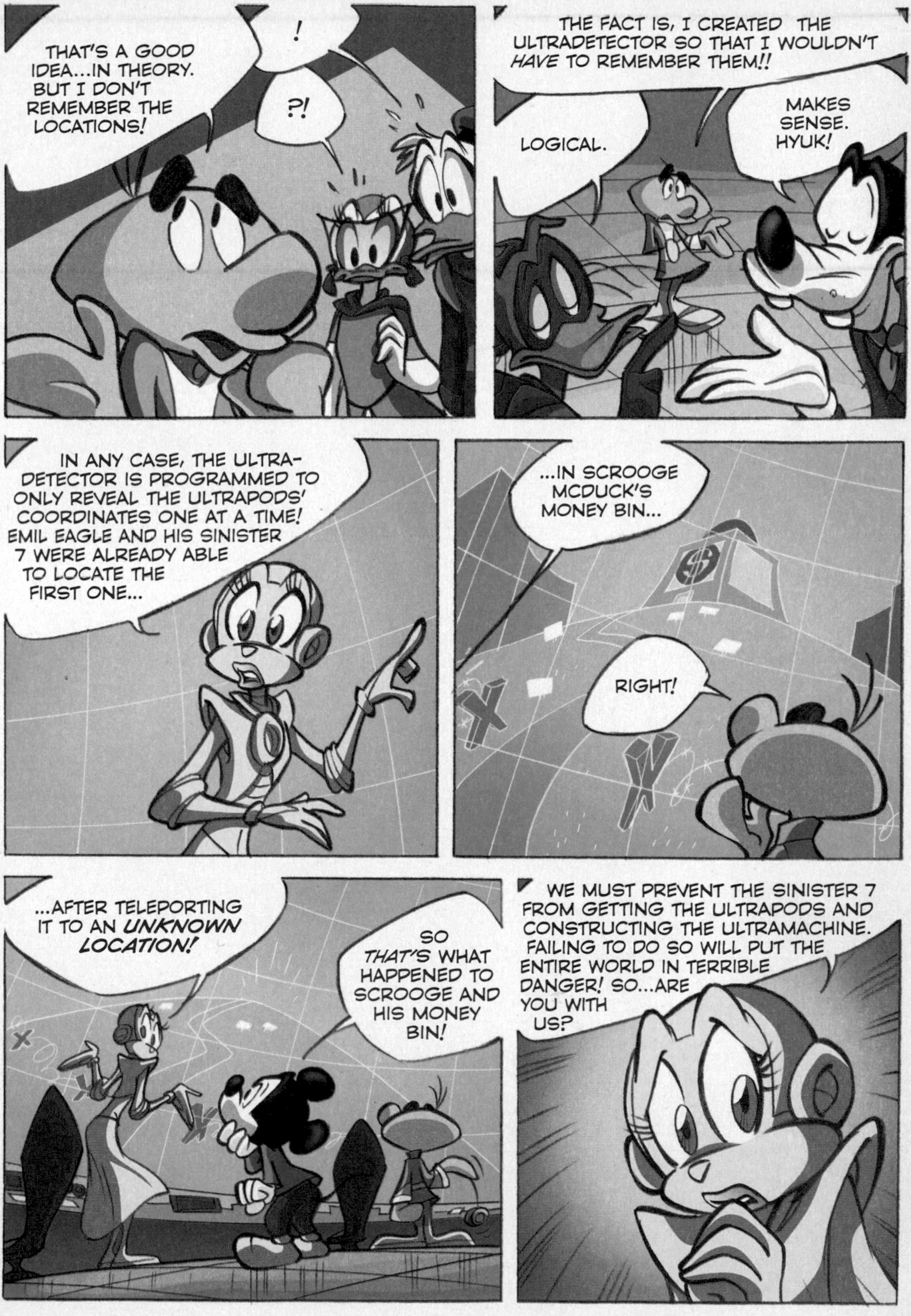
THAT'S A GOOD IDEA...IN THEORY. BUT I DON'T REMEMBER THE LOCATIONS!
!
?!
THE FACT IS, I CREATED THE ULTRADETECTOR SO THAT I WOULDN'T *HAVE* TO REMEMBER THEM!!
LOGICAL.
MAKES SENSE. HYUK!
IN ANY CASE, THE ULTRA-DETECTOR IS PROGRAMMED TO ONLY REVEAL THE ULTRAPODS' COORDINATES ONE AT A TIME! EMIL EAGLE AND HIS SINISTER 7 WERE ALREADY ABLE TO LOCATE THE FIRST ONE...
...IN SCROOGE MCDUCK'S MONEY BIN...
RIGHT!
...AFTER TELEPORTING IT TO AN *UNKNOWN LOCATION!*
SO *THAT'S* WHAT HAPPENED TO SCROOGE AND HIS MONEY BIN!
WE MUST PREVENT THE SINISTER 7 FROM GETTING THE ULTRAPODS AND CONSTRUCTING THE ULTRAMACHINE. FAILING TO DO SO WILL PUT THE ENTIRE WORLD IN TERRIBLE DANGER! SO...ARE YOU WITH US?

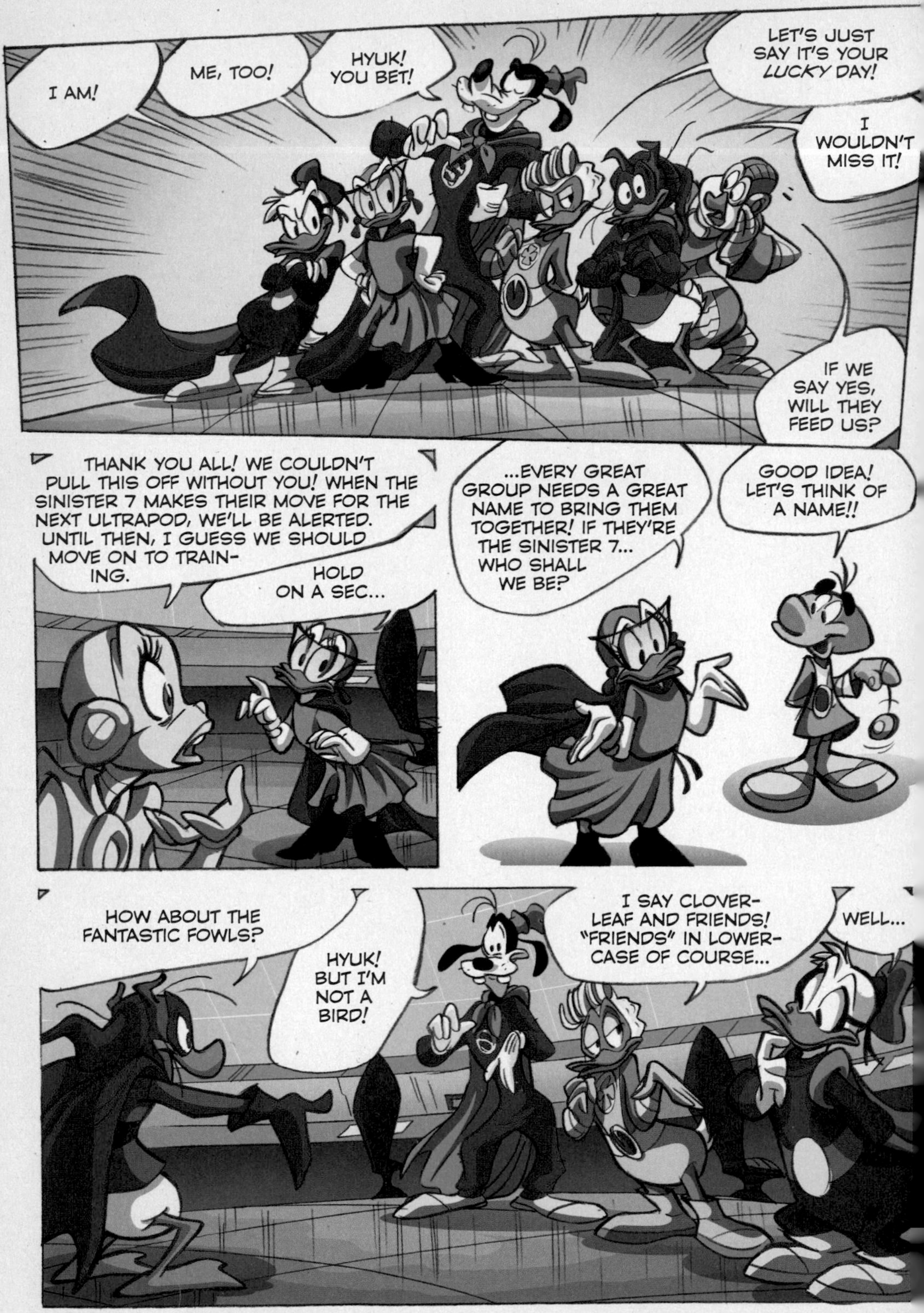
I AM!
ME, TOO!
HYUK! YOU BET!
LET'S JUST SAY IT'S YOUR LUCKY DAY!
I WOULDN'T MISS IT!
IF WE SAY YES, WILL THEY FEED US?
THANK YOU ALL! WE COULDN'T PULL THIS OFF WITHOUT YOU! WHEN THE SINISTER 7 MAKES THEIR MOVE FOR THE NEXT ULTRAPOD, WE'LL BE ALERTED. UNTIL THEN, I GUESS WE SHOULD MOVE ON TO TRAINING.
HOLD ON A SEC...
...EVERY GREAT GROUP NEEDS A GREAT NAME TO BRING THEM TOGETHER! IF THEY'RE THE SINISTER 7... WHO SHALL WE BE?
GOOD IDEA! LET'S THINK OF A NAME!!
HOW ABOUT THE FANTASTIC FOWLS?
HYUK! BUT I'M NOT A BIRD!
I SAY CLOVERLEAF AND FRIENDS! "FRIENDS" IN LOWERCASE OF COURSE...
WELL...

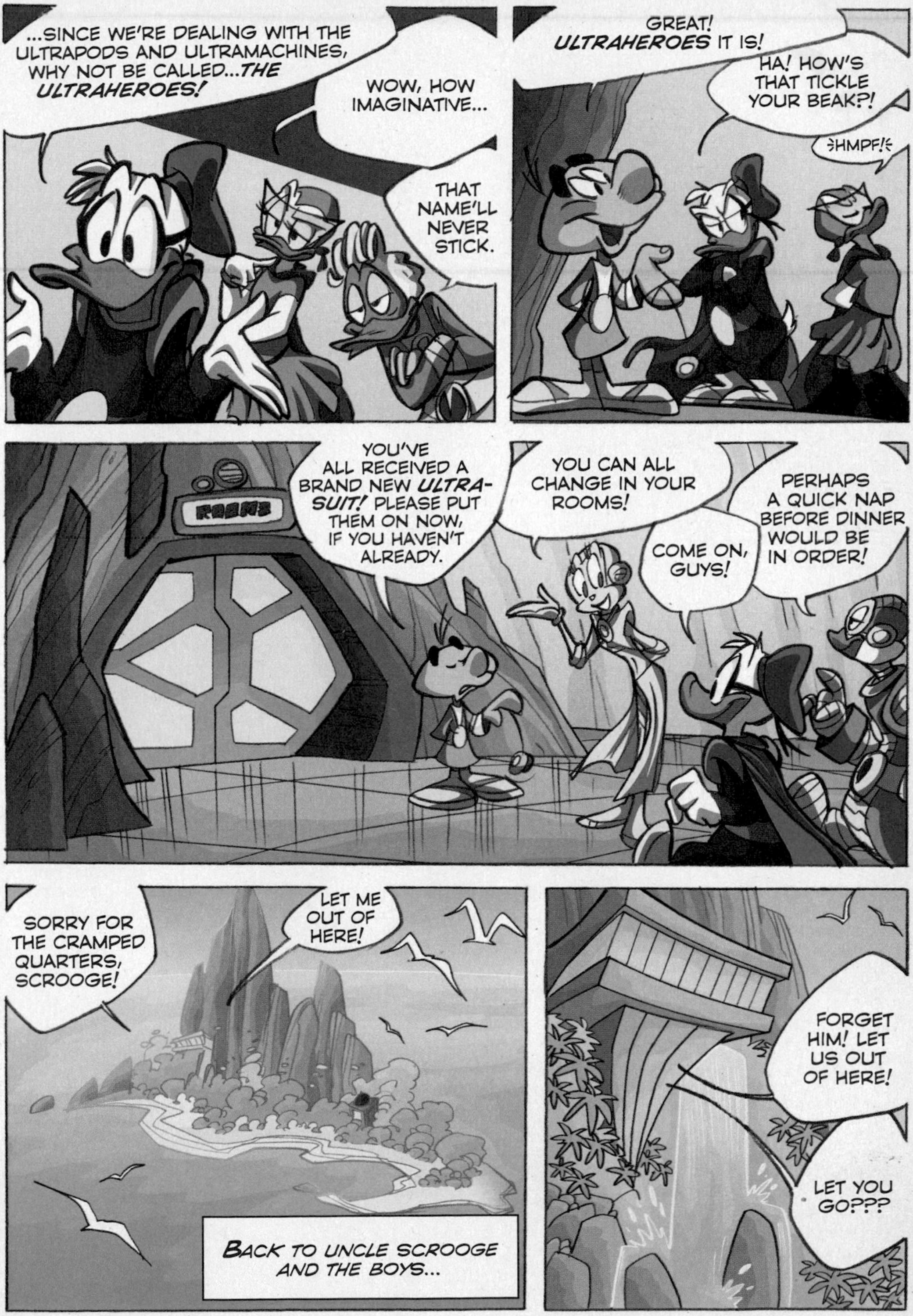
...SINCE WE'RE DEALING WITH THE ULTRAPODS AND ULTRAMACHINES, WHY NOT BE CALLED...*THE ULTRAHEROES!*
WOW, HOW IMAGINATIVE...
THAT NAME'LL NEVER STICK.
GREAT! *ULTRAHEROES* IT IS!
HA! HOW'S THAT TICKLE YOUR BEAK?!
HMPF!
ROOMS
YOU'VE ALL RECEIVED A BRAND NEW *ULTRA-SUIT!* PLEASE PUT THEM ON NOW, IF YOU HAVEN'T ALREADY.
YOU CAN ALL CHANGE IN YOUR ROOMS!
COME ON, GUYS!
PERHAPS A QUICK NAP BEFORE DINNER WOULD BE IN ORDER!
SORRY FOR THE CRAMPED QUARTERS, SCROOGE!
LET ME OUT OF HERE!
BACK TO UNCLE SCROOGE AND THE BOYS...
FORGET HIM! LET US OUT OF HERE!
LET YOU GO???

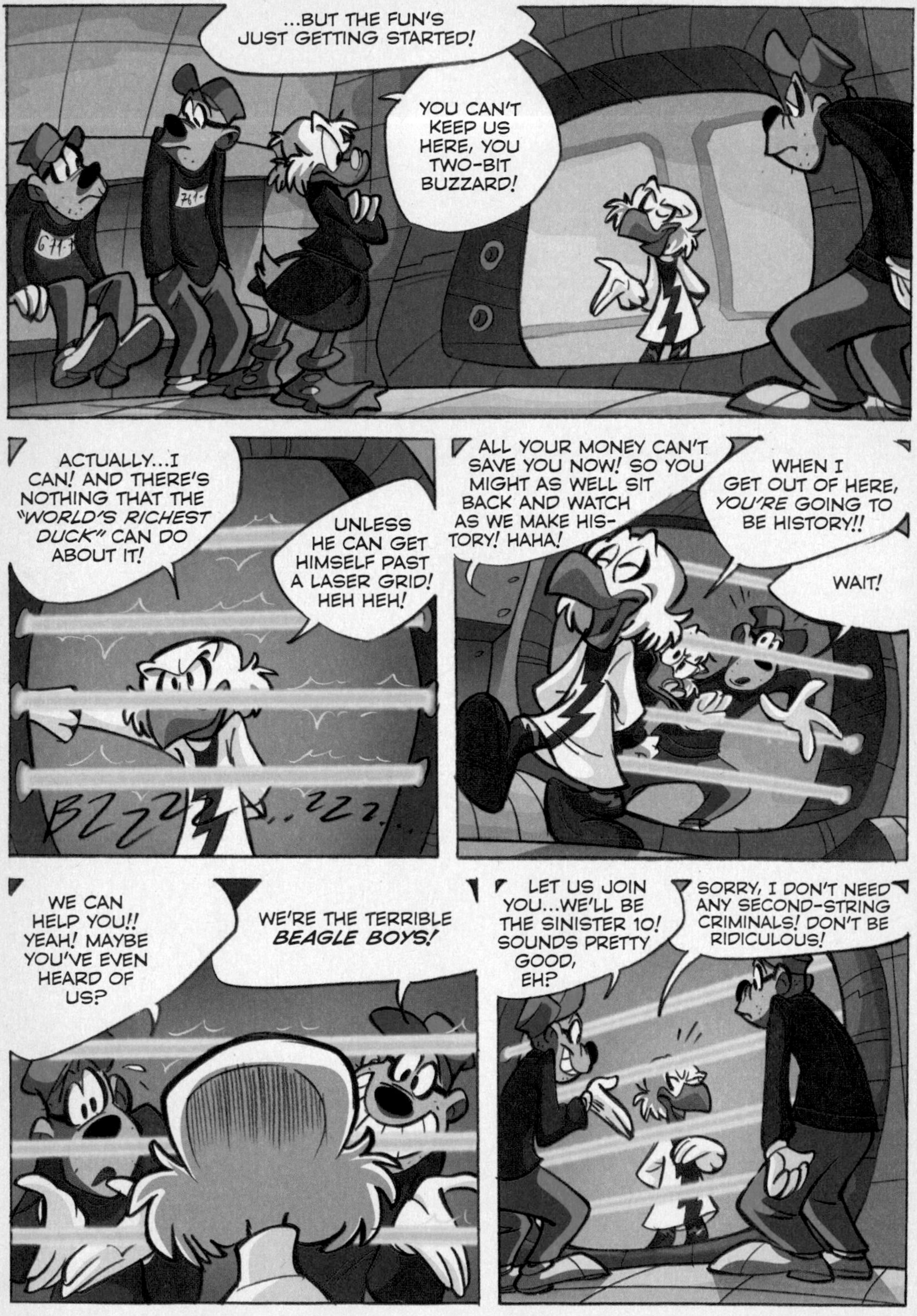
...BUT THE FUN'S JUST GETTING STARTED!
YOU CAN'T KEEP US HERE, YOU TWO-BIT BUZZARD!
ACTUALLY...I CAN! AND THERE'S NOTHING THAT THE *"WORLD'S RICHEST DUCK"* CAN DO ABOUT IT!
UNLESS HE CAN GET HIMSELF PAST A LASER GRID! HEH HEH!
BZZZZ...ZZZ...
ALL YOUR MONEY CAN'T SAVE YOU NOW! SO YOU MIGHT AS WELL SIT BACK AND WATCH AS WE MAKE HIS-TORY! HAHA!
WHEN I GET OUT OF HERE, *YOU'RE* GOING TO BE HISTORY!!
WAIT!
WE CAN HELP YOU!! YEAH! MAYBE YOU'VE EVEN HEARD OF US?
WE'RE THE TERRIBLE ***BEAGLE BOYS!***
LET US JOIN YOU...WE'LL BE THE SINISTER 10! SOUNDS PRETTY GOOD, EH?
SORRY, I DON'T NEED ANY SECOND-STRING CRIMINALS! DON'T BE RIDICULOUS!

BUT IF I EVER DO WANT SOMEONE TO BUNGLE EVEN THE SIMPLEST OF JOBS, I'LL KNOW EXACTLY WHERE TO LOOK!

DANG! THAT WAS DOWNRIGHT HURTFUL...

BLESS ME BAGPIPES! THE ONLY THING TERRIBLE ABOUT YOU THREE IS HOW INCOMPETENT YOU ARE!

UM, EEGA BEEVA, IS THERE ANYTHING I CAN DO TO HELP?

LIKE WHAT?

I DON'T KNOW, BUT THERE MUST BE SOMETHING I CAN BE GOOD FOR...

UHHH MAYBE. I'LL LET YOU KNOW.

IT'S LOCATED AT DUCKBURG STADIUM! THERE'S CURRENTLY A GAME GOING ON THERE...WHICH SHOULD MAKE THIS EVEN MORE FUN!

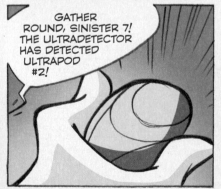

GATHER ROUND, SINISTER 7! THE ULTRADETECTOR HAS DETECTED ULTRAPOD #2!

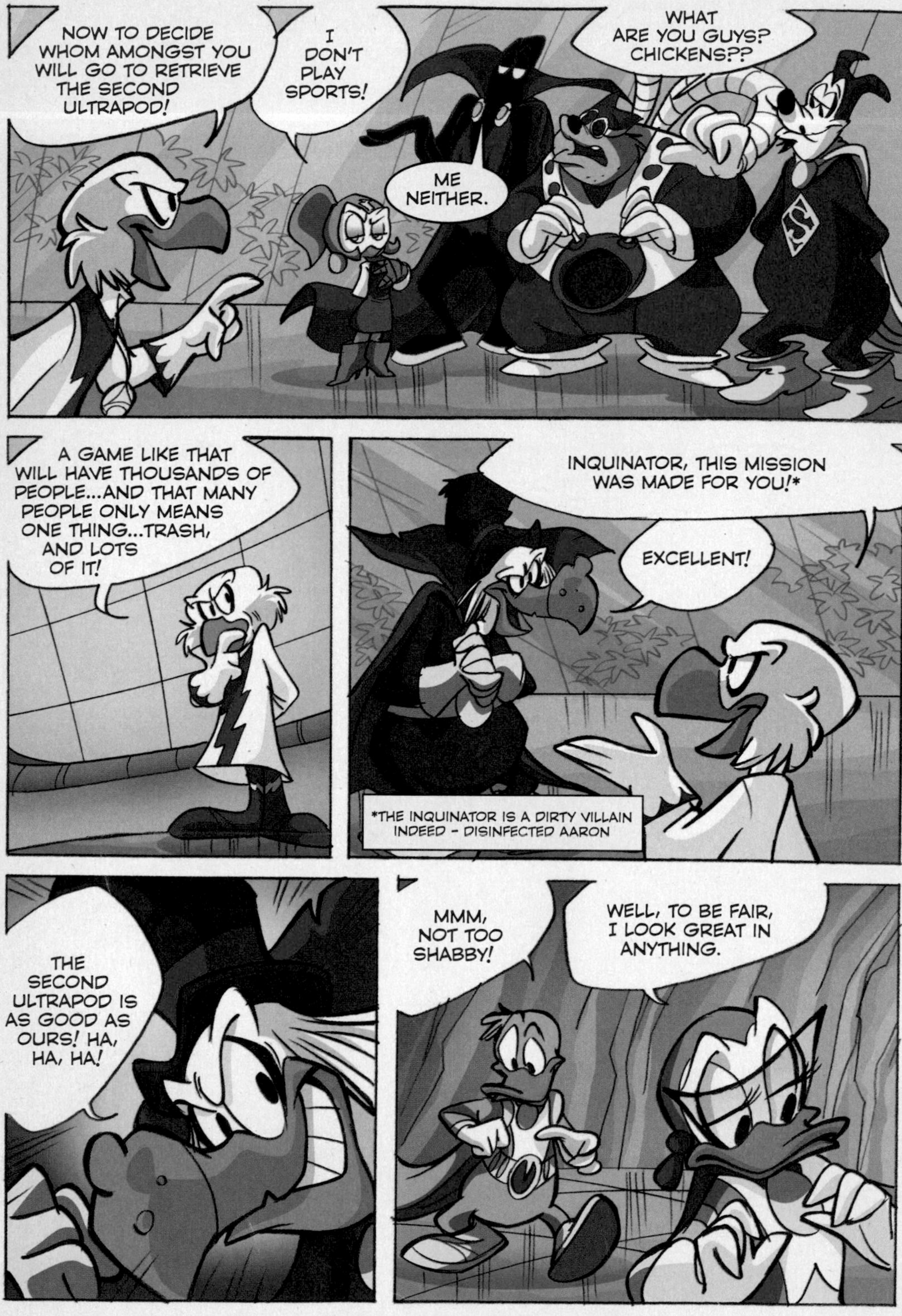
NOW TO DECIDE WHOM AMONGST YOU WILL GO TO RETRIEVE THE SECOND ULTRAPOD!
I DON'T PLAY SPORTS!
ME NEITHER.
WHAT ARE YOU GUYS? CHICKENS??
A GAME LIKE THAT WILL HAVE THOUSANDS OF PEOPLE...AND THAT MANY PEOPLE ONLY MEANS ONE THING...TRASH, AND LOTS OF IT!
INQUINATOR, THIS MISSION WAS MADE FOR YOU!*
EXCELLENT!
*THE INQUINATOR IS A DIRTY VILLAIN INDEED - DISINFECTED AARON
THE SECOND ULTRAPOD IS AS GOOD AS OURS! HA, HA, HA!
MMM, NOT TOO SHABBY!
WELL, TO BE FAIR, I LOOK GREAT IN ANYTHING.

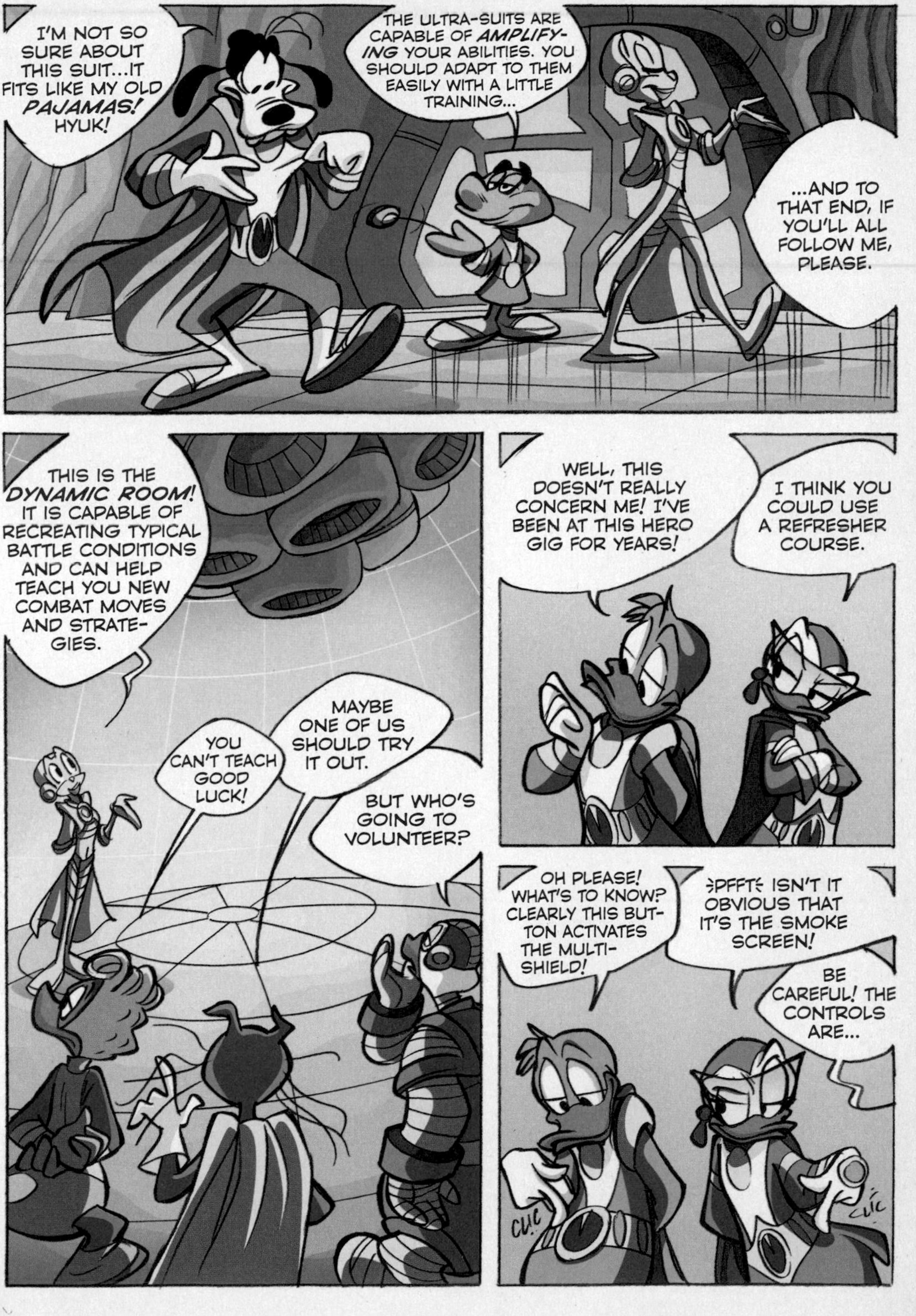
I'M NOT SO SURE ABOUT THIS SUIT...IT FITS LIKE MY OLD PAJAMAS! HYUK!
THE ULTRA-SUITS ARE CAPABLE OF AMPLIFYING YOUR ABILITIES. YOU SHOULD ADAPT TO THEM EASILY WITH A LITTLE TRAINING...
...AND TO THAT END, IF YOU'LL ALL FOLLOW ME, PLEASE.
THIS IS THE DYNAMIC ROOM! IT IS CAPABLE OF RECREATING TYPICAL BATTLE CONDITIONS AND CAN HELP TEACH YOU NEW COMBAT MOVES AND STRATEGIES.
YOU CAN'T TEACH GOOD LUCK!
MAYBE ONE OF US SHOULD TRY IT OUT.
BUT WHO'S GOING TO VOLUNTEER?
WELL, THIS DOESN'T REALLY CONCERN ME! I'VE BEEN AT THIS HERO GIG FOR YEARS!
I THINK YOU COULD USE A REFRESHER COURSE.
OH PLEASE! WHAT'S TO KNOW? CLEARLY THIS BUTTON ACTIVATES THE MULTI-SHIELD!
PFFT! ISN'T IT OBVIOUS THAT IT'S THE SMOKE SCREEN!
BE CAREFUL! THE CONTROLS ARE...
CLIC
CLIC

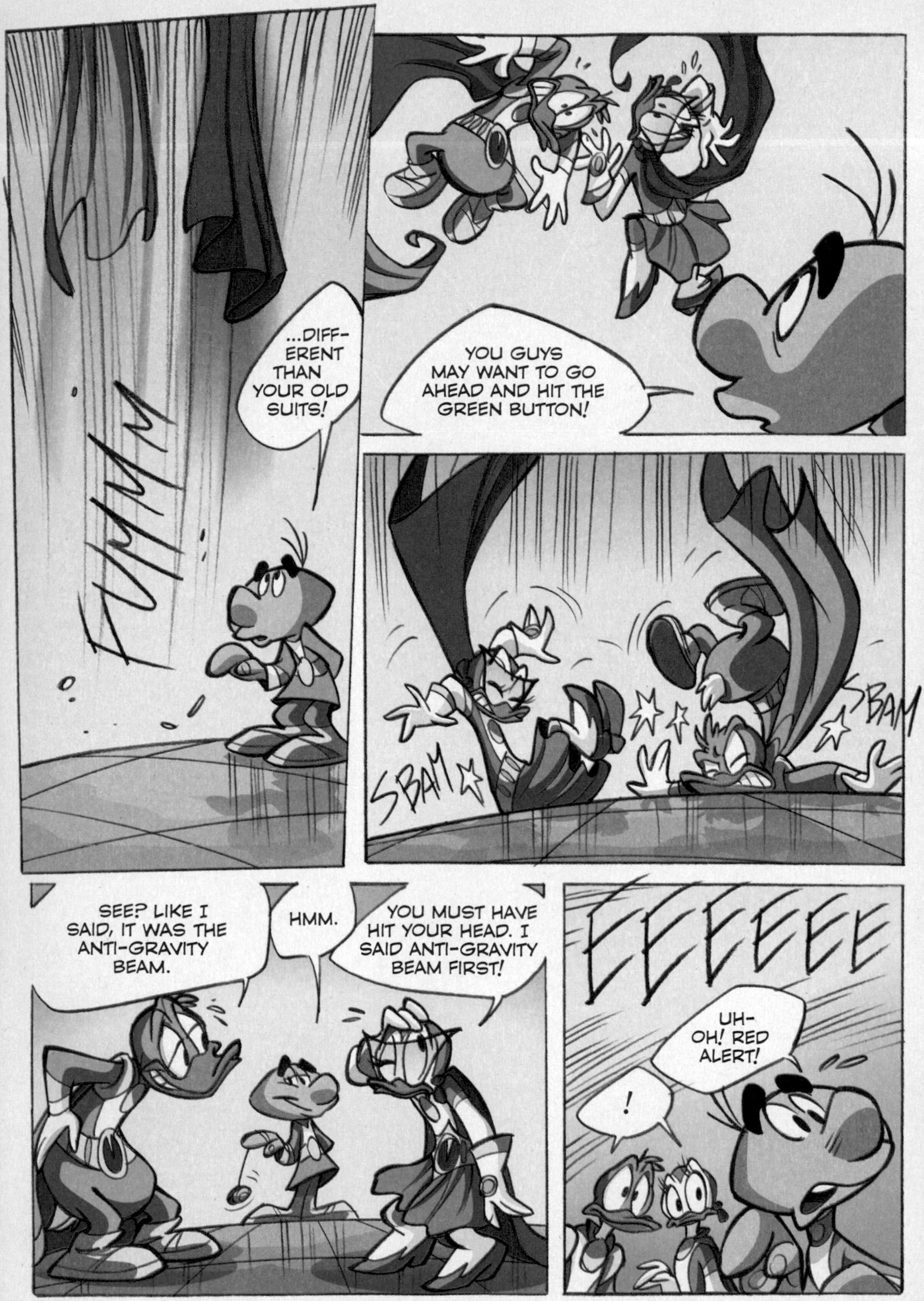
FUMMM
...DIFF-ERENT THAN YOUR OLD SUITS!
YOU GUYS MAY WANT TO GO AHEAD AND HIT THE GREEN BUTTON!
SBAM
SBAM
SEE? LIKE I SAID, IT WAS THE ANTI-GRAVITY BEAM.
HMM.
YOU MUST HAVE HIT YOUR HEAD. I SAID ANTI-GRAVITY BEAM FIRST!
EEEEEE
UH-OH! RED ALERT!
!

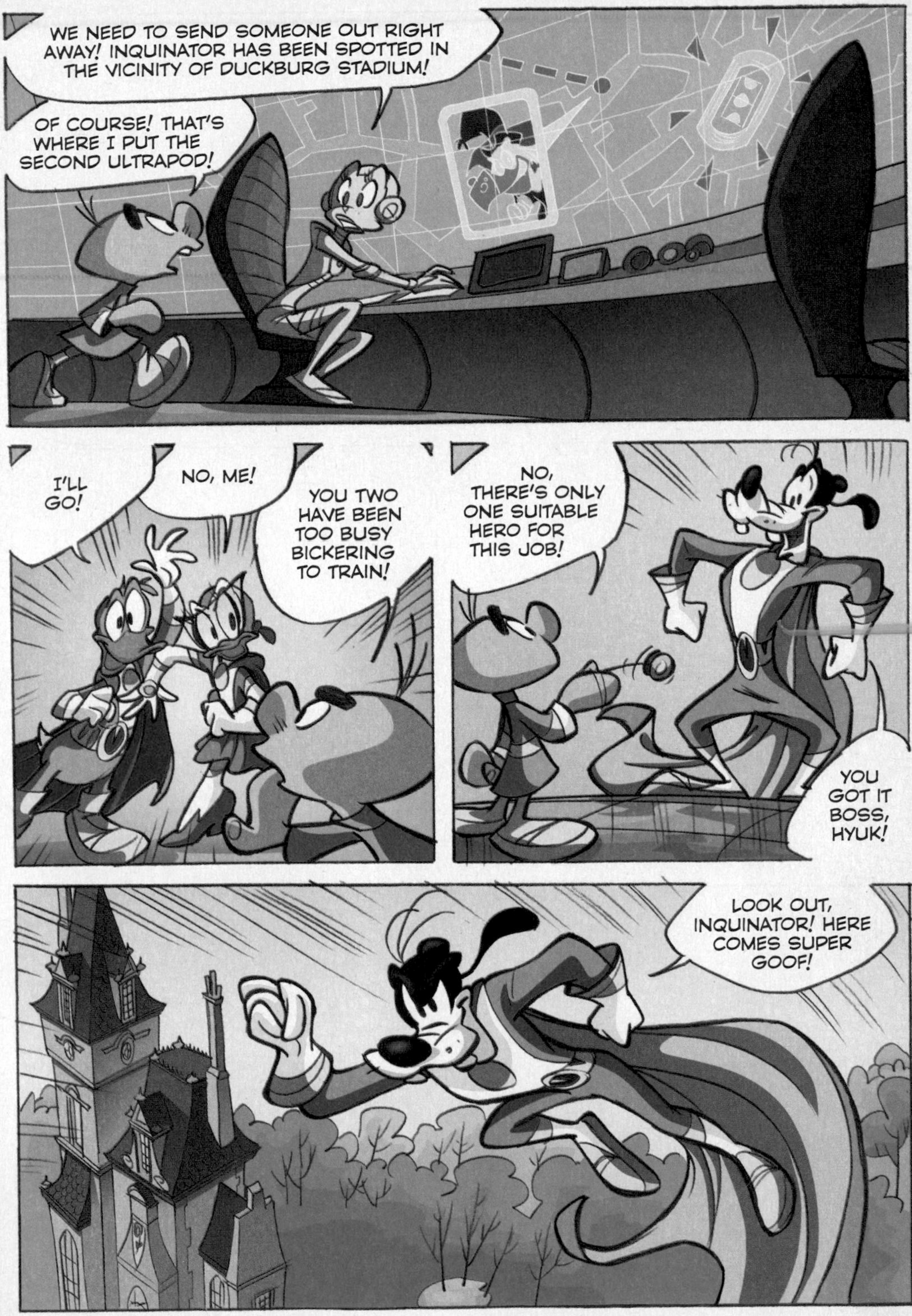
WE NEED TO SEND SOMEONE OUT RIGHT AWAY! INQUINATOR HAS BEEN SPOTTED IN THE VICINITY OF DUCKBURG STADIUM!
OF COURSE! THAT'S WHERE I PUT THE SECOND ULTRAPOD!
I'LL GO!
NO, ME!
YOU TWO HAVE BEEN TOO BUSY BICKERING TO TRAIN!
NO, THERE'S ONLY ONE SUITABLE HERO FOR THIS JOB!
YOU GOT IT BOSS, HYUK!
LOOK OUT, INQUINATOR! HERE COMES SUPER GOOF!

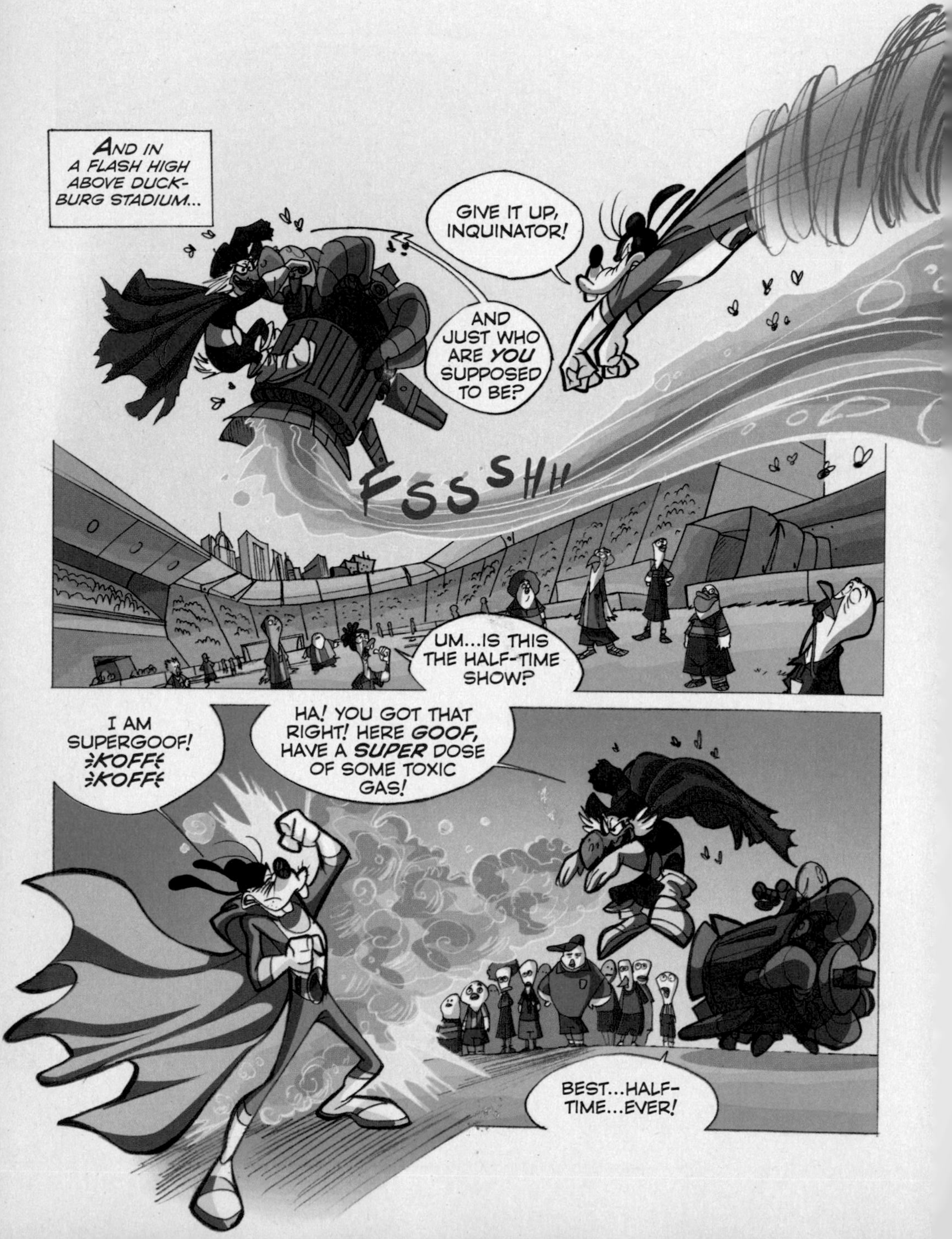
AND IN A FLASH HIGH ABOVE DUCKBURG STADIUM...
GIVE IT UP, INQUINATOR!
AND JUST WHO ARE YOU SUPPOSED TO BE?
FSSSHH
UM...IS THIS THE HALF-TIME SHOW?
I AM SUPERGOOF! KOFF KOFF
HA! YOU GOT THAT RIGHT! HERE GOOF, HAVE A SUPER DOSE OF SOME TOXIC GAS!
BEST...HALF-TIME...EVER!

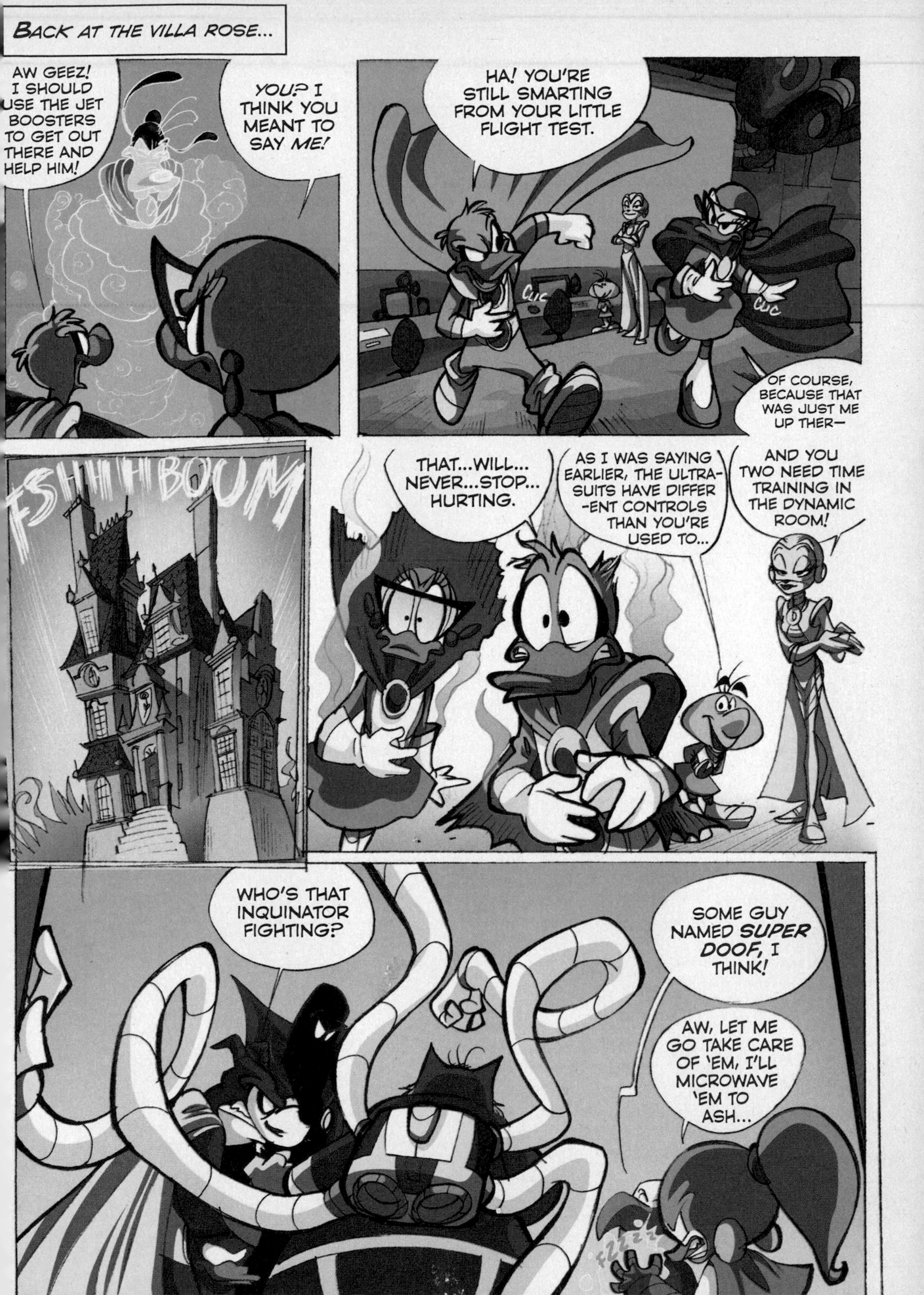
BACK AT THE VILLA ROSE...
AW GEEZ! I SHOULD USE THE JET BOOSTERS TO GET OUT THERE AND HELP HIM!
YOU? I THINK YOU MEANT TO SAY ME!
HA! YOU'RE STILL SMARTING FROM YOUR LITTLE FLIGHT TEST.
CLIC
CLIC
OF COURSE, BECAUSE THAT WAS JUST ME UP THER—
FSHHHHBOOM
THAT...WILL... NEVER...STOP... HURTING.
AS I WAS SAYING EARLIER, THE ULTRA-SUITS HAVE DIFFER -ENT CONTROLS THAN YOU'RE USED TO...
AND YOU TWO NEED TIME TRAINING IN THE DYNAMIC ROOM!
WHO'S THAT INQUINATOR FIGHTING?
SOME GUY NAMED SUPER DOOF, I THINK!
AW, LET ME GO TAKE CARE OF 'EM, I'LL MICROWAVE 'EM TO ASH...
fzzzz

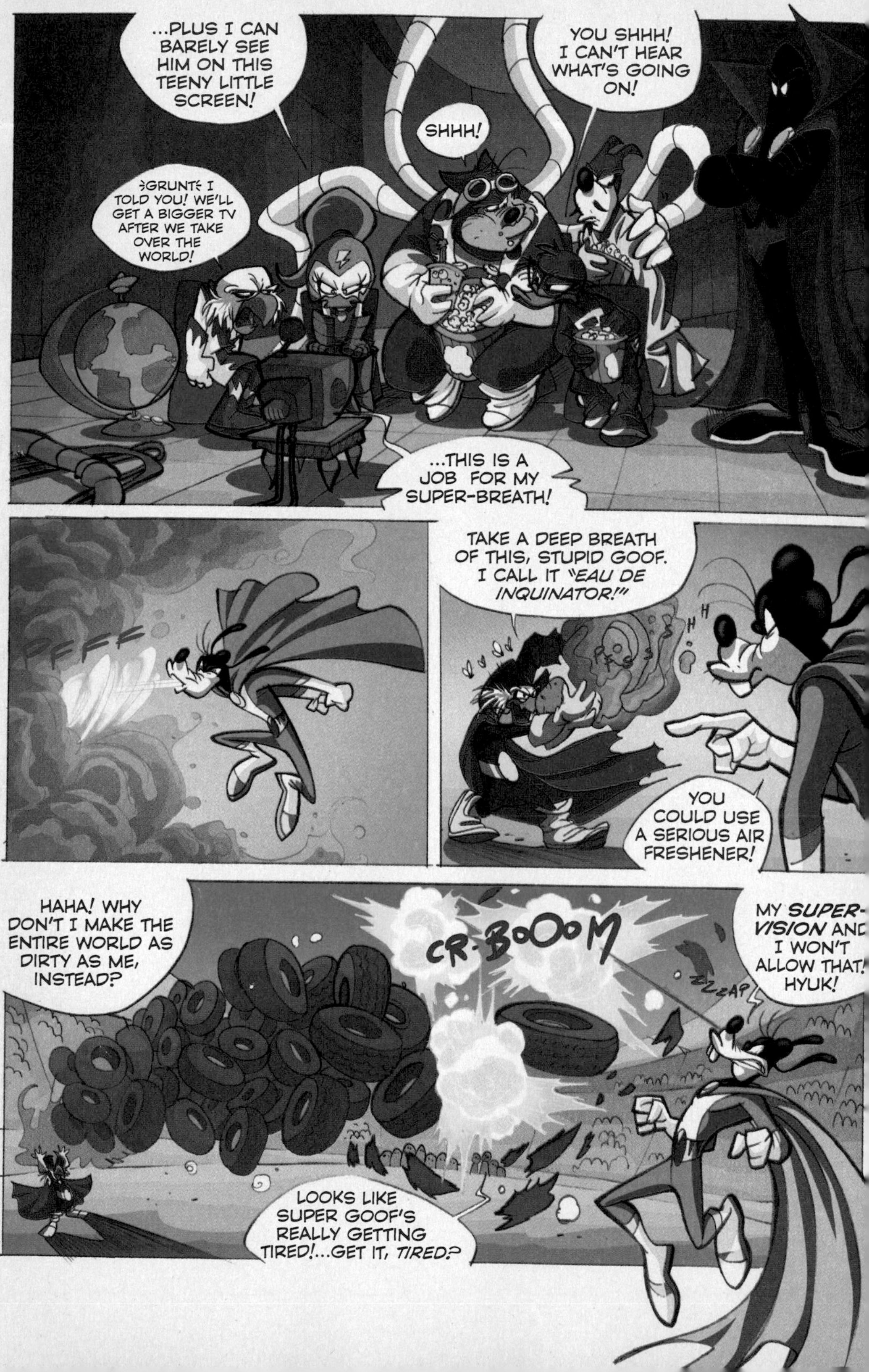
...PLUS I CAN BARELY SEE HIM ON THIS TEENY LITTLE SCREEN!
YOU SHHH! I CAN'T HEAR WHAT'S GOING ON!
SHHH!
GRUNT I TOLD YOU! WE'LL GET A BIGGER TV AFTER WE TAKE OVER THE WORLD!
...THIS IS A JOB FOR MY SUPER-BREATH!
PFFFF
TAKE A DEEP BREATH OF THIS, STUPID GOOF. I CALL IT "EAU DE INQUINATOR!"
YOU COULD USE A SERIOUS AIR FRESHENER!
HAHA! WHY DON'T I MAKE THE ENTIRE WORLD AS DIRTY AS ME, INSTEAD?
CR-BOOOM
MY SUPER-VISION AND I WON'T ALLOW THAT! HYUK!
ZZZAP
LOOKS LIKE SUPER GOOF'S REALLY GETTING TIRED!...GET IT, TIRED?

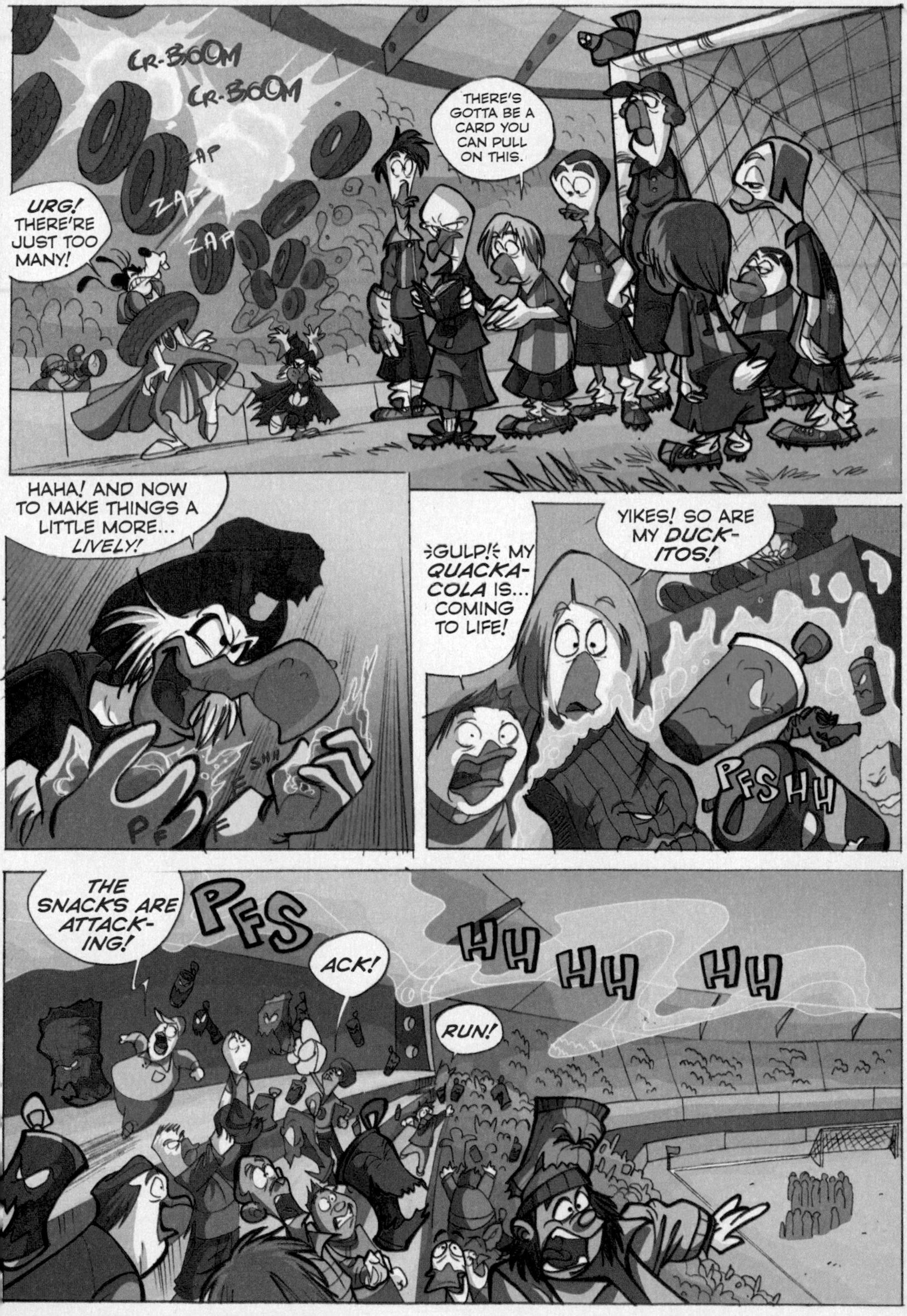
CR-BOOM
CR-BOOM
ZAP
ZAP
ZAP
URG! THERE'RE JUST TOO MANY!
THERE'S GOTTA BE A CARD YOU CAN PULL ON THIS.
HAHA! AND NOW TO MAKE THINGS A LITTLE MORE... LIVELY!
PF
YIKES! SO ARE MY DUCK-ITOS!
GULP! MY QUACKA-COLA IS... COMING TO LIFE!
PFSHH
THE SNACKS ARE ATTACK-ING!
PFS
HH HH HH
ACK!
RUN!

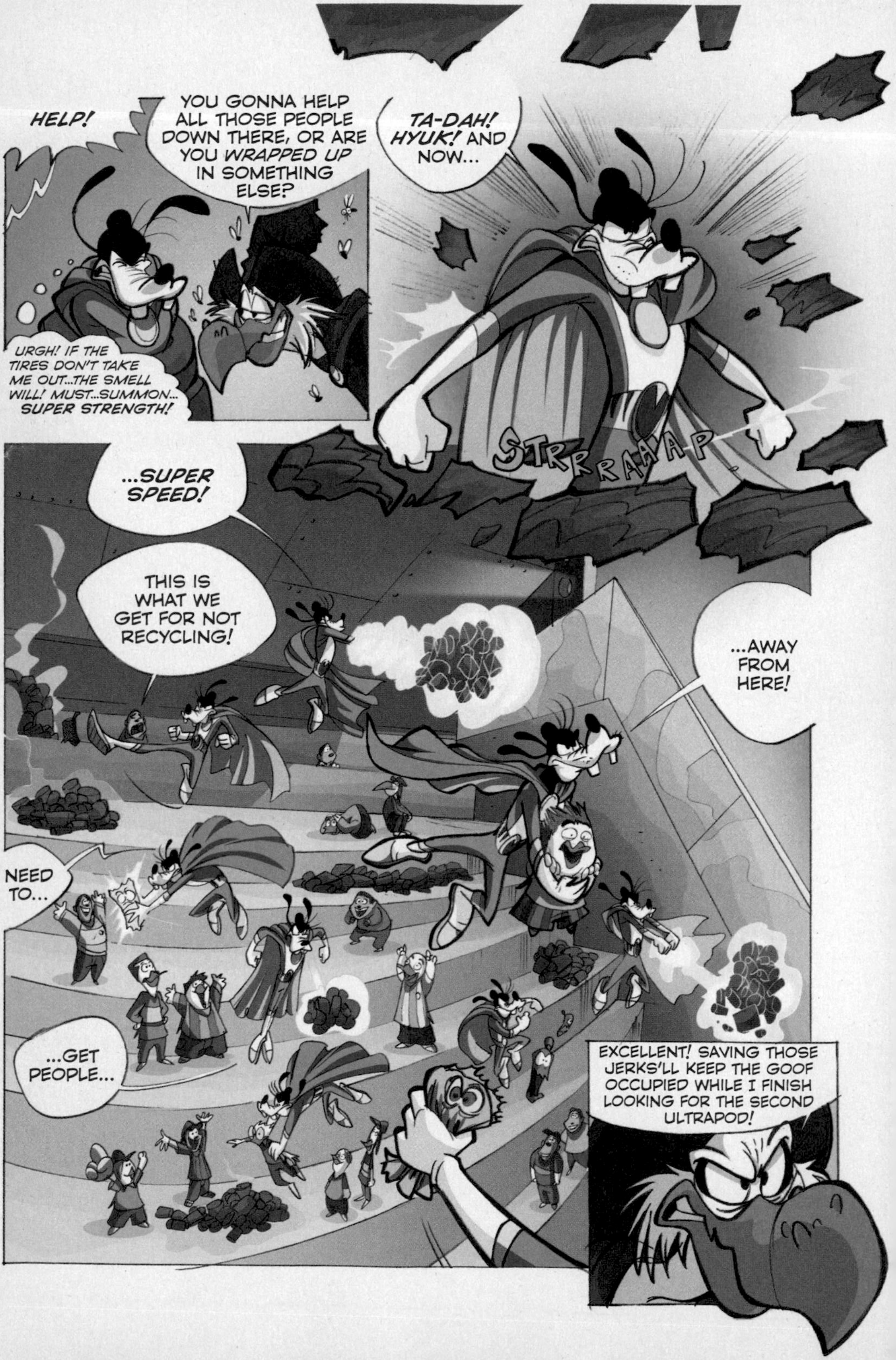

HELP!
YOU GONNA HELP ALL THOSE PEOPLE DOWN THERE, OR ARE YOU WRAPPED UP IN SOMETHING ELSE?
URGH! IF THE TIRES DON'T TAKE ME OUT...THE SMELL WILL! MUST...SUMMON... SUPER STRENGTH!
TA-DAH! HYUK! AND NOW...
STRRRAAAAP
...SUPER SPEED!
THIS IS WHAT WE GET FOR NOT RECYCLING!
NEED TO...
...GET PEOPLE...
...AWAY FROM HERE!
EXCELLENT! SAVING THOSE JERKS'LL KEEP THE GOOF OCCUPIED WHILE I FINISH LOOKING FOR THE SECOND ULTRAPOD!

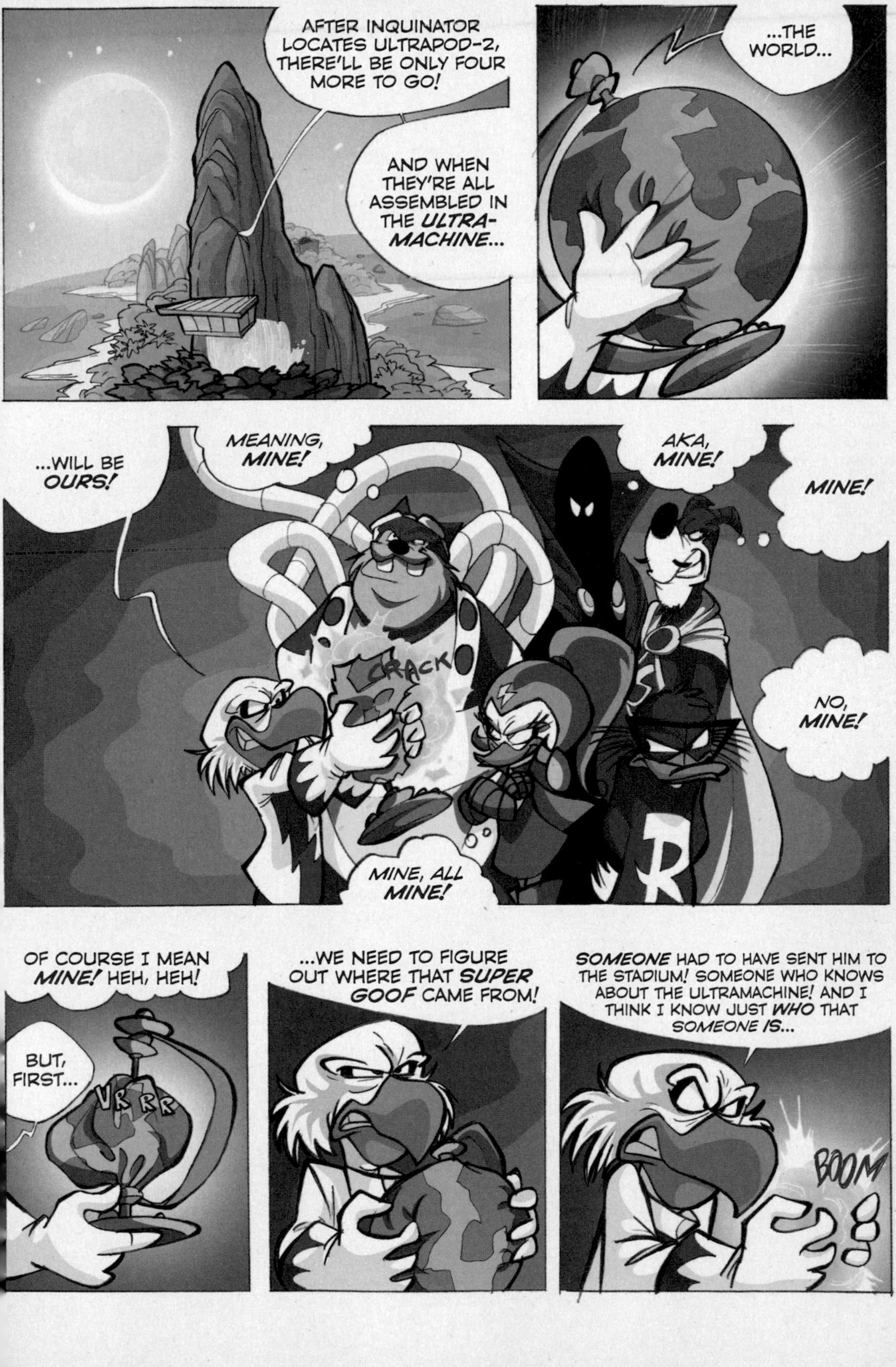
AFTER INQUINATOR LOCATES ULTRAPOD-2, THERE'LL BE ONLY FOUR MORE TO GO!
AND WHEN THEY'RE ALL ASSEMBLED IN THE *ULTRA-MACHINE*...
...THE WORLD...
...WILL BE *OURS!*
MEANING, *MINE!*
AKA, *MINE!*
MINE!
CRACK
NO, *MINE!*
MINE, ALL *MINE!*
OF COURSE I MEAN *MINE!* HEH, HEH!
BUT, FIRST...
VRRR
...WE NEED TO FIGURE OUT WHERE THAT *SUPER GOOF* CAME FROM!
SOMEONE HAD TO HAVE SENT HIM TO THE STADIUM! SOMEONE WHO KNOWS ABOUT THE ULTRAMACHINE! AND I THINK I KNOW JUST *WHO* THAT SOMEONE *IS*...
BOOM

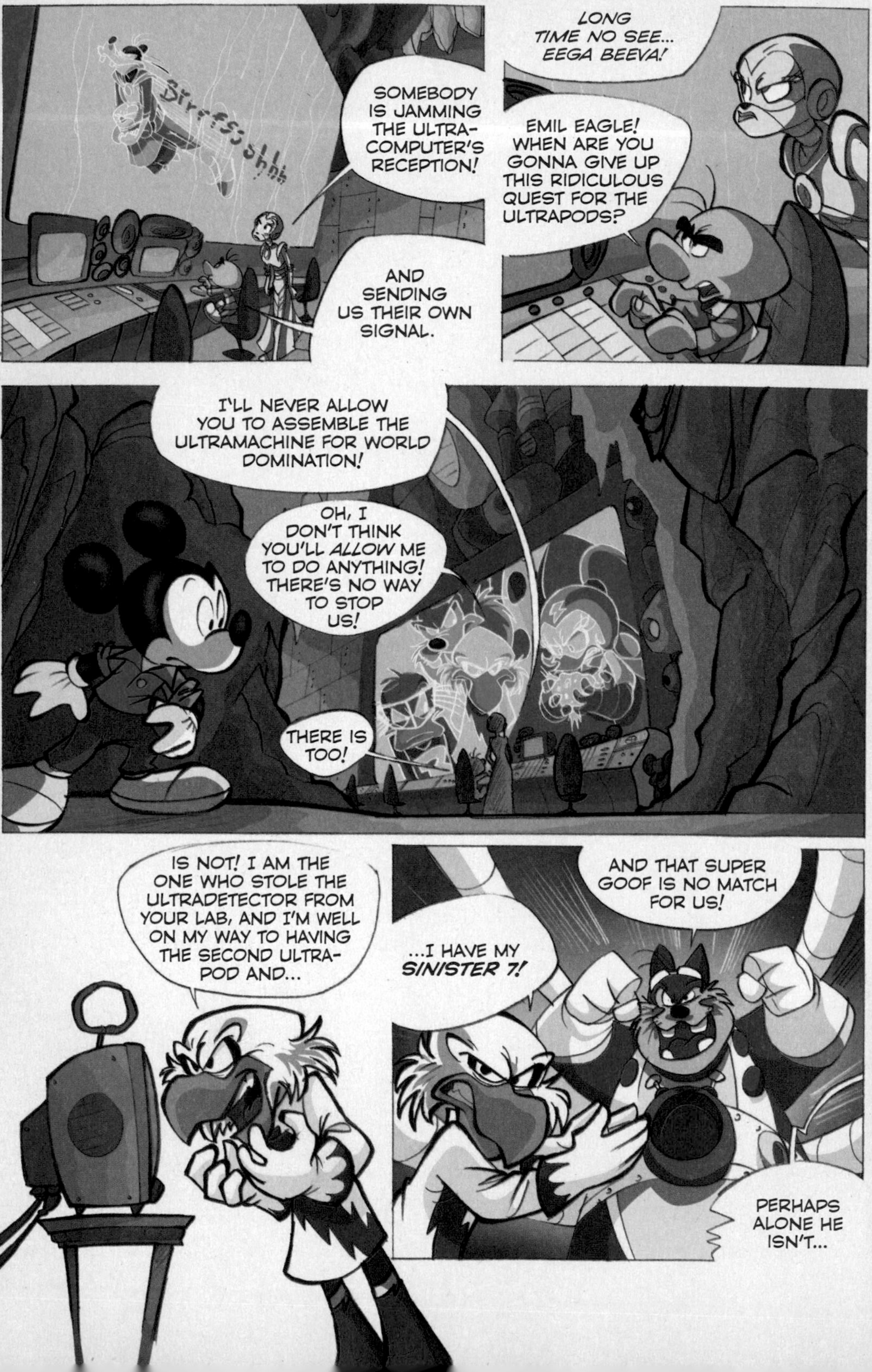
SOMEBODY IS JAMMING THE ULTRA-COMPUTER'S RECEPTION!
AND SENDING US THEIR OWN SIGNAL.
LONG TIME NO SEE... EEGA BEEVA!
EMIL EAGLE! WHEN ARE YOU GONNA GIVE UP THIS RIDICULOUS QUEST FOR THE ULTRAPODS?
I'LL NEVER ALLOW YOU TO ASSEMBLE THE ULTRAMACHINE FOR WORLD DOMINATION!
OH, I DON'T THINK YOU'LL *ALLOW* ME TO DO ANYTHING! THERE'S NO WAY TO STOP US!
THERE IS TOO!
IS NOT! I AM THE ONE WHO STOLE THE ULTRADETECTOR FROM YOUR LAB, AND I'M WELL ON MY WAY TO HAVING THE SECOND ULTRA-POD AND...
...I HAVE MY ***SINISTER 7!***
AND THAT SUPER GOOF IS NO MATCH FOR US!
PERHAPS ALONE HE ISN'T...

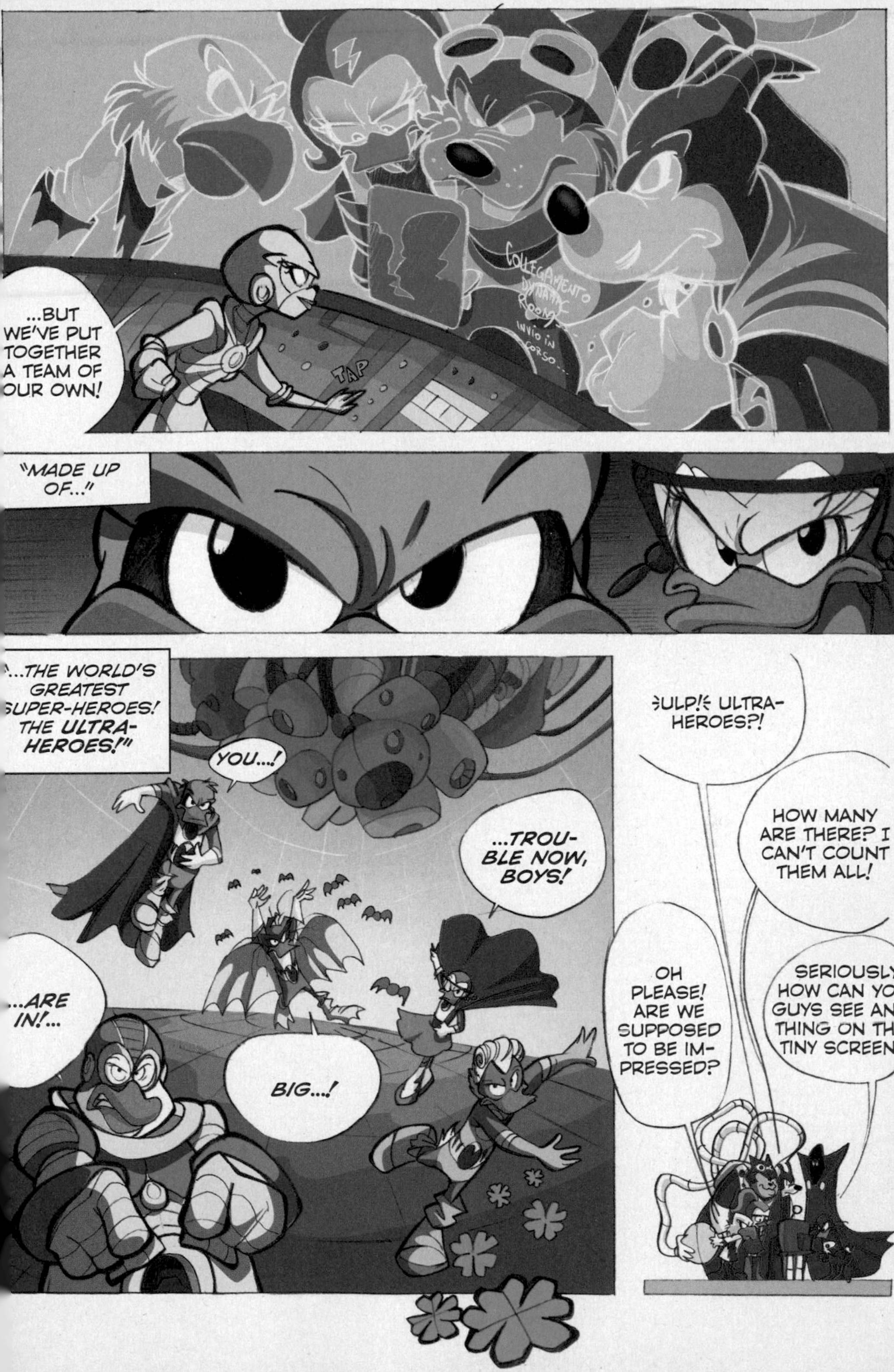
...BUT WE'VE PUT TOGETHER A TEAM OF OUR OWN!
TAP
"MADE UP OF..."
"...THE WORLD'S GREATEST SUPER-HEROES! THE ULTRA-HEROES!"
YOU...!
...ARE IN!...
BIG...!
...TROUBLE NOW, BOYS!
GULP! ULTRA-HEROES?!
HOW MANY ARE THERE? I CAN'T COUNT THEM ALL!
OH PLEASE! ARE WE SUPPOSED TO BE IMPRESSED?
SERIOUSLY! HOW CAN YOU GUYS SEE ANYTHING ON THIS TINY SCREEN?

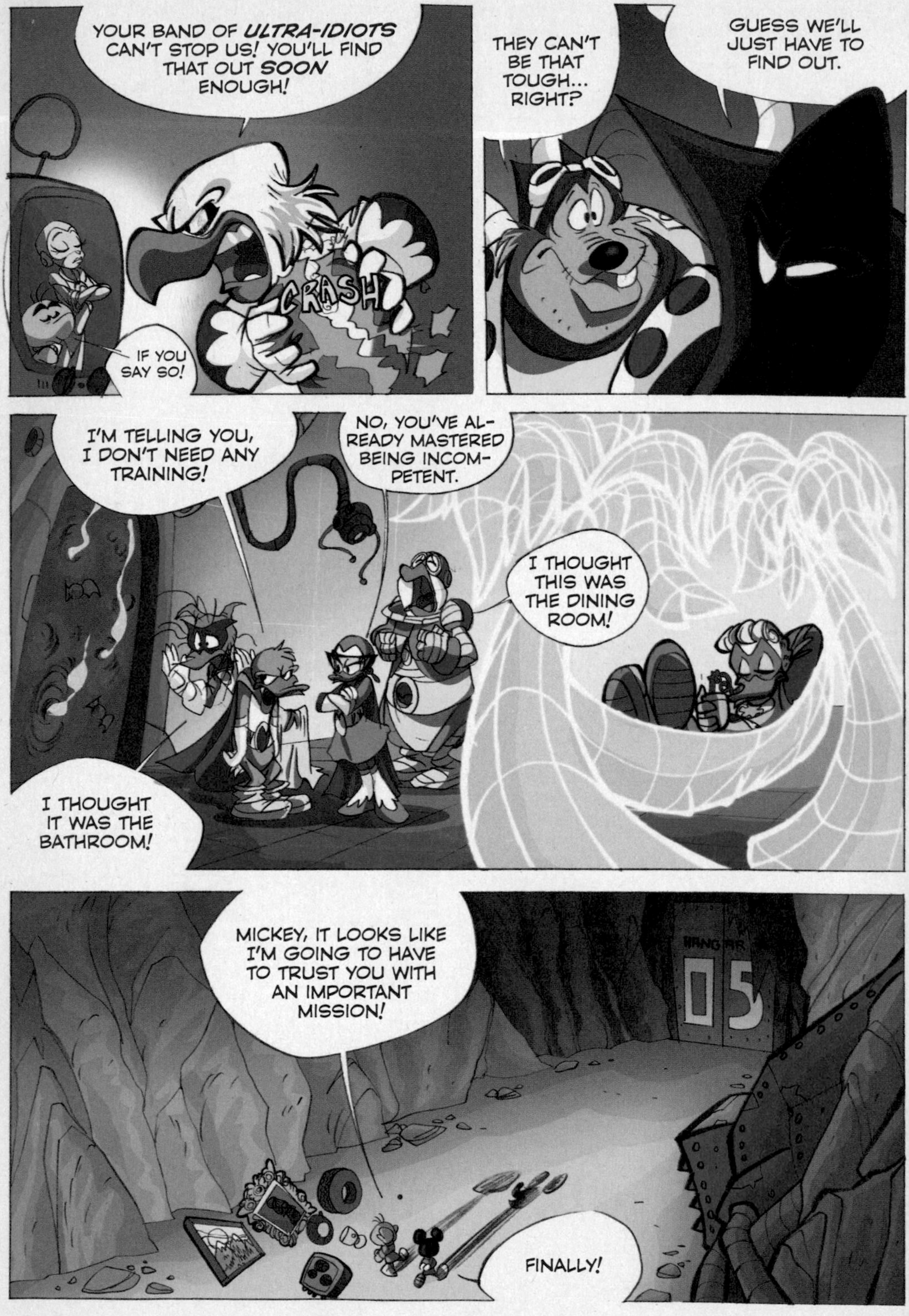
YOUR BAND OF *ULTRA-IDIOTS* CAN'T STOP US! YOU'LL FIND THAT OUT *SOON* ENOUGH!
CRASH
IF YOU SAY SO!
THEY CAN'T BE THAT TOUGH... RIGHT?
GUESS WE'LL JUST HAVE TO FIND OUT.
I'M TELLING YOU, I DON'T NEED ANY TRAINING!
NO, YOU'VE AL-READY MASTERED BEING INCOM-PETENT.
I THOUGHT THIS WAS THE DINING ROOM!
I THOUGHT IT WAS THE BATHROOM!
MICKEY, IT LOOKS LIKE I'M GOING TO HAVE TO TRUST YOU WITH AN IMPORTANT MISSION!
05
FINALLY!

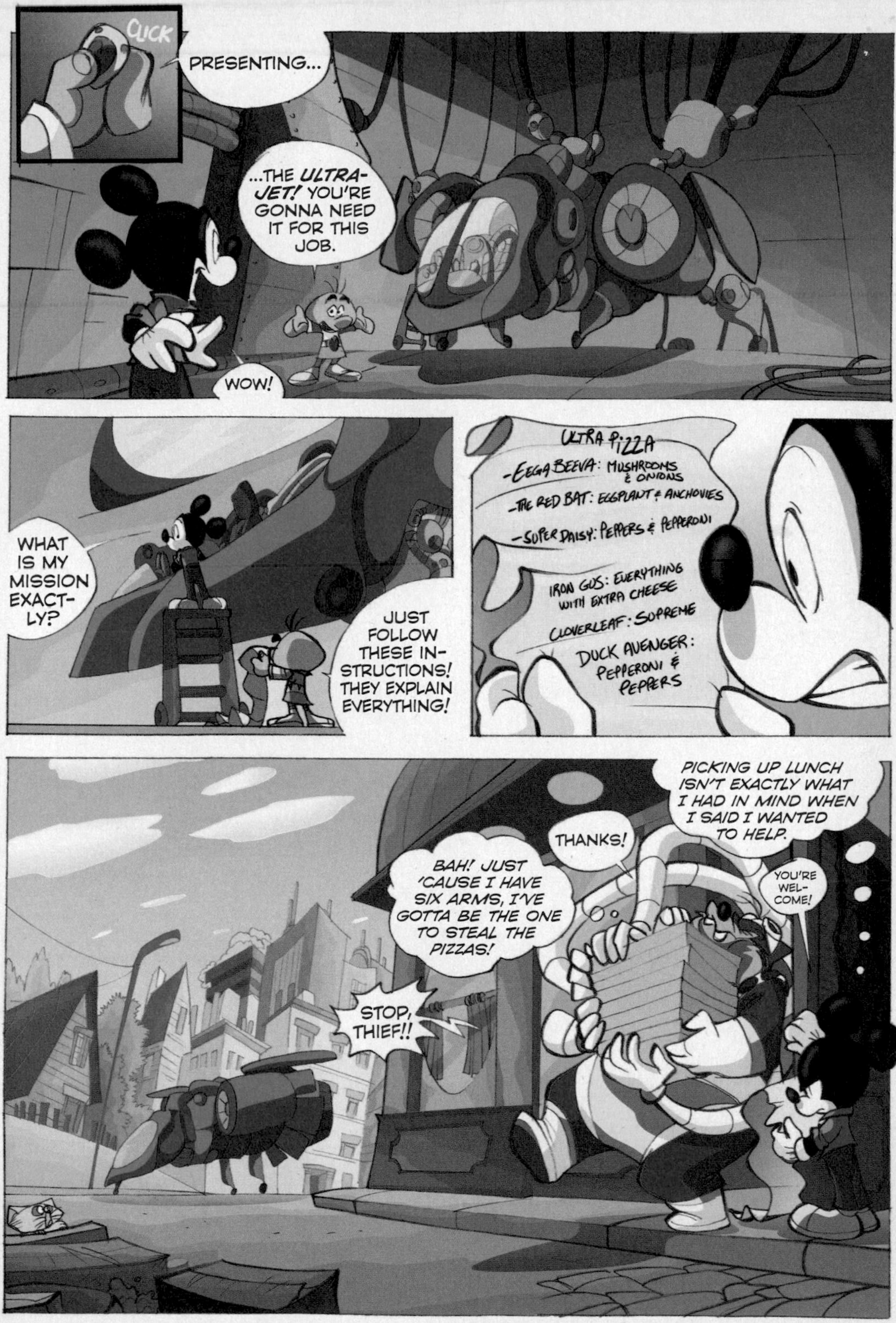
CLICK
PRESENTING...
...THE ULTRA-JET! YOU'RE GONNA NEED IT FOR THIS JOB.
WOW!
WHAT IS MY MISSION EXACTLY?
JUST FOLLOW THESE INSTRUCTIONS! THEY EXPLAIN EVERYTHING!
ULTRA PIZZA
-EEGA BEEVA: MUSHROOMS & ONIONS
-THE RED BAT: EGGPLANT & ANCHOVIES
-SUPER DAISY: PEPPERS & PEPPERONI
IRON GUS: EVERYTHING WITH EXTRA CHEESE
CLOVERLEAF: SUPREME
DUCK AVENGER: PEPPERONI & PEPPERS
PICKING UP LUNCH ISN'T EXACTLY WHAT I HAD IN MIND WHEN I SAID I WANTED TO HELP.
THANKS!
YOU'RE WELCOME!
BAH! JUST 'CAUSE I HAVE SIX ARMS, I'VE GOTTA BE THE ONE TO STEAL THE PIZZAS!
STOP, THIEF!!

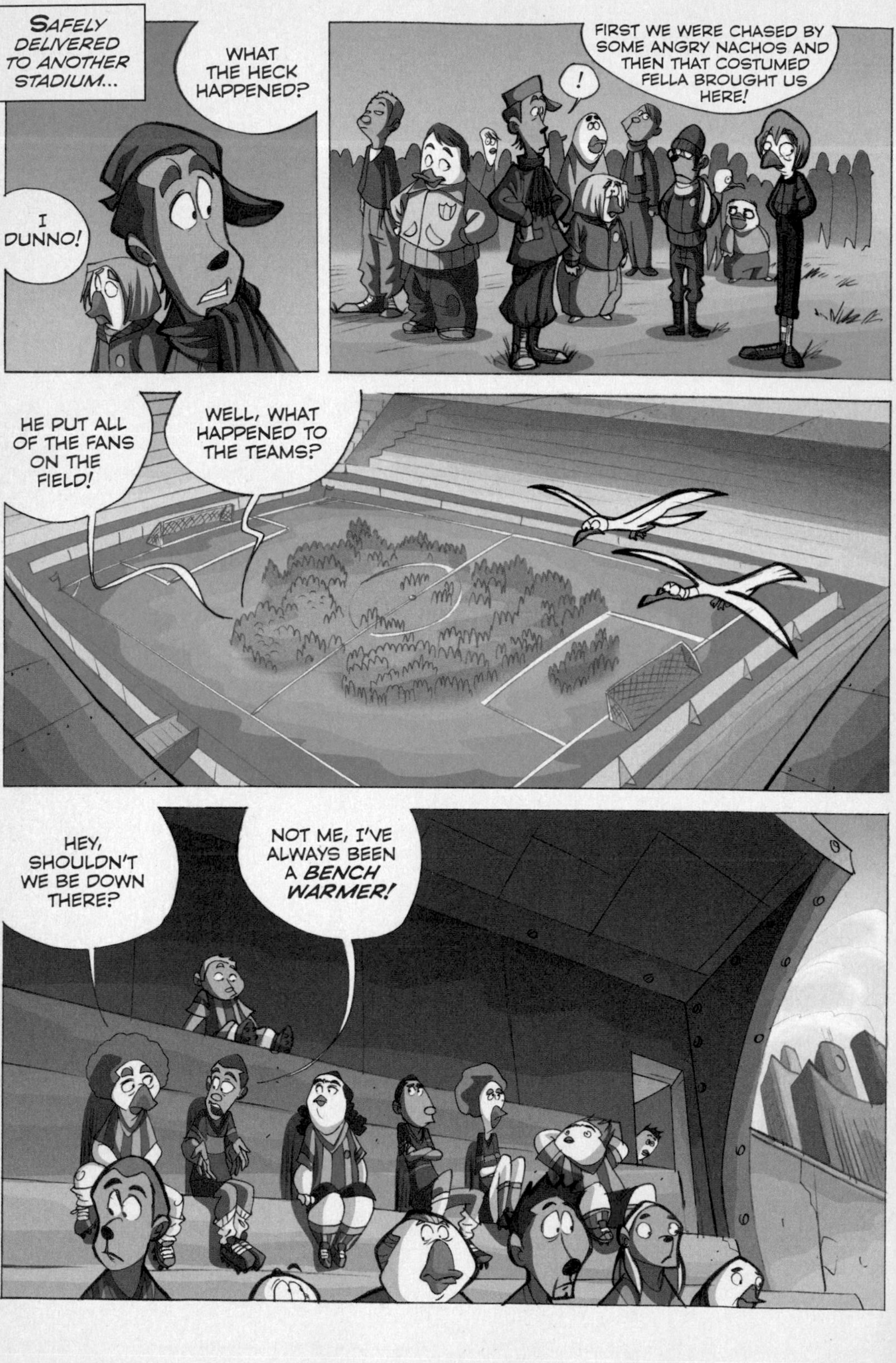
SAFELY DELIVERED TO ANOTHER STADIUM...
WHAT THE HECK HAPPENED?
I DUNNO!
FIRST WE WERE CHASED BY SOME ANGRY NACHOS AND THEN THAT COSTUMED FELLA BROUGHT US HERE!
!
WELL, WHAT HAPPENED TO THE TEAMS?
HE PUT ALL OF THE FANS ON THE FIELD!
HEY, SHOULDN'T WE BE DOWN THERE?
NOT ME, I'VE ALWAYS BEEN A *BENCH WARMER!*

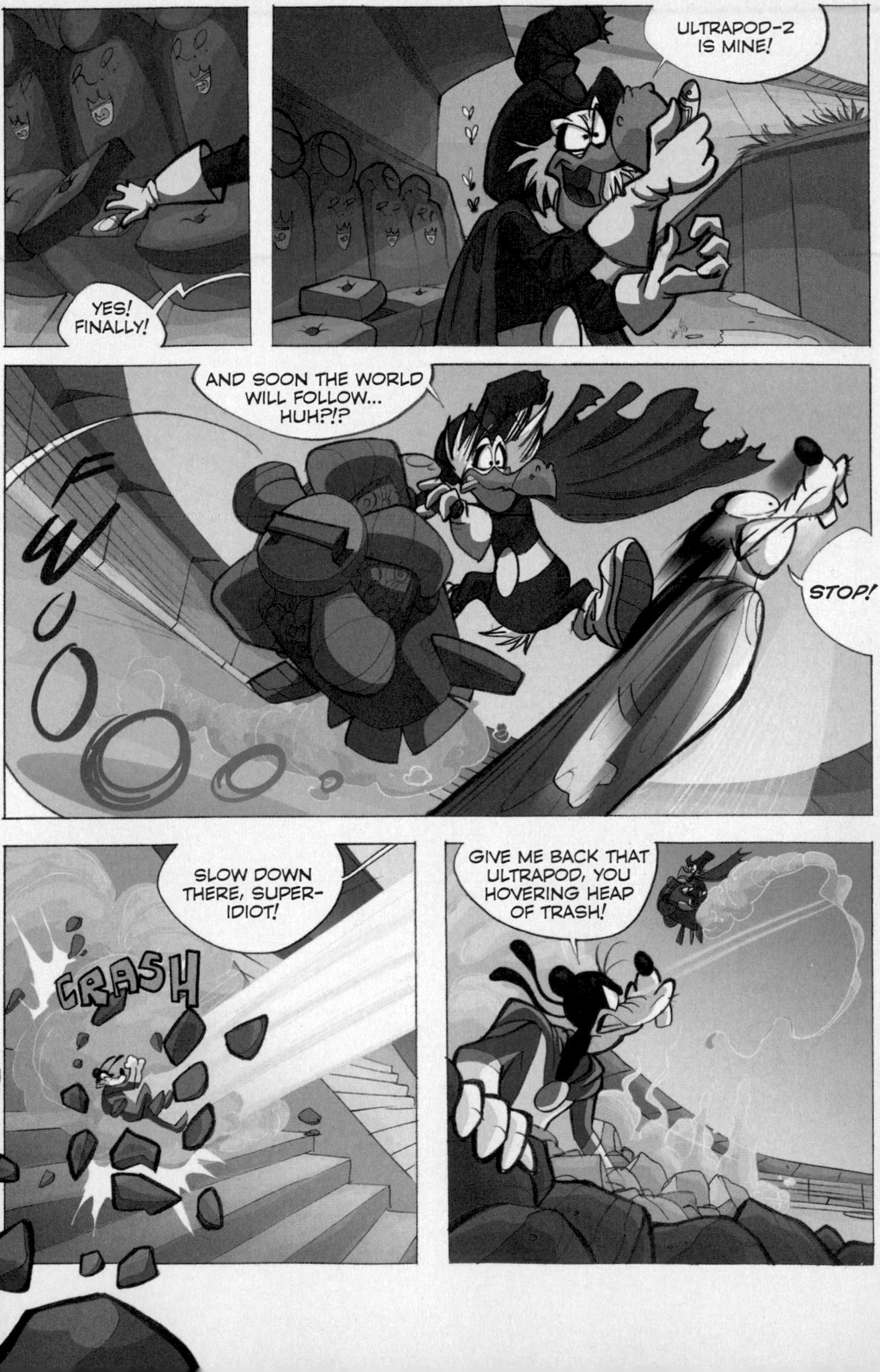
YES! FINALLY!
ULTRAPOD-2 IS MINE!
AND SOON THE WORLD WILL FOLLOW... HUH?!?
FWOOOOO
STOP!
SLOW DOWN THERE, SUPER-IDIOT!
CRASH
GIVE ME BACK THAT ULTRAPOD, YOU HOVERING HEAP OF TRASH!

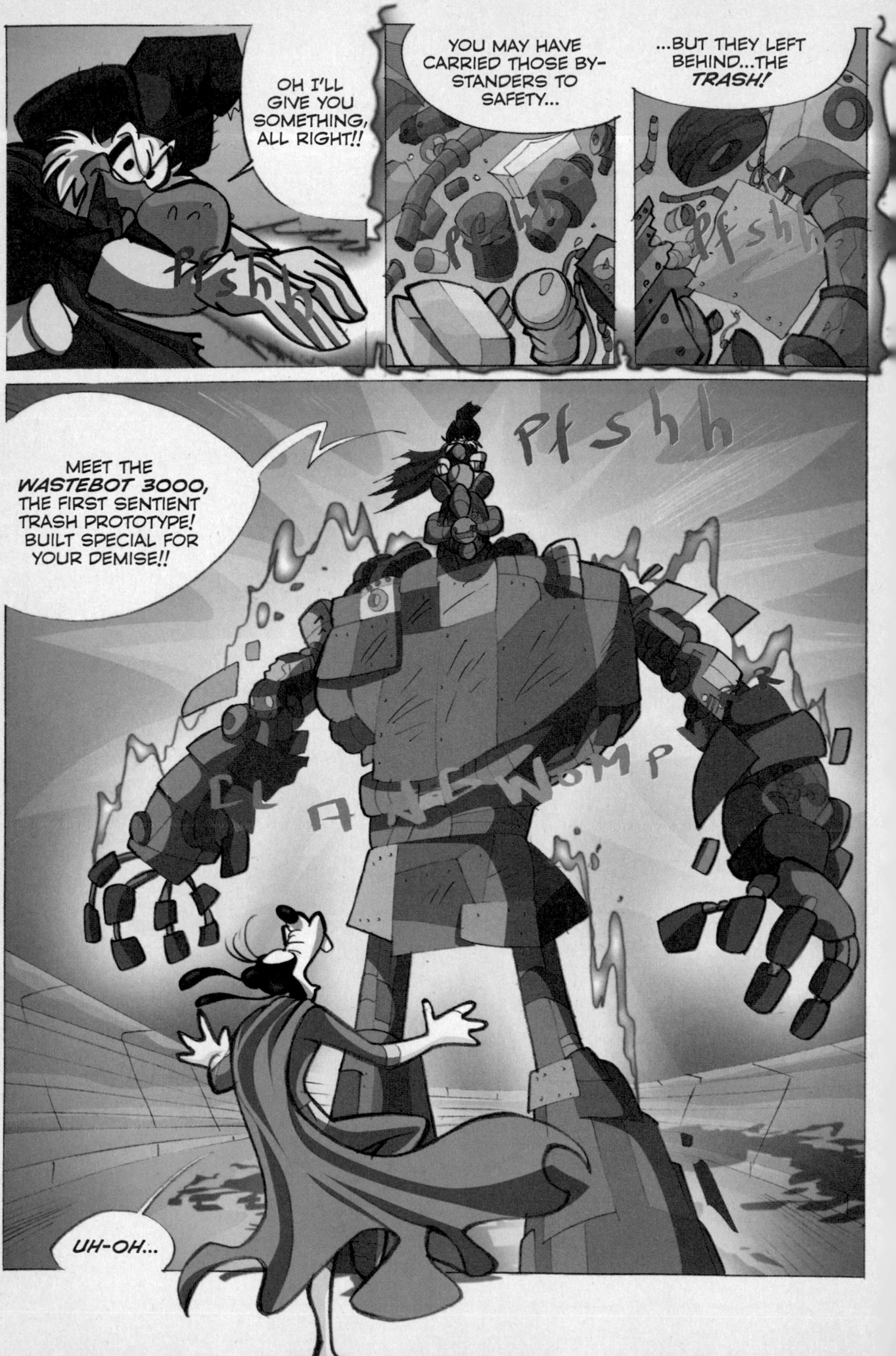
OH I'LL GIVE YOU SOMETHING, ALL RIGHT!!
PFSHH
YOU MAY HAVE CARRIED THOSE BY-STANDERS TO SAFETY...
PFSHH
...BUT THEY LEFT BEHIND...THE TRASH!
PFSHH
MEET THE WASTEBOT 3000, THE FIRST SENTIENT TRASH PROTOTYPE! BUILT SPECIAL FOR YOUR DEMISE!!
PFSHH
CLANGWOMP
UH-OH...

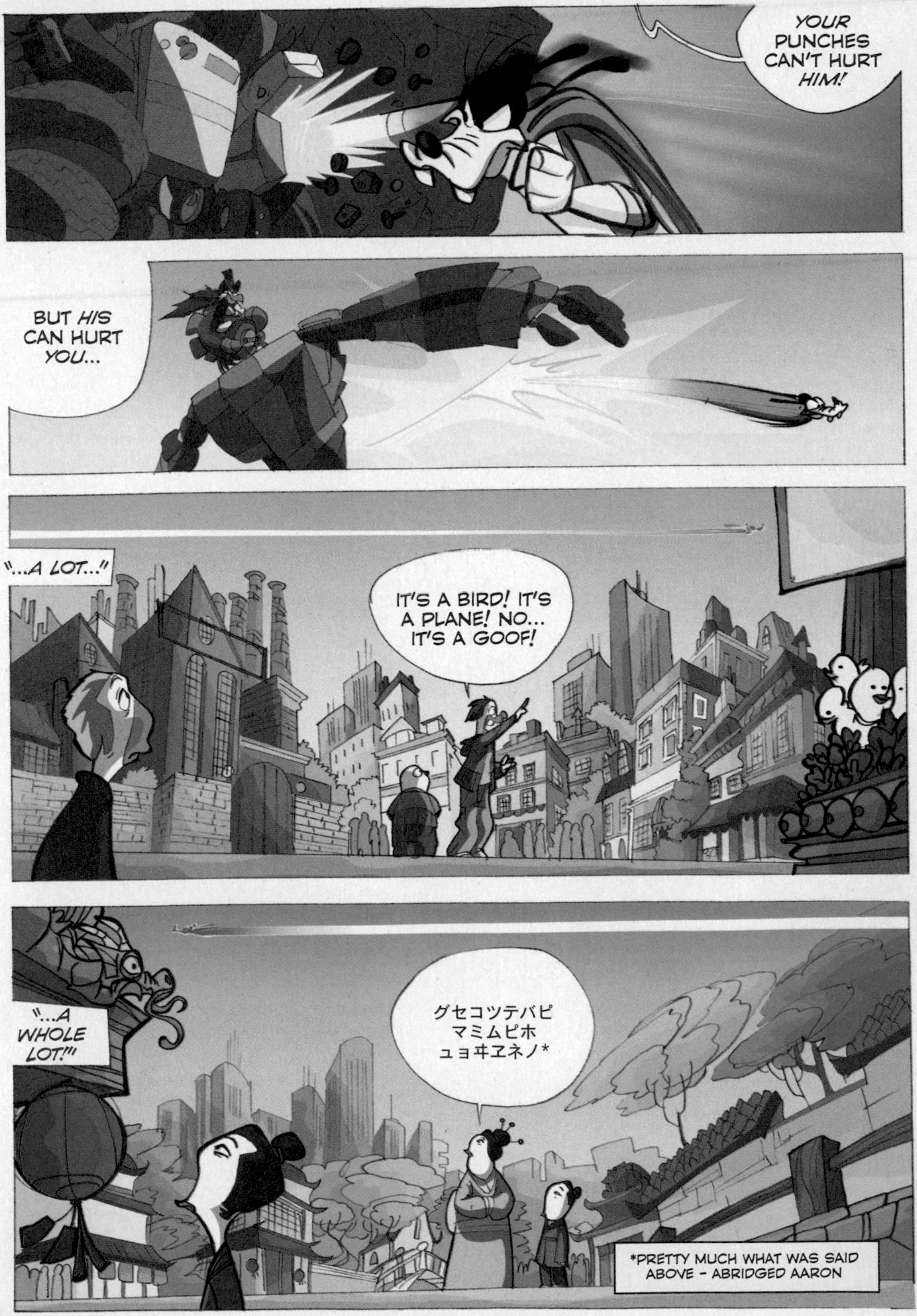
YOUR PUNCHES CAN'T HURT HIM!
BUT HIS CAN HURT YOU...
"...A LOT..."
IT'S A BIRD! IT'S A PLANE! NO... IT'S A GOOF!
"...A WHOLE LOT!"
グセコツテバピ
マミムピホ
ュョヰヱネノ*
*PRETTY MUCH WHAT WAS SAID ABOVE - ABRIDGED AARON

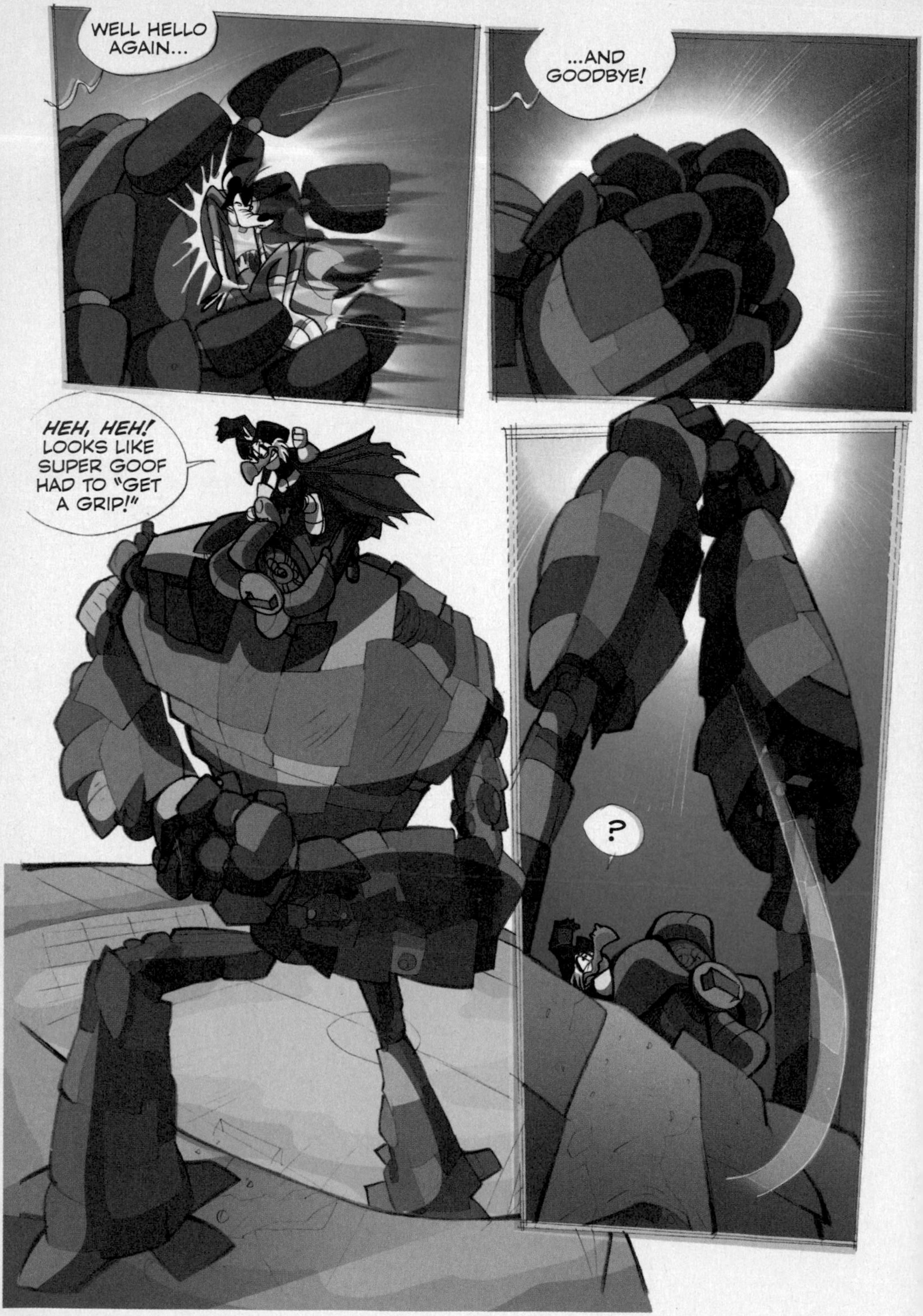

WELL HELLO AGAIN...
...AND GOODBYE!
HEH, HEH! LOOKS LIKE SUPER GOOF HAD TO "GET A GRIP!"
?

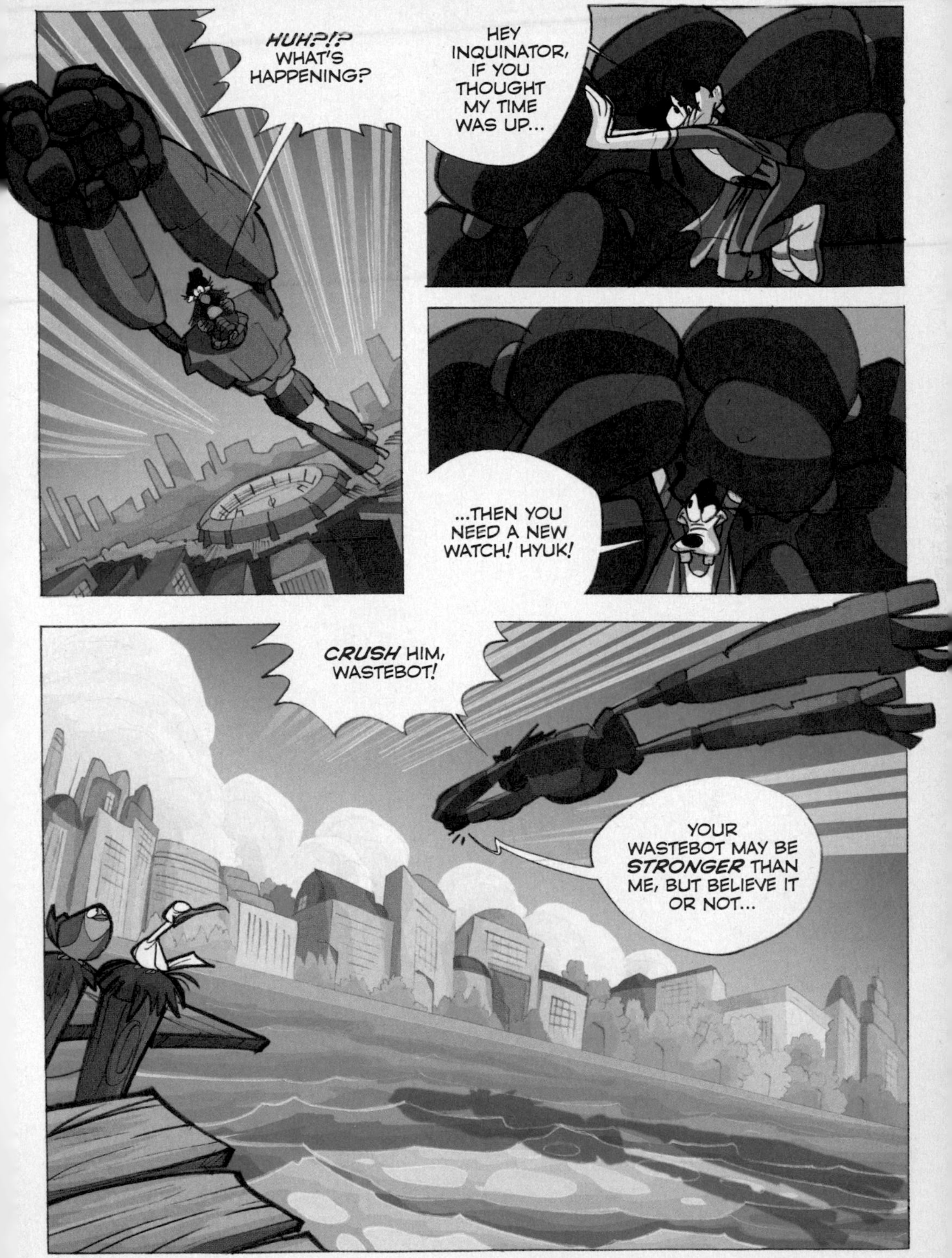
HUH?!? WHAT'S HAPPENING?
HEY INQUINATOR, IF YOU THOUGHT MY TIME WAS UP...
...THEN YOU NEED A NEW WATCH! HYUK!
CRUSH HIM, WASTEBOT!
YOUR WASTEBOT MAY BE STRONGER THAN ME, BUT BELIEVE IT OR NOT...

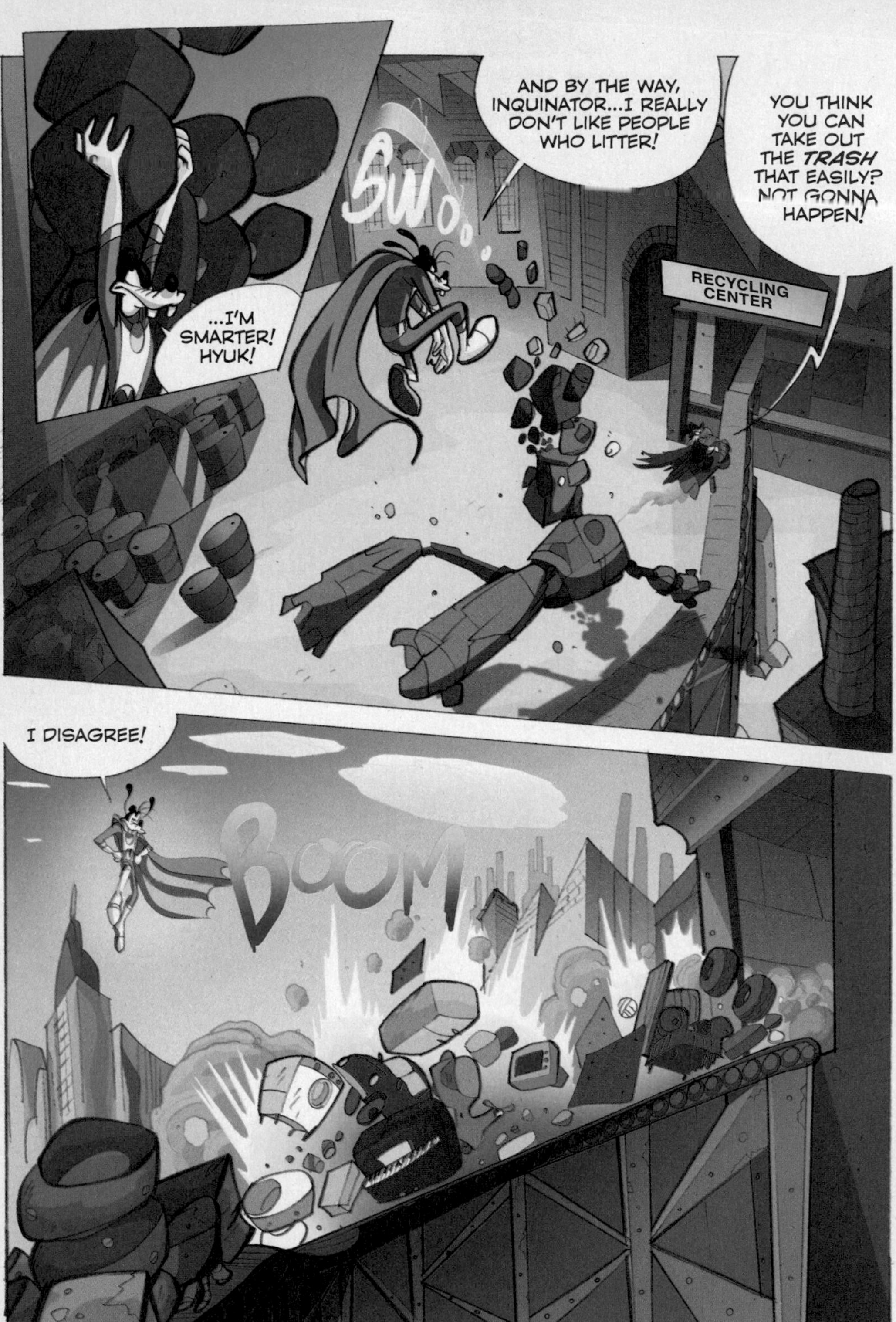
...I'M SMARTER! HYUK!
AND BY THE WAY, INQUINATOR...I REALLY DON'T LIKE PEOPLE WHO LITTER!
SWOOO
YOU THINK YOU CAN TAKE OUT THE TRASH THAT EASILY? NOT GONNA HAPPEN!
RECYCLING CENTER
I DISAGREE!
BOOM

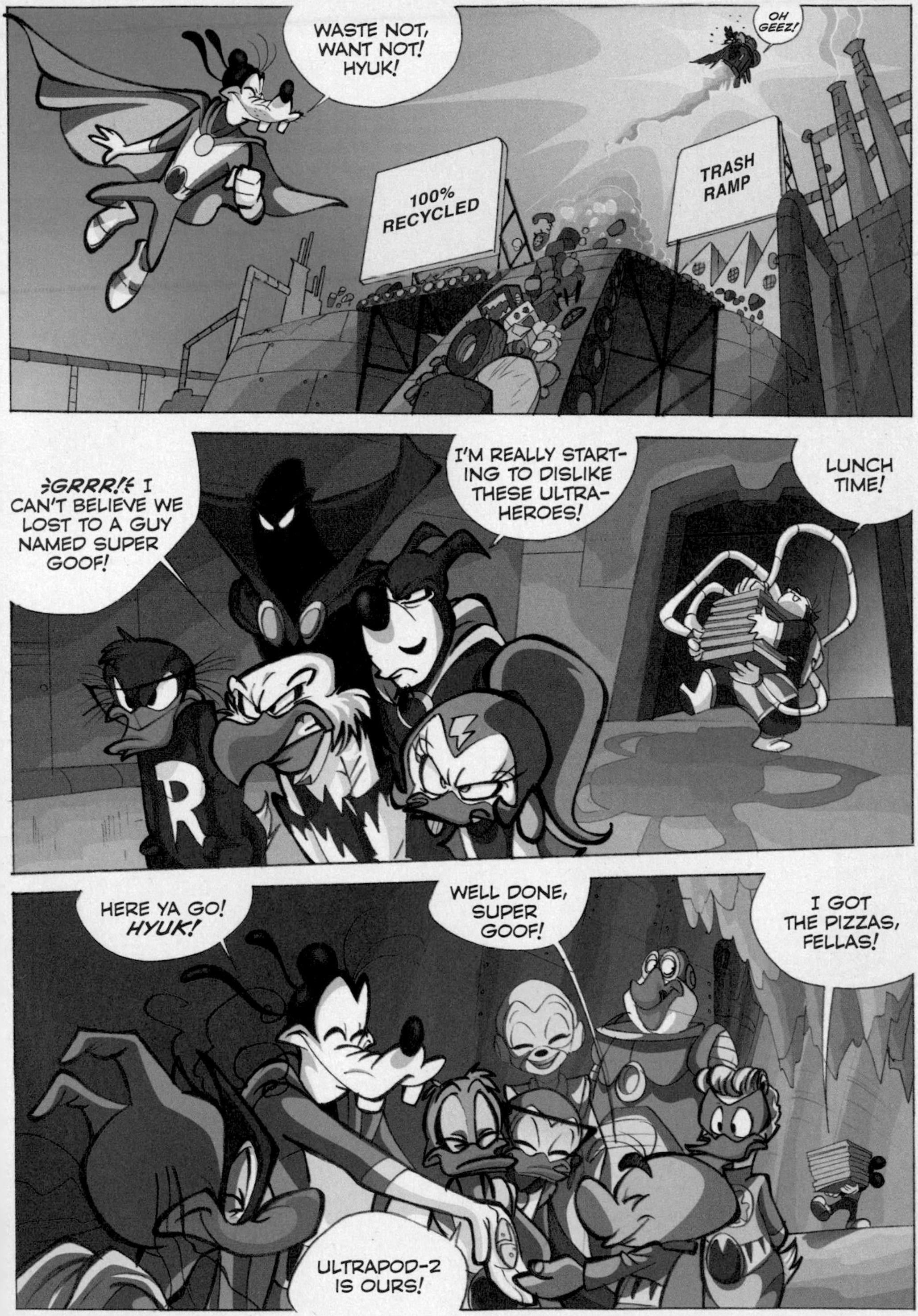
WASTE NOT, WANT NOT! HYUK!
OH GEEZ!
100% RECYCLED
TRASH RAMP
GRRR! I CAN'T BELIEVE WE LOST TO A GUY NAMED SUPER GOOF!
I'M REALLY STARTING TO DISLIKE THESE ULTRA-HEROES!
LUNCH TIME!
R
HERE YA GO! HYUK!
WELL DONE, SUPER GOOF!
I GOT THE PIZZAS, FELLAS!
ULTRAPOD-2 IS OURS!

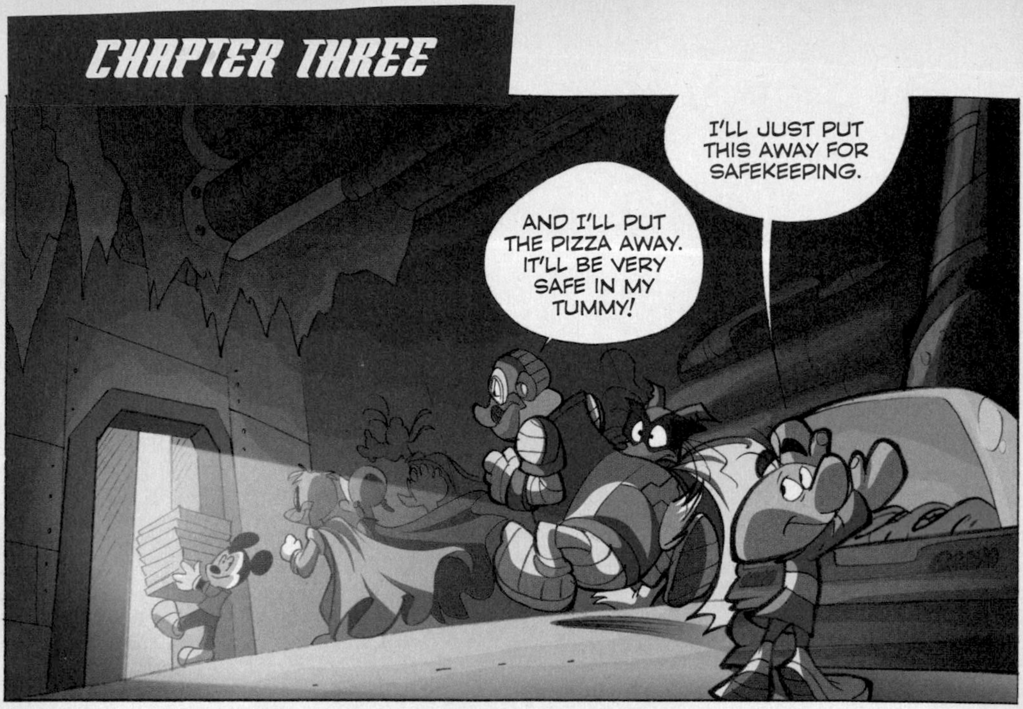
CHAPTER THREE
I'LL JUST PUT THIS AWAY FOR SAFEKEEPING.
AND I'LL PUT THE PIZZA AWAY. IT'LL BE VERY SAFE IN MY TUMMY!

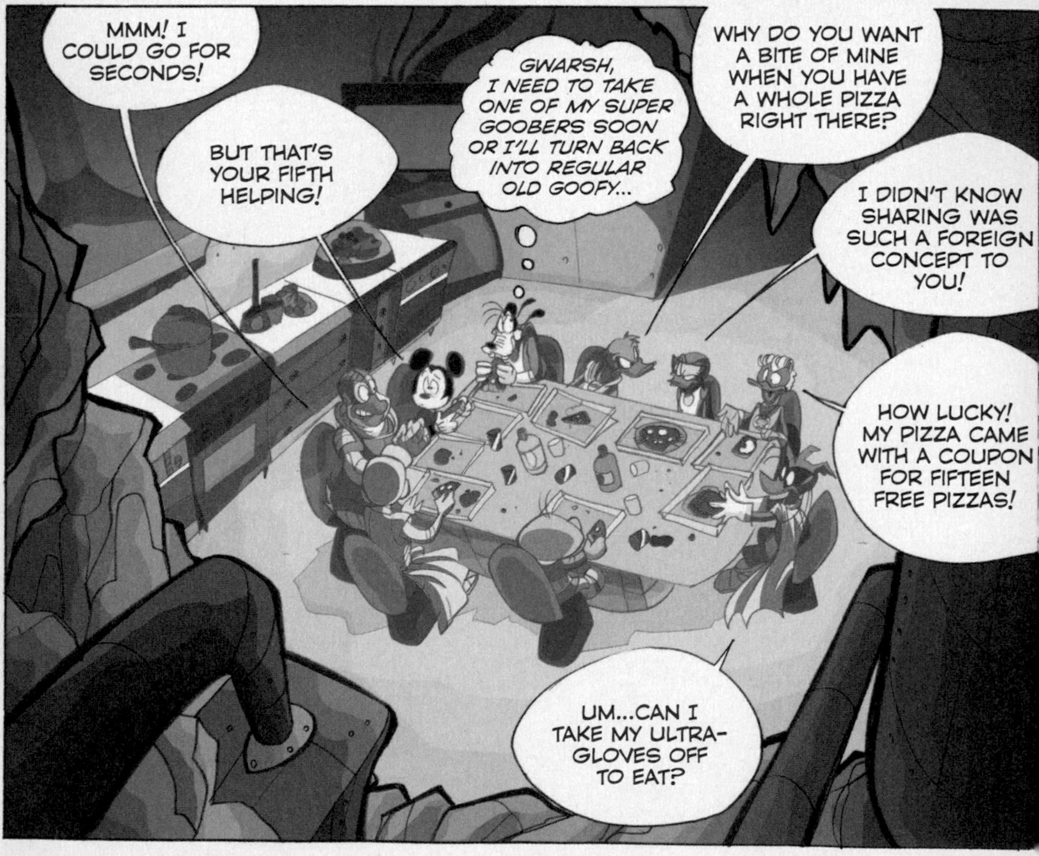
MMM! I COULD GO FOR SECONDS!
BUT THAT'S YOUR FIFTH HELPING!
GWARSH, I NEED TO TAKE ONE OF MY SUPER GOOBERS SOON OR I'LL TURN BACK INTO REGULAR OLD GOOFY...
WHY DO YOU WANT A BITE OF MINE WHEN YOU HAVE A WHOLE PIZZA RIGHT THERE?
I DIDN'T KNOW SHARING WAS SUCH A FOREIGN CONCEPT TO YOU!
HOW LUCKY! MY PIZZA CAME WITH A COUPON FOR FIFTEEN FREE PIZZAS!
UM...CAN I TAKE MY ULTRA-GLOVES OFF TO EAT?

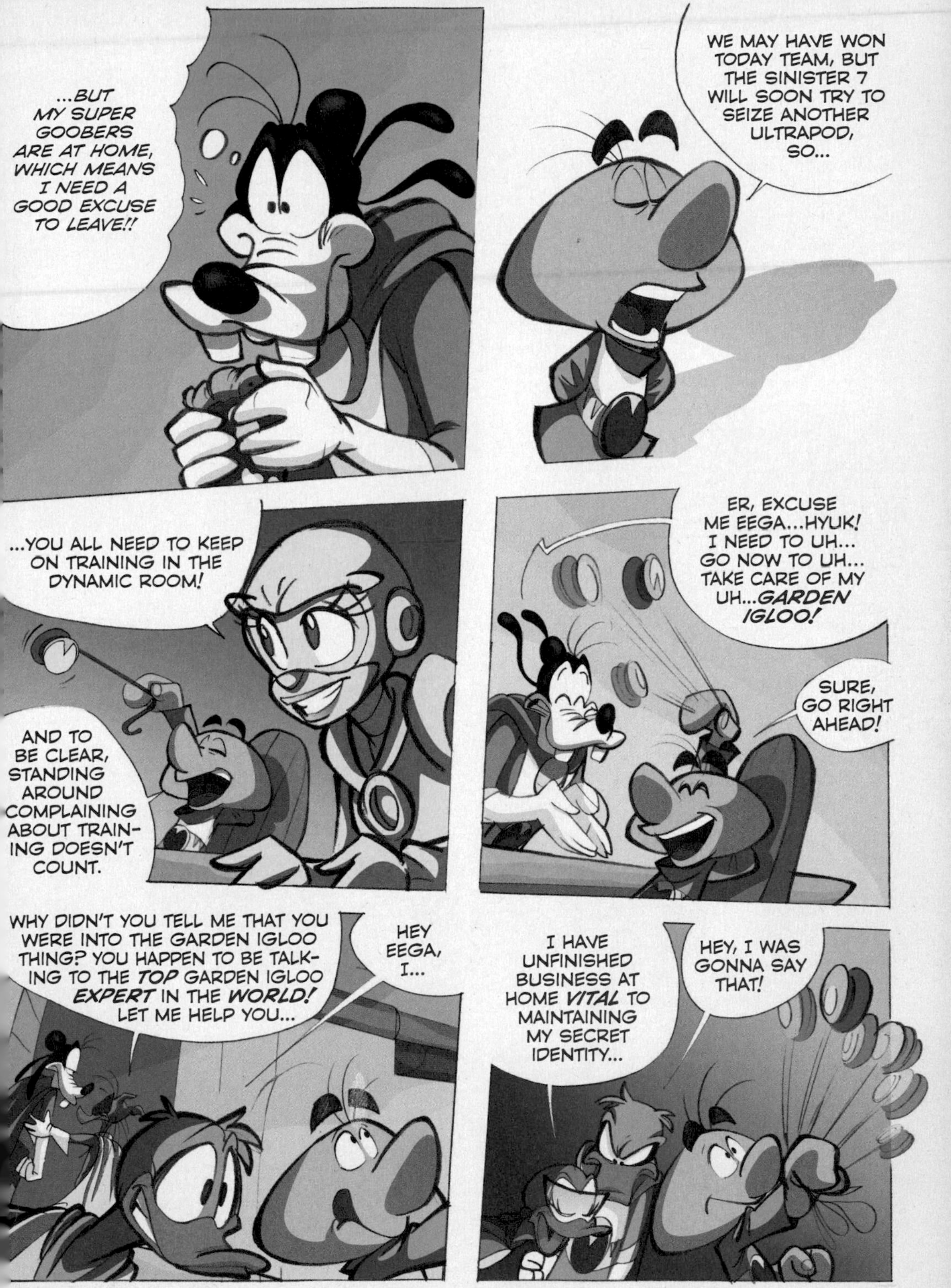
...BUT MY SUPER GOOBERS ARE AT HOME, WHICH MEANS I NEED A GOOD EXCUSE TO LEAVE!!
WE MAY HAVE WON TODAY TEAM, BUT THE SINISTER 7 WILL SOON TRY TO SEIZE ANOTHER ULTRAPOD, SO...
...YOU ALL NEED TO KEEP ON TRAINING IN THE DYNAMIC ROOM!
AND TO BE CLEAR, STANDING AROUND COMPLAINING ABOUT TRAINING DOESN'T COUNT.
ER, EXCUSE ME EEGA...HYUK! I NEED TO UH... GO NOW TO UH... TAKE CARE OF MY UH...GARDEN IGLOO!
SURE, GO RIGHT AHEAD!
WHY DIDN'T YOU TELL ME THAT YOU WERE INTO THE GARDEN IGLOO THING? YOU HAPPEN TO BE TALKING TO THE TOP GARDEN IGLOO EXPERT IN THE WORLD! LET ME HELP YOU...
HEY EEGA, I...
I HAVE UNFINISHED BUSINESS AT HOME VITAL TO MAINTAINING MY SECRET IDENTITY...
HEY, I WAS GONNA SAY THAT!

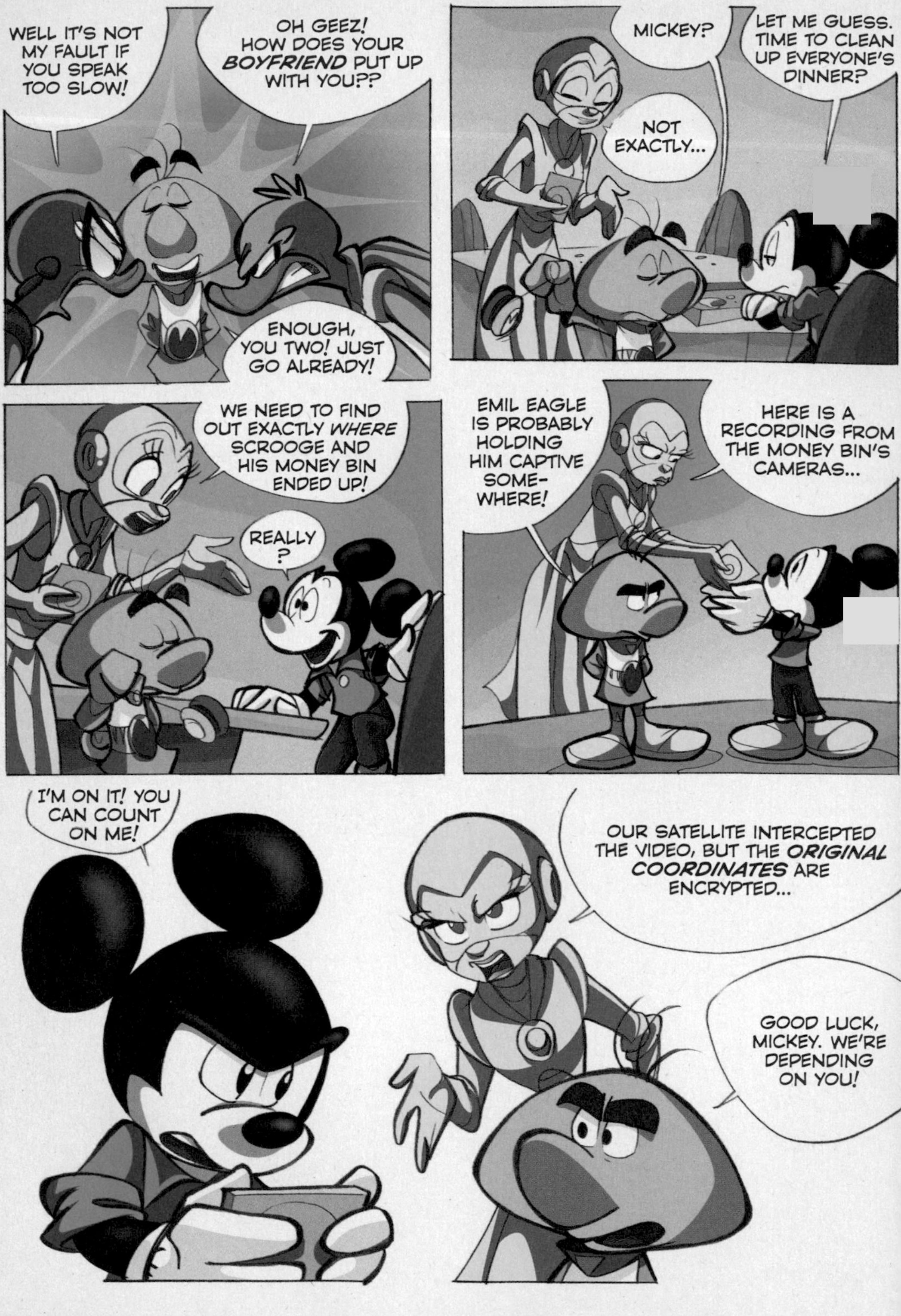
WELL IT'S NOT MY FAULT IF YOU SPEAK TOO SLOW!
OH GEEZ! HOW DOES YOUR BOYFRIEND PUT UP WITH YOU??
ENOUGH, YOU TWO! JUST GO ALREADY!
MICKEY?
LET ME GUESS. TIME TO CLEAN UP EVERYONE'S DINNER?
NOT EXACTLY...
WE NEED TO FIND OUT EXACTLY WHERE SCROOGE AND HIS MONEY BIN ENDED UP!
REALLY?
EMIL EAGLE IS PROBABLY HOLDING HIM CAPTIVE SOME-WHERE!
HERE IS A RECORDING FROM THE MONEY BIN'S CAMERAS...
I'M ON IT! YOU CAN COUNT ON ME!
OUR SATELLITE INTERCEPTED THE VIDEO, BUT THE ORIGINAL COORDINATES ARE ENCRYPTED...
GOOD LUCK, MICKEY. WE'RE DEPENDING ON YOU!

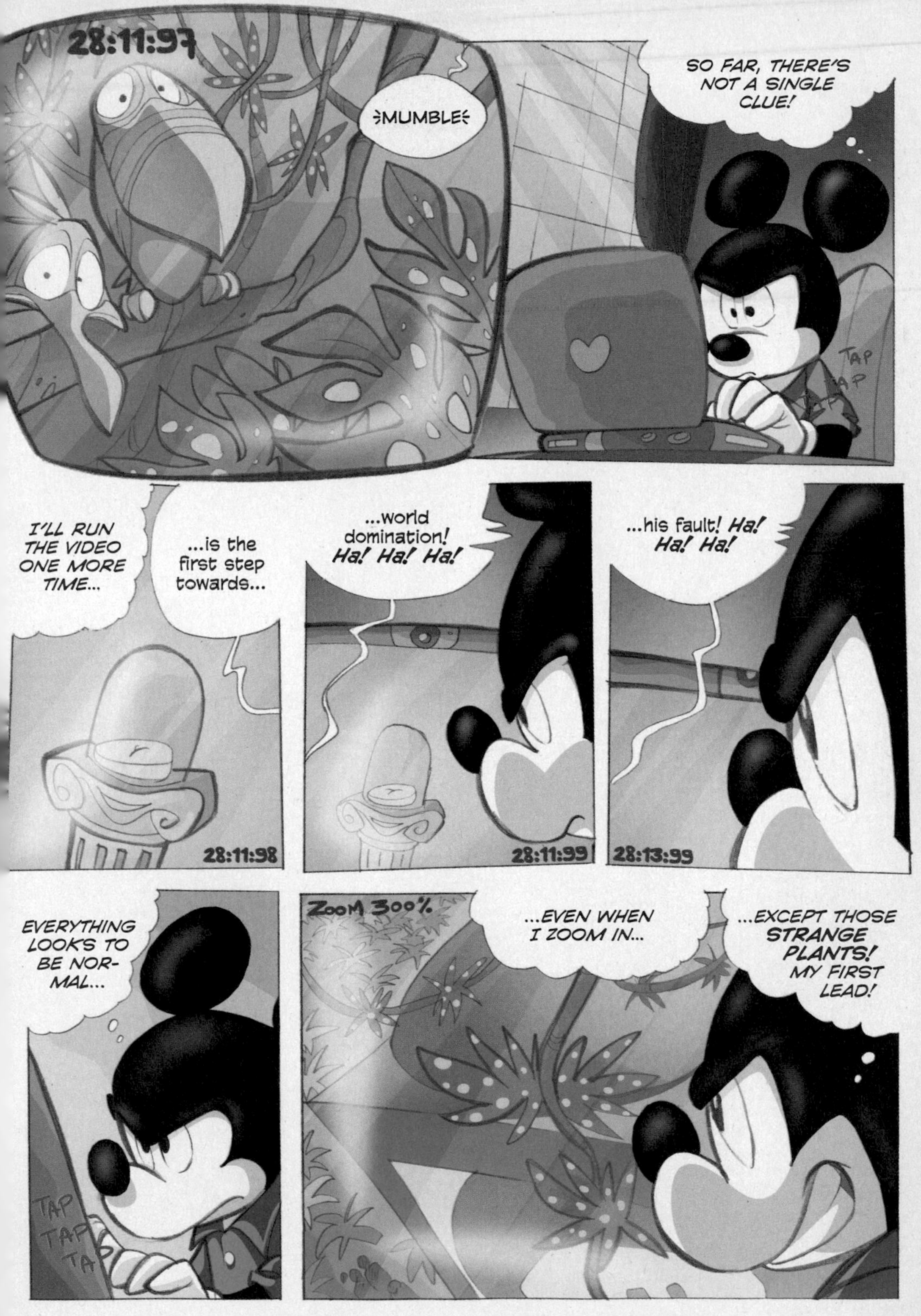
28:11:97
MUMBLE
SO FAR, THERE'S NOT A SINGLE CLUE!
TAP TAP TAP
I'LL RUN THE VIDEO ONE MORE TIME...
...is the first step towards...
28:11:98
...world domination! Ha! Ha! Ha!
28:11:99
...his fault! Ha! Ha! Ha!
28:13:99
EVERYTHING LOOKS TO BE NOR-MAL...
TAP TAP TAP
ZOOM 300%
...EVEN WHEN I ZOOM IN...
...EXCEPT THOSE STRANGE PLANTS! MY FIRST LEAD!

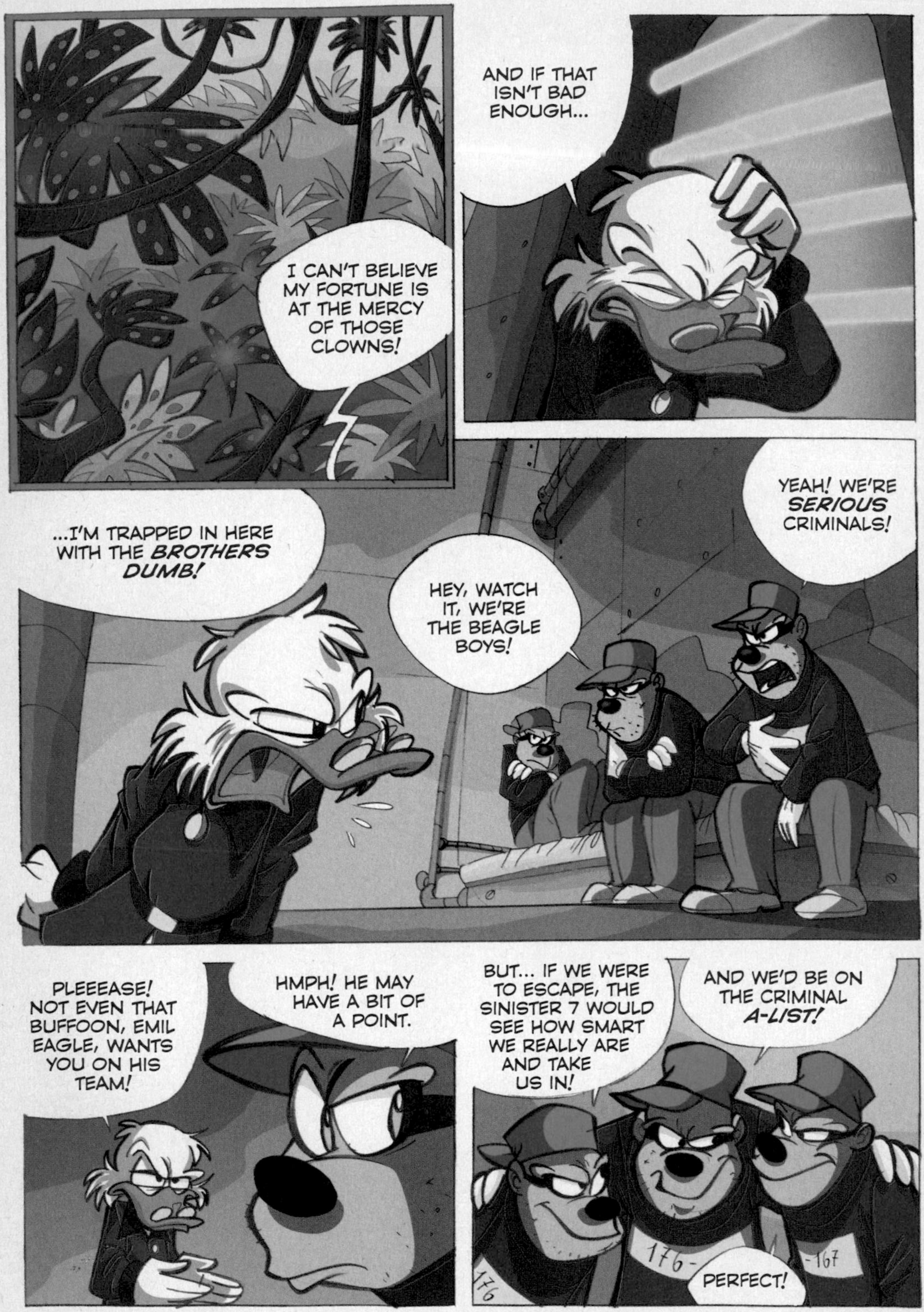
I CAN'T BELIEVE MY FORTUNE IS AT THE MERCY OF THOSE CLOWNS!
AND IF THAT ISN'T BAD ENOUGH...
...I'M TRAPPED IN HERE WITH THE BROTHERS DUMB!
HEY, WATCH IT, WE'RE THE BEAGLE BOYS!
YEAH! WE'RE SERIOUS CRIMINALS!
PLEEEASE! NOT EVEN THAT BUFFOON, EMIL EAGLE, WANTS YOU ON HIS TEAM!
HMPH! HE MAY HAVE A BIT OF A POINT.
BUT... IF WE WERE TO ESCAPE, THE SINISTER 7 WOULD SEE HOW SMART WE REALLY ARE AND TAKE US IN!
AND WE'D BE ON THE CRIMINAL A-LIST!
176
176-
-167
PERFECT!

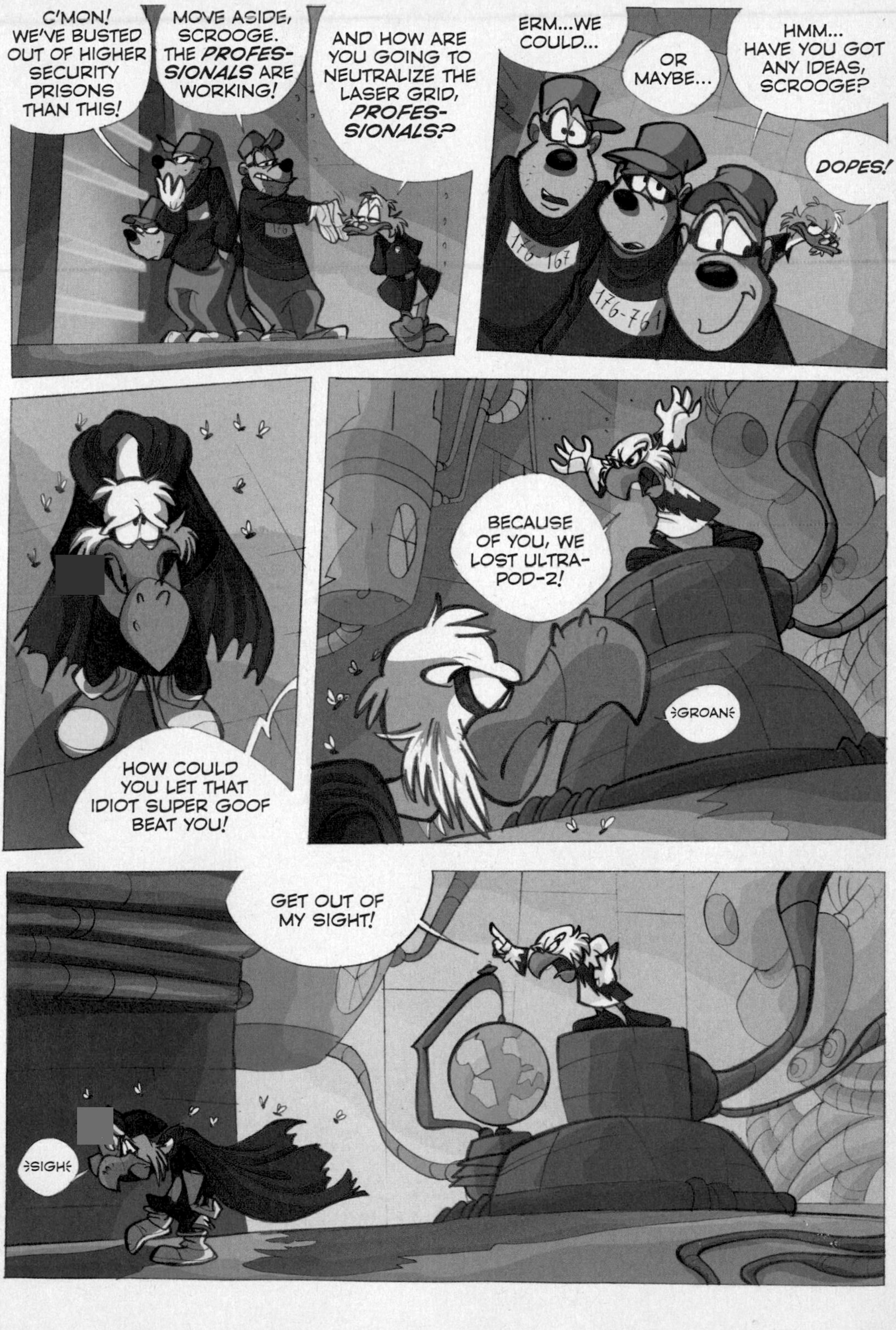
C'MON! WE'VE BUSTED OUT OF HIGHER SECURITY PRISONS THAN THIS!
MOVE ASIDE, SCROOGE. THE *PROFESSIONALS* ARE WORKING!
AND HOW ARE YOU GOING TO NEUTRALIZE THE LASER GRID, *PROFESSIONALS?*
ERM...WE COULD...
OR MAYBE...
HMM... HAVE YOU GOT ANY IDEAS, SCROOGE?
DOPES!
HOW COULD YOU LET THAT IDIOT SUPER GOOF BEAT YOU!
BECAUSE OF YOU, WE LOST ULTRA-POD-2!
GROAN
GET OUT OF MY SIGHT!
SIGH

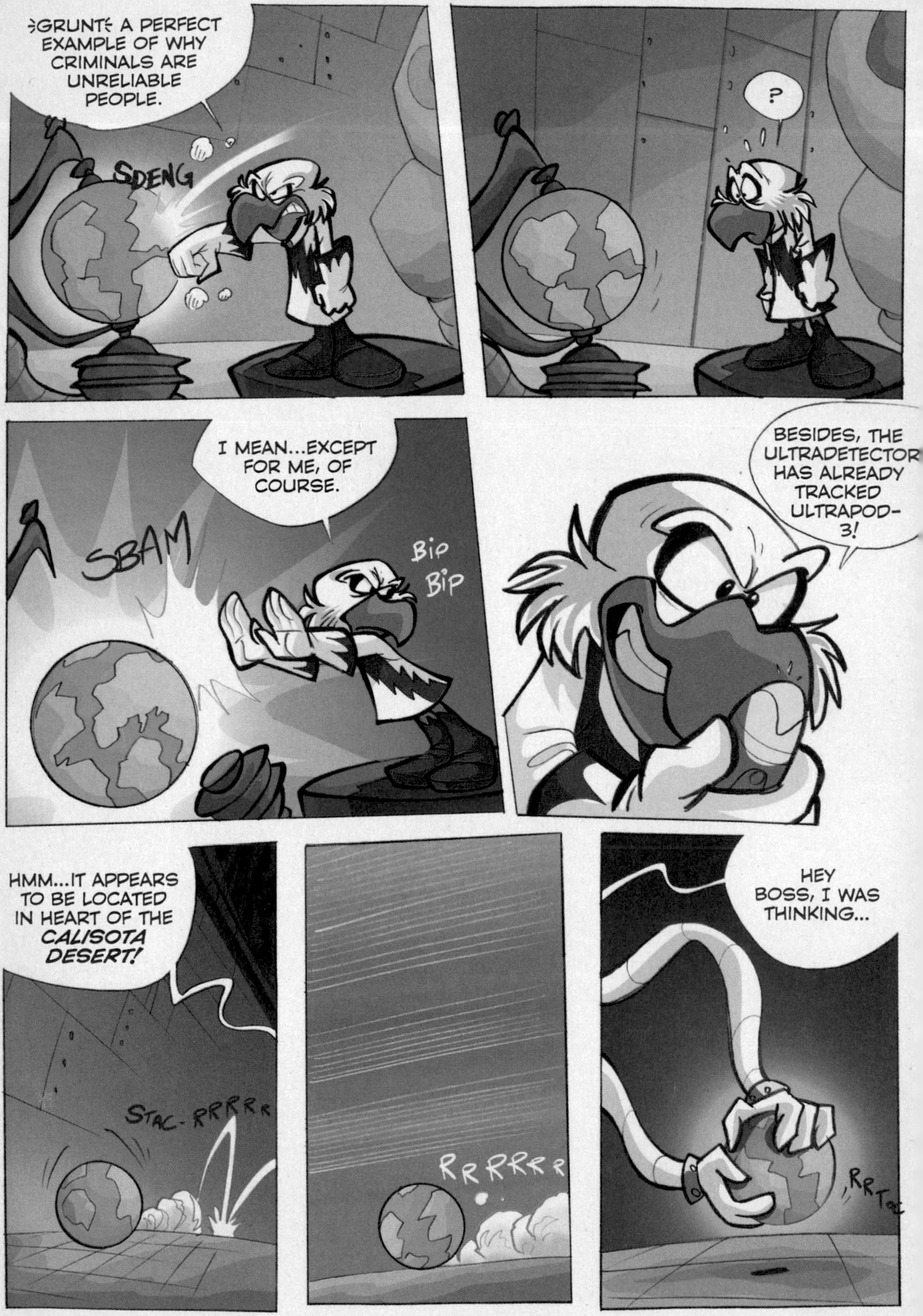

⋟GRUNT⋞ A PERFECT EXAMPLE OF WHY CRIMINALS ARE UNRELIABLE PEOPLE.
SDENG
?
I MEAN...EXCEPT FOR ME, OF COURSE.
SBAM
BIP BIP
BESIDES, THE ULTRADETECTOR HAS ALREADY TRACKED ULTRAPOD-3!
HMM...IT APPEARS TO BE LOCATED IN HEART OF THE CALISOTA DESERT!
STAC-RRRRR
RRRRRR
HEY BOSS, I WAS THINKING...
RRTOC

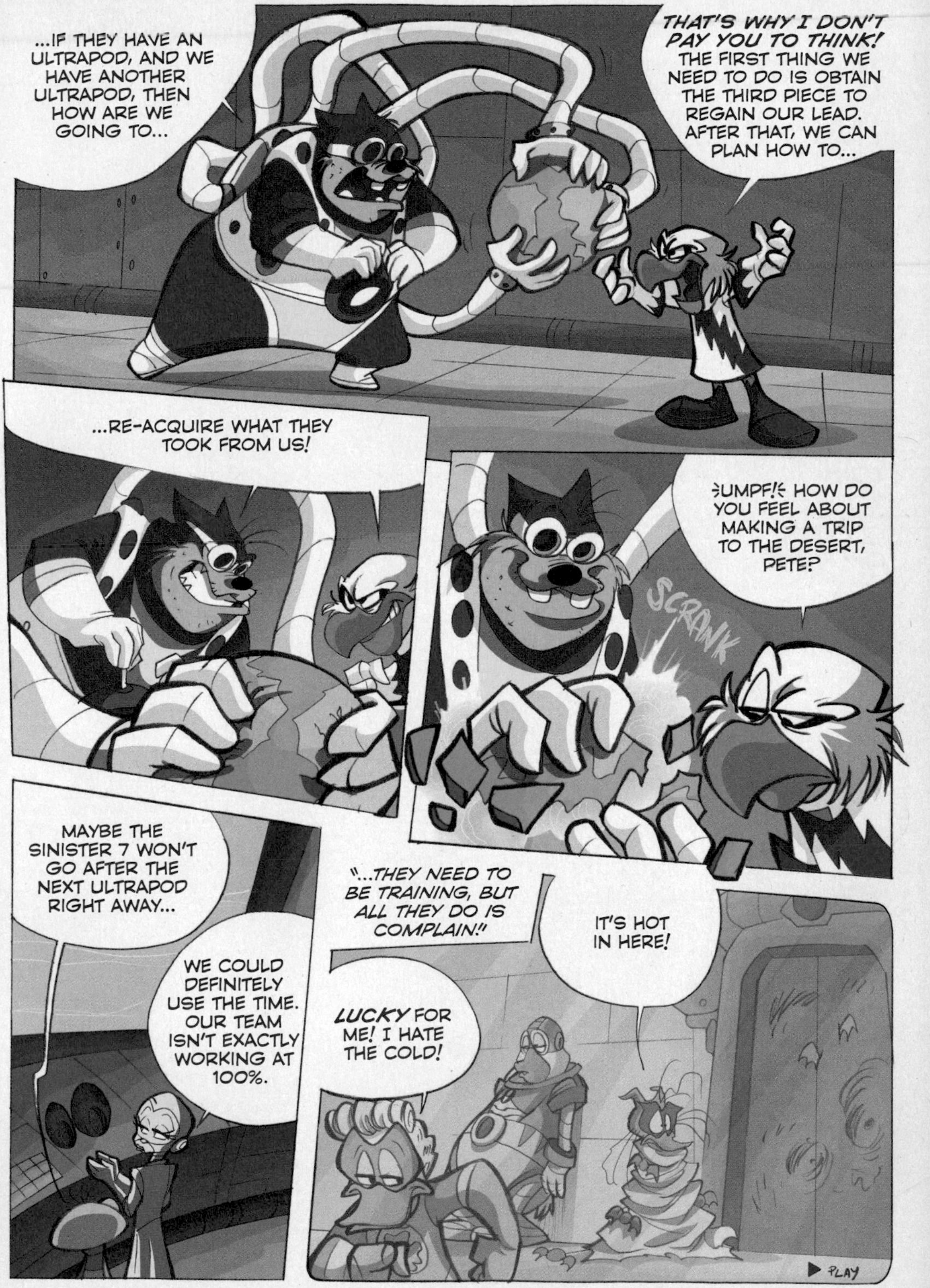
...IF THEY HAVE AN ULTRAPOD, AND WE HAVE ANOTHER ULTRAPOD, THEN HOW ARE WE GOING TO...
THAT'S WHY I DON'T PAY YOU TO THINK! THE FIRST THING WE NEED TO DO IS OBTAIN THE THIRD PIECE TO REGAIN OUR LEAD. AFTER THAT, WE CAN PLAN HOW TO...
...RE-ACQUIRE WHAT THEY TOOK FROM US!
SCRANK
HUMPF! HOW DO YOU FEEL ABOUT MAKING A TRIP TO THE DESERT, PETE?
MAYBE THE SINISTER 7 WON'T GO AFTER THE NEXT ULTRAPOD RIGHT AWAY...
WE COULD DEFINITELY USE THE TIME. OUR TEAM ISN'T EXACTLY WORKING AT 100%.
"...*THEY NEED TO BE TRAINING, BUT ALL THEY DO IS COMPLAIN!*"
IT'S HOT IN HERE!
LUCKY FOR ME! I HATE THE COLD!
PLAY

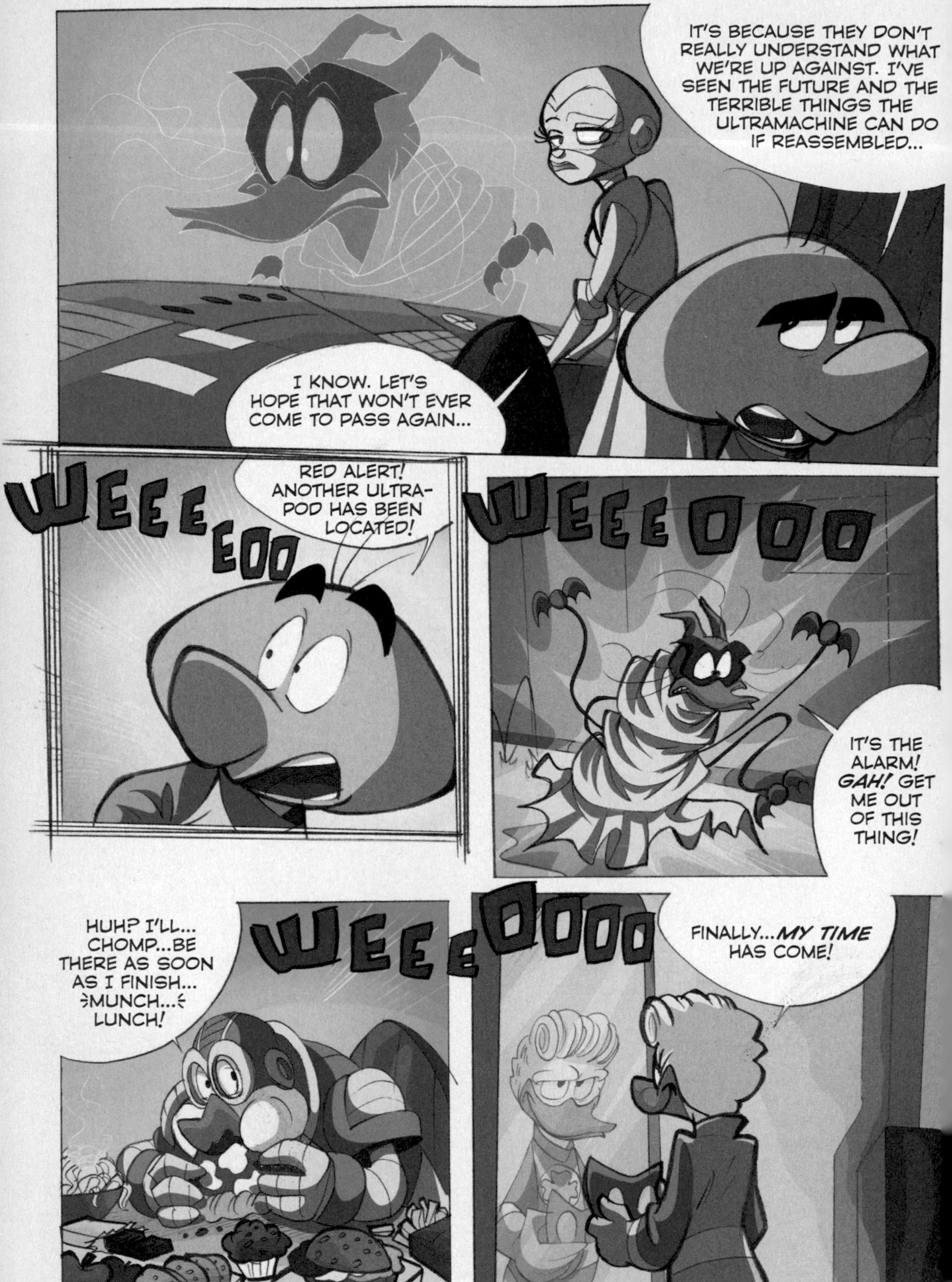
IT'S BECAUSE THEY DON'T REALLY UNDERSTAND WHAT WE'RE UP AGAINST. I'VE SEEN THE FUTURE AND THE TERRIBLE THINGS THE ULTRAMACHINE CAN DO IF REASSEMBLED...
I KNOW. LET'S HOPE THAT WON'T EVER COME TO PASS AGAIN...
WEEEEOO
RED ALERT! ANOTHER ULTRA-POD HAS BEEN LOCATED!
WEEEOOO
IT'S THE ALARM! *GAH!* GET ME OUT OF THIS THING!
HUH? I'LL... CHOMP...BE THERE AS SOON AS I FINISH... MUNCH... LUNCH!
WEEEOOOO
FINALLY...*MY TIME* HAS COME!

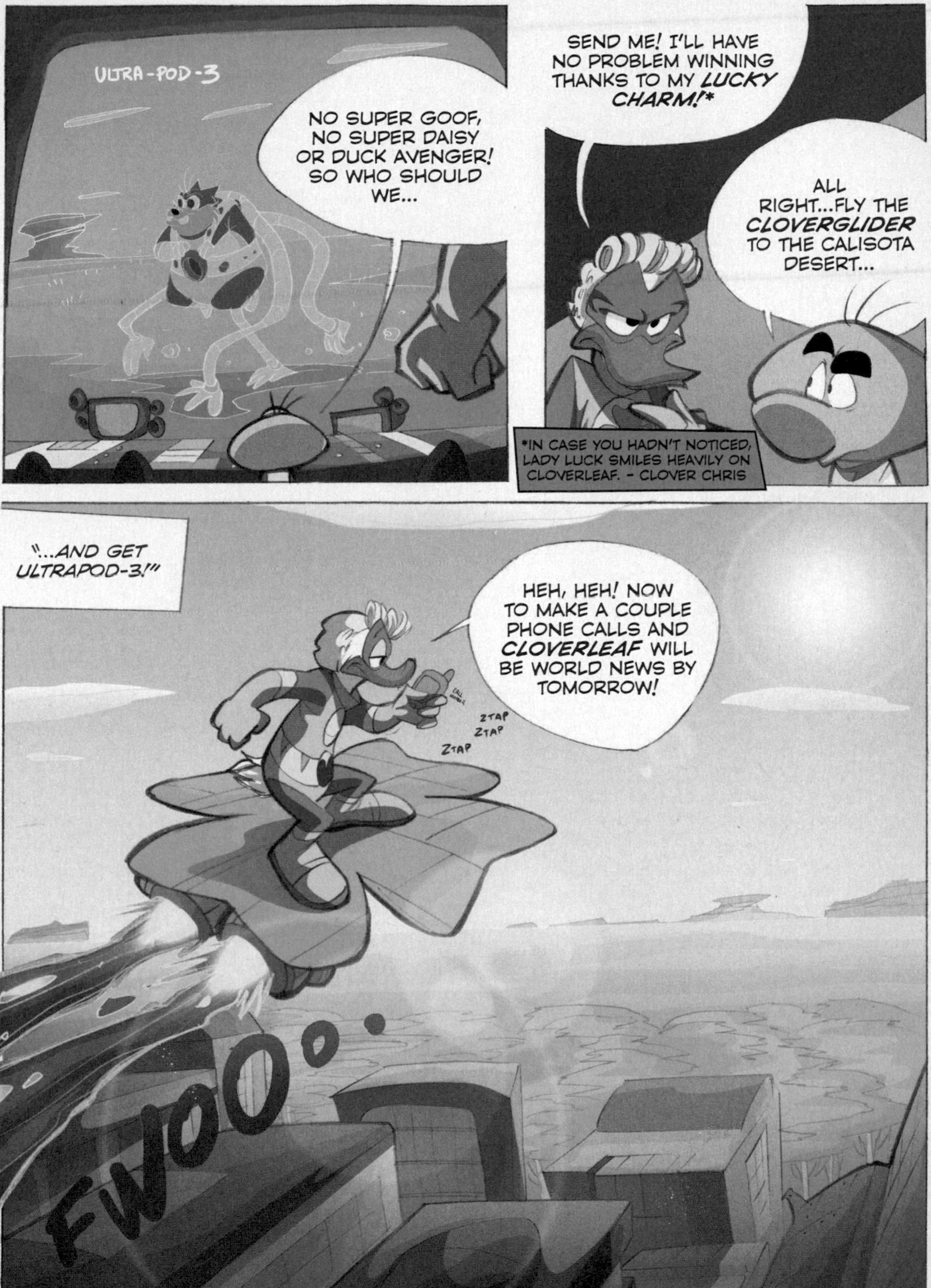
ULTRA-POD-3
NO SUPER GOOF, NO SUPER DAISY OR DUCK AVENGER! SO WHO SHOULD WE...
SEND ME! I'LL HAVE NO PROBLEM WINNING THANKS TO MY *LUCKY CHARM!**
ALL RIGHT...FLY THE *CLOVERGLIDER* TO THE CALISOTA DESERT...
*IN CASE YOU HADN'T NOTICED, LADY LUCK SMILES HEAVILY ON CLOVERLEAF. - CLOVER CHRIS
"...AND GET ULTRAPOD-3!"
HEH, HEH! NOW TO MAKE A COUPLE PHONE CALLS AND *CLOVERLEAF* WILL BE WORLD NEWS BY TOMORROW!
ZTAP ZTAP ZTAP
FWOOO..

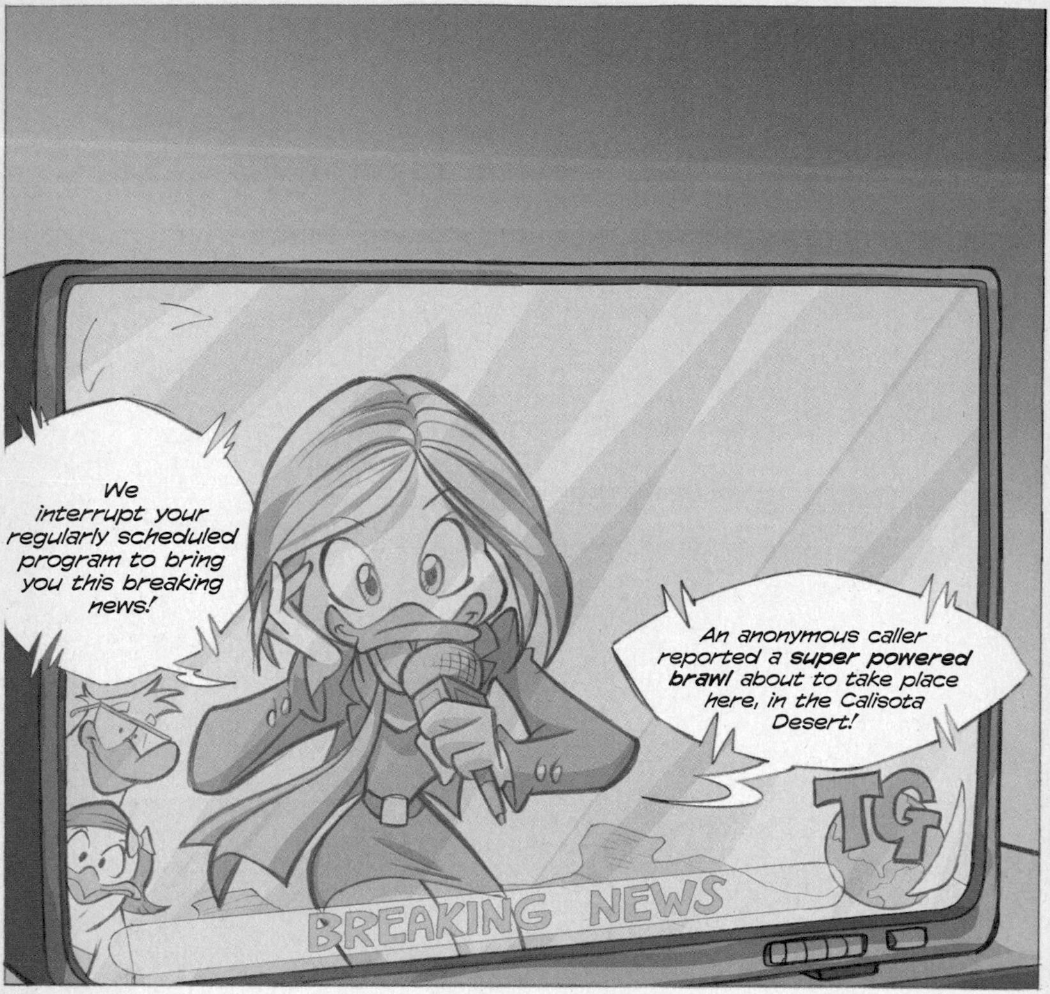
We interrupt your regularly scheduled program to bring you this breaking news!
An anonymous caller reported a super powered brawl about to take place here, in the Calisota Desert!
TG
BREAKING NEWS

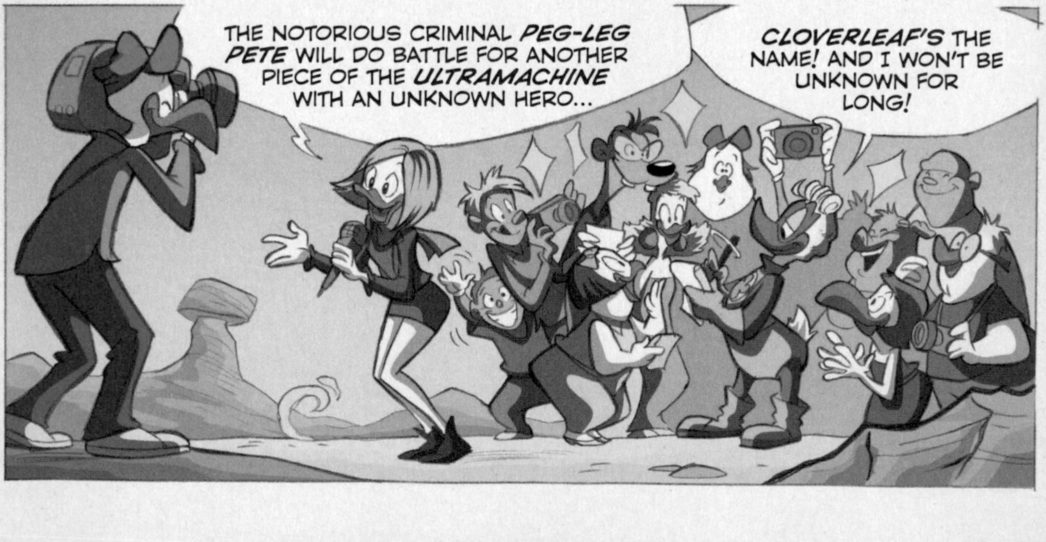
THE NOTORIOUS CRIMINAL PEG-LEG PETE WILL DO BATTLE FOR ANOTHER PIECE OF THE ULTRAMACHINE WITH AN UNKNOWN HERO...
CLOVERLEAF'S THE NAME! AND I WON'T BE UNKNOWN FOR LONG!

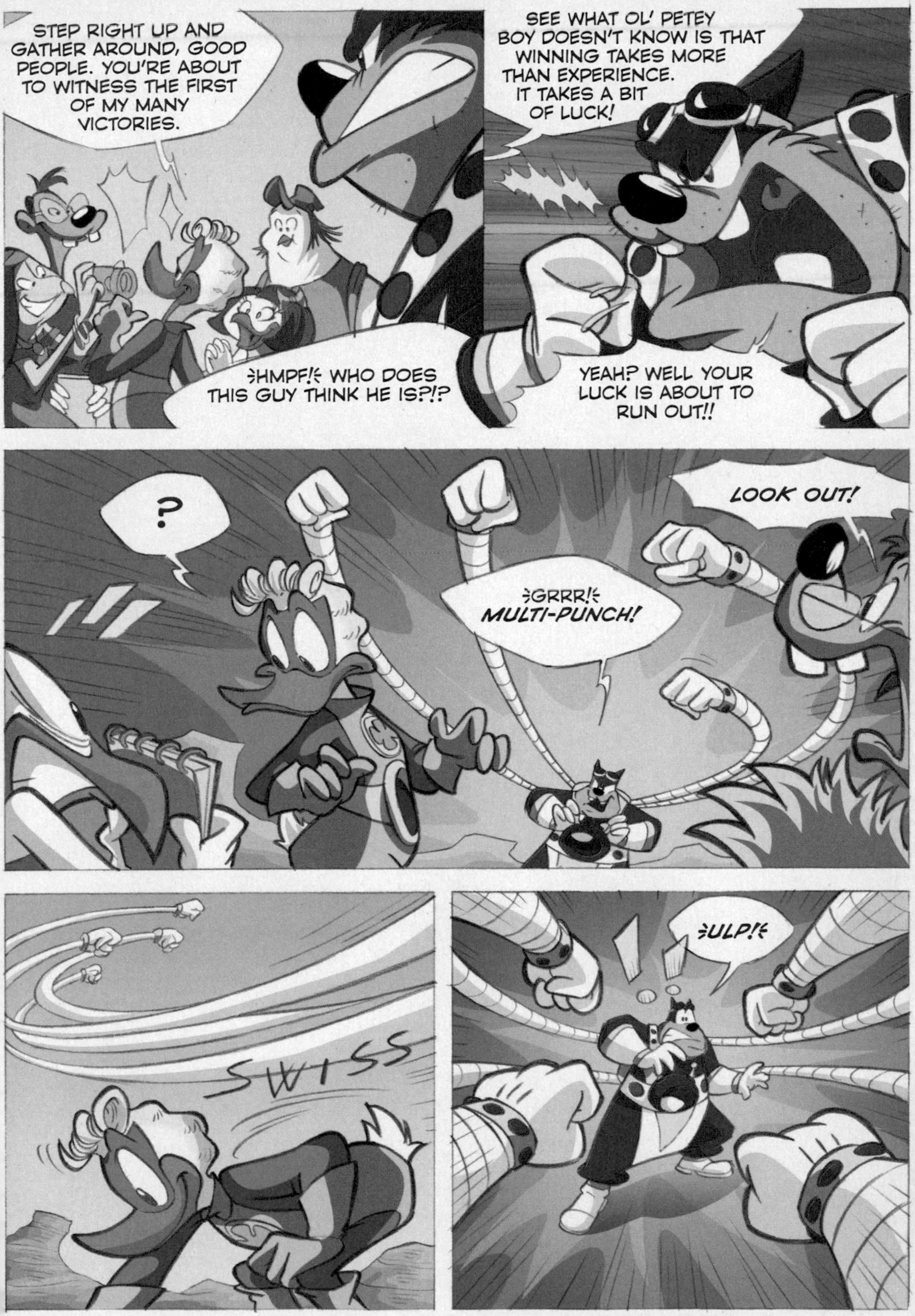
STEP RIGHT UP AND GATHER AROUND, GOOD PEOPLE. YOU'RE ABOUT TO WITNESS THE FIRST OF MY MANY VICTORIES.
SEE WHAT OL' PETEY BOY DOESN'T KNOW IS THAT WINNING TAKES MORE THAN EXPERIENCE. IT TAKES A BIT OF LUCK!
HMPF! WHO DOES THIS GUY THINK HE IS?!?
YEAH? WELL YOUR LUCK IS ABOUT TO RUN OUT!!
?
GRRR! MULTI-PUNCH!
LOOK OUT!
SWISS
ULP!

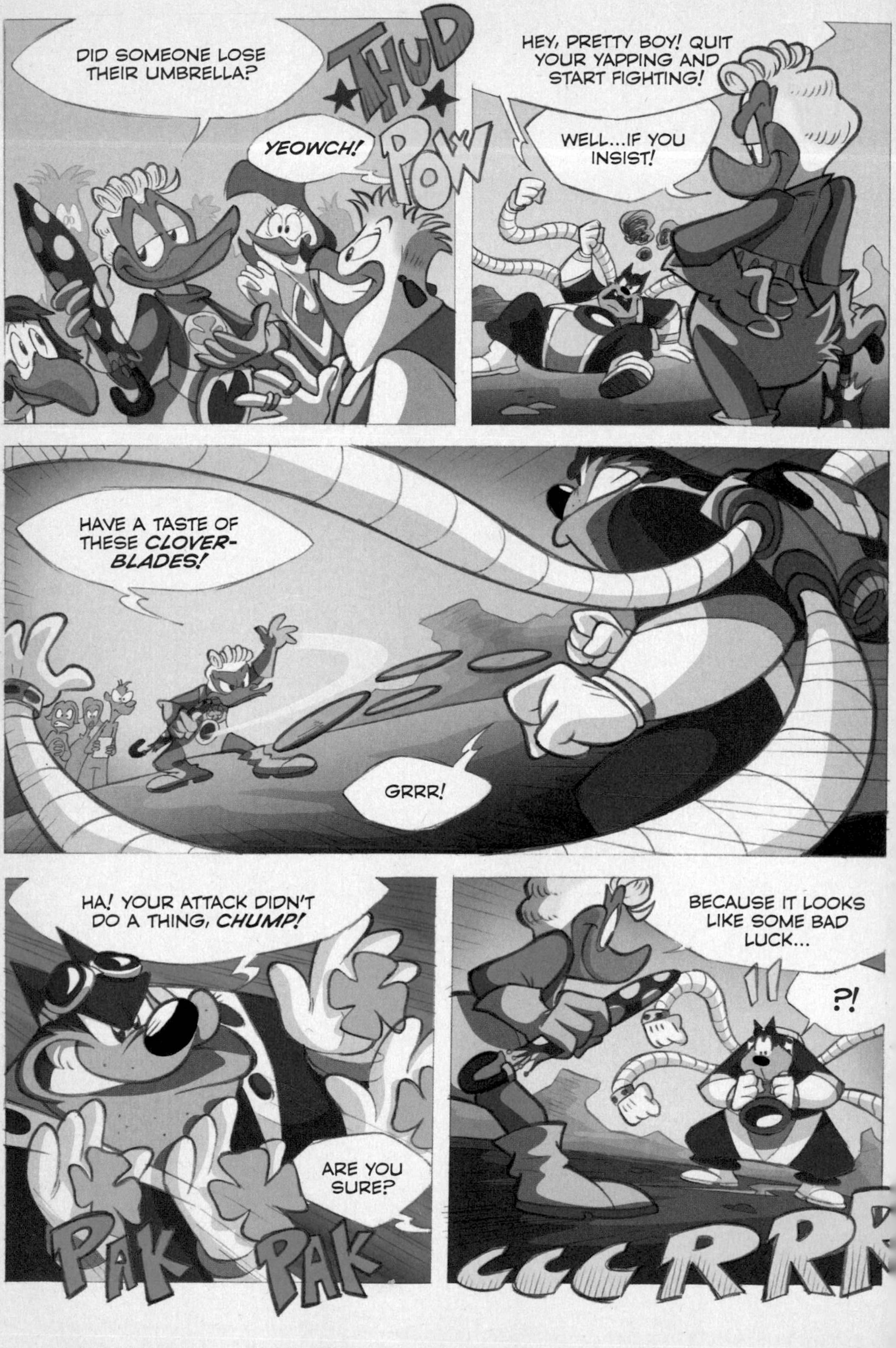
DID SOMEONE LOSE THEIR UMBRELLA?
THUD
YEOWCH!
POW
HEY, PRETTY BOY! QUIT YOUR YAPPING AND START FIGHTING!
WELL...IF YOU INSIST!
HAVE A TASTE OF THESE *CLOVER-BLADES!*
GRRR!
HA! YOUR ATTACK DIDN'T DO A THING, *CHUMP!*
ARE YOU SURE?
PAK PAK
BECAUSE IT LOOKS LIKE SOME BAD LUCK...
?!
CCCRRR

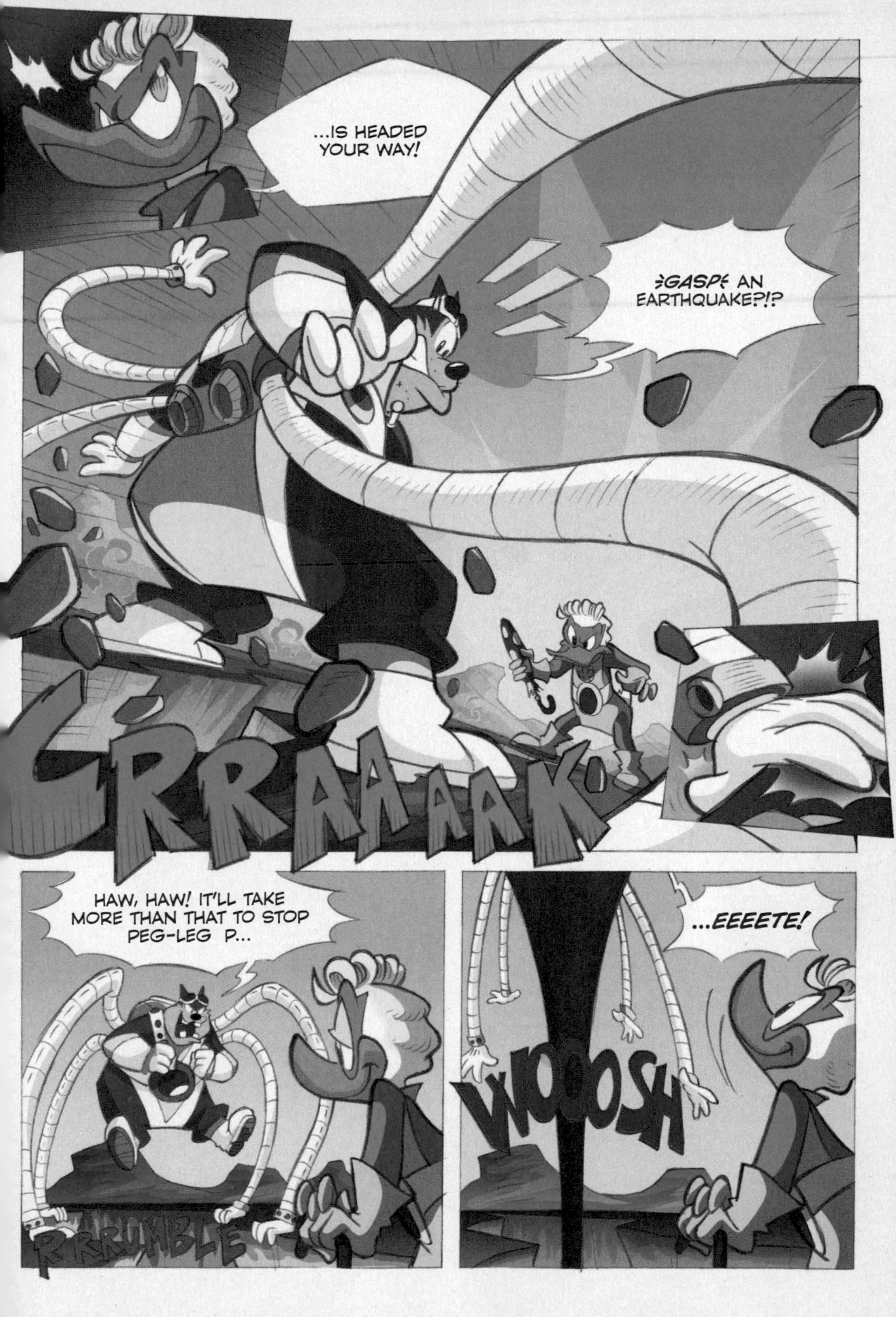
...IS HEADED YOUR WAY!
GASP AN EARTHQUAKE?!?
CRRAAAAK
HAW, HAW! IT'LL TAKE MORE THAN THAT TO STOP PEG-LEG P...
RRRUMBLE
...EEEETE!
WOOOSH

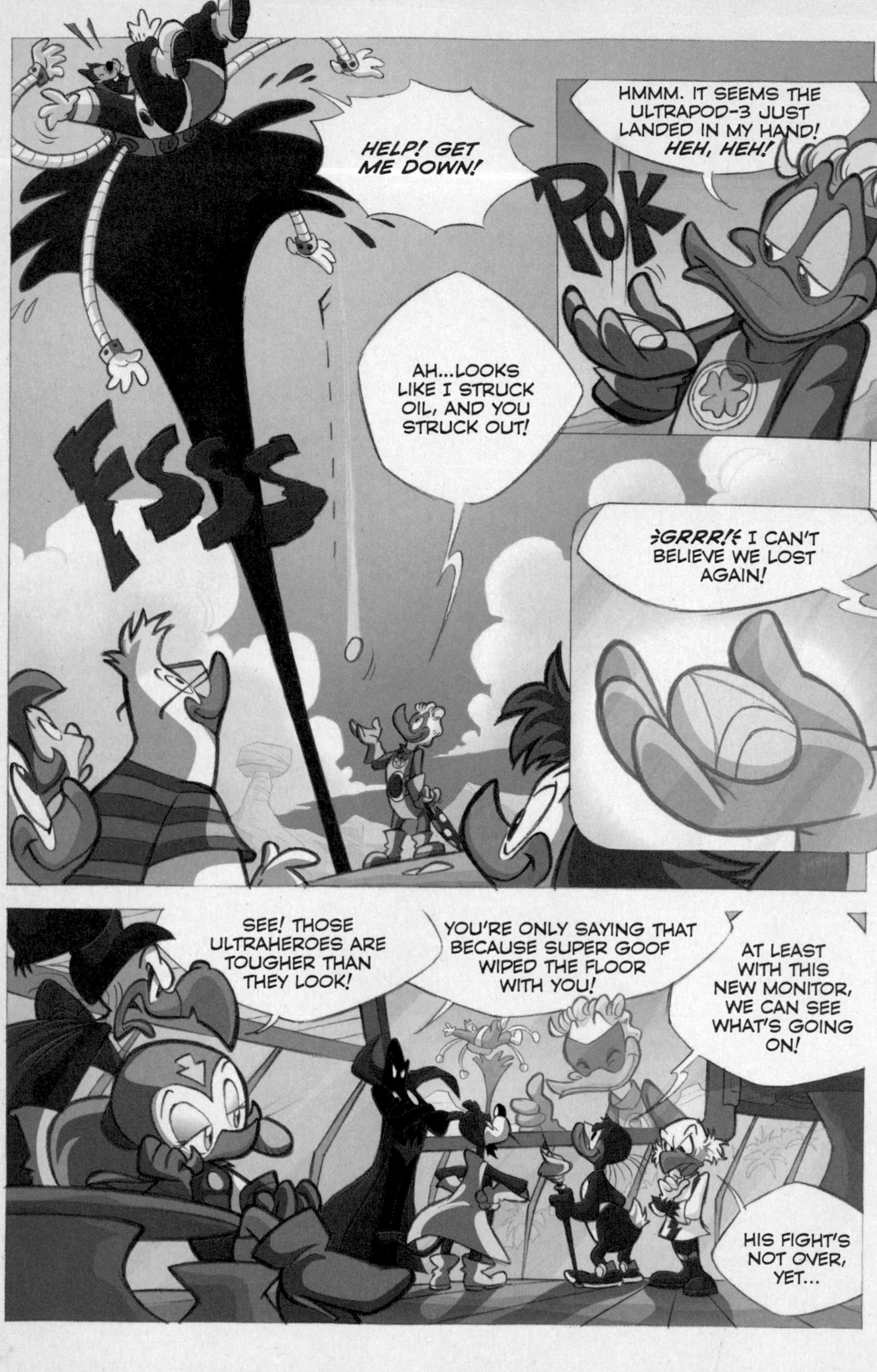
HELP! GET ME DOWN!
HMMM. IT SEEMS THE ULTRAPOD-3 JUST LANDED IN MY HAND! HEH, HEH!
POK
FSSS
AH...LOOKS LIKE I STRUCK OIL, AND YOU STRUCK OUT!
GRRR! I CAN'T BELIEVE WE LOST AGAIN!
SEE! THOSE ULTRAHEROES ARE TOUGHER THAN THEY LOOK!
YOU'RE ONLY SAYING THAT BECAUSE SUPER GOOF WIPED THE FLOOR WITH YOU!
AT LEAST WITH THIS NEW MONITOR, WE CAN SEE WHAT'S GOING ON!
HIS FIGHT'S NOT OVER, YET...

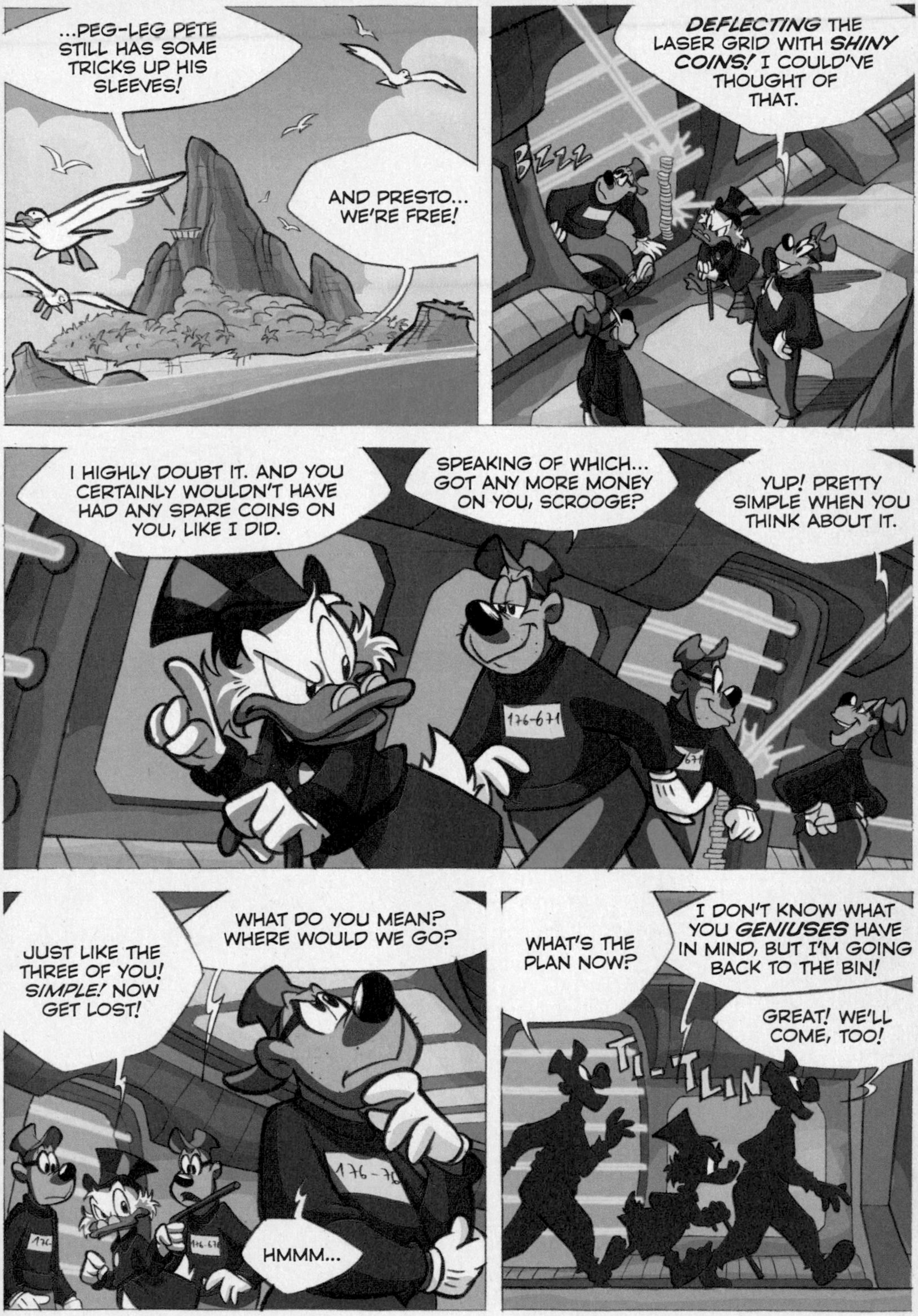
...PEG-LEG PETE STILL HAS SOME TRICKS UP HIS SLEEVES!
AND PRESTO... WE'RE FREE!
DEFLECTING THE LASER GRID WITH SHINY COINS! I COULD'VE THOUGHT OF THAT.
BZZZ
I HIGHLY DOUBT IT. AND YOU CERTAINLY WOULDN'T HAVE HAD ANY SPARE COINS ON YOU, LIKE I DID.
SPEAKING OF WHICH... GOT ANY MORE MONEY ON YOU, SCROOGE?
YUP! PRETTY SIMPLE WHEN YOU THINK ABOUT IT.
176-671
JUST LIKE THE THREE OF YOU! SIMPLE! NOW GET LOST!
WHAT DO YOU MEAN? WHERE WOULD WE GO?
HMMM...
WHAT'S THE PLAN NOW?
I DON'T KNOW WHAT YOU GENIUSES HAVE IN MIND, BUT I'M GOING BACK TO THE BIN!
GREAT! WE'LL COME, TOO!
TI-TLIN

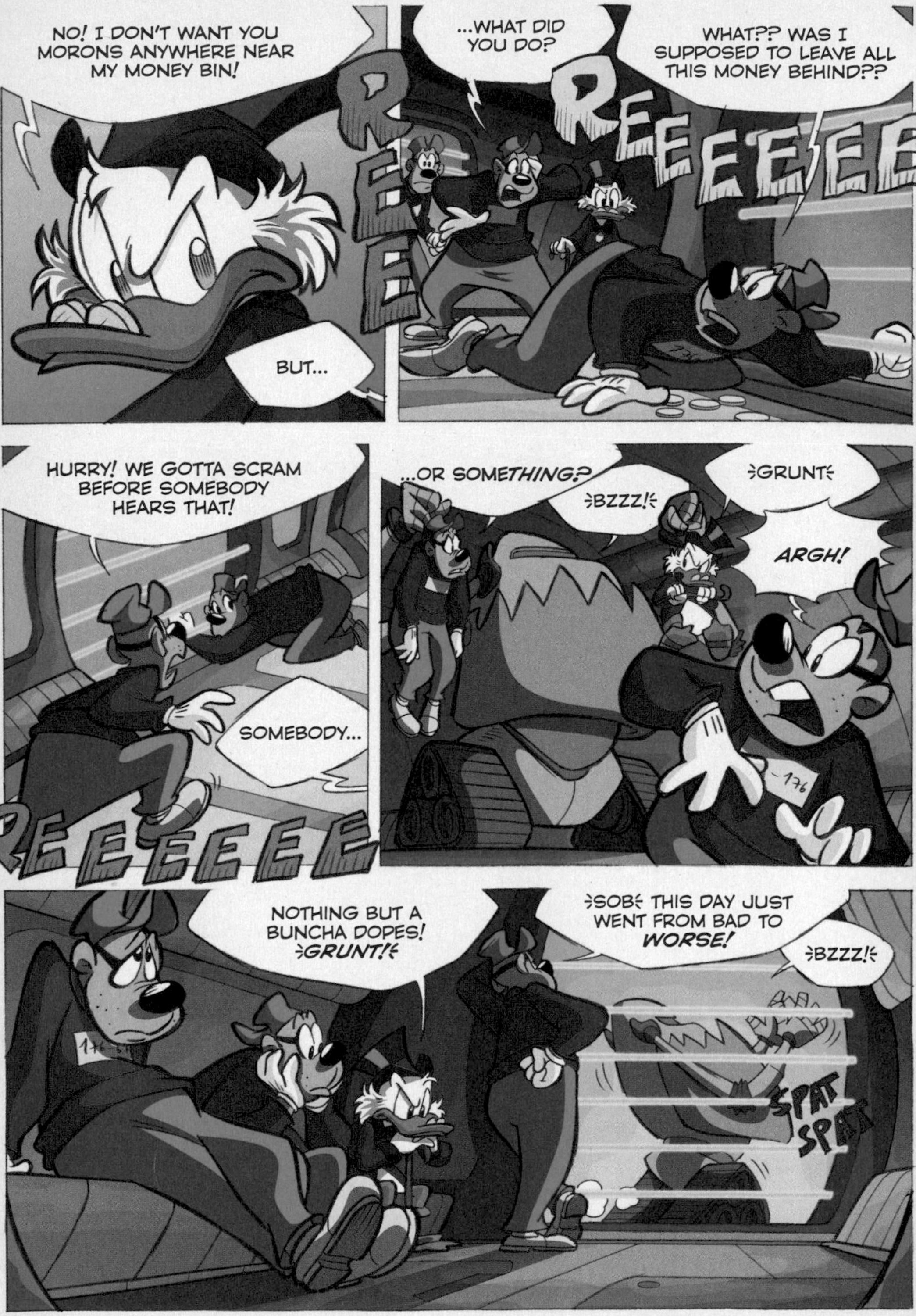
NO! I DON'T WANT YOU MORONS ANYWHERE NEAR MY MONEY BIN!
BUT...
REE
...WHAT DID YOU DO?
WHAT?? WAS I SUPPOSED TO LEAVE ALL THIS MONEY BEHIND??
REEEEEEE
HURRY! WE GOTTA SCRAM BEFORE SOMEBODY HEARS THAT!
SOMEBODY...
REEEEEEE
...OR SOMETHING?
BZZZ!
GRUNT
ARGH!
NOTHING BUT A BUNCHA DOPES! GRUNT!
SOB THIS DAY JUST WENT FROM BAD TO WORSE!
BZZZ!
SPAT SPAT

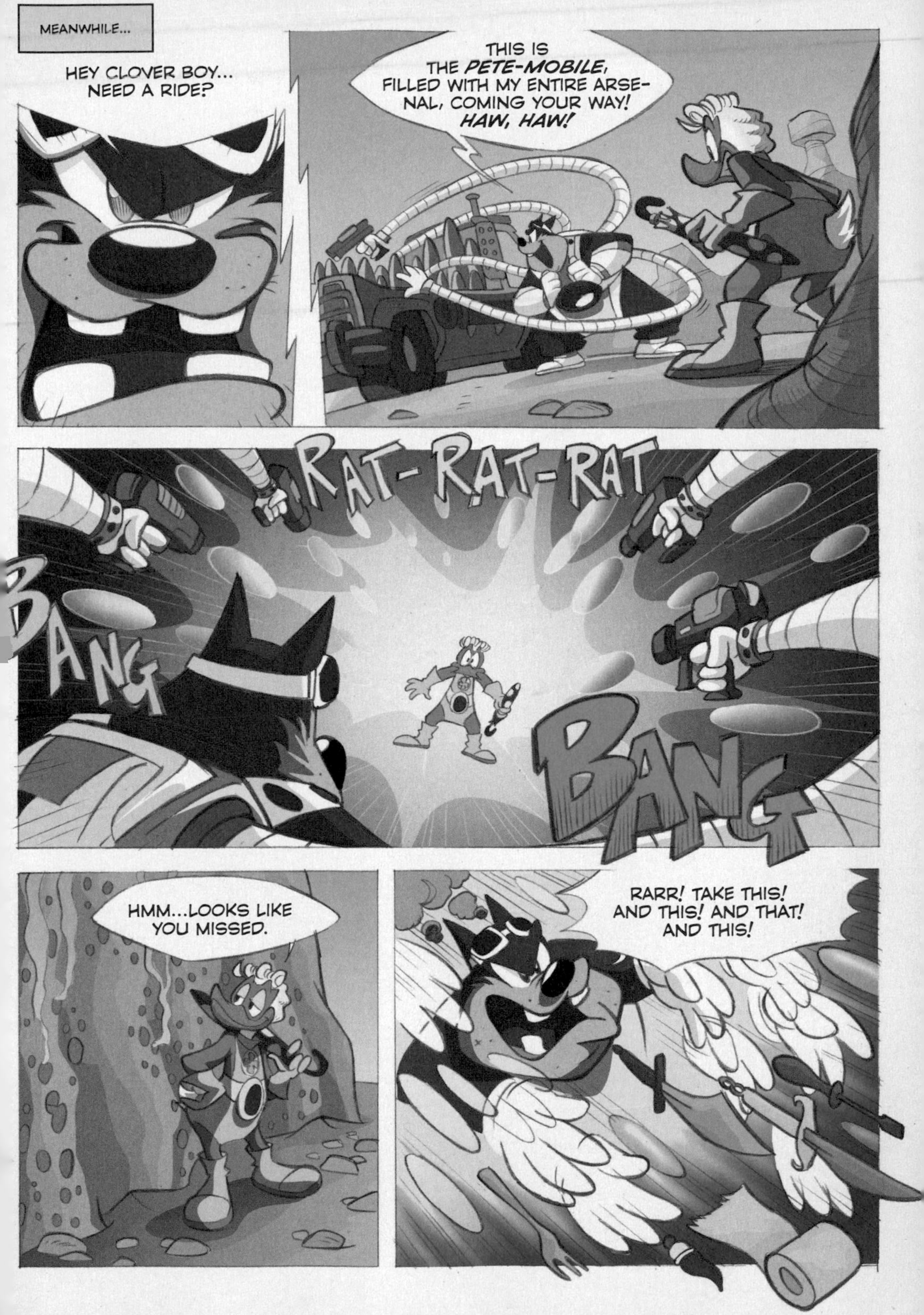
MEANWHILE...
HEY CLOVER BOY... NEED A RIDE?
THIS IS THE *PETE-MOBILE*, FILLED WITH MY ENTIRE ARSE-NAL, COMING YOUR WAY! *HAW, HAW!*
RAT-RAT-RAT
BANG
BANG
HMM...LOOKS LIKE YOU MISSED.
RARR! TAKE THIS! AND THIS! AND THAT! AND THIS!

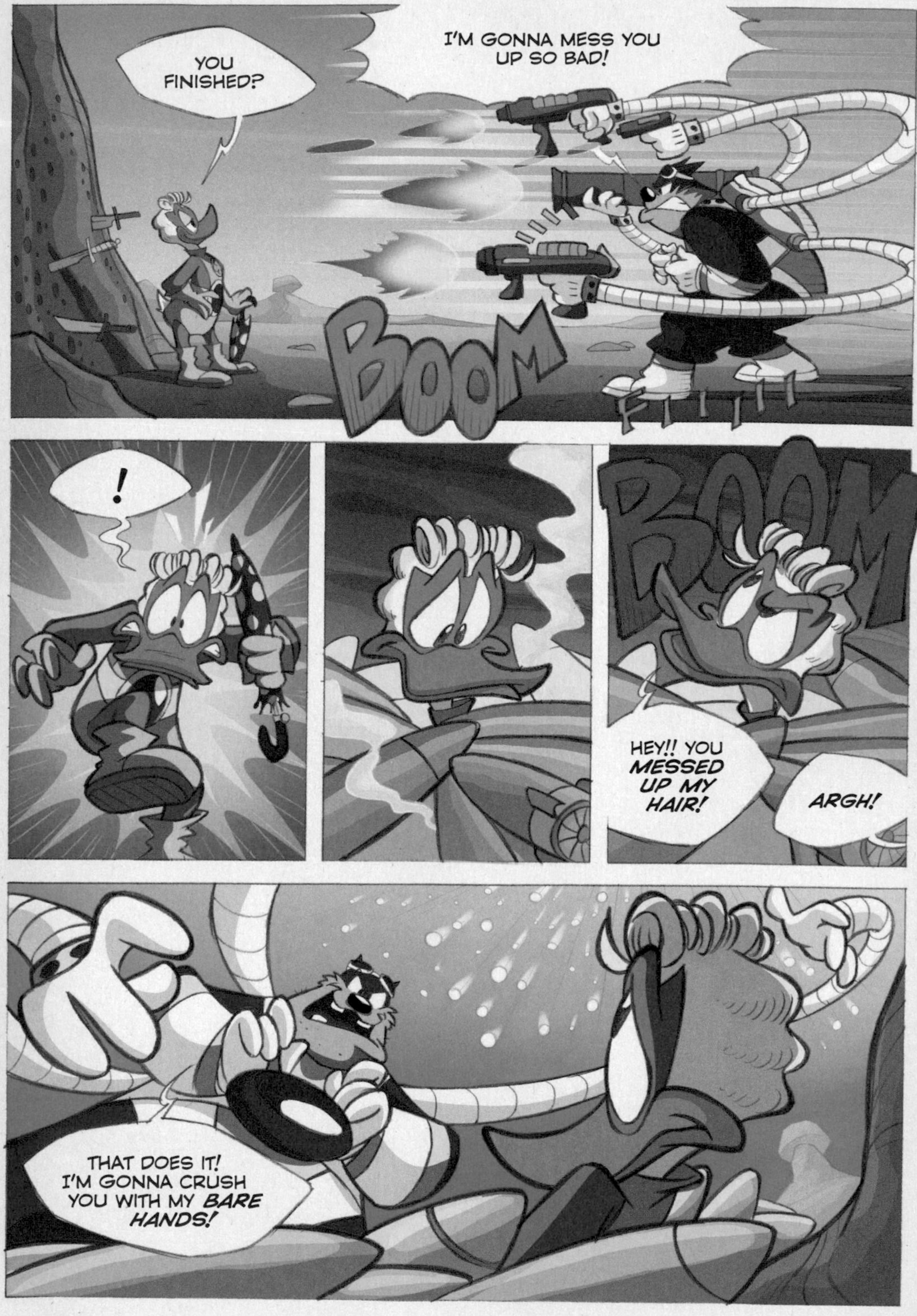
YOU FINISHED?
I'M GONNA MESS YOU UP SO BAD!
BOOM
!
BOOM
HEY!! YOU *MESSED UP MY HAIR!*
ARGH!
THAT DOES IT! I'M GONNA CRUSH YOU WITH MY *BARE HANDS!*

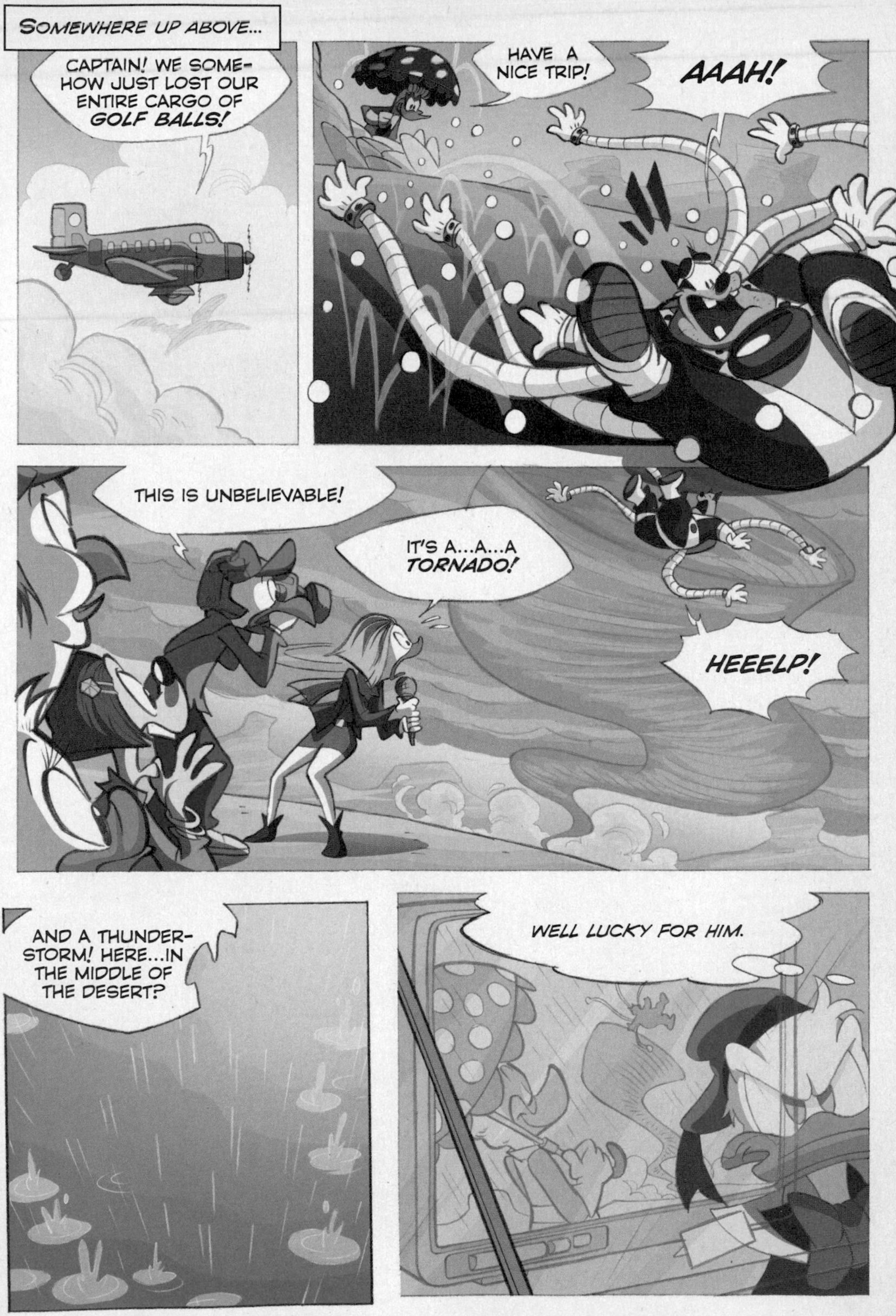
SOMEWHERE UP ABOVE...
CAPTAIN! WE SOMEHOW JUST LOST OUR ENTIRE CARGO OF GOLF BALLS!
HAVE A NICE TRIP!
AAAH!
THIS IS UNBELIEVABLE!
IT'S A...A...A TORNADO!
HEEELP!
AND A THUNDERSTORM! HERE...IN THE MIDDLE OF THE DESERT?
WELL LUCKY FOR HIM.

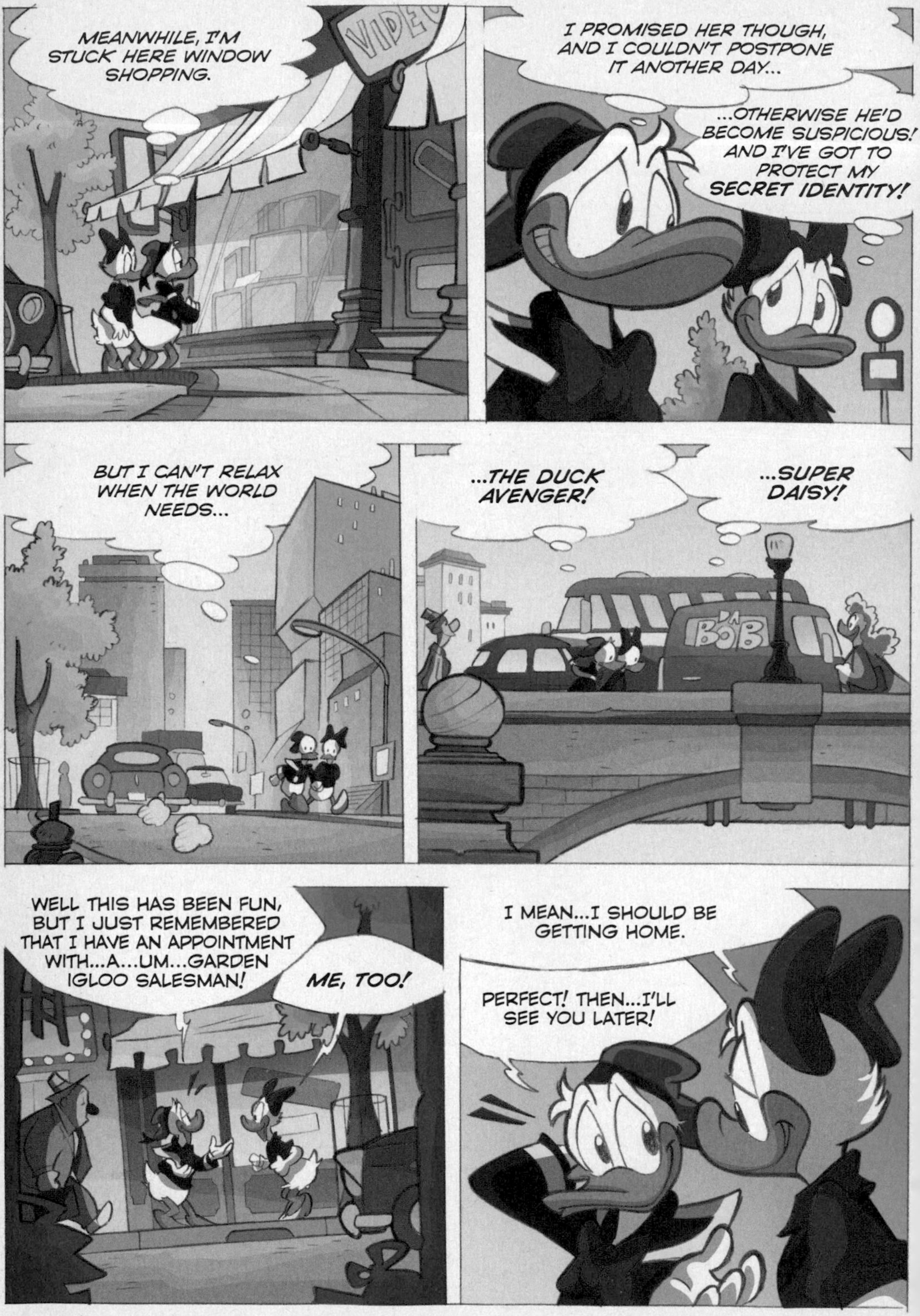
MEANWHILE, I'M STUCK HERE WINDOW SHOPPING.
VIDEO
I PROMISED HER THOUGH, AND I COULDN'T POSTPONE IT ANOTHER DAY...
...OTHERWISE HE'D BECOME SUSPICIOUS! AND I'VE GOT TO PROTECT MY SECRET IDENTITY!
BUT I CAN'T RELAX WHEN THE WORLD NEEDS...
...THE DUCK AVENGER!
...SUPER DAISY!
WELL THIS HAS BEEN FUN, BUT I JUST REMEMBERED THAT I HAVE AN APPOINTMENT WITH...A...UM...GARDEN IGLOO SALESMAN!
ME, TOO!
I MEAN...I SHOULD BE GETTING HOME.
PERFECT! THEN...I'LL SEE YOU LATER!

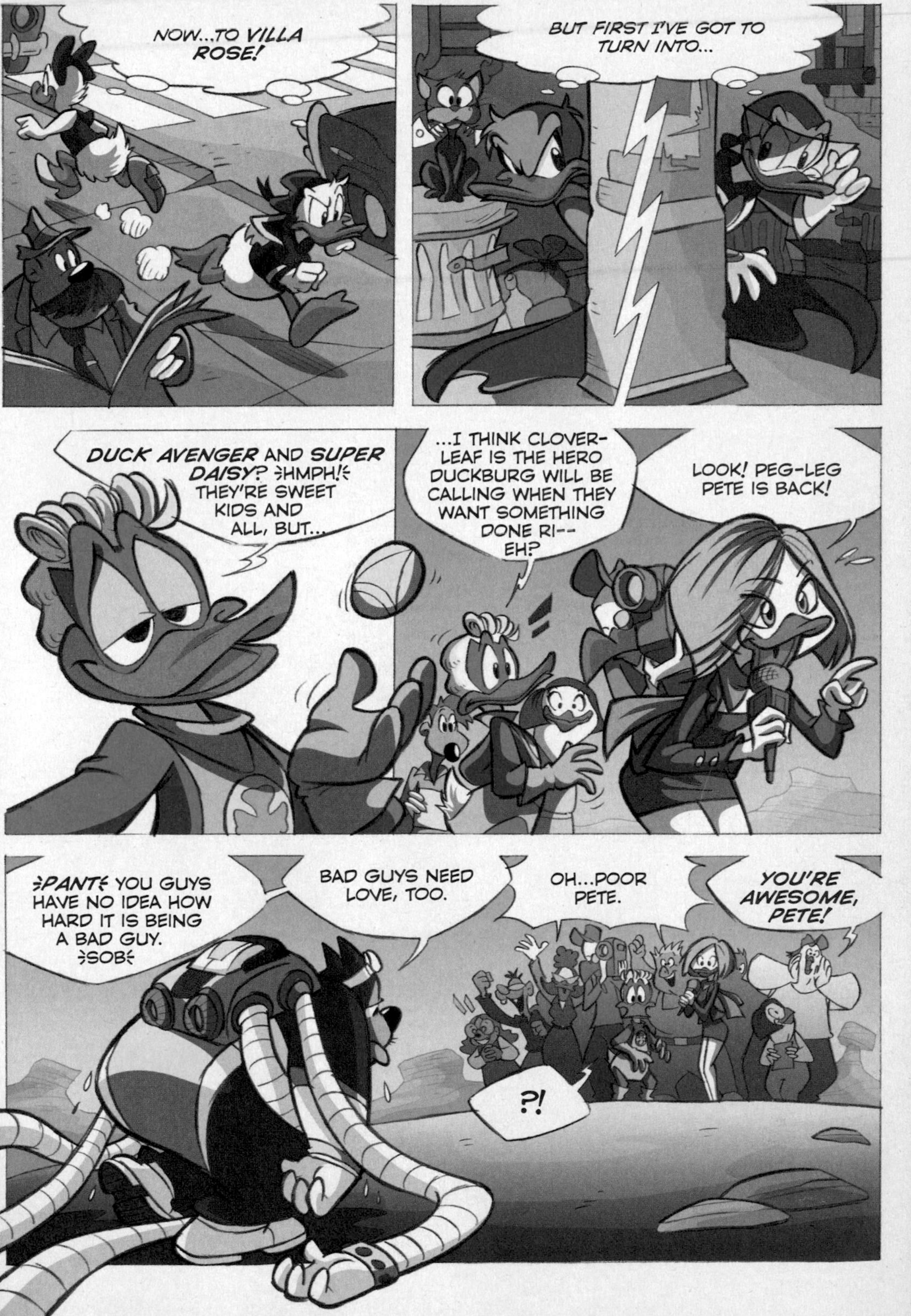
NOW...TO VILLA ROSE!
BUT FIRST I'VE GOT TO TURN INTO...
DUCK AVENGER AND SUPER DAISY? ⸗HMPH!⸗ THEY'RE SWEET KIDS AND ALL, BUT...
...I THINK CLOVER-LEAF IS THE HERO DUCKBURG WILL BE CALLING WHEN THEY WANT SOMETHING DONE RI--
EH?
LOOK! PEG-LEG PETE IS BACK!
⸗PANT⸗ YOU GUYS HAVE NO IDEA HOW HARD IT IS BEING A BAD GUY. ⸗SOB⸗
BAD GUYS NEED LOVE, TOO.
OH...POOR PETE.
YOU'RE AWESOME, PETE!
?!

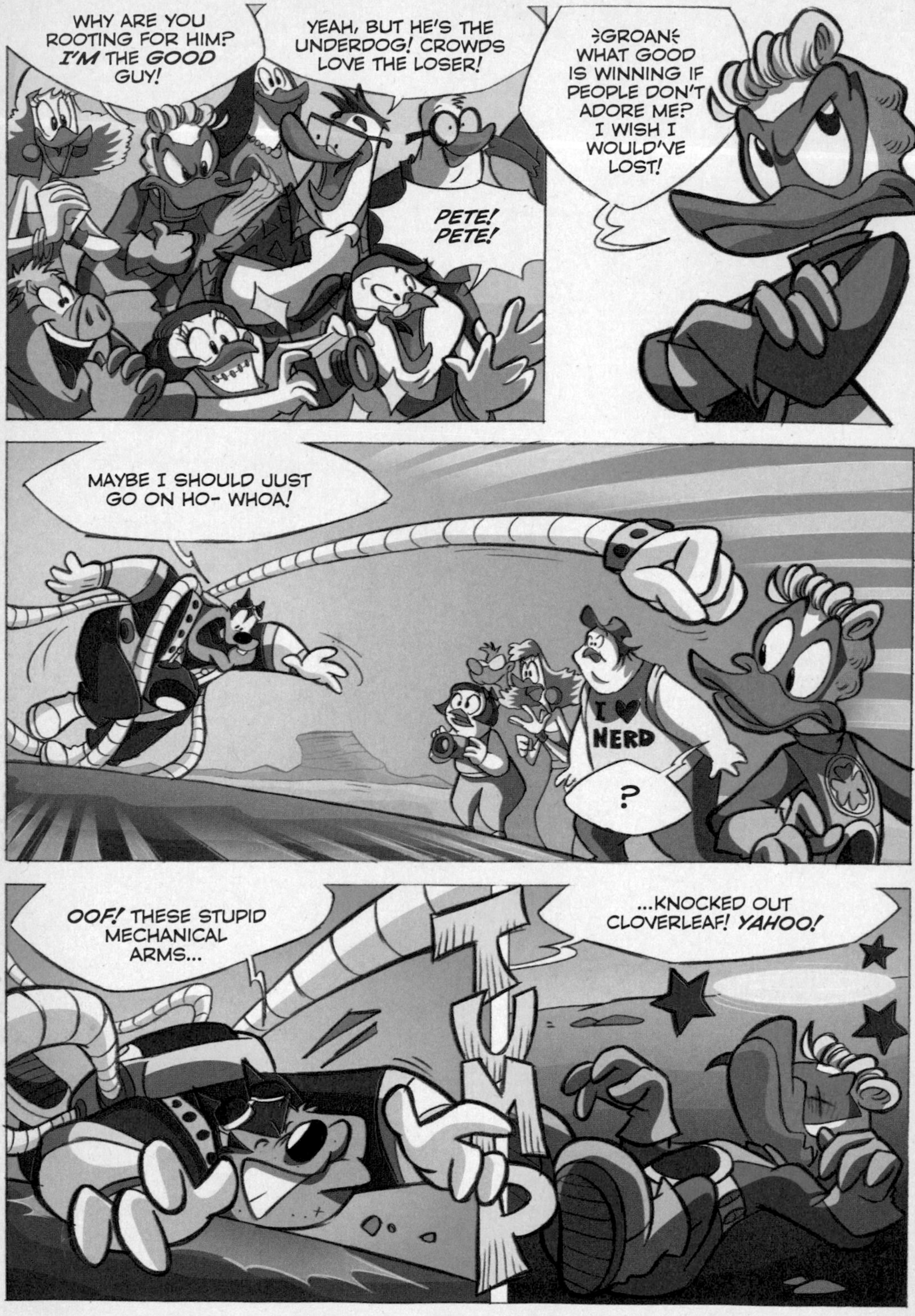
WHY ARE YOU ROOTING FOR HIM? *I'M* THE *GOOD* GUY!
YEAH, BUT HE'S THE UNDERDOG! CROWDS LOVE THE LOSER!
PETE! PETE!
≶GROAN≷ WHAT GOOD IS WINNING IF PEOPLE DON'T ADORE ME? I WISH I WOULD'VE LOST!
MAYBE I SHOULD JUST GO ON HO- WHOA!
I ♥ NERD
?
OOF! THESE STUPID MECHANICAL ARMS...
THUMP
...KNOCKED OUT CLOVERLEAF! *YAHOO!*

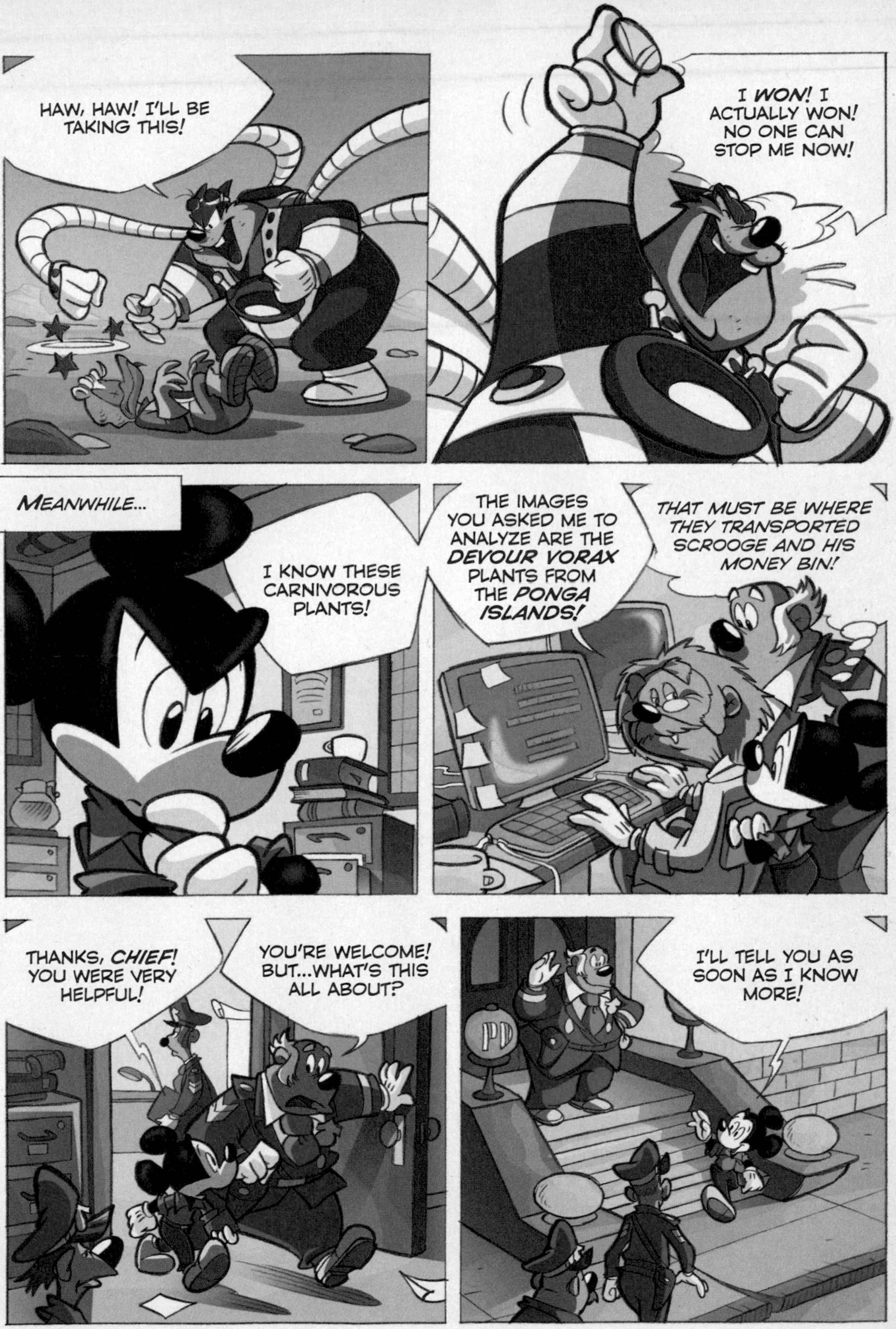
HAW, HAW! I'LL BE TAKING THIS!
I *WON*! I ACTUALLY WON! NO ONE CAN STOP ME NOW!
MEANWHILE...
I KNOW THESE CARNIVOROUS PLANTS!
THE IMAGES YOU ASKED ME TO ANALYZE ARE THE ***DEVOUR VORAX*** PLANTS FROM THE ***PONGA ISLANDS!***
THAT MUST BE WHERE THEY TRANSPORTED SCROOGE AND HIS MONEY BIN!
THANKS, ***CHIEF!*** YOU WERE VERY HELPFUL!
YOU'RE WELCOME! BUT...WHAT'S THIS ALL ABOUT?
I'LL TELL YOU AS SOON AS I KNOW MORE!

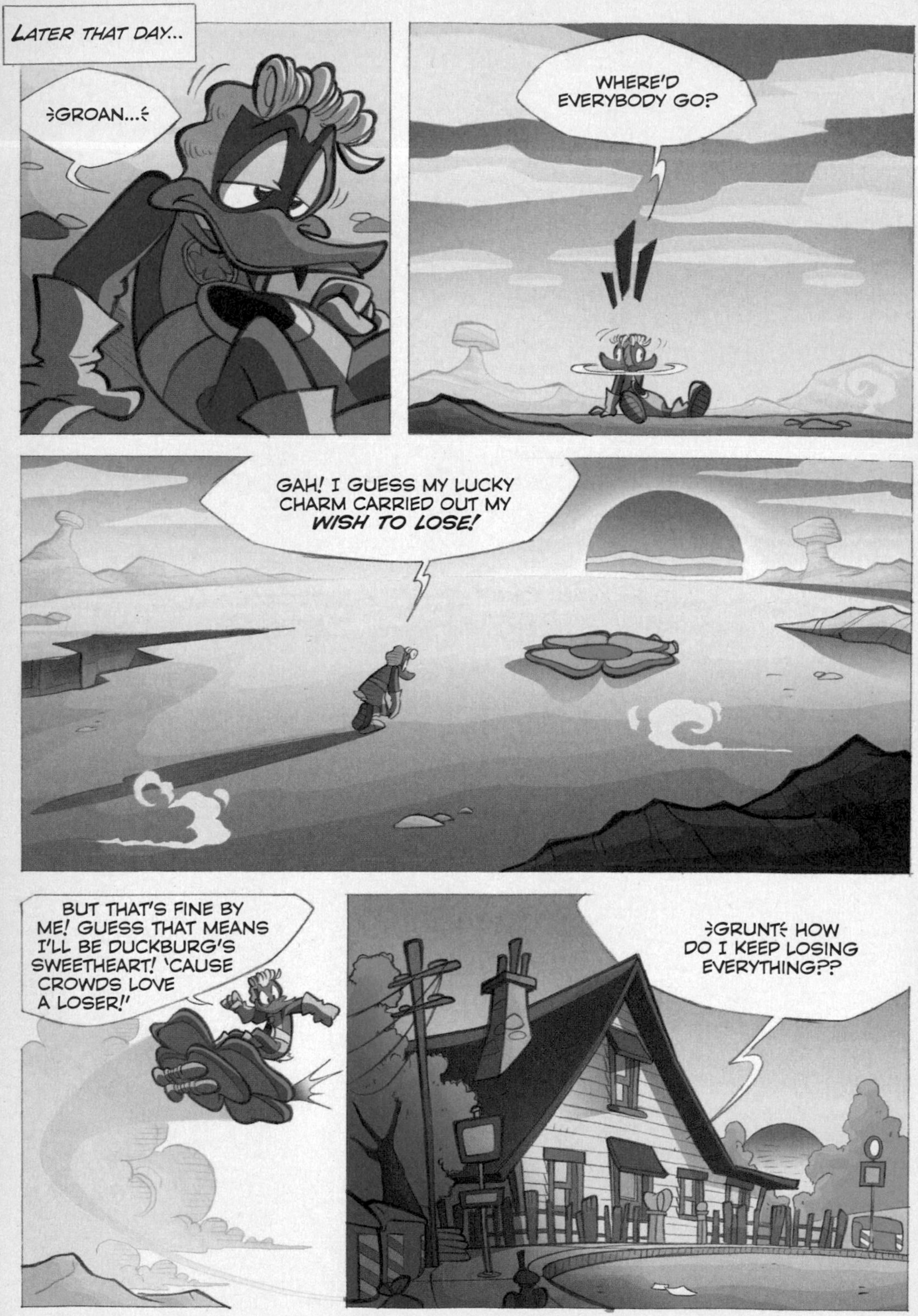
LATER THAT DAY...
GROAN...
WHERE'D EVERYBODY GO?
GAH! I GUESS MY LUCKY CHARM CARRIED OUT MY WISH TO LOSE!
BUT THAT'S FINE BY ME! GUESS THAT MEANS I'LL BE DUCKBURG'S SWEETHEART! 'CAUSE CROWDS LOVE A LOSER!'
GRUNT HOW DO I KEEP LOSING EVERYTHING??

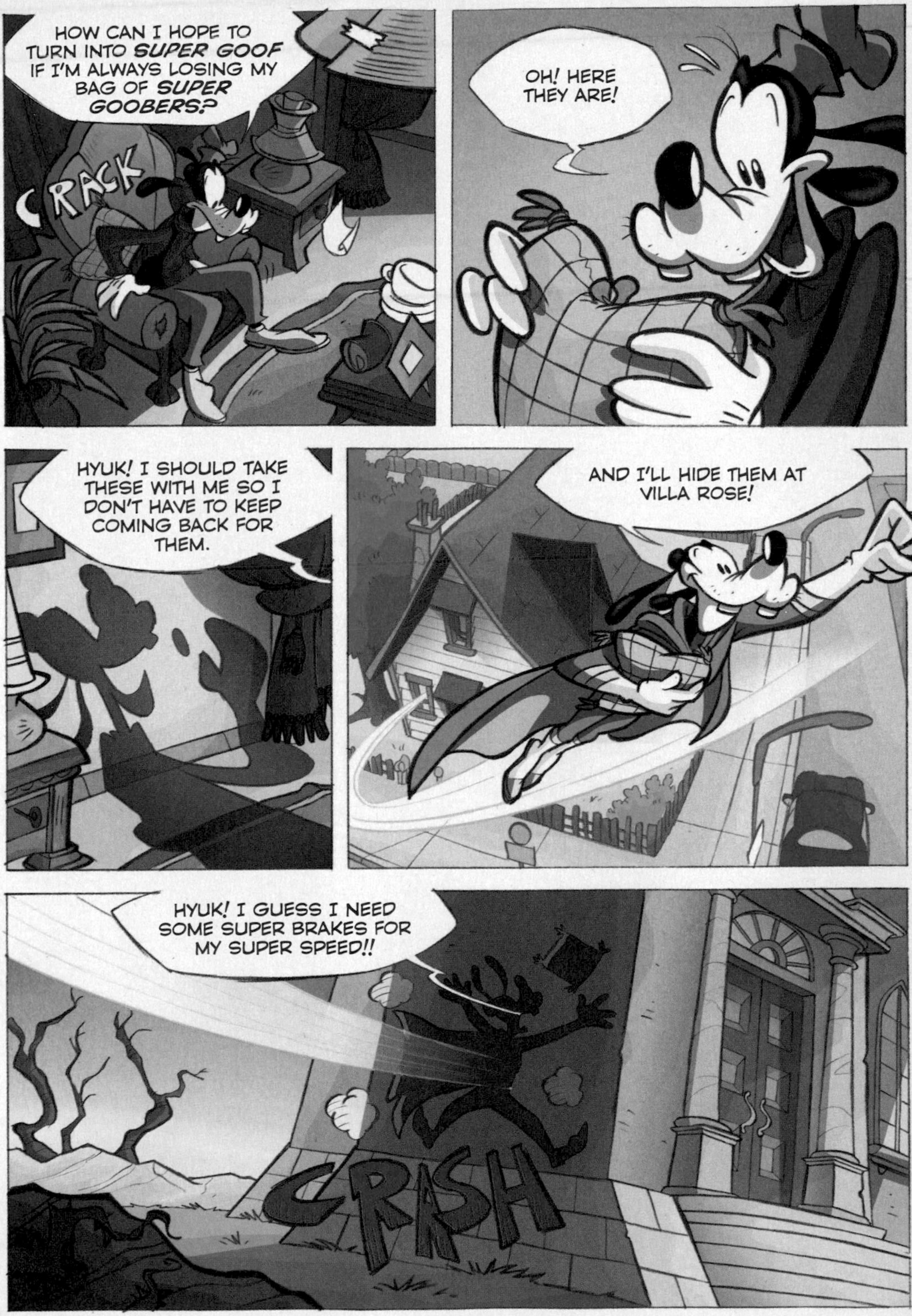

HOW CAN I HOPE TO TURN INTO SUPER GOOF IF I'M ALWAYS LOSING MY BAG OF SUPER GOOBERS?
CRACK
OH! HERE THEY ARE!
HYUK! I SHOULD TAKE THESE WITH ME SO I DON'T HAVE TO KEEP COMING BACK FOR THEM.
AND I'LL HIDE THEM AT VILLA ROSE!
HYUK! I GUESS I NEED SOME SUPER BRAKES FOR MY SUPER SPEED!!
CRASH

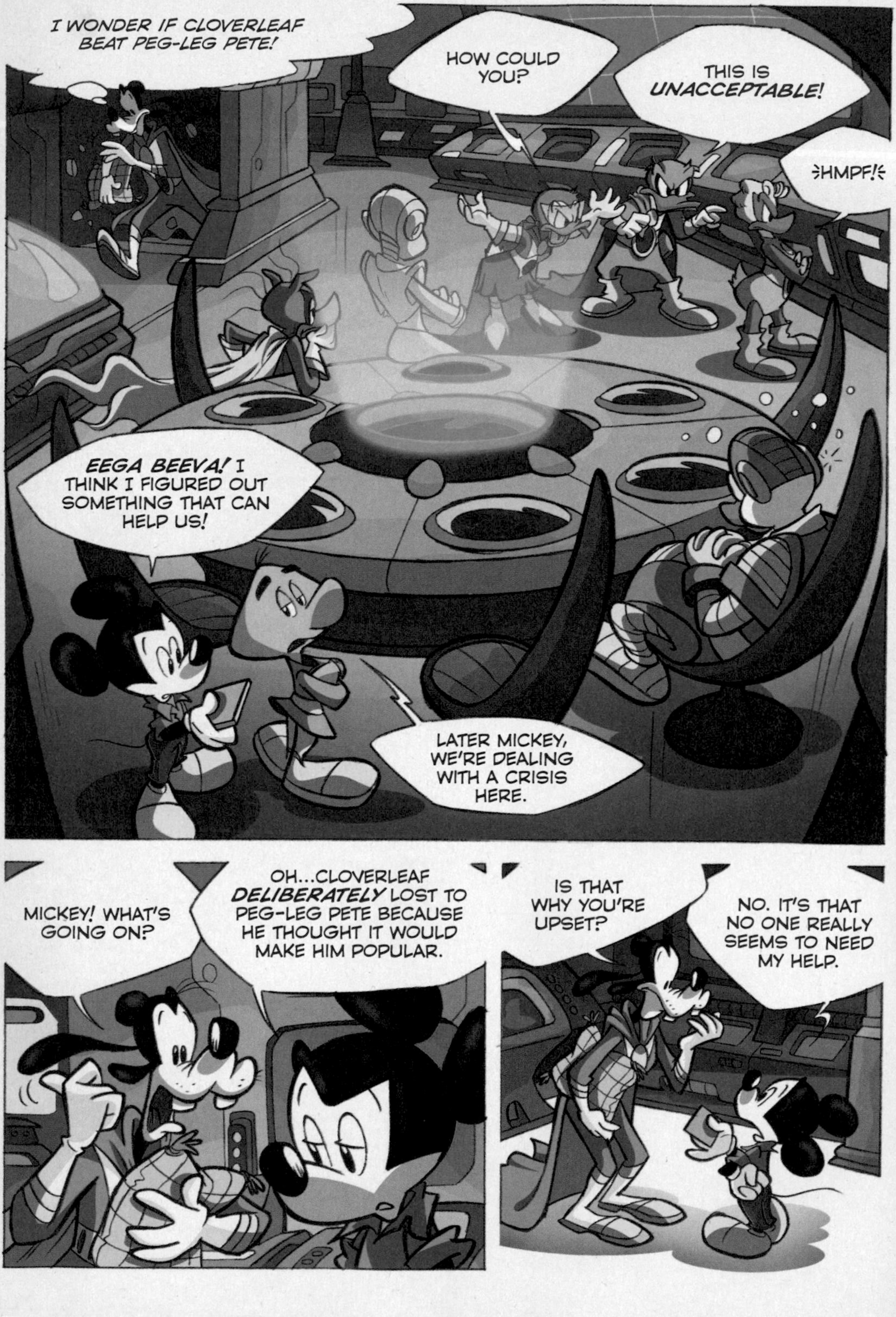
I WONDER IF CLOVERLEAF BEAT PEG-LEG PETE!
HOW COULD YOU?
THIS IS UNACCEPTABLE!
HMPF!
EEGA BEEVA! I THINK I FIGURED OUT SOMETHING THAT CAN HELP US!
LATER MICKEY, WE'RE DEALING WITH A CRISIS HERE.
MICKEY! WHAT'S GOING ON?
OH...CLOVERLEAF DELIBERATELY LOST TO PEG-LEG PETE BECAUSE HE THOUGHT IT WOULD MAKE HIM POPULAR.
IS THAT WHY YOU'RE UPSET?
NO. IT'S THAT NO ONE REALLY SEEMS TO NEED MY HELP.

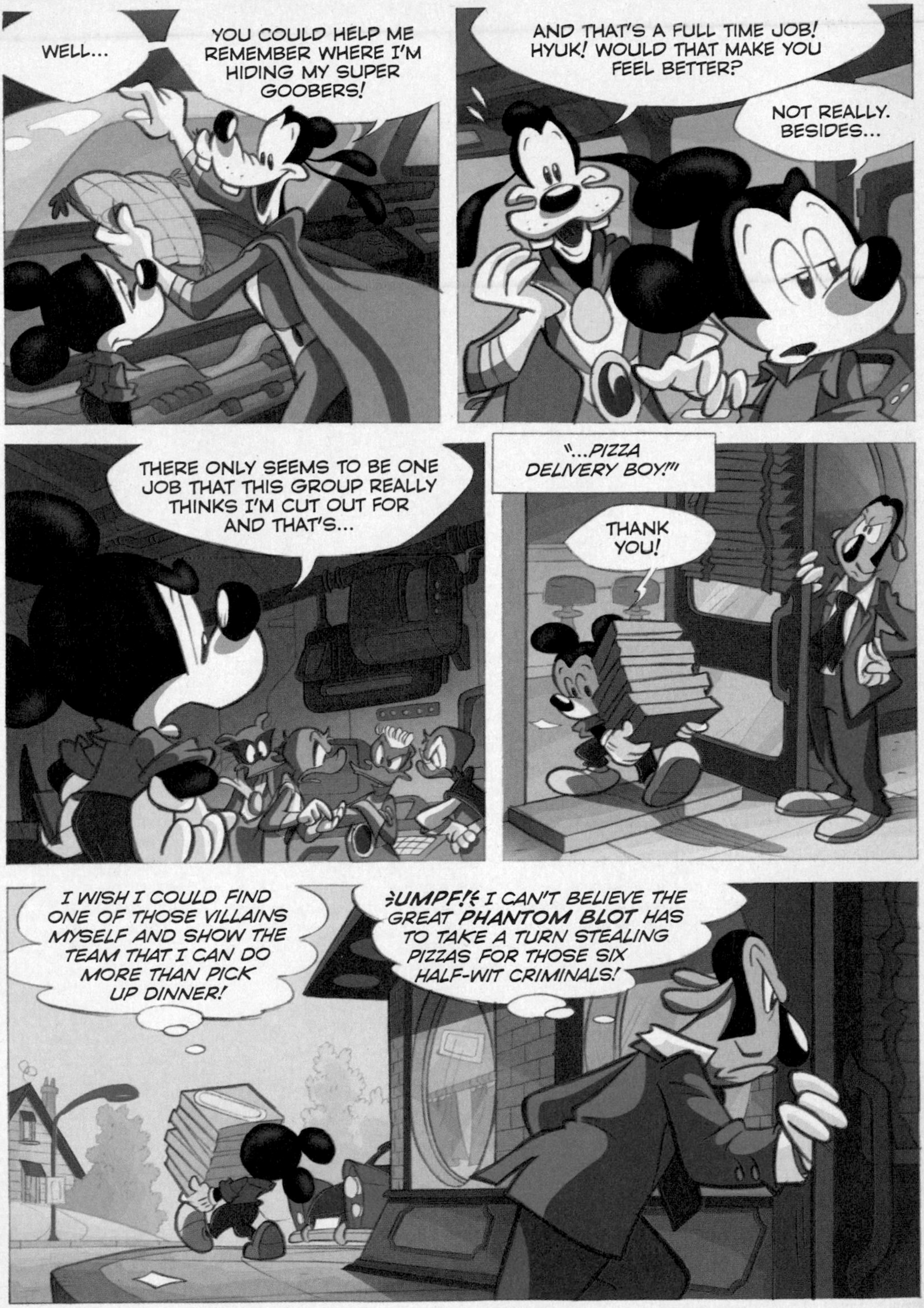
WELL...
YOU COULD HELP ME REMEMBER WHERE I'M HIDING MY SUPER GOOBERS!
AND THAT'S A FULL TIME JOB! HYUK! WOULD THAT MAKE YOU FEEL BETTER?
NOT REALLY. BESIDES...
THERE ONLY SEEMS TO BE ONE JOB THAT THIS GROUP REALLY THINKS I'M CUT OUT FOR AND THAT'S...
"...PIZZA DELIVERY BOY!"
THANK YOU!
I WISH I COULD FIND ONE OF THOSE VILLAINS MYSELF AND SHOW THE TEAM THAT I CAN DO MORE THAN PICK UP DINNER!
UMPF! I CAN'T BELIEVE THE GREAT PHANTOM BLOT HAS TO TAKE A TURN STEALING PIZZAS FOR THOSE SIX HALF-WIT CRIMINALS!

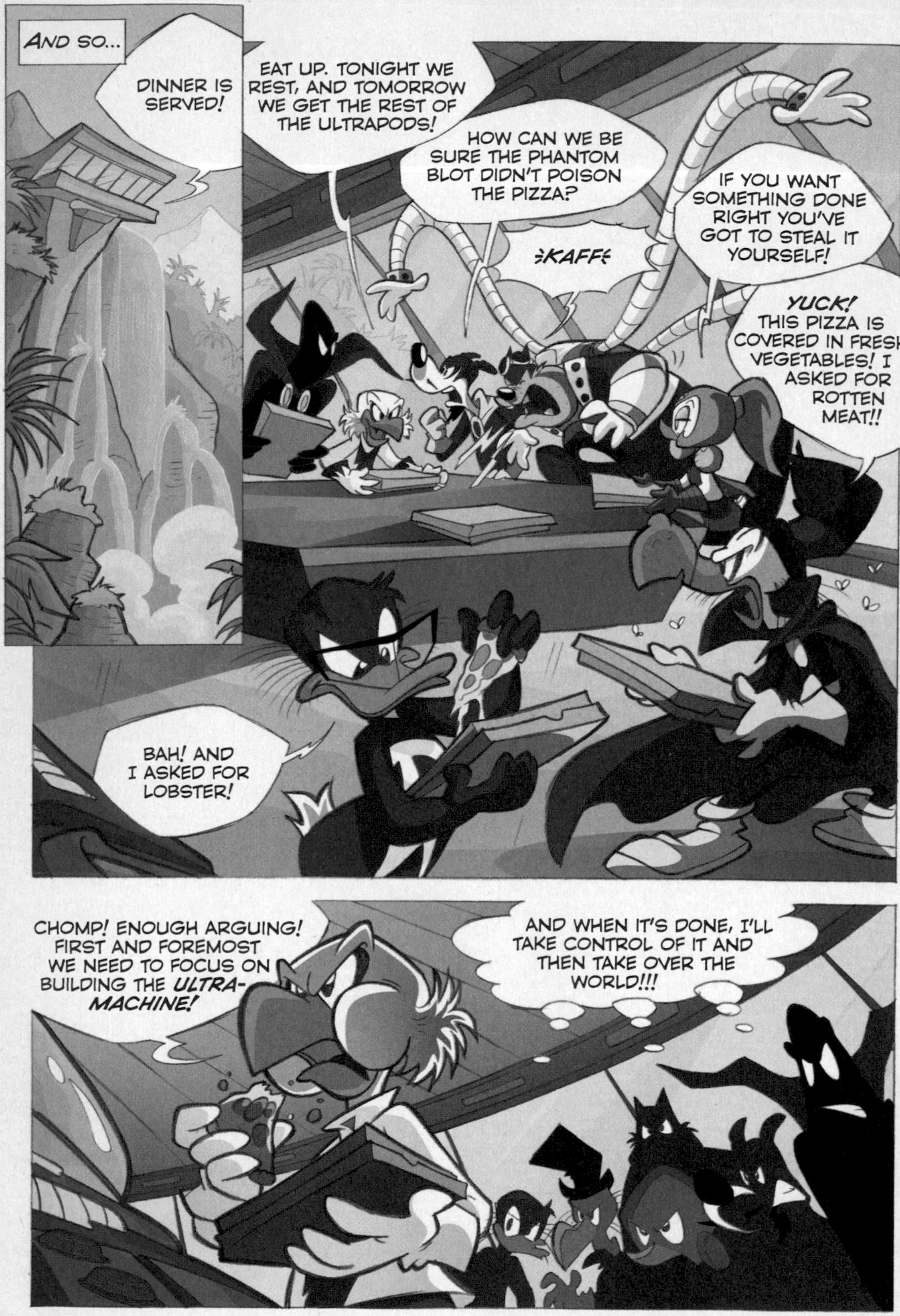
AND SO...
DINNER IS SERVED!
EAT UP. TONIGHT WE REST, AND TOMORROW WE GET THE REST OF THE ULTRAPODS!
HOW CAN WE BE SURE THE PHANTOM BLOT DIDN'T POISON THE PIZZA?
KAFF
IF YOU WANT SOMETHING DONE RIGHT YOU'VE GOT TO STEAL IT YOURSELF!
YUCK! THIS PIZZA IS COVERED IN FRESH VEGETABLES! I ASKED FOR ROTTEN MEAT!!
BAH! AND I ASKED FOR LOBSTER!
CHOMP! ENOUGH ARGUING! FIRST AND FOREMOST WE NEED TO FOCUS ON BUILDING THE ULTRA-MACHINE!
AND WHEN IT'S DONE, I'LL TAKE CONTROL OF IT AND THEN TAKE OVER THE WORLD!!!

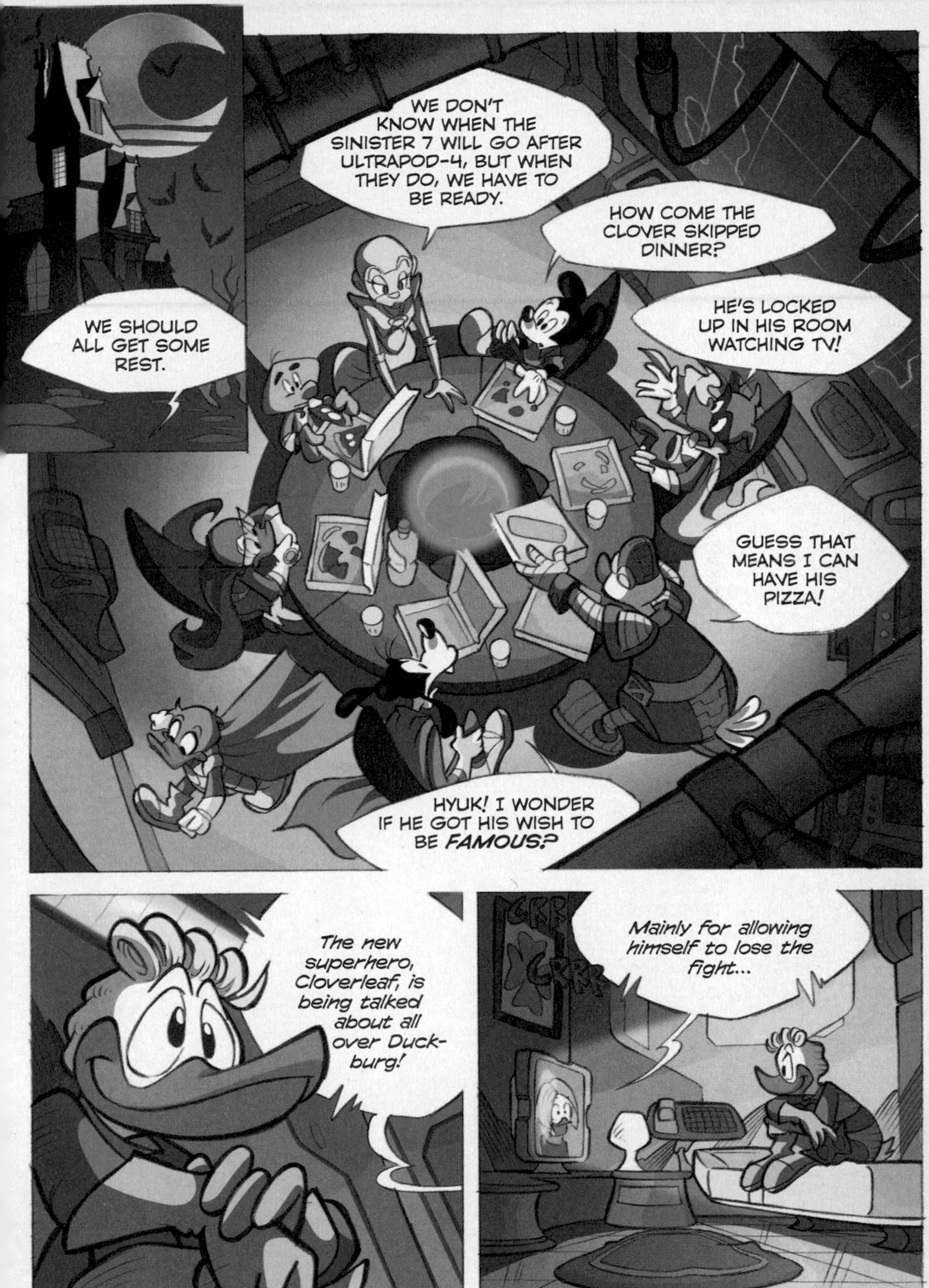
WE SHOULD ALL GET SOME REST.
WE DON'T KNOW WHEN THE SINISTER 7 WILL GO AFTER ULTRAPOD-4, BUT WHEN THEY DO, WE HAVE TO BE READY.
HOW COME THE CLOVER SKIPPED DINNER?
HE'S LOCKED UP IN HIS ROOM WATCHING TV!
GUESS THAT MEANS I CAN HAVE HIS PIZZA!
HYUK! I WONDER IF HE GOT HIS WISH TO BE *FAMOUS?*
The new superhero, Cloverleaf, is being talked about all over Duck-burg!
GRR GRR
Mainly for allowing himself to lose the fight...

STAK
...thereby becoming a *laughing stock*...
CRASH
WHAT'S THAT? YOU'D LIKE TO BUY A GARDEN *IGLOO?* HALF AN HOUR? GOTCHA!
...*CRACKLE*... *FZZZ*...
I NEED TO LEAVE FOR A WHILE! I KNOW IT'LL BE TOUGH WITHOUT ME... BUT HANG IN THERE, I'LL BE BACK!
HEY...
...WASN'T IT HIS TURN TO DO *LAUNDRY* TONIGHT?
GRUNT WHEN WILL I LEARN TO KEEP MY MOUTH SHUT?
ALTHOUGH WITH EEGA BEEVA'S *SUPERSTRONG ULTRA-DETERGENT,* THE CLOTHES GOT DONE IN A JIFF!

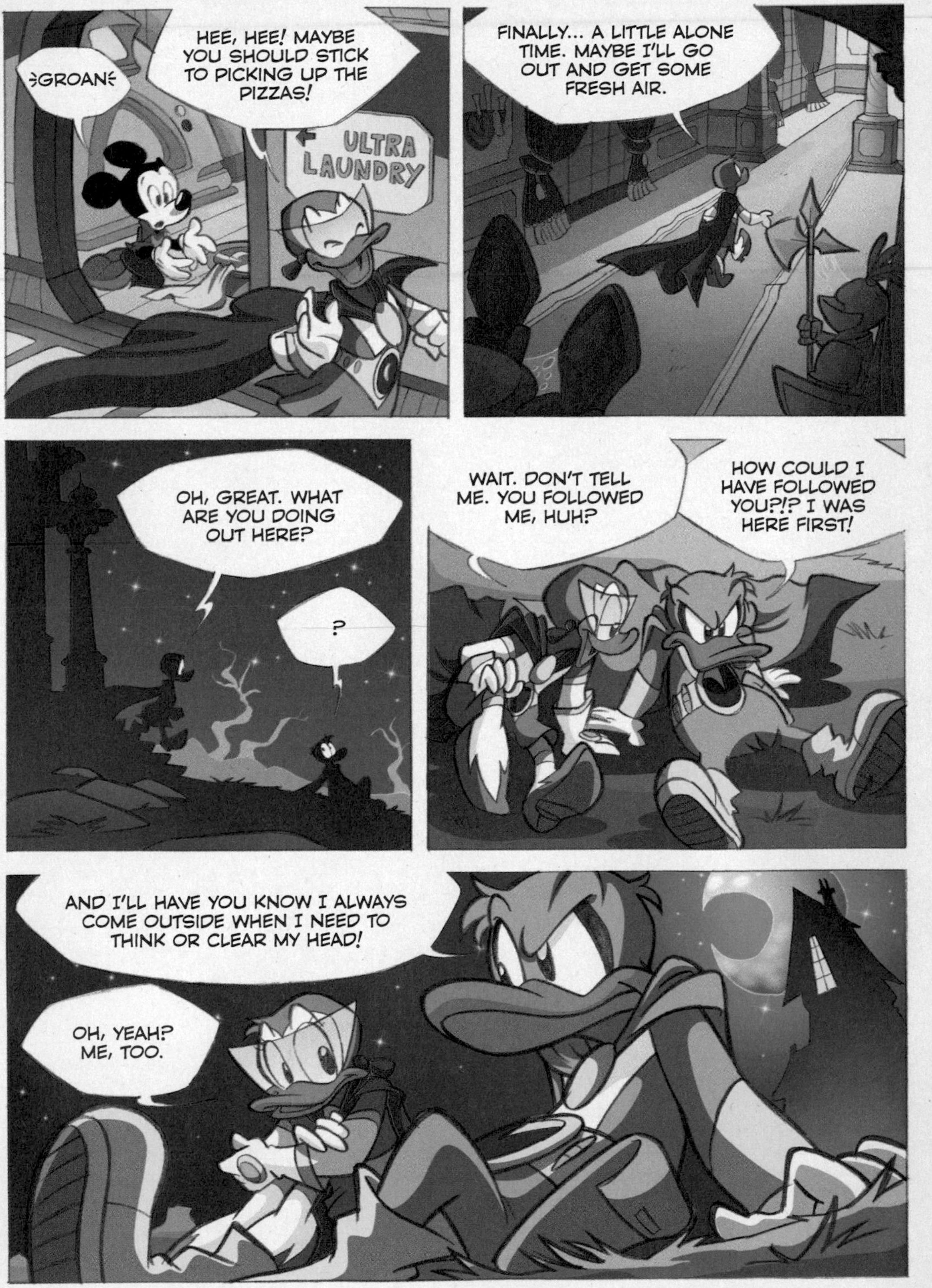

ƸGROANƷ
HEE, HEE! MAYBE YOU SHOULD STICK TO PICKING UP THE PIZZAS!
ULTRA LAUNDRY
FINALLY... A LITTLE ALONE TIME. MAYBE I'LL GO OUT AND GET SOME FRESH AIR.
OH, GREAT. WHAT ARE YOU DOING OUT HERE?
?
WAIT. DON'T TELL ME. YOU FOLLOWED ME, HUH?
HOW COULD I HAVE FOLLOWED YOU?!? I WAS HERE FIRST!
AND I'LL HAVE YOU KNOW I ALWAYS COME OUTSIDE WHEN I NEED TO THINK OR CLEAR MY HEAD!
OH, YEAH? ME, TOO.

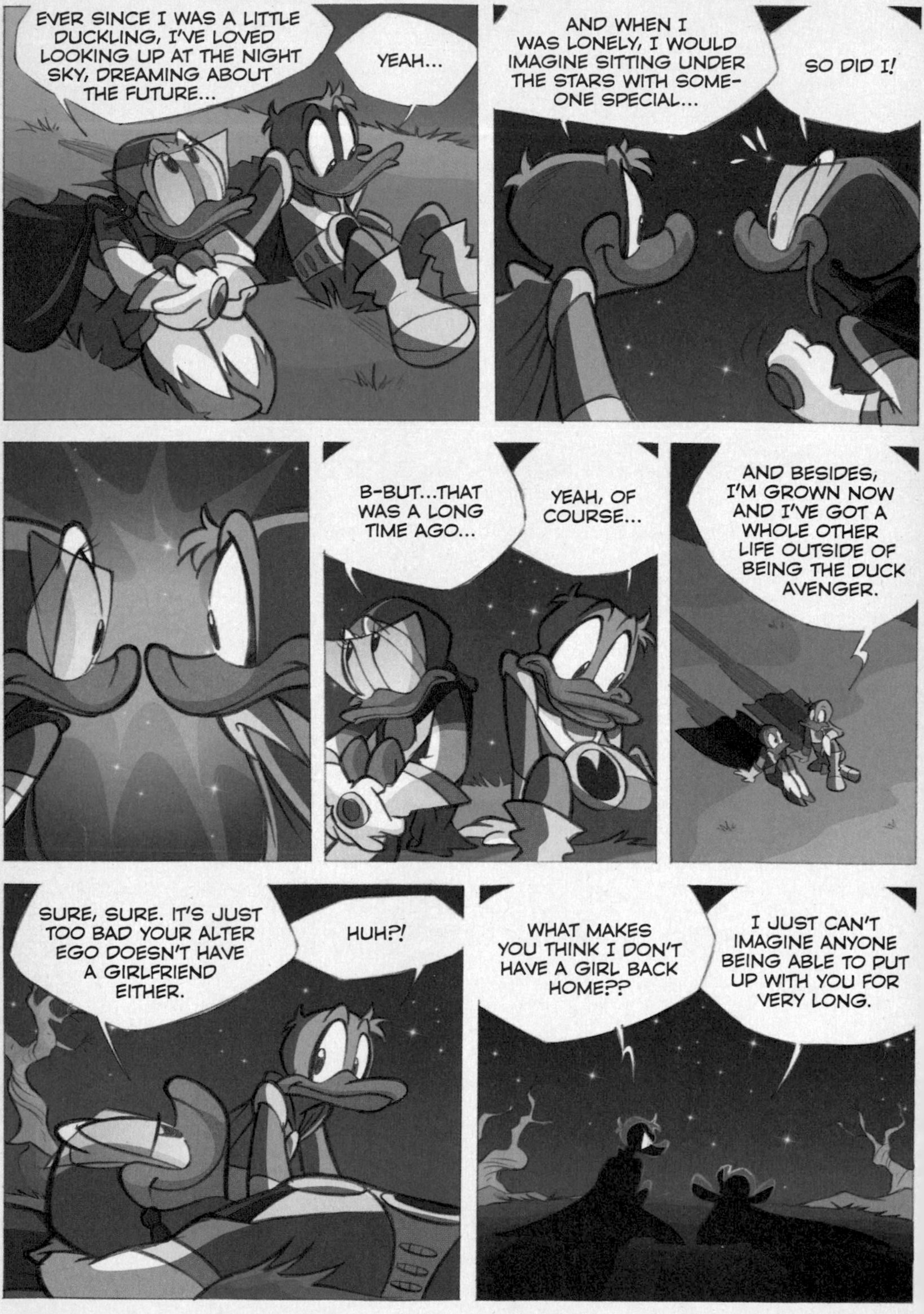
EVER SINCE I WAS A LITTLE DUCKLING, I'VE LOVED LOOKING UP AT THE NIGHT SKY, DREAMING ABOUT THE FUTURE...
YEAH...
AND WHEN I WAS LONELY, I WOULD IMAGINE SITTING UNDER THE STARS WITH SOME-ONE SPECIAL...
SO DID I!
B-BUT...THAT WAS A LONG TIME AGO...
YEAH, OF COURSE...
AND BESIDES, I'M GROWN NOW AND I'VE GOT A WHOLE OTHER LIFE OUTSIDE OF BEING THE DUCK AVENGER.
SURE, SURE. IT'S JUST TOO BAD YOUR ALTER EGO DOESN'T HAVE A GIRLFRIEND EITHER.
HUH?!
WHAT MAKES YOU THINK I DON'T HAVE A GIRL BACK HOME??
I JUST CAN'T IMAGINE ANYONE BEING ABLE TO PUT UP WITH YOU FOR VERY LONG.

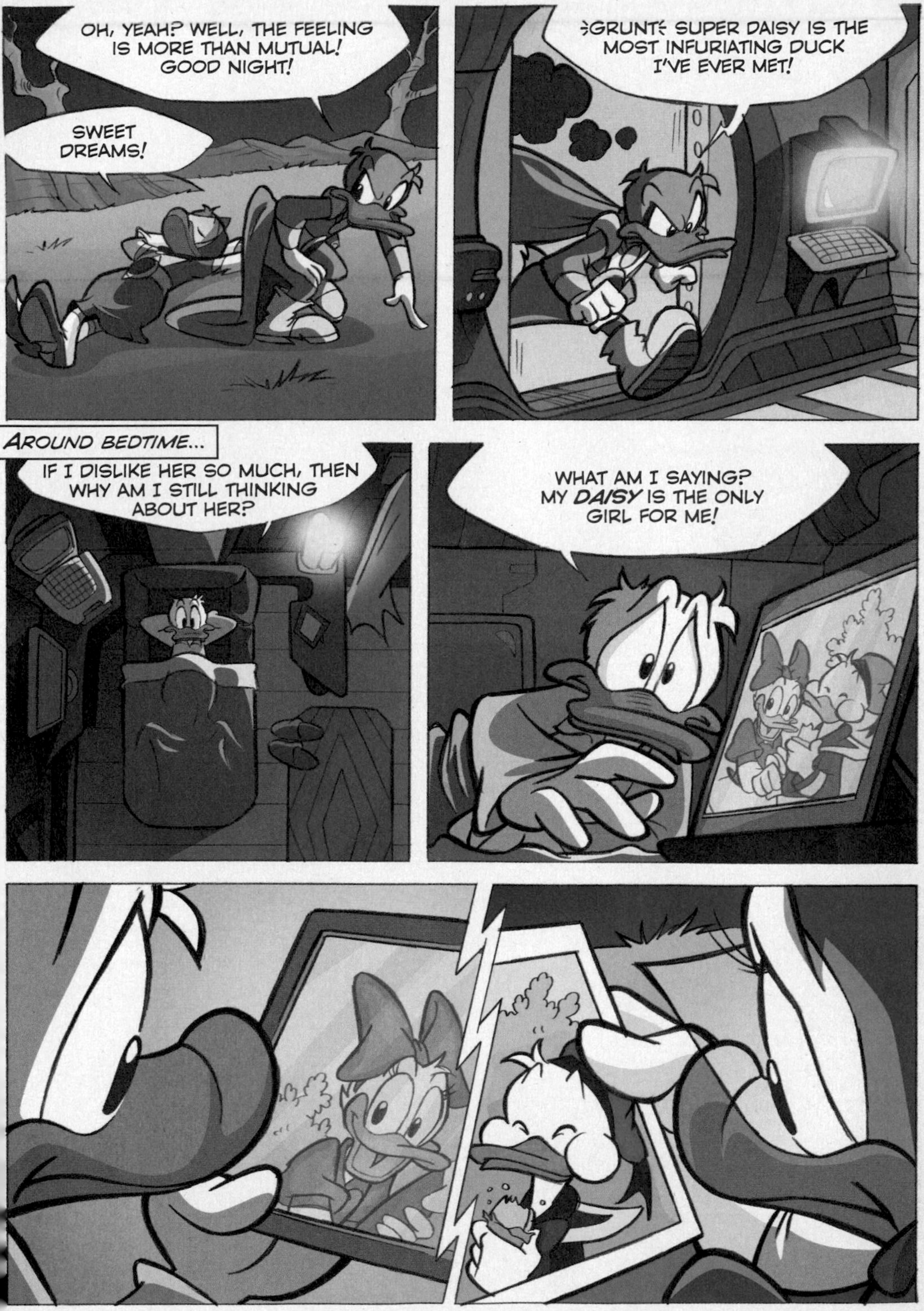

OH, YEAH? WELL, THE FEELING IS MORE THAN MUTUAL! GOOD NIGHT!
SWEET DREAMS!
GRUNT SUPER DAISY IS THE MOST INFURIATING DUCK I'VE EVER MET!
AROUND BEDTIME...
IF I DISLIKE HER SO MUCH, THEN WHY AM I STILL THINKING ABOUT HER?
WHAT AM I SAYING? MY DAISY IS THE ONLY GIRL FOR ME!

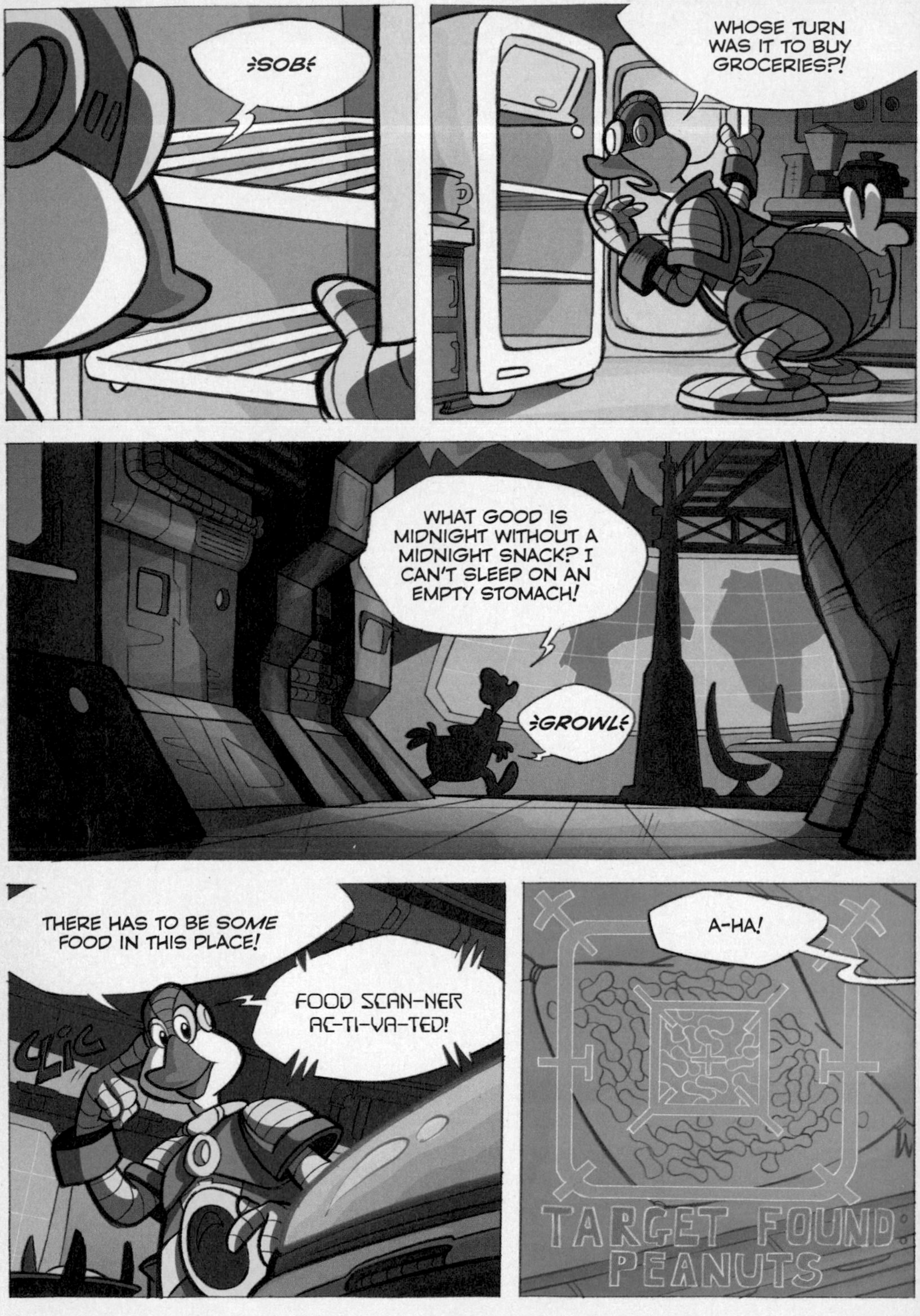

SOB
WHOSE TURN WAS IT TO BUY GROCERIES?!
WHAT GOOD IS MIDNIGHT WITHOUT A MIDNIGHT SNACK? I CAN'T SLEEP ON AN EMPTY STOMACH!
GROWL
THERE HAS TO BE SOME FOOD IN THIS PLACE!
CLIC
FOOD SCAN-NER AC-TI-VA-TED!
A-HA!
TARGET FOUND:
PEANUTS

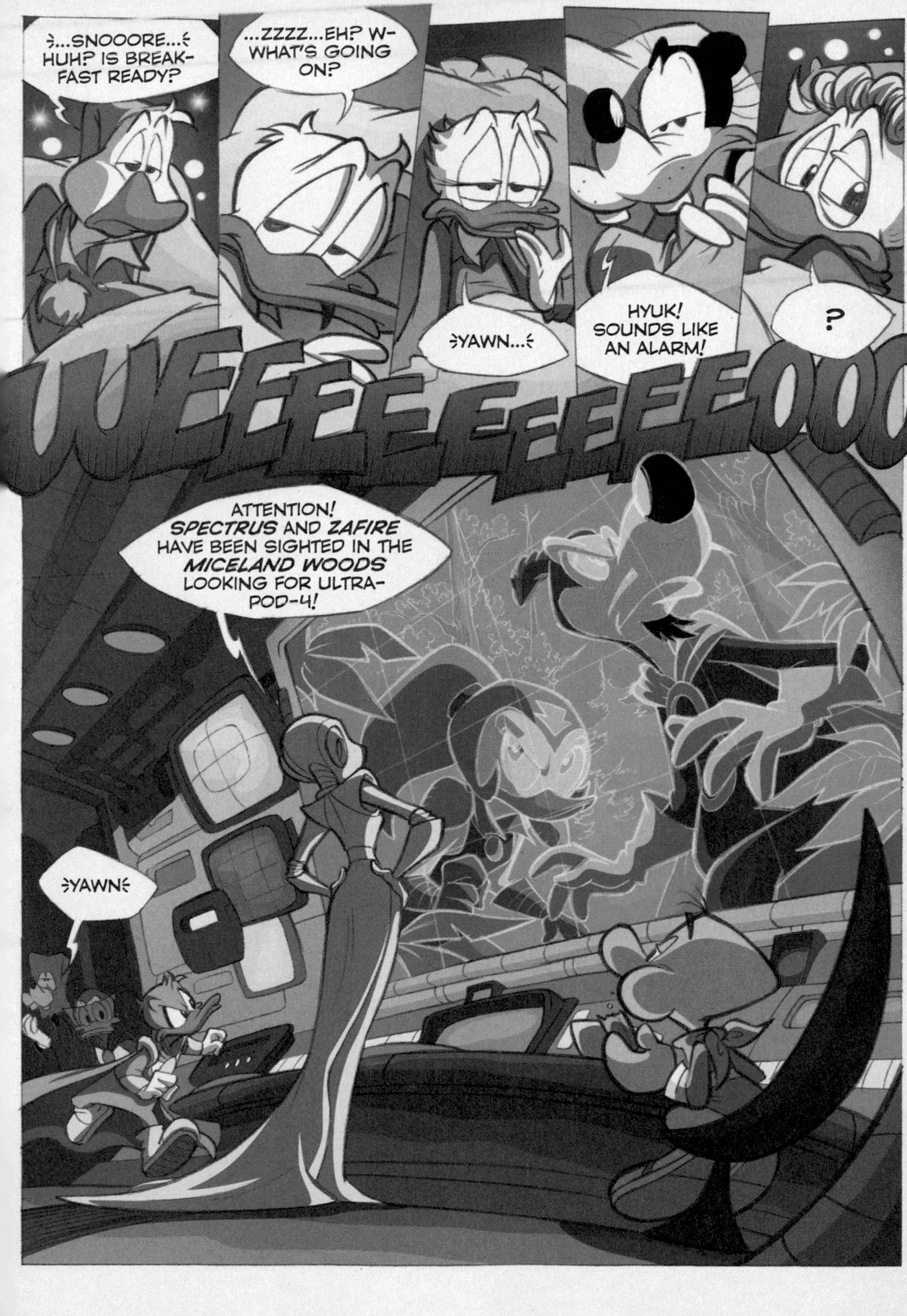
...SNOOORE... HUH? IS BREAK-FAST READY?
...ZZZZ...EH? W-WHAT'S GOING ON?
YAWN...
HYUK! SOUNDS LIKE AN ALARM!
?
WEEEEEEEEEOOO
ATTENTION! SPECTRUS AND ZAFIRE HAVE BEEN SIGHTED IN THE MICELAND WOODS LOOKING FOR ULTRA-POD-4!
YAWN

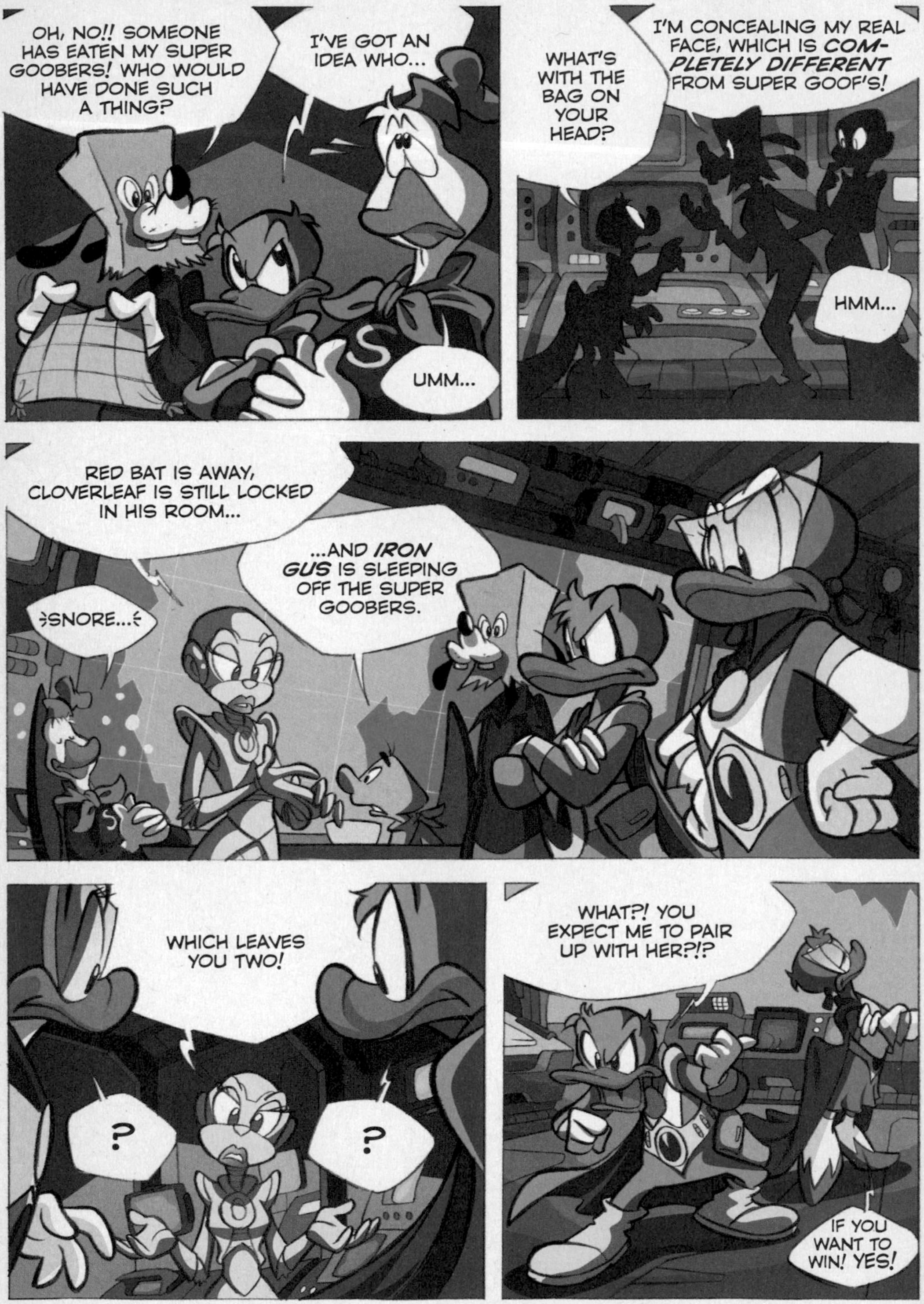
OH, NO!! SOMEONE HAS EATEN MY SUPER GOOBERS! WHO WOULD HAVE DONE SUCH A THING?
I'VE GOT AN IDEA WHO...
UMM...
WHAT'S WITH THE BAG ON YOUR HEAD?
I'M CONCEALING MY REAL FACE, WHICH IS *COMPLETELY DIFFERENT* FROM SUPER GOOF'S!
HMM...
RED BAT IS AWAY, CLOVERLEAF IS STILL LOCKED IN HIS ROOM...
...AND *IRON GUS* IS SLEEPING OFF THE SUPER GOOBERS.
SNORE...
WHICH LEAVES YOU TWO!
?
?
WHAT?! YOU EXPECT ME TO PAIR UP WITH HER?!?
IF YOU WANT TO WIN! YES!

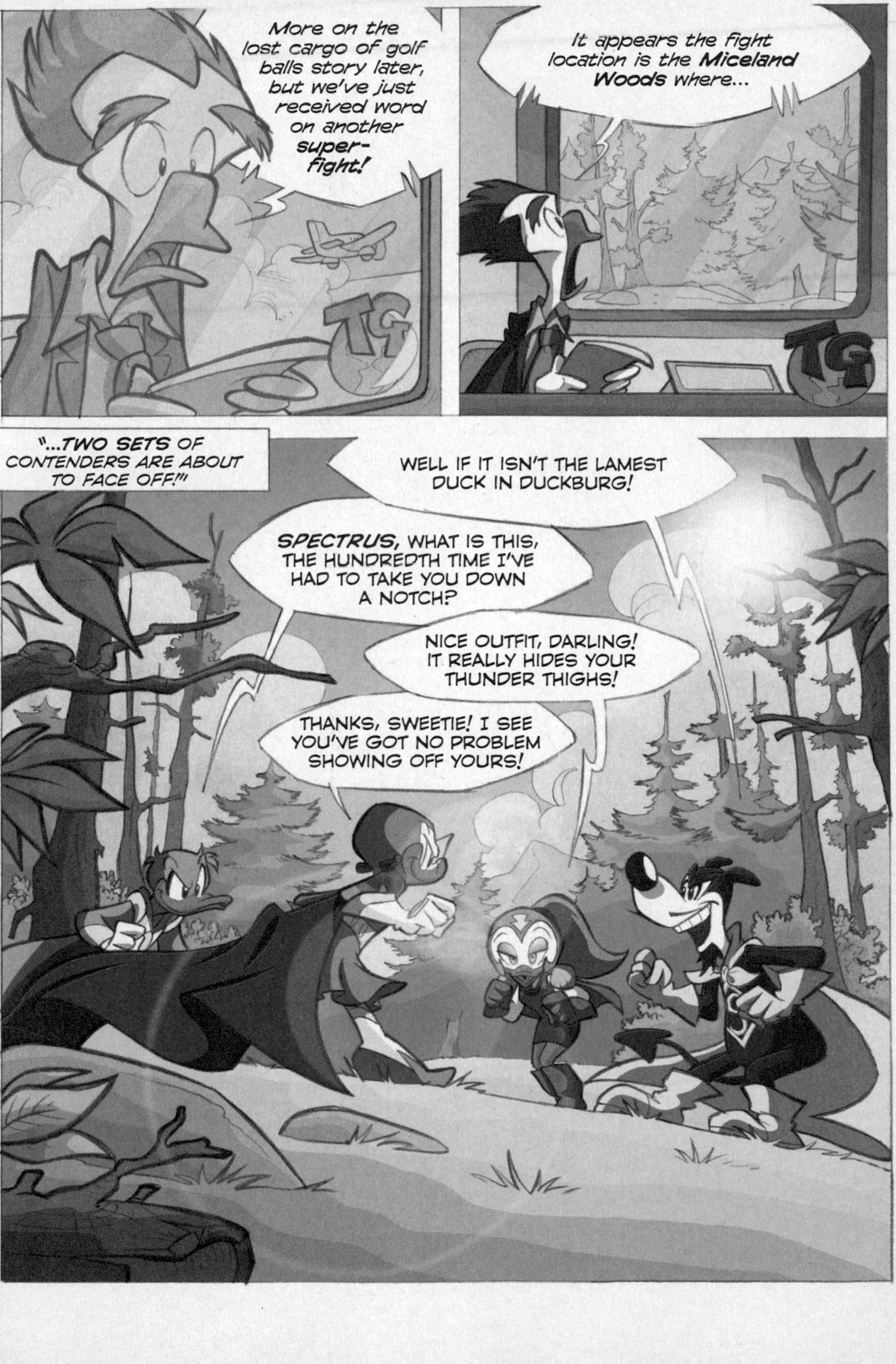
More on the lost cargo of golf balls story later, but we've just received word on another super-fight!
It appears the fight location is the Miceland Woods where...
"...TWO SETS OF CONTENDERS ARE ABOUT TO FACE OFF!"
WELL IF IT ISN'T THE LAMEST DUCK IN DUCKBURG!
SPECTRUS, WHAT IS THIS, THE HUNDREDTH TIME I'VE HAD TO TAKE YOU DOWN A NOTCH?
NICE OUTFIT, DARLING! IT REALLY HIDES YOUR THUNDER THIGHS!
THANKS, SWEETIE! I SEE YOU'VE GOT NO PROBLEM SHOWING OFF YOURS!

CHAPTER FOUR

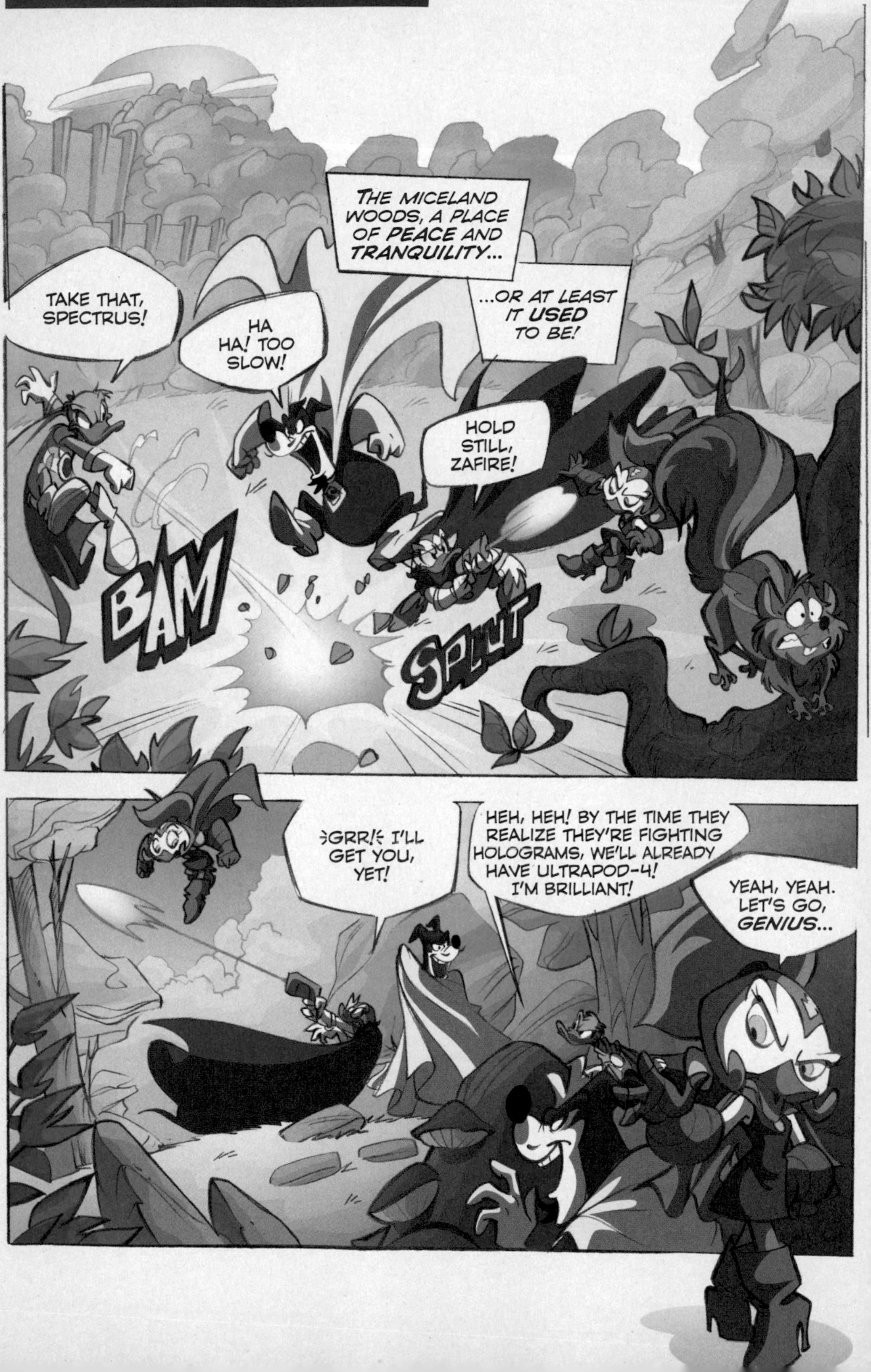
THE MICELAND WOODS, A PLACE OF PEACE AND TRANQUILITY...
...OR AT LEAST IT USED TO BE!
TAKE THAT, SPECTRUS!
HA HA! TOO SLOW!
HOLD STILL, ZAFIRE!
BAM
SPLUT
GRR! I'LL GET YOU, YET!
HEH, HEH! BY THE TIME THEY REALIZE THEY'RE FIGHTING HOLOGRAMS, WE'LL ALREADY HAVE ULTRAPOD-4! I'M BRILLIANT!
YEAH, YEAH. LET'S GO, GENIUS...

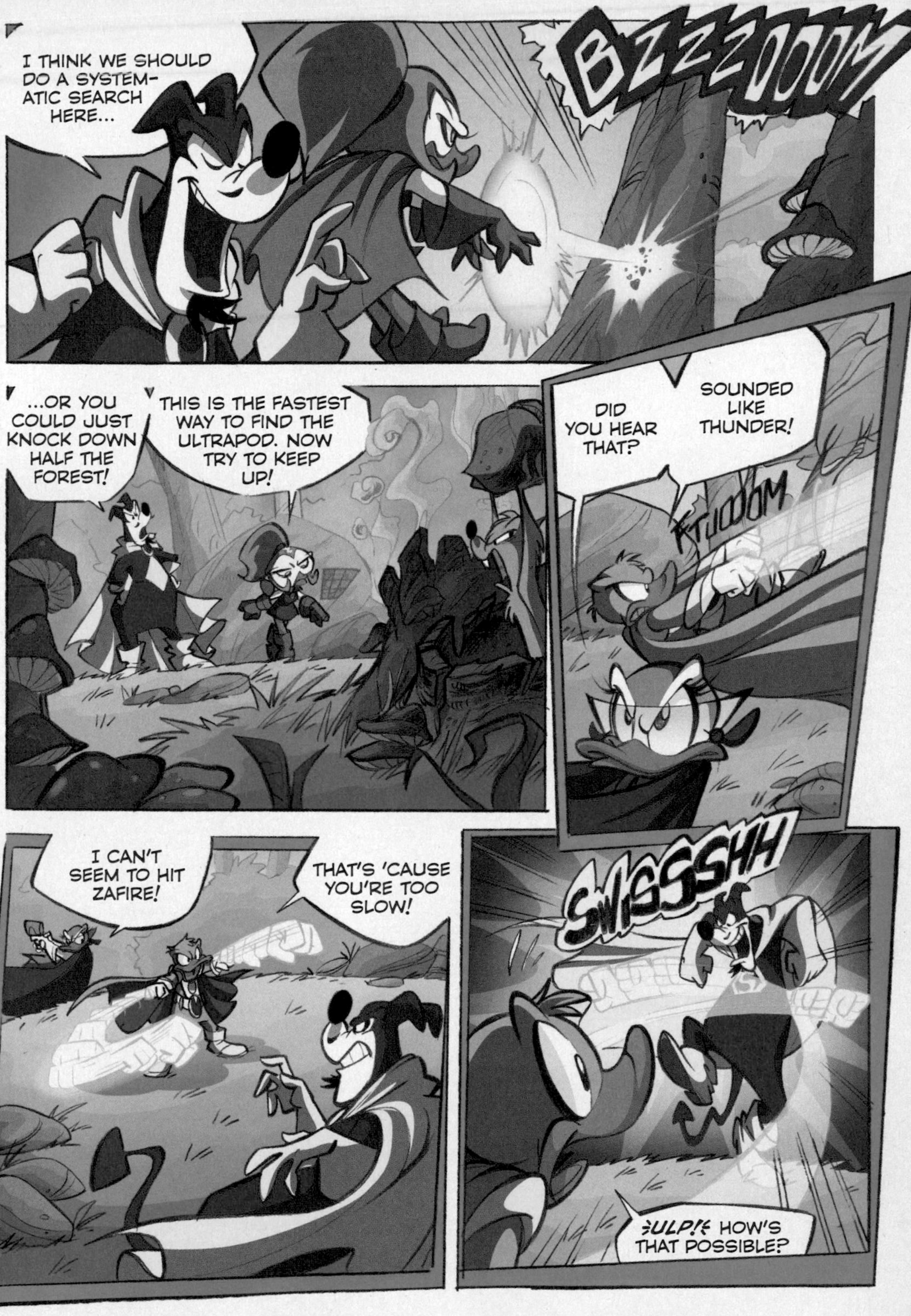

I THINK WE SHOULD DO A SYSTEMATIC SEARCH HERE...
BZZZOOOM
...OR YOU COULD JUST KNOCK DOWN HALF THE FOREST!
THIS IS THE FASTEST WAY TO FIND THE ULTRAPOD. NOW TRY TO KEEP UP!
DID YOU HEAR THAT?
SOUNDED LIKE THUNDER!
KTUOOOM
I CAN'T SEEM TO HIT ZAFIRE!
THAT'S 'CAUSE YOU'RE TOO SLOW!
SWISSSHH
ULP! HOW'S THAT POSSIBLE?

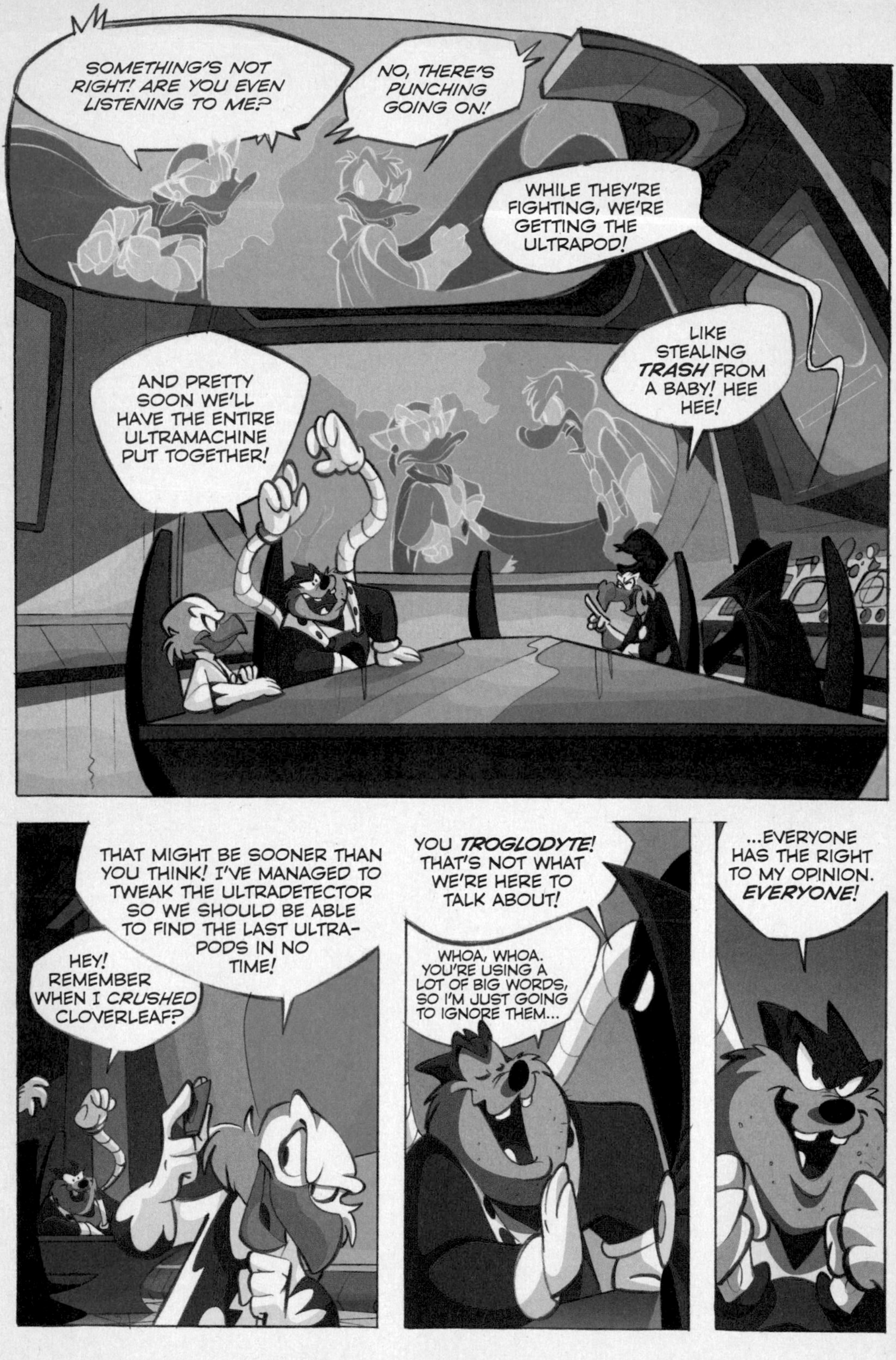
SOMETHING'S NOT RIGHT! ARE YOU EVEN LISTENING TO ME?
NO, THERE'S PUNCHING GOING ON!
WHILE THEY'RE FIGHTING, WE'RE GETTING THE ULTRAPOD!
AND PRETTY SOON WE'LL HAVE THE ENTIRE ULTRAMACHINE PUT TOGETHER!
LIKE STEALING TRASH FROM A BABY! HEE HEE!
THAT MIGHT BE SOONER THAN YOU THINK! I'VE MANAGED TO TWEAK THE ULTRADETECTOR SO WE SHOULD BE ABLE TO FIND THE LAST ULTRA-PODS IN NO TIME!
HEY! REMEMBER WHEN I CRUSHED CLOVERLEAF?
YOU TROGLODYTE! THAT'S NOT WHAT WE'RE HERE TO TALK ABOUT!
WHOA, WHOA. YOU'RE USING A LOT OF BIG WORDS, SO I'M JUST GOING TO IGNORE THEM...
...EVERYONE HAS THE RIGHT TO MY OPINION. EVERYONE!

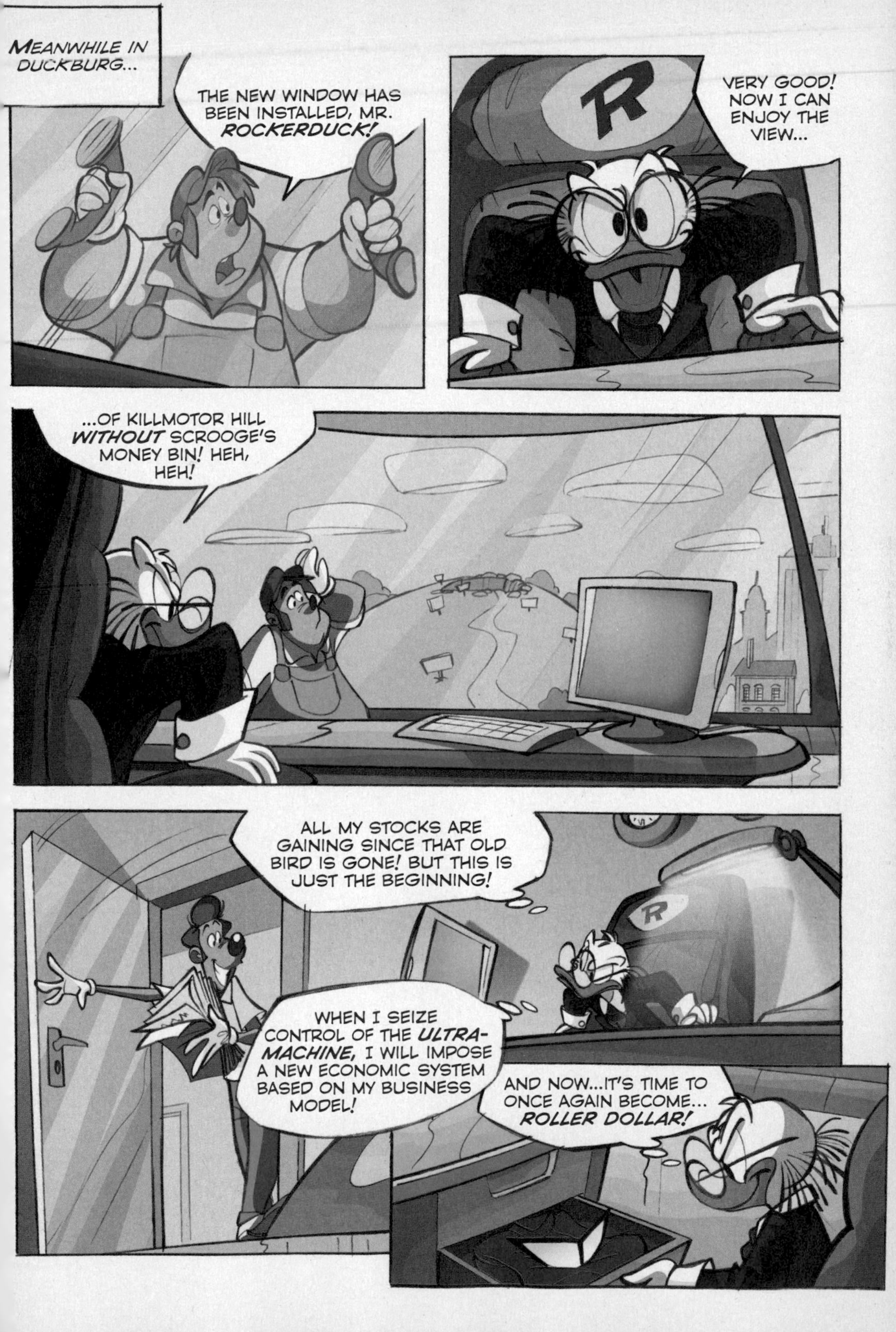
MEANWHILE IN DUCKBURG...
THE NEW WINDOW HAS BEEN INSTALLED, MR. ROCKERDUCK!
VERY GOOD! NOW I CAN ENJOY THE VIEW...
...OF KILLMOTOR HILL WITHOUT SCROOGE'S MONEY BIN! HEH, HEH!
ALL MY STOCKS ARE GAINING SINCE THAT OLD BIRD IS GONE! BUT THIS IS JUST THE BEGINNING!
WHEN I SEIZE CONTROL OF THE ULTRA-MACHINE, I WILL IMPOSE A NEW ECONOMIC SYSTEM BASED ON MY BUSINESS MODEL!
AND NOW...IT'S TIME TO ONCE AGAIN BECOME... ROLLER DOLLAR!

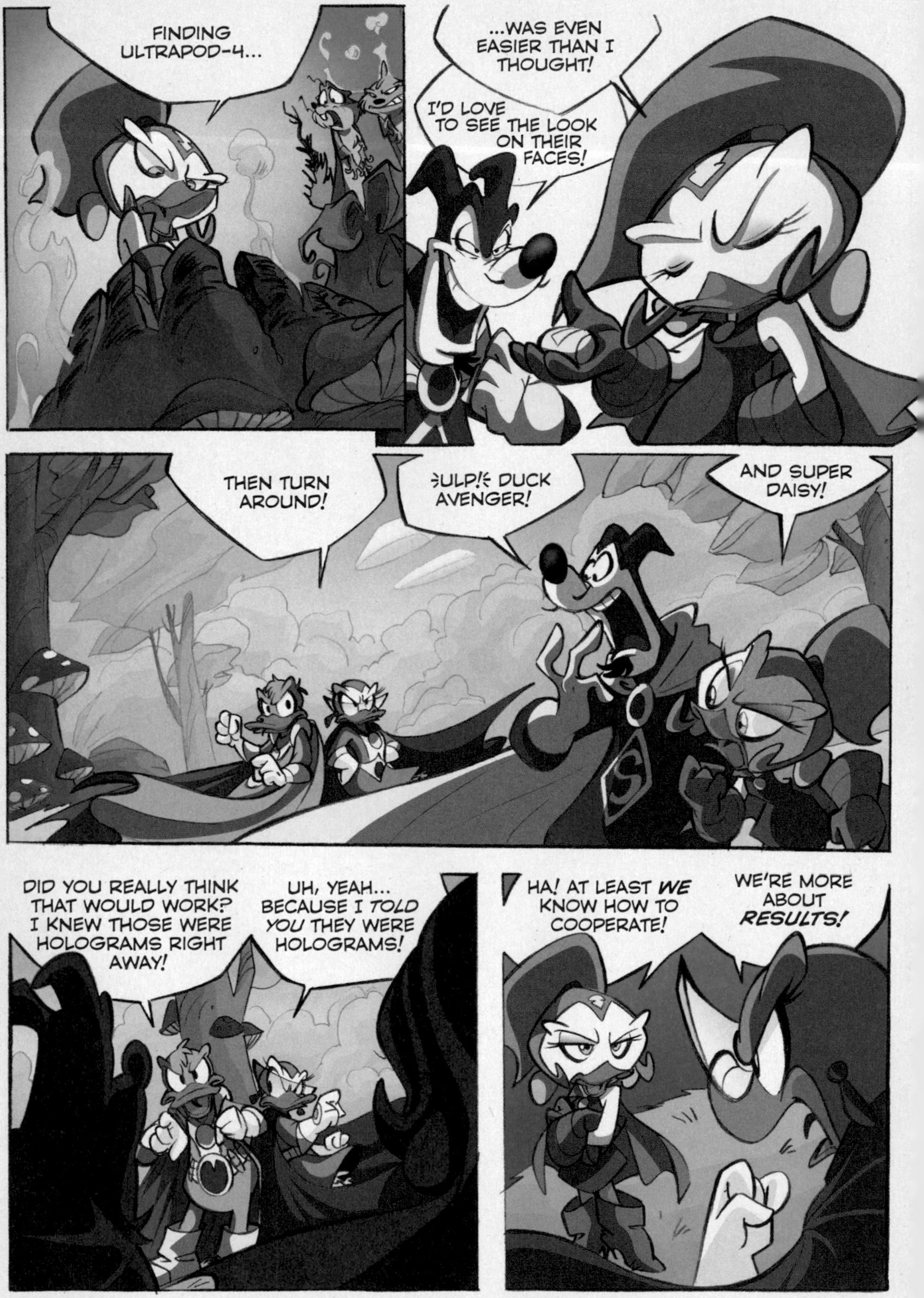
FINDING ULTRAPOD-4...
...WAS EVEN EASIER THAN I THOUGHT!
I'D LOVE TO SEE THE LOOK ON THEIR FACES!
THEN TURN AROUND!
GULP! DUCK AVENGER!
AND SUPER DAISY!
DID YOU REALLY THINK THAT WOULD WORK? I KNEW THOSE WERE HOLOGRAMS RIGHT AWAY!
UH, YEAH... BECAUSE I TOLD YOU THEY WERE HOLOGRAMS!
HA! AT LEAST WE KNOW HOW TO COOPERATE!
WE'RE MORE ABOUT RESULTS!

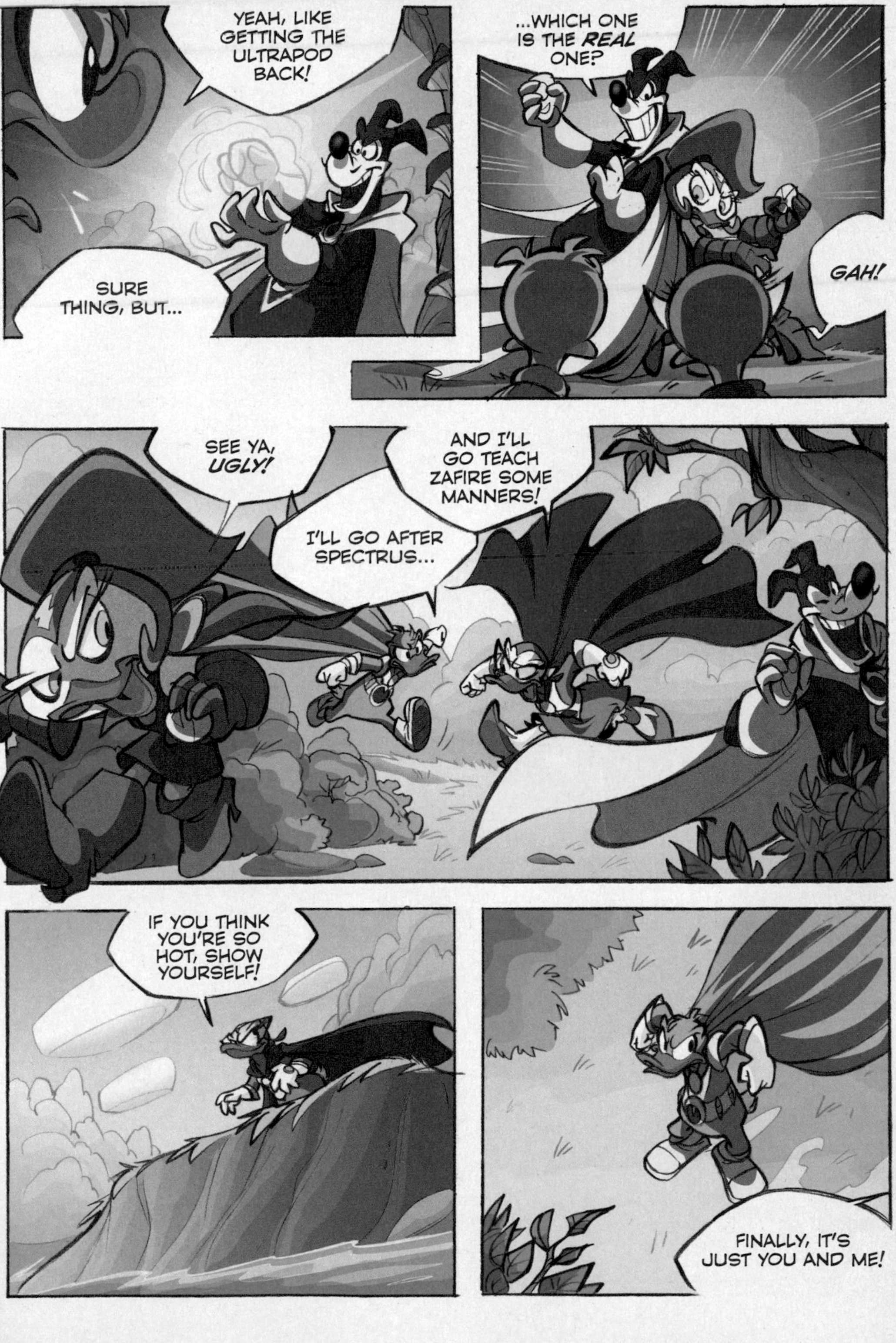
YEAH, LIKE GETTING THE ULTRAPOD BACK!
SURE THING, BUT...
...WHICH ONE IS THE REAL ONE?
GAH!
SEE YA, UGLY!
AND I'LL GO TEACH ZAFIRE SOME MANNERS!
I'LL GO AFTER SPECTRUS...
IF YOU THINK YOU'RE SO HOT, SHOW YOURSELF!
FINALLY, IT'S JUST YOU AND ME!

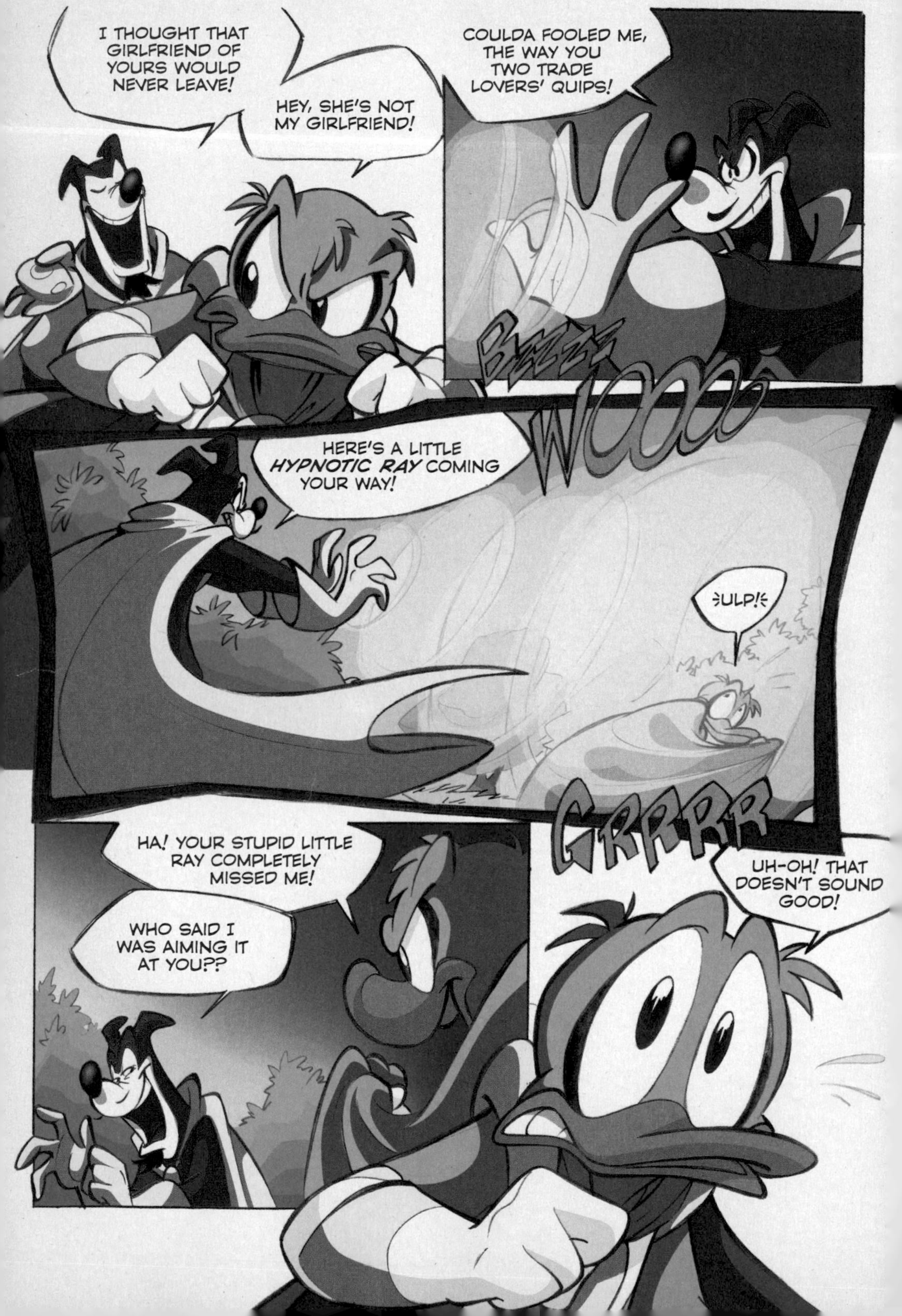

I THOUGHT THAT GIRLFRIEND OF YOURS WOULD NEVER LEAVE!
HEY, SHE'S NOT MY GIRLFRIEND!
COULDA FOOLED ME, THE WAY YOU TWO TRADE LOVERS' QUIPS!
BZZZ-WOOOO
HERE'S A LITTLE HYPNOTIC RAY COMING YOUR WAY!
ULP!
GRRRR
HA! YOUR STUPID LITTLE RAY COMPLETELY MISSED ME!
WHO SAID I WAS AIMING IT AT YOU??
UH-OH! THAT DOESN'T SOUND GOOD!

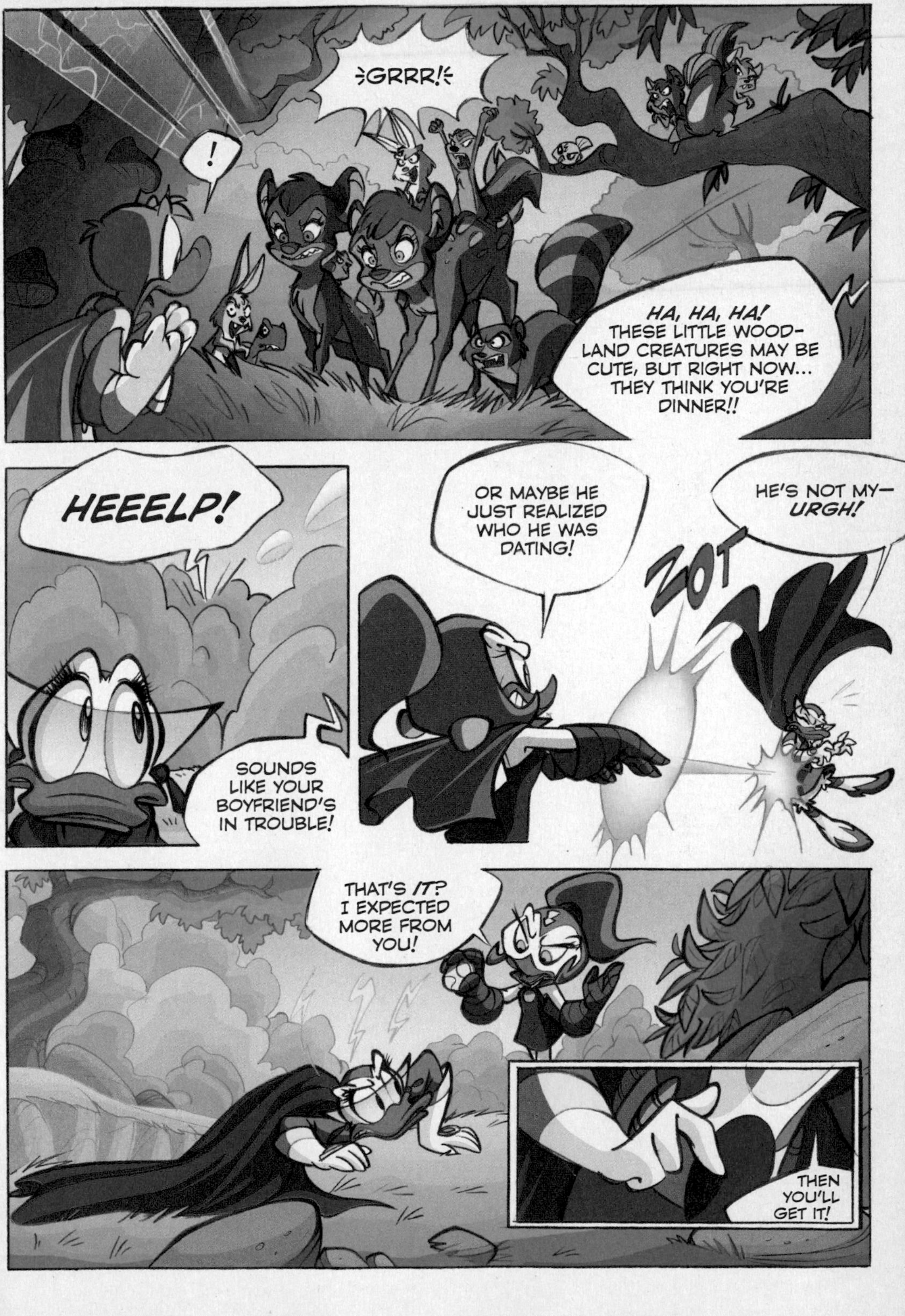

GRRR!
!
HA, HA, HA! THESE LITTLE WOODLAND CREATURES MAY BE CUTE, BUT RIGHT NOW... THEY THINK YOU'RE DINNER!!
HEEELP!
SOUNDS LIKE YOUR BOYFRIEND'S IN TROUBLE!
OR MAYBE HE JUST REALIZED WHO HE WAS DATING!
HE'S NOT MY— URGH!
ZOT
THAT'S IT? I EXPECTED MORE FROM YOU!
THEN YOU'LL GET IT!

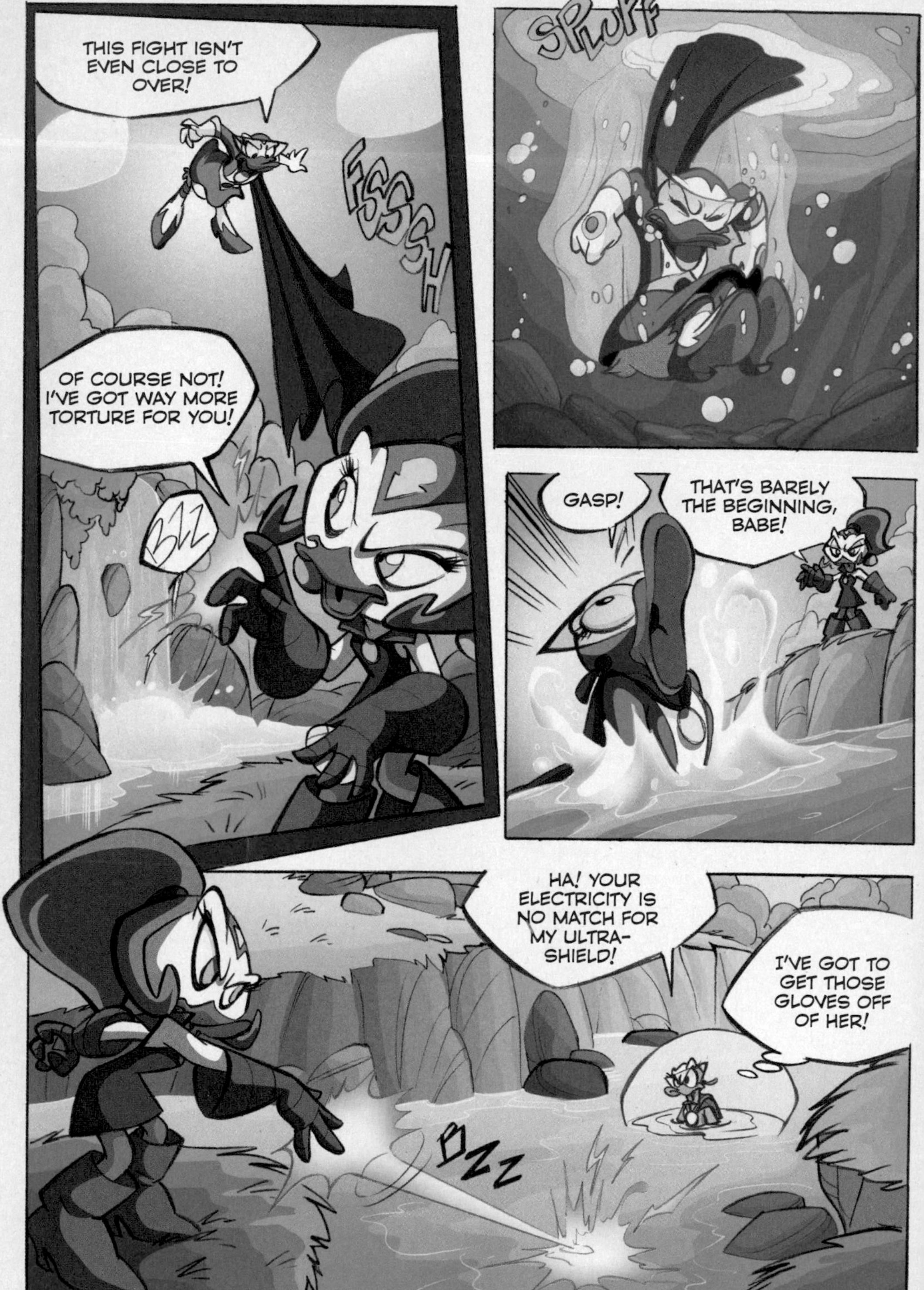
THIS FIGHT ISN'T EVEN CLOSE TO OVER!
FSSSH
OF COURSE NOT! I'VE GOT WAY MORE TORTURE FOR YOU!
BZZ
SPLUFF
GASP!
THAT'S BARELY THE BEGINNING, BABE!
HA! YOUR ELECTRICITY IS NO MATCH FOR MY ULTRA-SHIELD!
I'VE GOT TO GET THOSE GLOVES OFF OF HER!
BZZ

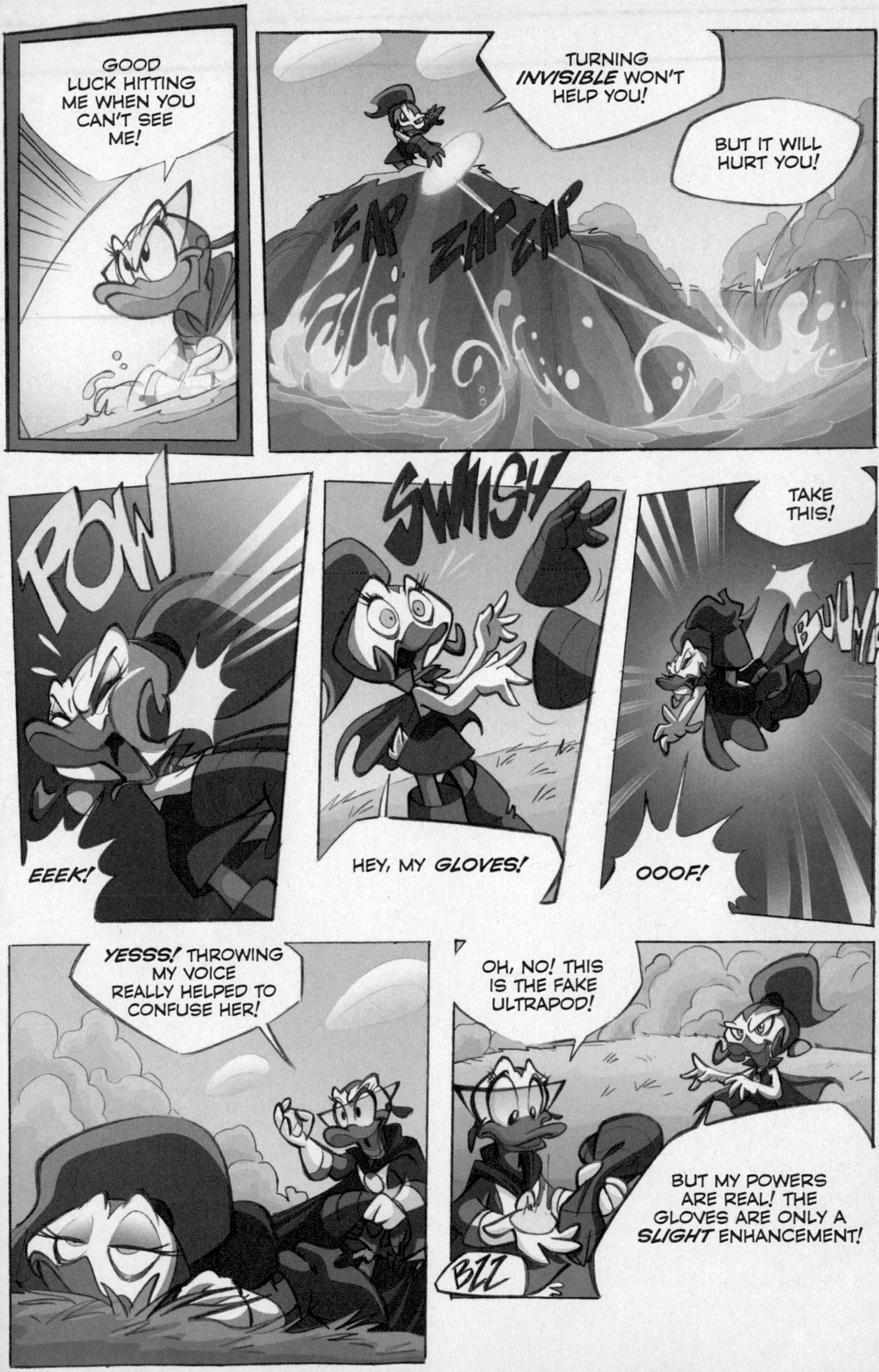
GOOD LUCK HITTING ME WHEN YOU CAN'T SEE ME!
TURNING *INVISIBLE* WON'T HELP YOU!
BUT IT WILL HURT YOU!
ZAP
ZAP
ZAP
POW
EEEK!
SWISH
HEY, MY *GLOVES!*
TAKE THIS!
BUMP
OOOF!
YESSS! THROWING MY VOICE REALLY HELPED TO CONFUSE HER!
OH, NO! THIS IS THE FAKE ULTRAPOD!
BUT MY POWERS ARE REAL! THE GLOVES ARE ONLY A *SLIGHT* ENHANCEMENT!
BZZ

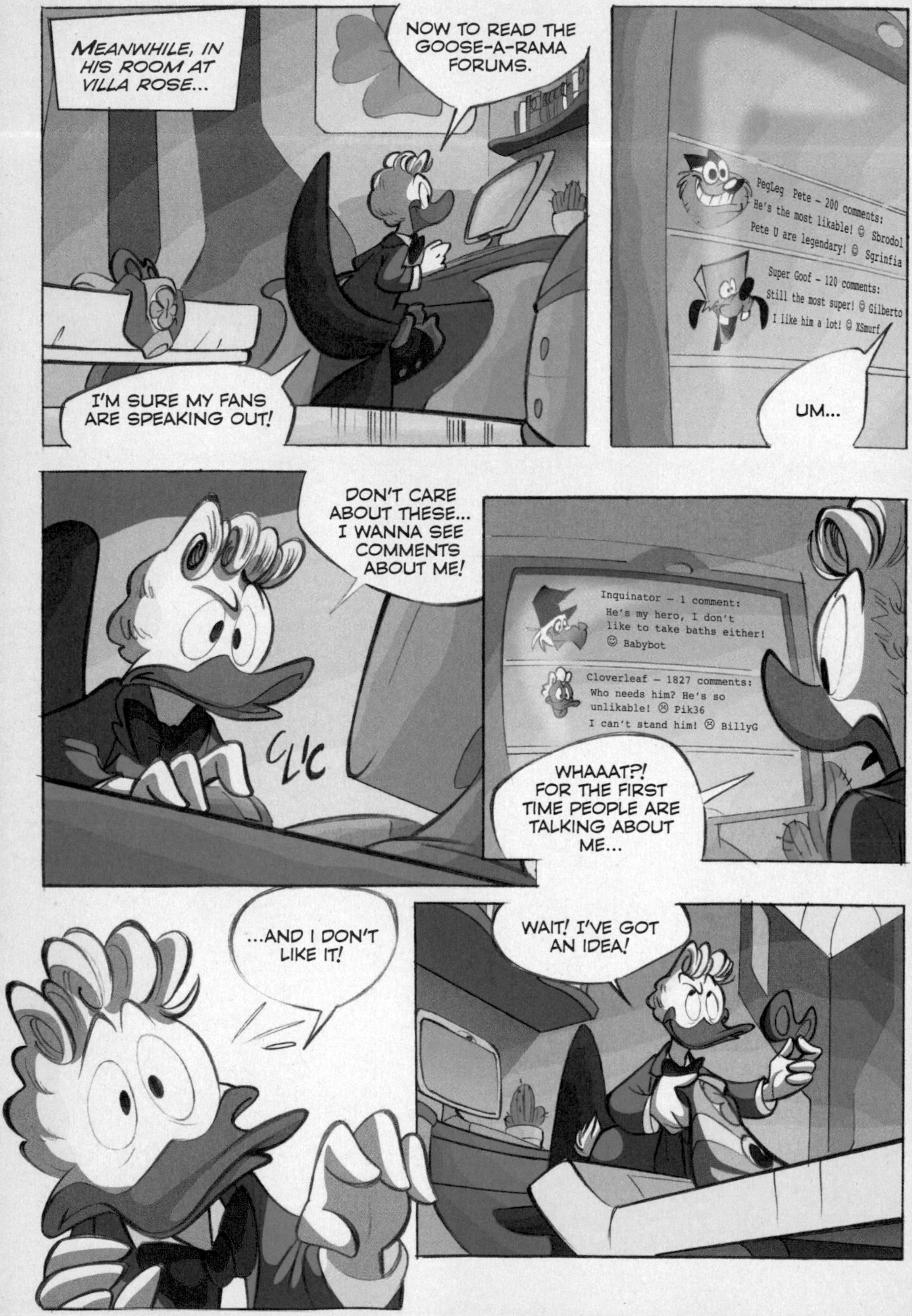
MEANWHILE, IN HIS ROOM AT VILLA ROSE...
NOW TO READ THE GOOSE-A-RAMA FORUMS.
I'M SURE MY FANS ARE SPEAKING OUT!
PegLeg Pete – 200 comments:
He's the most likable! ☺ Sbrodol
Pete U are legendary! ☺ Sgrinfia
Super Goof – 120 comments:
Still the most super! ☺ Gilberto
I like him a lot! ☺ XSmurf
UM...
DON'T CARE ABOUT THESE... I WANNA SEE COMMENTS ABOUT ME!
CLIC
Inquinator – 1 comment:
He's my hero, I don't like to take baths either! ☺ Babybot
Cloverleaf – 1827 comments:
Who needs him? He's so unlikable! ☹ Pik36
I can't stand him! ☹ BillyG
WHAAAT?! FOR THE FIRST TIME PEOPLE ARE TALKING ABOUT ME...
...AND I DON'T LIKE IT!
WAIT! I'VE GOT AN IDEA!

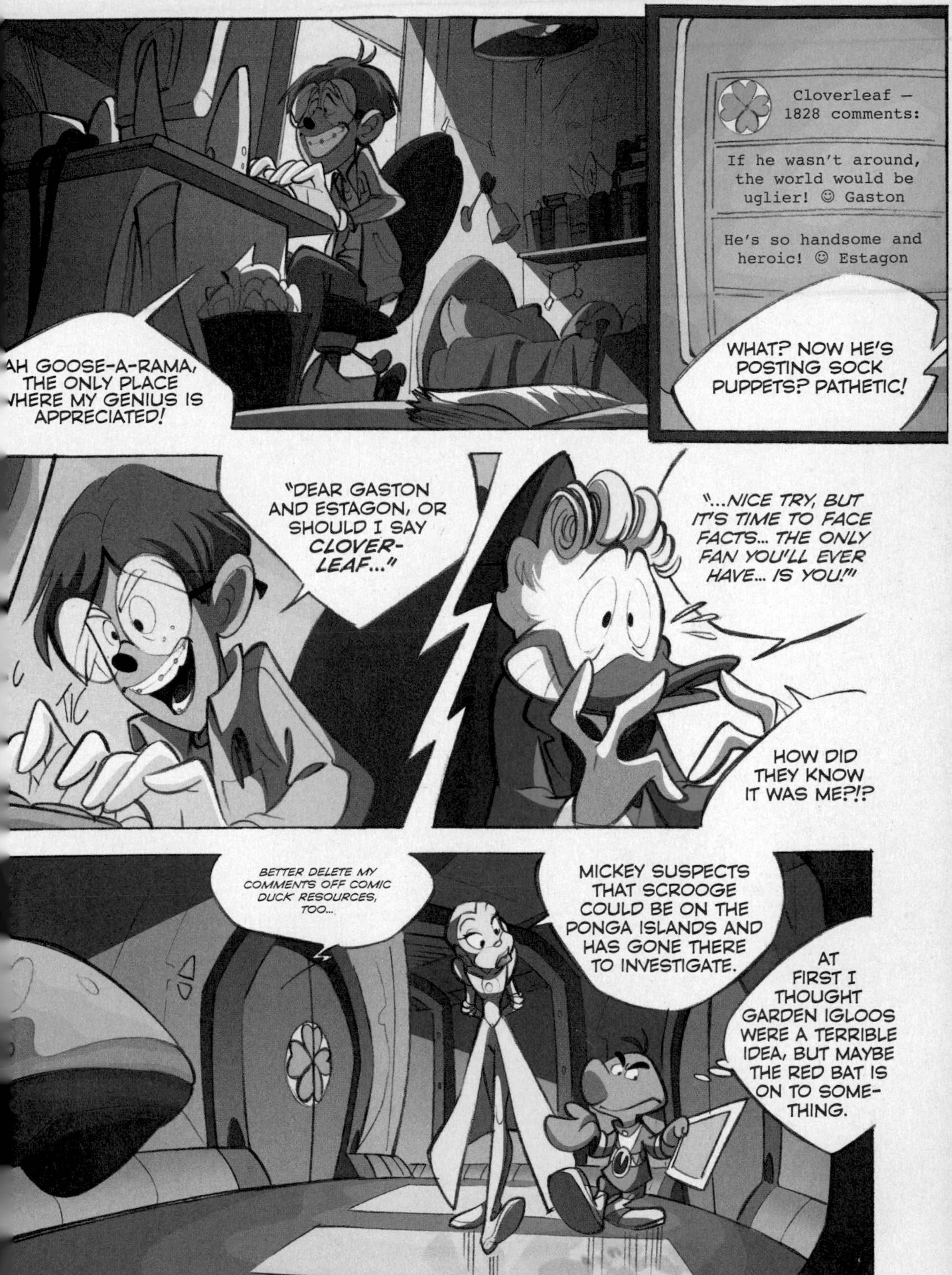
AH GOOSE-A-RAMA, THE ONLY PLACE HERE MY GENIUS IS APPRECIATED!
Cloverleaf — 1828 comments:
If he wasn't around, the world would be uglier! ☺ Gaston
He's so handsome and heroic! ☺ Estagon
WHAT? NOW HE'S POSTING SOCK PUPPETS? PATHETIC!
"DEAR GASTON AND ESTAGON, OR SHOULD I SAY *CLOVER-LEAF*..."
TIC
"...*NICE TRY, BUT IT'S TIME TO FACE FACTS... THE ONLY FAN YOU'LL EVER HAVE... IS YOU!*"
HOW DID THEY KNOW IT WAS ME?!?
BETTER DELETE MY COMMENTS OFF COMIC DUCK RESOURCES, TOO...
MICKEY SUSPECTS THAT SCROOGE COULD BE ON THE PONGA ISLANDS AND HAS GONE THERE TO INVESTIGATE.
AT FIRST I THOUGHT GARDEN IGLOOS WERE A TERRIBLE IDEA, BUT MAYBE THE RED BAT IS ON TO SOME-THING.

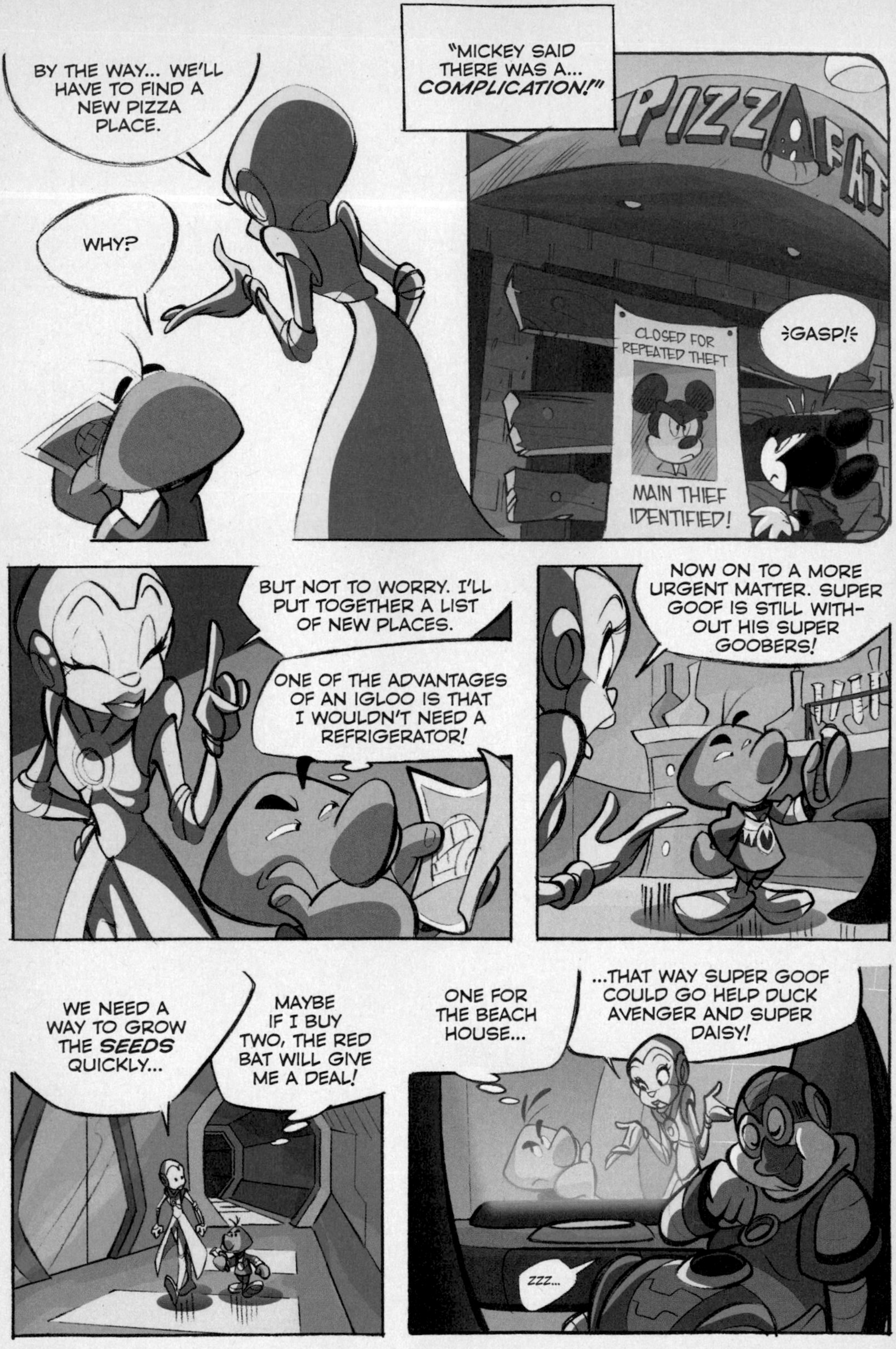
BY THE WAY... WE'LL HAVE TO FIND A NEW PIZZA PLACE.
WHY?
"MICKEY SAID THERE WAS A... *COMPLICATION!*"
PIZZA
CLOSED FOR REPEATED THEFT
MAIN THIEF IDENTIFIED!
GASP!
BUT NOT TO WORRY. I'LL PUT TOGETHER A LIST OF NEW PLACES.
ONE OF THE ADVANTAGES OF AN IGLOO IS THAT I WOULDN'T NEED A REFRIGERATOR!
NOW ON TO A MORE URGENT MATTER. SUPER GOOF IS STILL WITHOUT HIS SUPER GOOBERS!
WE NEED A WAY TO GROW THE *SEEDS* QUICKLY...
MAYBE IF I BUY TWO, THE RED BAT WILL GIVE ME A DEAL!
ONE FOR THE BEACH HOUSE...
...THAT WAY SUPER GOOF COULD GO HELP DUCK AVENGER AND SUPER DAISY!
ZZZ...

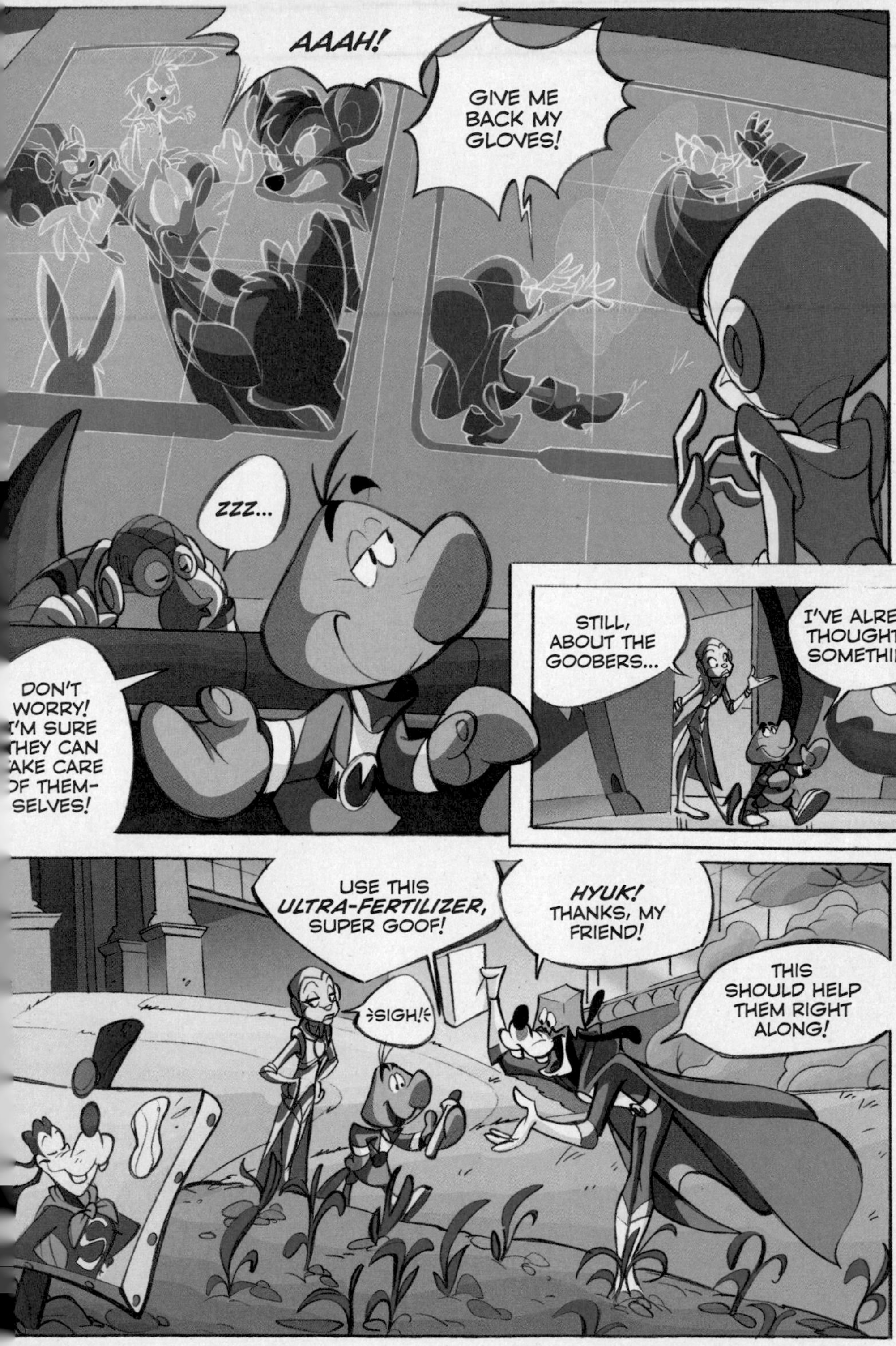
AAAH!
GIVE ME BACK MY GLOVES!
ZZZ...
DON'T WORRY! I'M SURE THEY CAN TAKE CARE OF THEM-SELVES!
STILL, ABOUT THE GOOBERS...
I'VE ALREADY THOUGHT OF SOMETHING!
USE THIS ULTRA-FERTILIZER, SUPER GOOF!
HYUK! THANKS, MY FRIEND!
SIGH!
THIS SHOULD HELP THEM RIGHT ALONG!

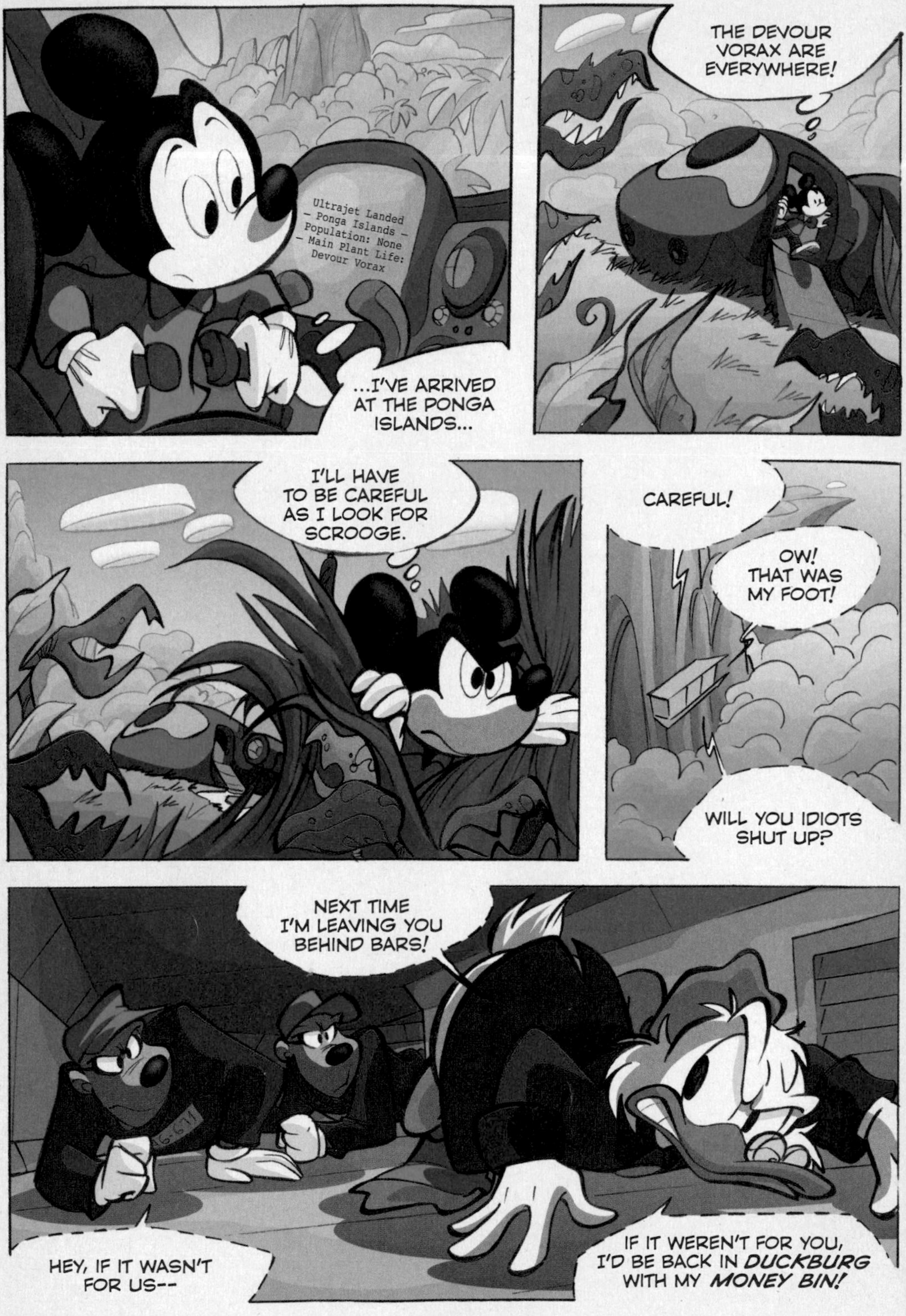
Ultrajet Landed
– Ponga Islands –
Population: None
– Main Plant Life:
Devour Vorax
...I'VE ARRIVED AT THE PONGA ISLANDS...
THE DEVOUR VORAX ARE EVERYWHERE!
I'LL HAVE TO BE CAREFUL AS I LOOK FOR SCROOGE.
CAREFUL!
OW! THAT WAS MY FOOT!
WILL YOU IDIOTS SHUT UP?
NEXT TIME I'M LEAVING YOU BEHIND BARS!
HEY, IF IT WASN'T FOR US--
IF IT WEREN'T FOR YOU, I'D BE BACK IN DUCKBURG WITH MY MONEY BIN!

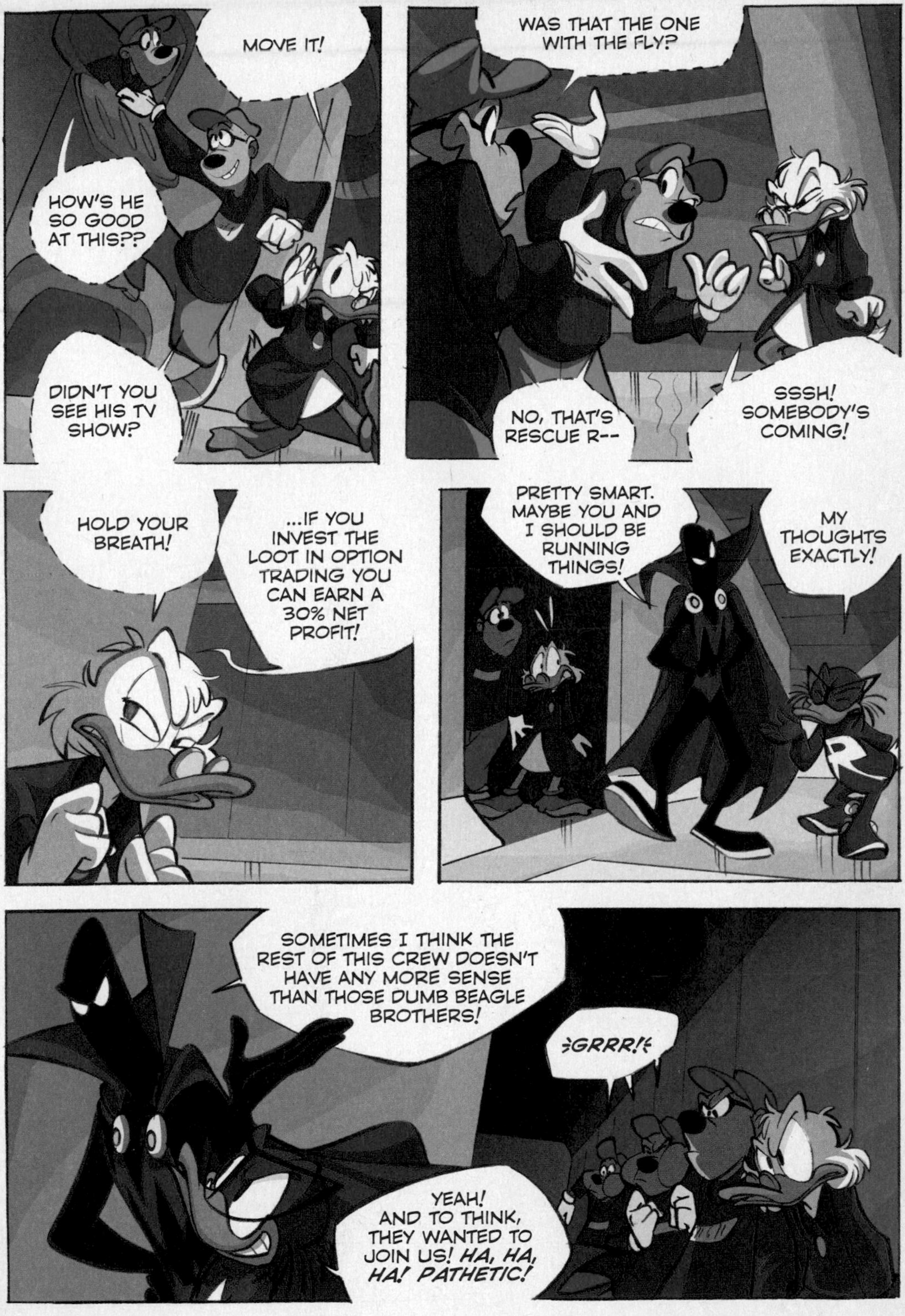

MOVE IT!
HOW'S HE SO GOOD AT THIS??
DIDN'T YOU SEE HIS TV SHOW?
WAS THAT THE ONE WITH THE FLY?
NO, THAT'S RESCUE R--
SSSH! SOMEBODY'S COMING!
HOLD YOUR BREATH!
...IF YOU INVEST THE LOOT IN OPTION TRADING YOU CAN EARN A 30% NET PROFIT!
PRETTY SMART. MAYBE YOU AND I SHOULD BE RUNNING THINGS!
MY THOUGHTS EXACTLY!
SOMETIMES I THINK THE REST OF THIS CREW DOESN'T HAVE ANY MORE SENSE THAN THOSE DUMB BEAGLE BROTHERS!
GRRR!
YEAH! AND TO THINK, THEY WANTED TO JOIN US! *HA, HA, HA! PATHETIC!*

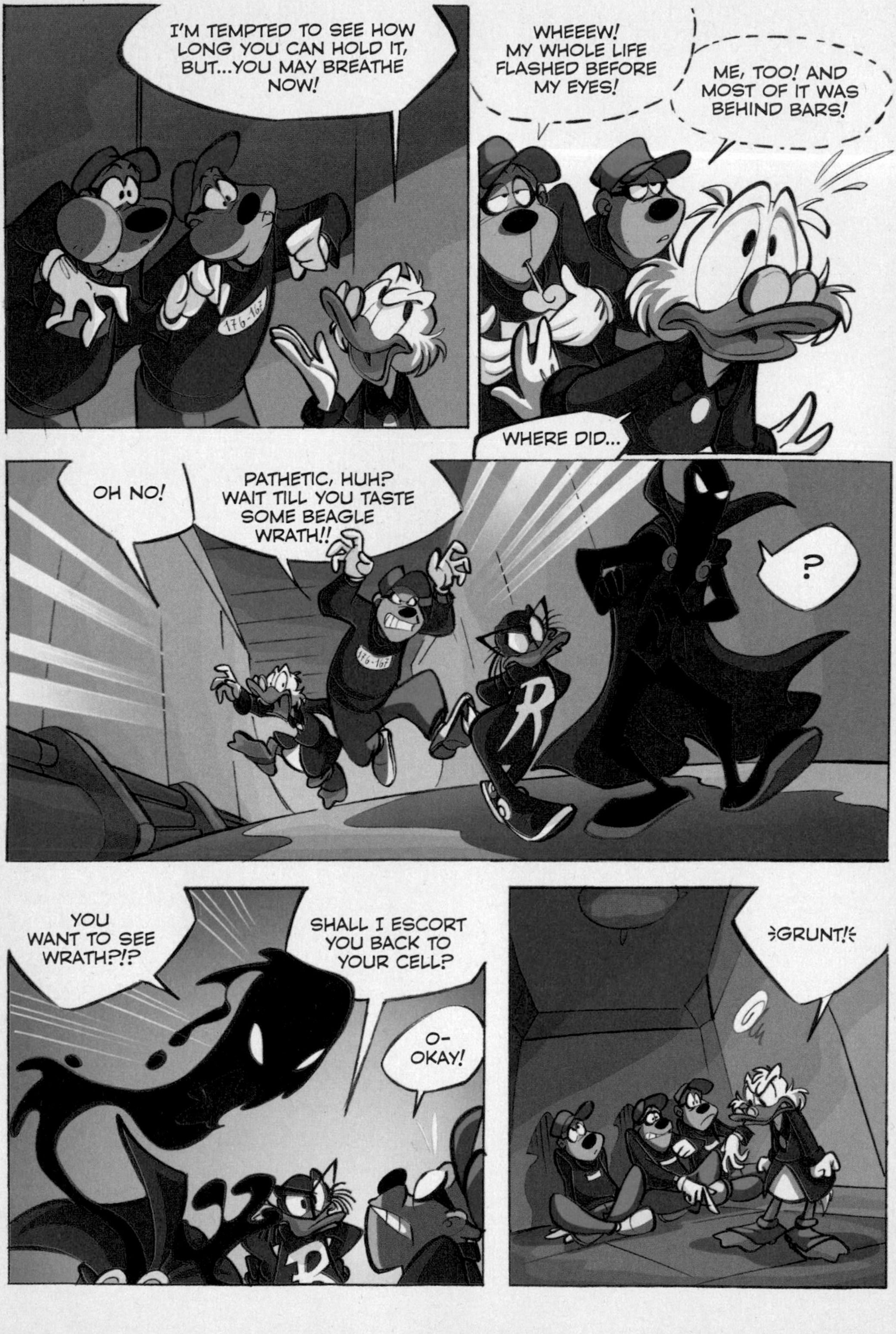
I'M TEMPTED TO SEE HOW LONG YOU CAN HOLD IT, BUT...YOU MAY BREATHE NOW!
WHEEEW! MY WHOLE LIFE FLASHED BEFORE MY EYES!
ME, TOO! AND MOST OF IT WAS BEHIND BARS!
176-167
WHERE DID...
OH NO!
PATHETIC, HUH? WAIT TILL YOU TASTE SOME BEAGLE WRATH!!
?
176-167
YOU WANT TO SEE WRATH?!?
SHALL I ESCORT YOU BACK TO YOUR CELL?
O-OKAY!
GRUNT!

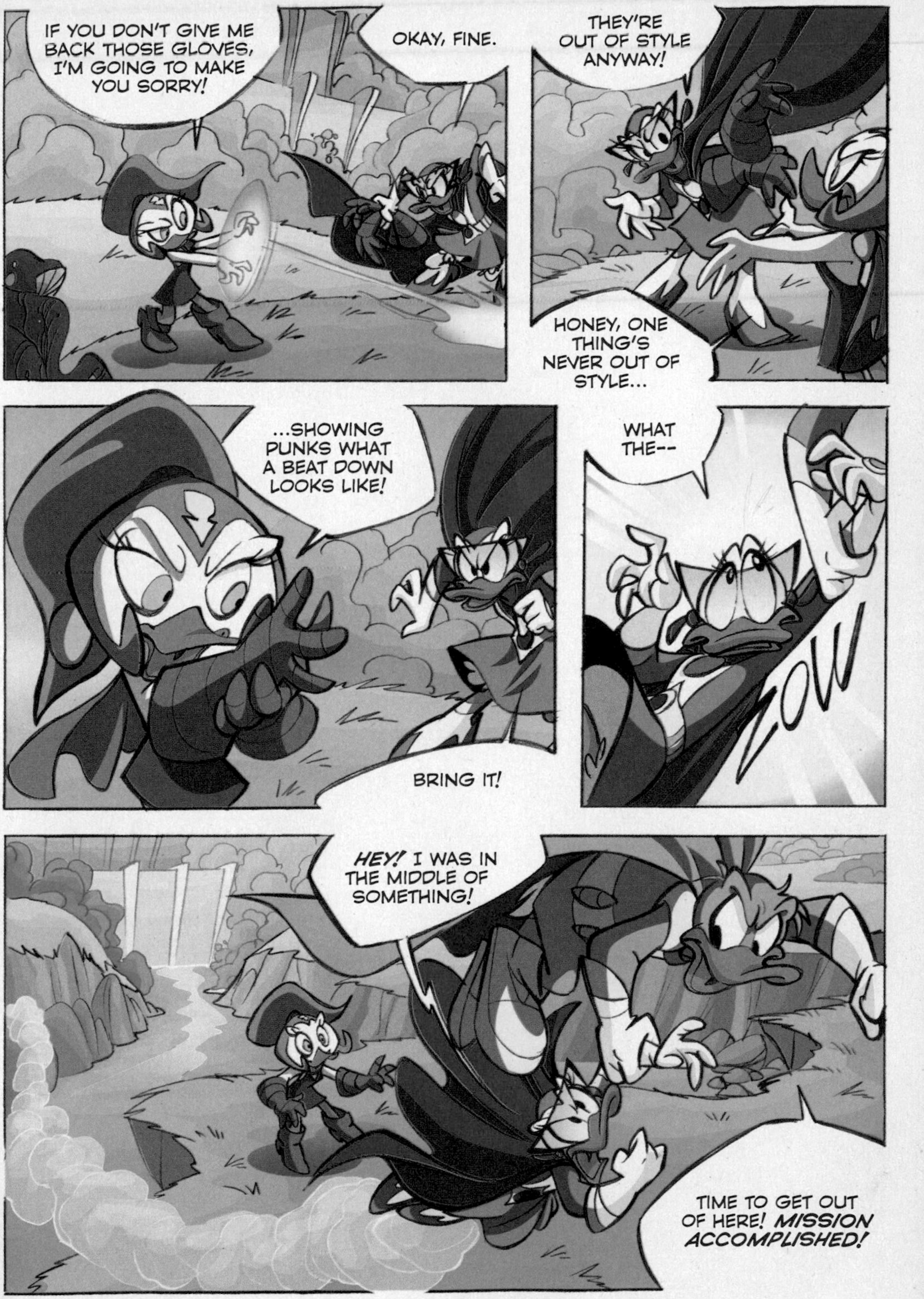
IF YOU DON'T GIVE ME BACK THOSE GLOVES, I'M GOING TO MAKE YOU SORRY!
OKAY, FINE.
THEY'RE OUT OF STYLE ANYWAY!
HONEY, ONE THING'S NEVER OUT OF STYLE...
...SHOWING PUNKS WHAT A BEAT DOWN LOOKS LIKE!
BRING IT!
WHAT THE--
ZOW
HEY! I WAS IN THE MIDDLE OF SOMETHING!
TIME TO GET OUT OF HERE! MISSION ACCOMPLISHED!

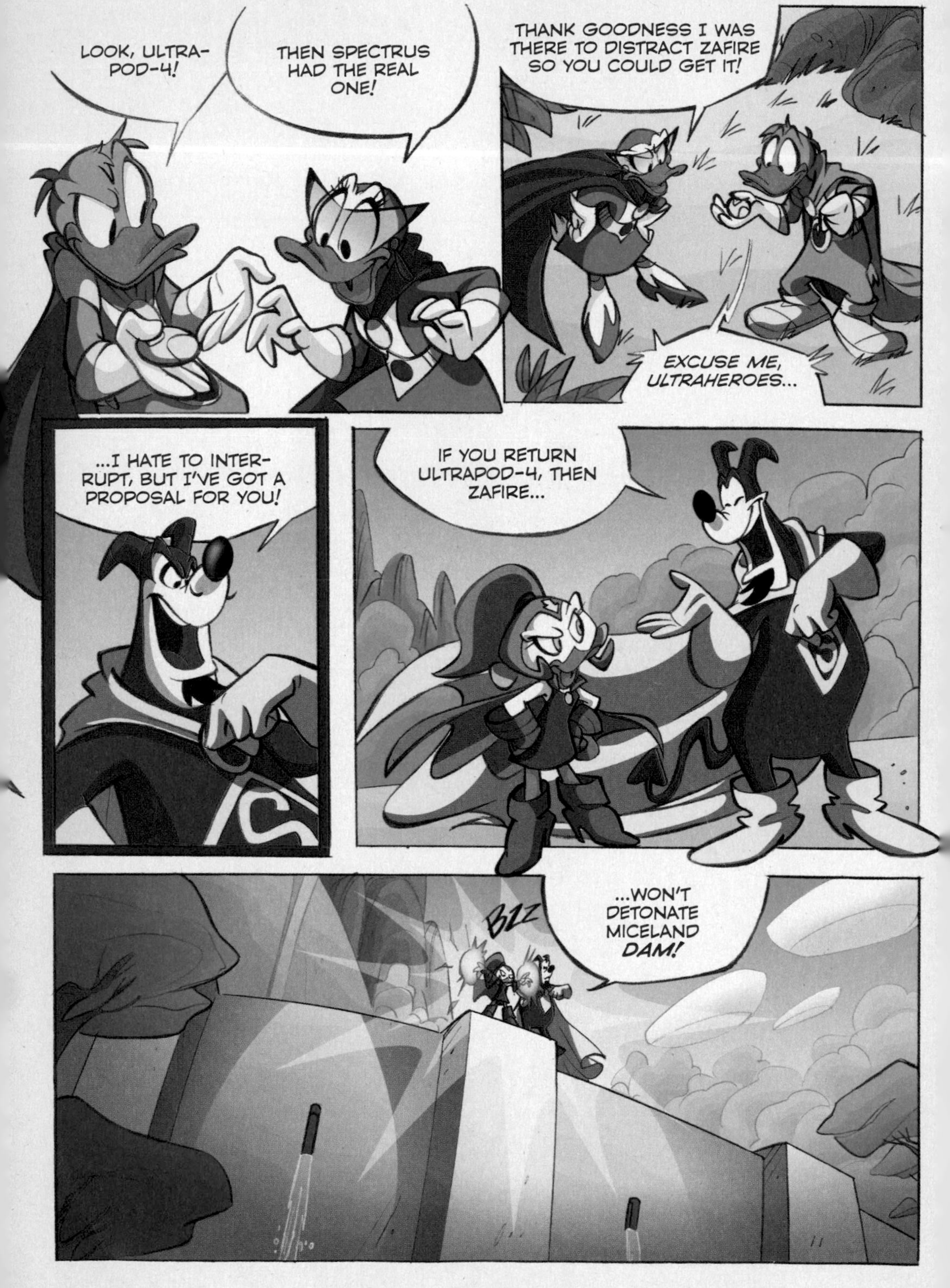
LOOK, ULTRA-POD-4!
THEN SPECTRUS HAD THE REAL ONE!
THANK GOODNESS I WAS THERE TO DISTRACT ZAFIRE SO YOU COULD GET IT!
EXCUSE ME, ULTRAHEROES...
...I HATE TO INTER-RUPT, BUT I'VE GOT A PROPOSAL FOR YOU!
IF YOU RETURN ULTRAPOD-4, THEN ZAFIRE...
BZZ
...WON'T DETONATE MICELAND DAM!

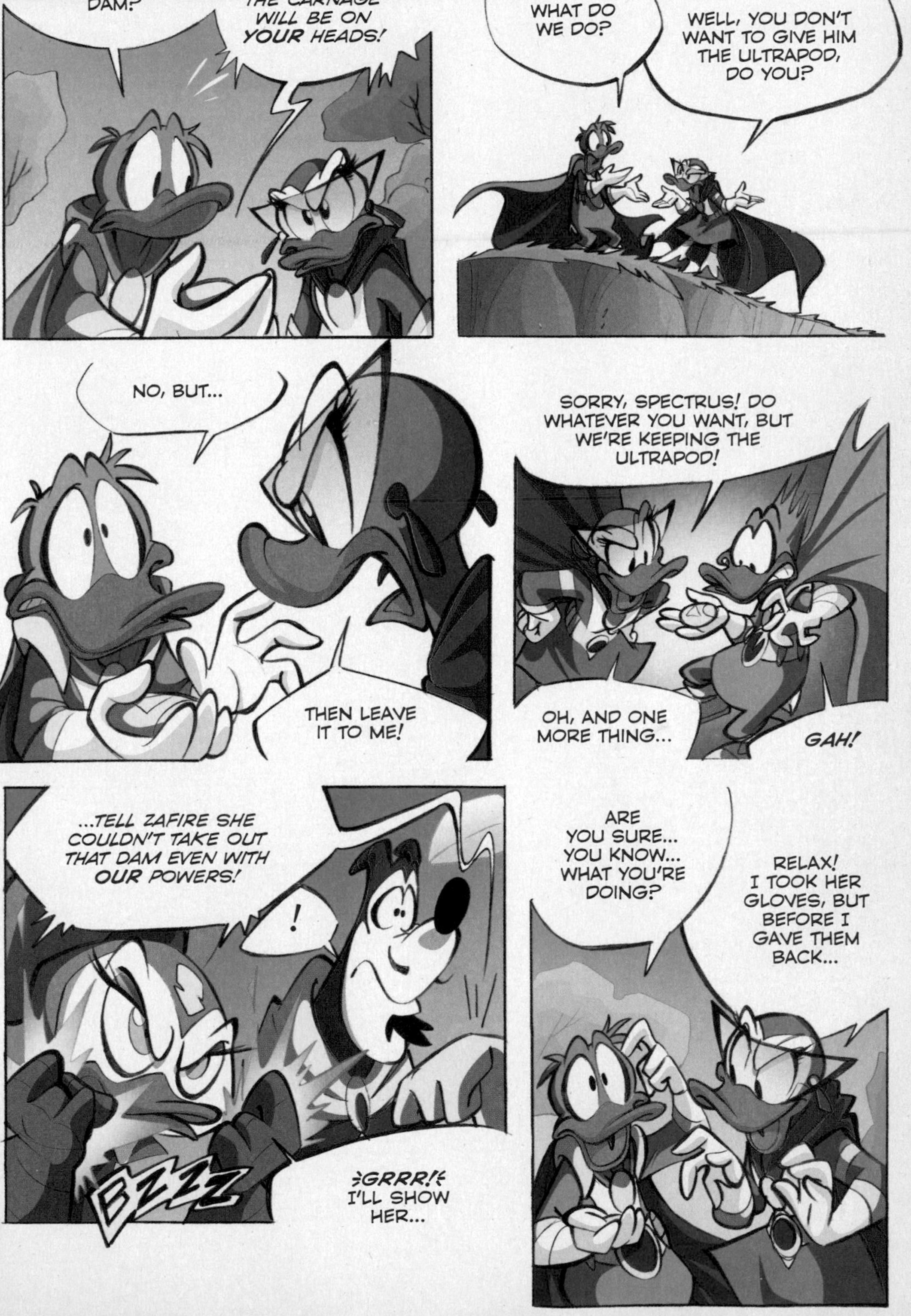

GULP! SHE'LL... BLOW UP THE DAM?
THAT'S RIGHT, AND THE CARNAGE WILL BE ON YOUR HEADS!
WHAT DO WE DO?
WELL, YOU DON'T WANT TO GIVE HIM THE ULTRAPOD, DO YOU?
NO, BUT...
THEN LEAVE IT TO ME!
SORRY, SPECTRUS! DO WHATEVER YOU WANT, BUT WE'RE KEEPING THE ULTRAPOD!
OH, AND ONE MORE THING...
GAH!
...TELL ZAFIRE SHE COULDN'T TAKE OUT THAT DAM EVEN WITH OUR POWERS!
!
BZZZ
GRRR! I'LL SHOW HER...
ARE YOU SURE... YOU KNOW... WHAT YOU'RE DOING?
RELAX! I TOOK HER GLOVES, BUT BEFORE I GAVE THEM BACK...

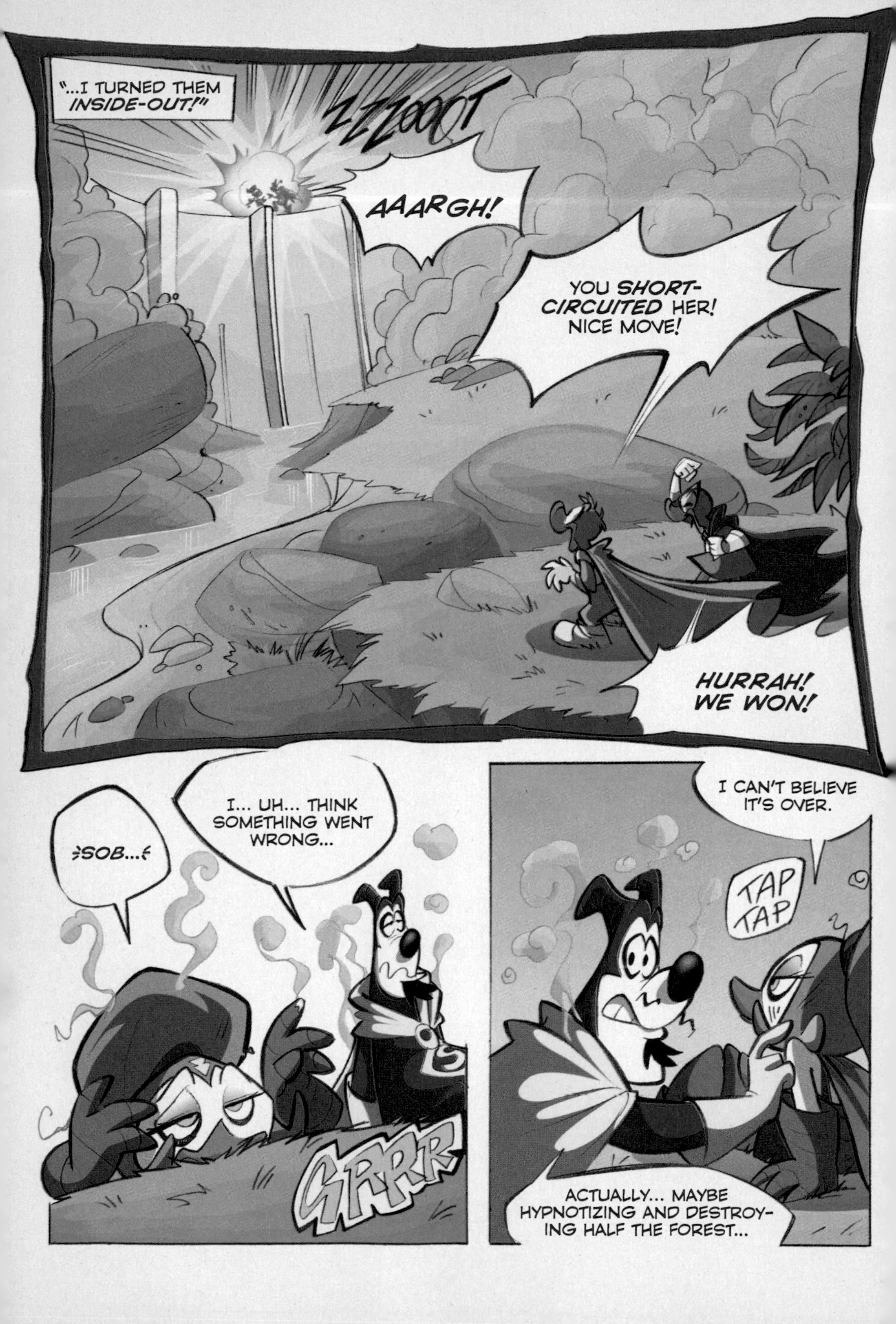
"...I TURNED THEM INSIDE-OUT!"
ZZZOOOT
AAARGH!
YOU SHORT-CIRCUITED HER! NICE MOVE!
HURRAH! WE WON!
≈SOB...≈
I... UH... THINK SOMETHING WENT WRONG...
SPRRR
I CAN'T BELIEVE IT'S OVER.
TAP TAP
ACTUALLY... MAYBE HYPNOTIZING AND DESTROY-ING HALF THE FOREST...

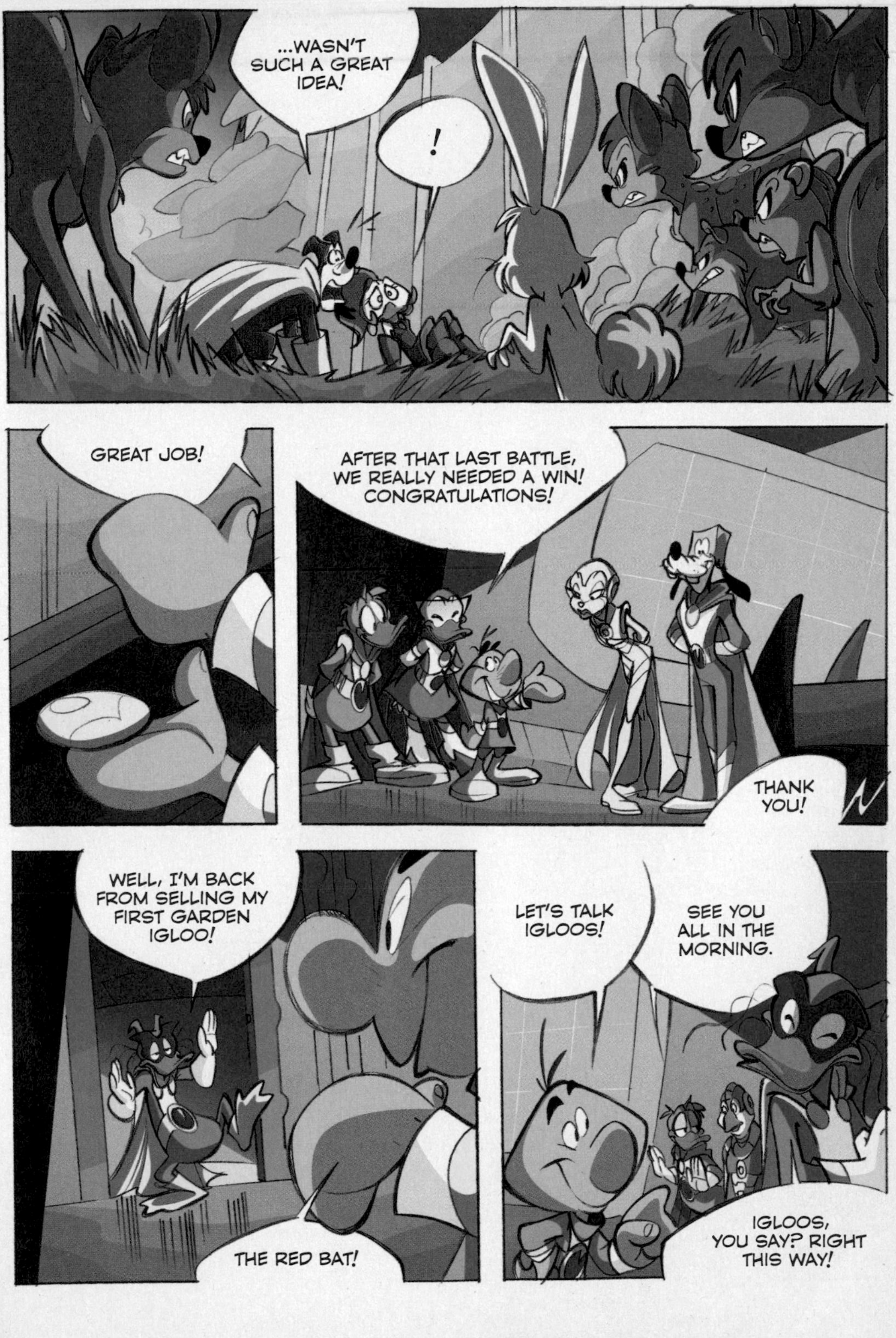
...WASN'T SUCH A GREAT IDEA!
!
GREAT JOB!
AFTER THAT LAST BATTLE, WE REALLY NEEDED A WIN! CONGRATULATIONS!
THANK YOU!
WELL, I'M BACK FROM SELLING MY FIRST GARDEN IGLOO!
THE RED BAT!
LET'S TALK IGLOOS!
SEE YOU ALL IN THE MORNING.
IGLOOS, YOU SAY? RIGHT THIS WAY!

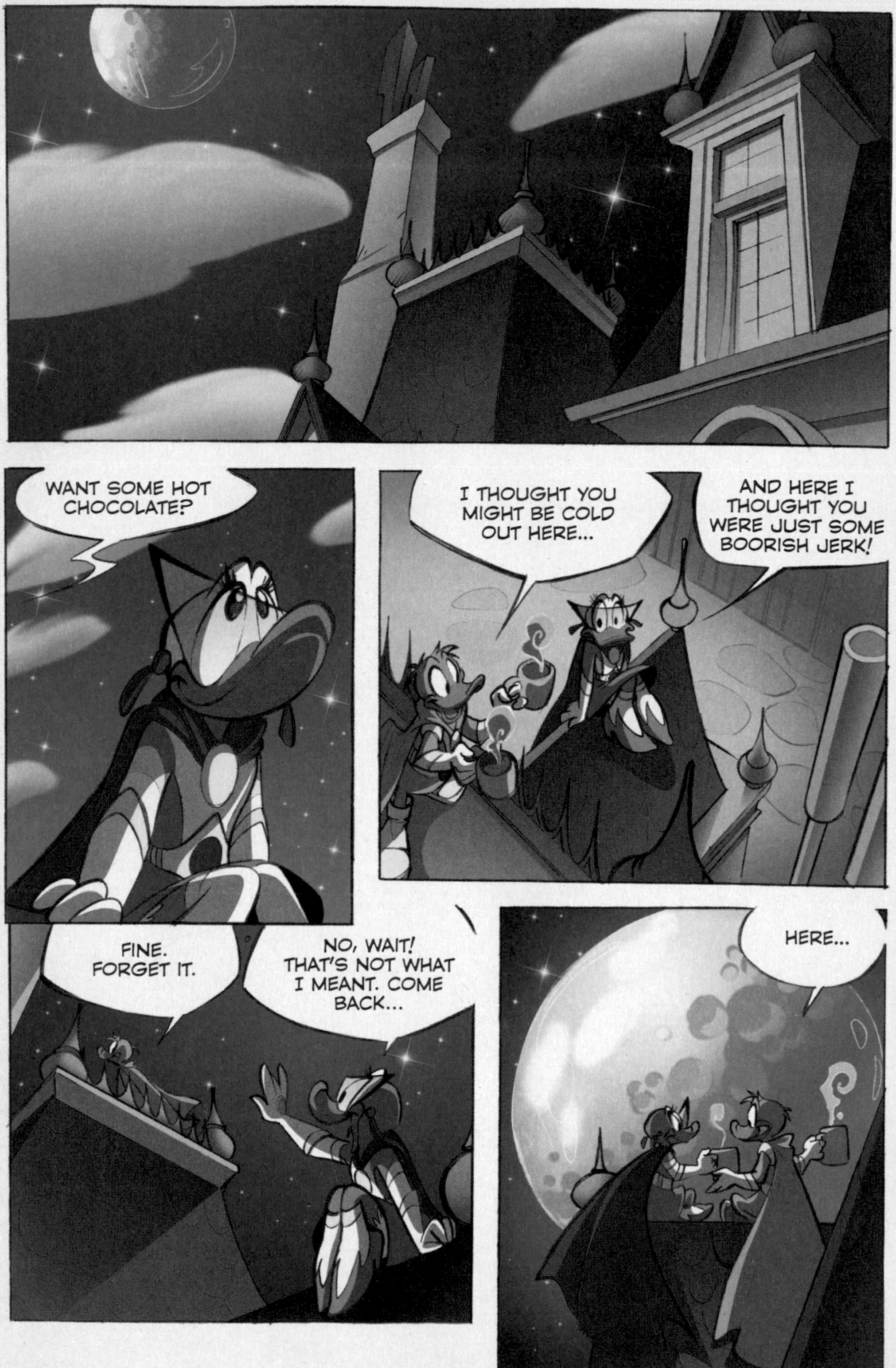
WANT SOME HOT CHOCOLATE?
I THOUGHT YOU MIGHT BE COLD OUT HERE...
AND HERE I THOUGHT YOU WERE JUST SOME BOORISH JERK!
FINE. FORGET IT.
NO, WAIT! THAT'S NOT WHAT I MEANT. COME BACK...
HERE...

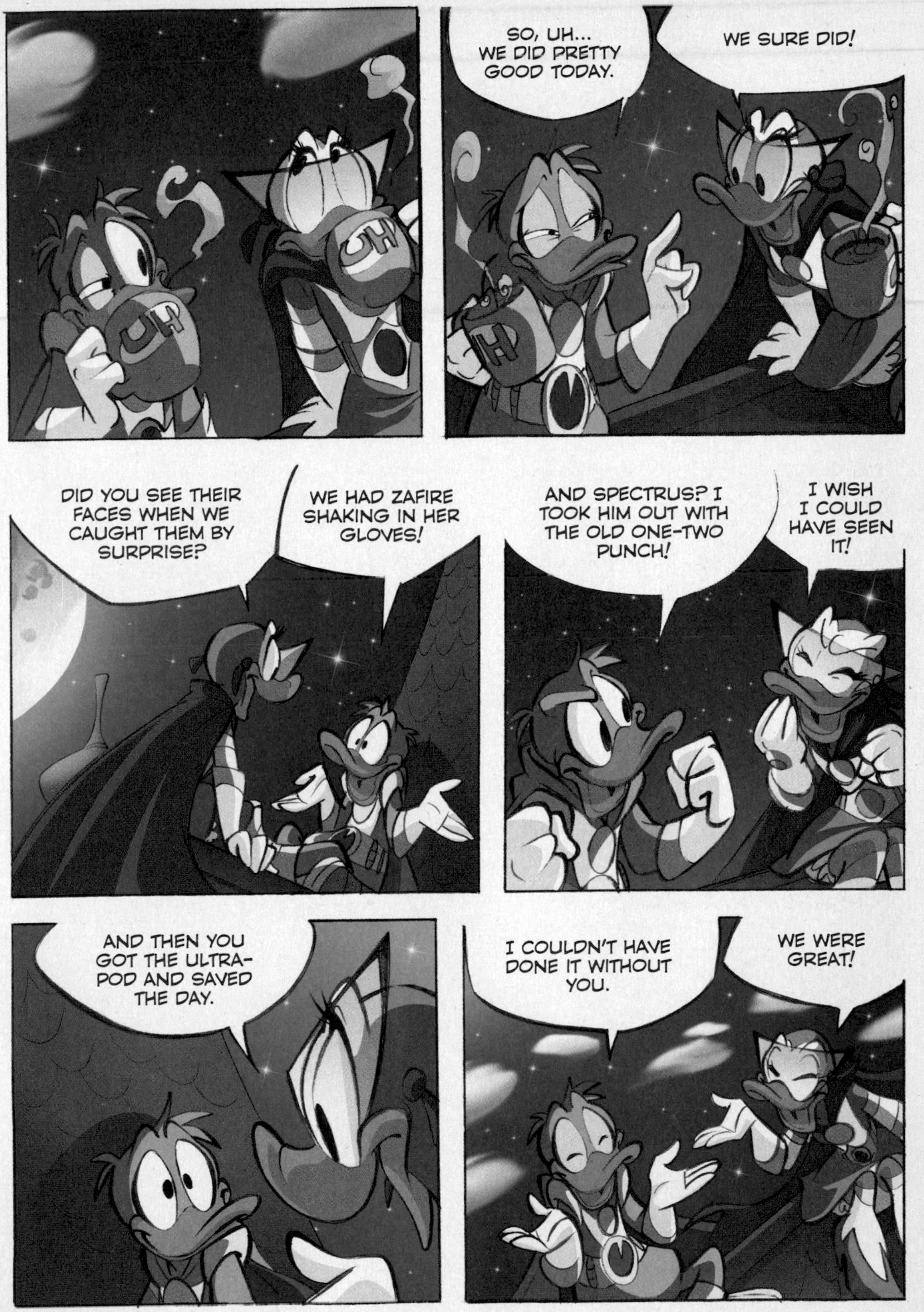
SO, UH... WE DID PRETTY GOOD TODAY.
WE SURE DID!
DID YOU SEE THEIR FACES WHEN WE CAUGHT THEM BY SURPRISE?
WE HAD ZAFIRE SHAKING IN HER GLOVES!
AND SPECTRUS? I TOOK HIM OUT WITH THE OLD ONE-TWO PUNCH!
I WISH I COULD HAVE SEEN IT!
AND THEN YOU GOT THE ULTRA-POD AND SAVED THE DAY.
I COULDN'T HAVE DONE IT WITHOUT YOU.
WE WERE GREAT!

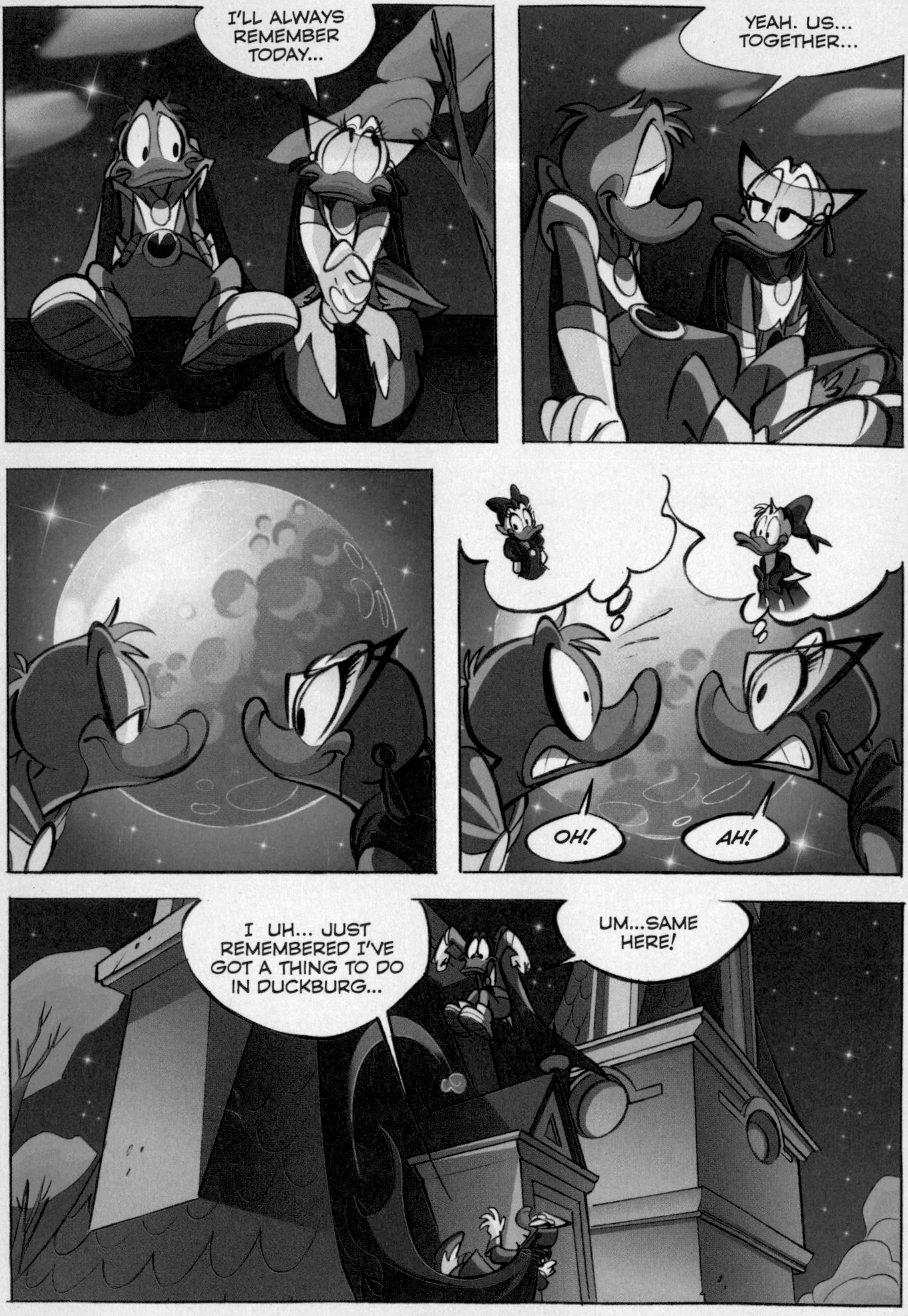
I'LL ALWAYS REMEMBER TODAY...
YEAH. US... TOGETHER...
OH!
AH!
I UH... JUST REMEMBERED I'VE GOT A THING TO DO IN DUCKBURG...
UM...SAME HERE!

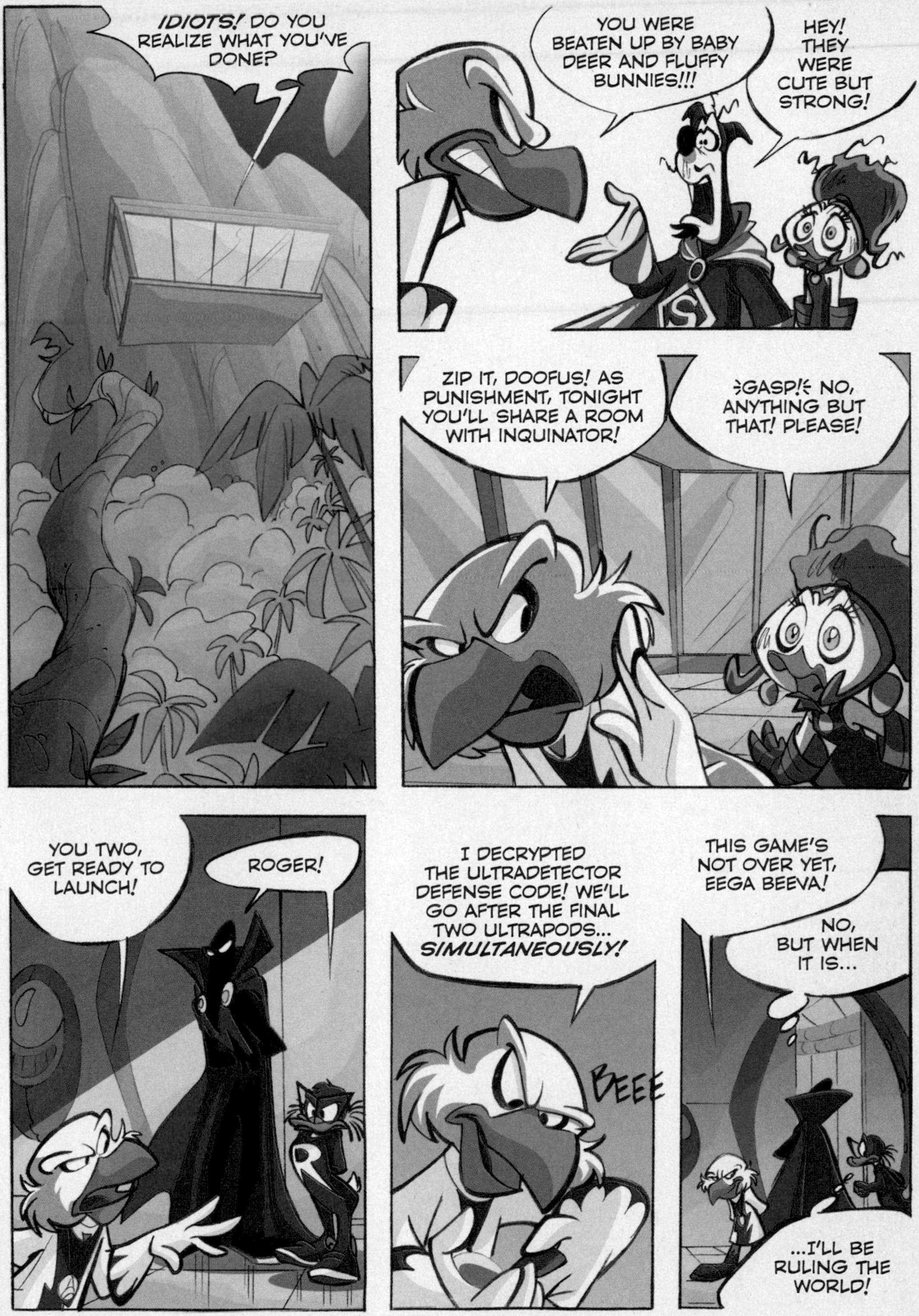
IDIOTS! DO YOU REALIZE WHAT YOU'VE DONE?
YOU WERE BEATEN UP BY BABY DEER AND FLUFFY BUNNIES!!!
HEY! THEY WERE CUTE BUT STRONG!
ZIP IT, DOOFUS! AS PUNISHMENT, TONIGHT YOU'LL SHARE A ROOM WITH INQUINATOR!
GASP! NO, ANYTHING BUT THAT! PLEASE!
YOU TWO, GET READY TO LAUNCH!
ROGER!
I DECRYPTED THE ULTRADETECTOR DEFENSE CODE! WE'LL GO AFTER THE FINAL TWO ULTRAPODS... SIMULTANEOUSLY!
BEEE
THIS GAME'S NOT OVER YET, EEGA BEEVA!
NO, BUT WHEN IT IS...
...I'LL BE RULING THE WORLD!

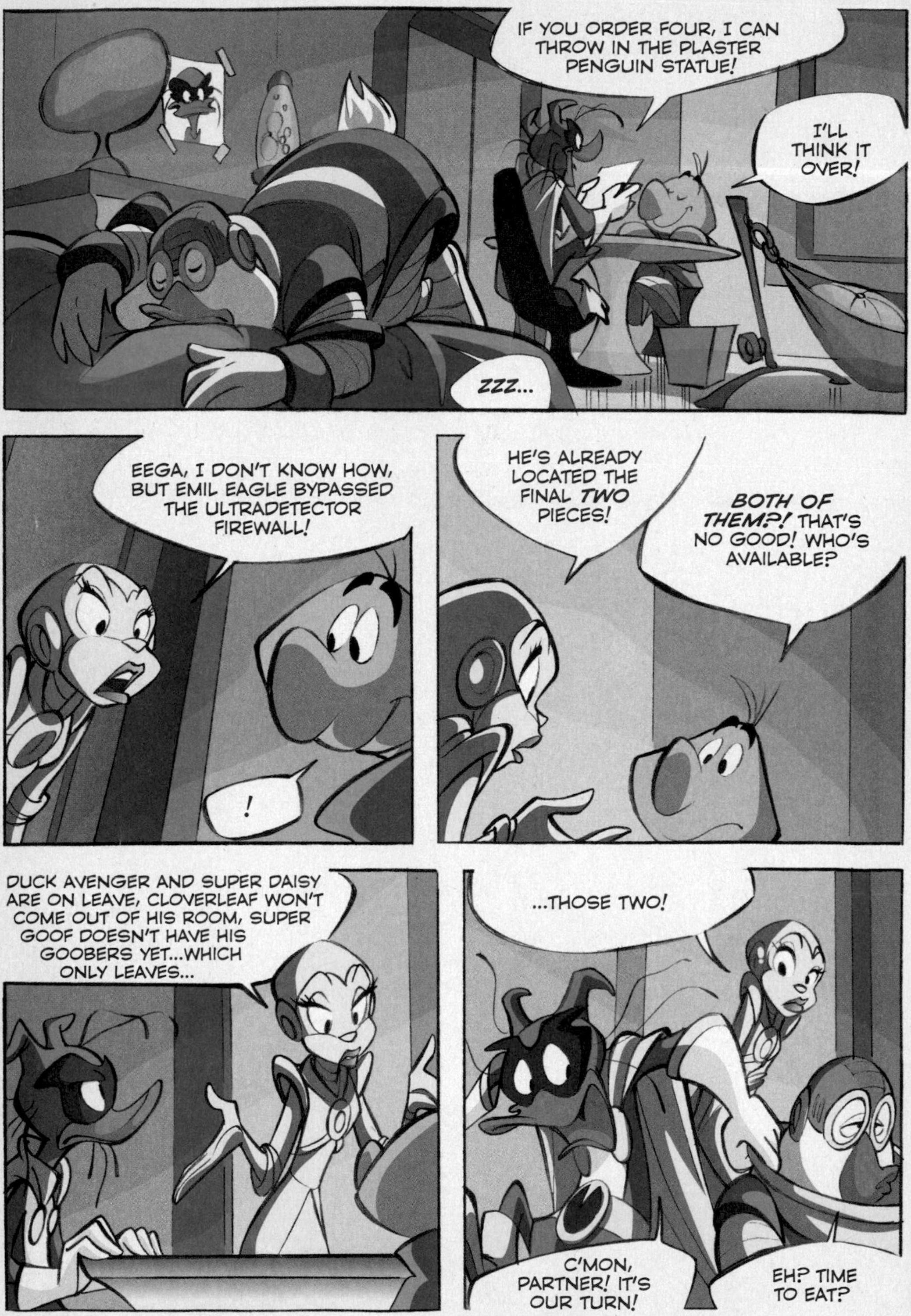
IF YOU ORDER FOUR, I CAN THROW IN THE PLASTER PENGUIN STATUE!
I'LL THINK IT OVER!
ZZZ...
EEGA, I DON'T KNOW HOW, BUT EMIL EAGLE BYPASSED THE ULTRADETECTOR FIREWALL!
!
HE'S ALREADY LOCATED THE FINAL TWO PIECES!
BOTH OF THEM?! THAT'S NO GOOD! WHO'S AVAILABLE?
DUCK AVENGER AND SUPER DAISY ARE ON LEAVE, CLOVERLEAF WON'T COME OUT OF HIS ROOM, SUPER GOOF DOESN'T HAVE HIS GOOBERS YET...WHICH ONLY LEAVES...
...THOSE TWO!
C'MON, PARTNER! IT'S OUR TURN!
EH? TIME TO EAT?

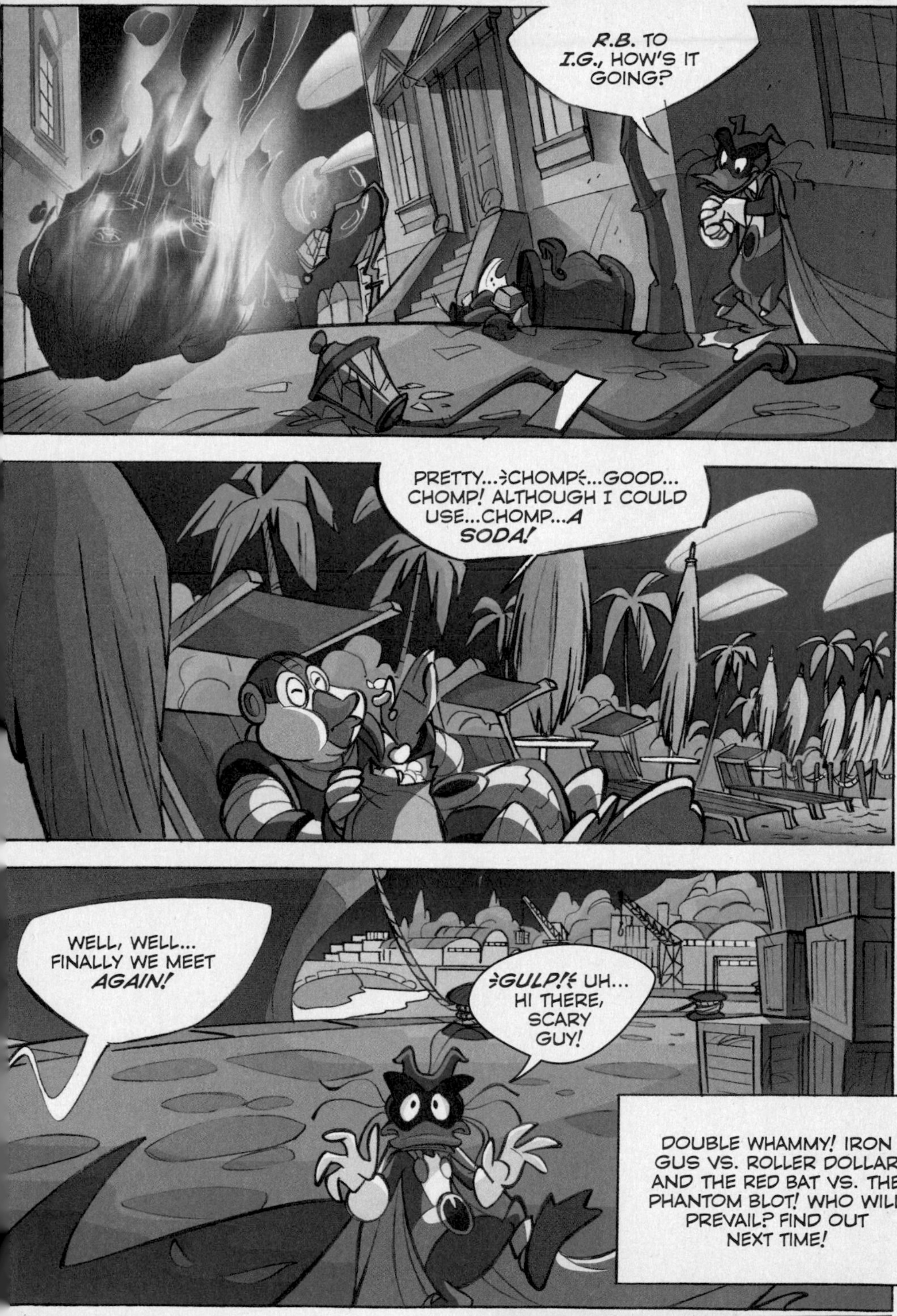
R.B. TO I.G., HOW'S IT GOING?
PRETTY...¦CHOMP¦...GOOD... CHOMP! ALTHOUGH I COULD USE...CHOMP...A SODA!
WELL, WELL... FINALLY WE MEET AGAIN!
¦GULP!¦ UH... HI THERE, SCARY GUY!
DOUBLE WHAMMY! IRON GUS VS. ROLLER DOLLAR AND THE RED BAT VS. THE PHANTOM BLOT! WHO WILL PREVAIL? FIND OUT NEXT TIME!

TO BE CONTINUED...

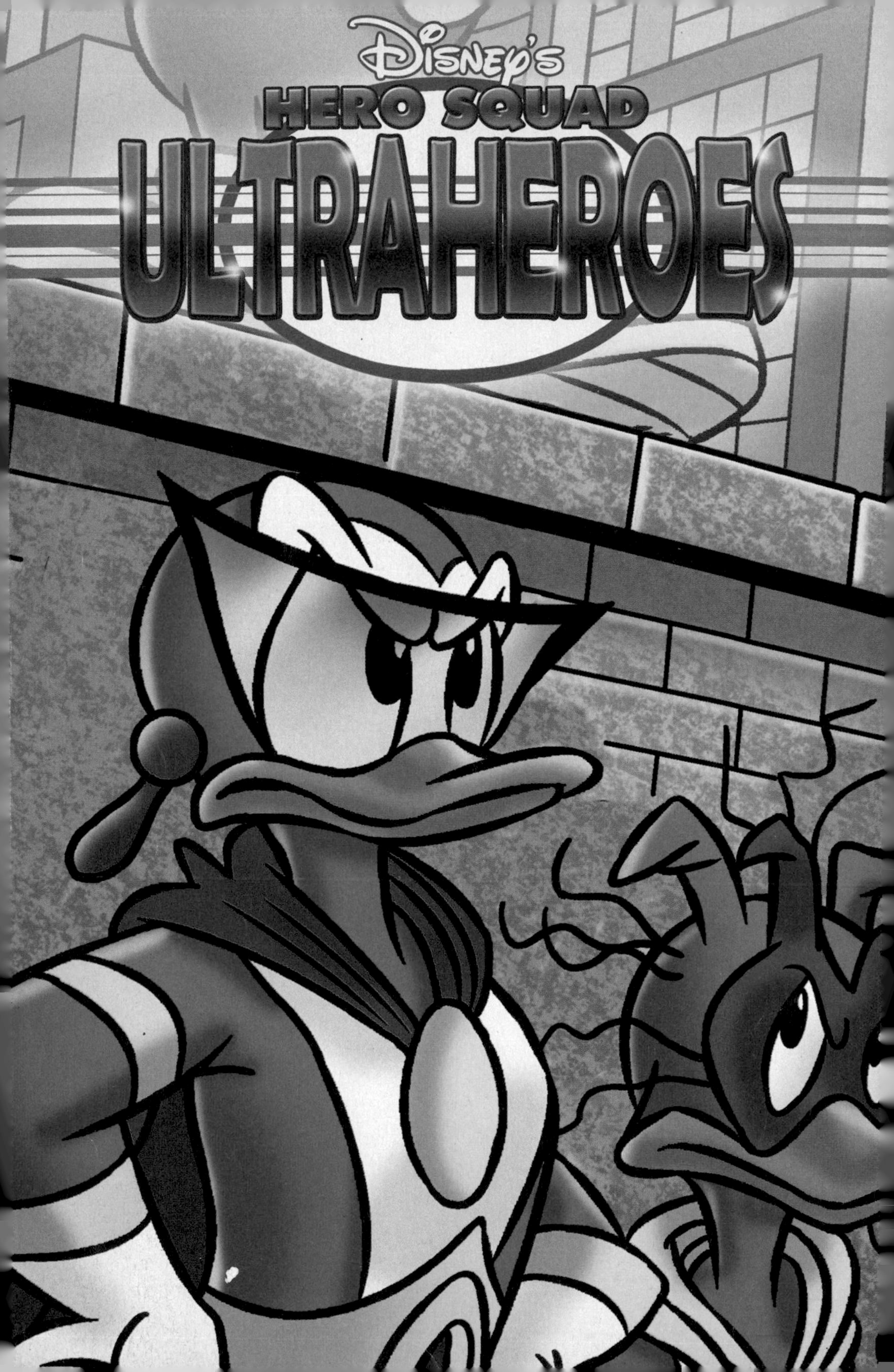
Disney's
HERO SQUAD
ULTRAHEROES

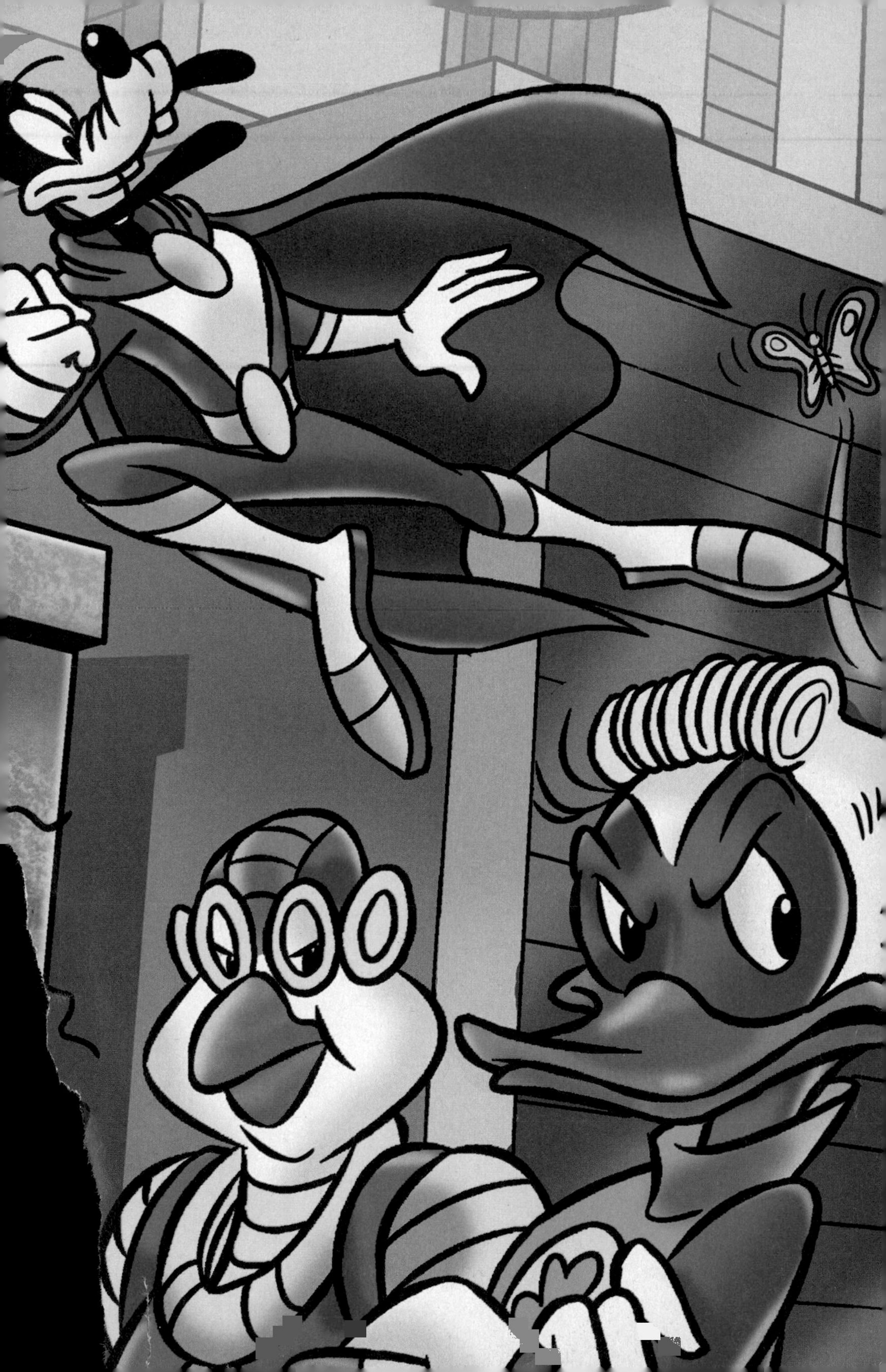

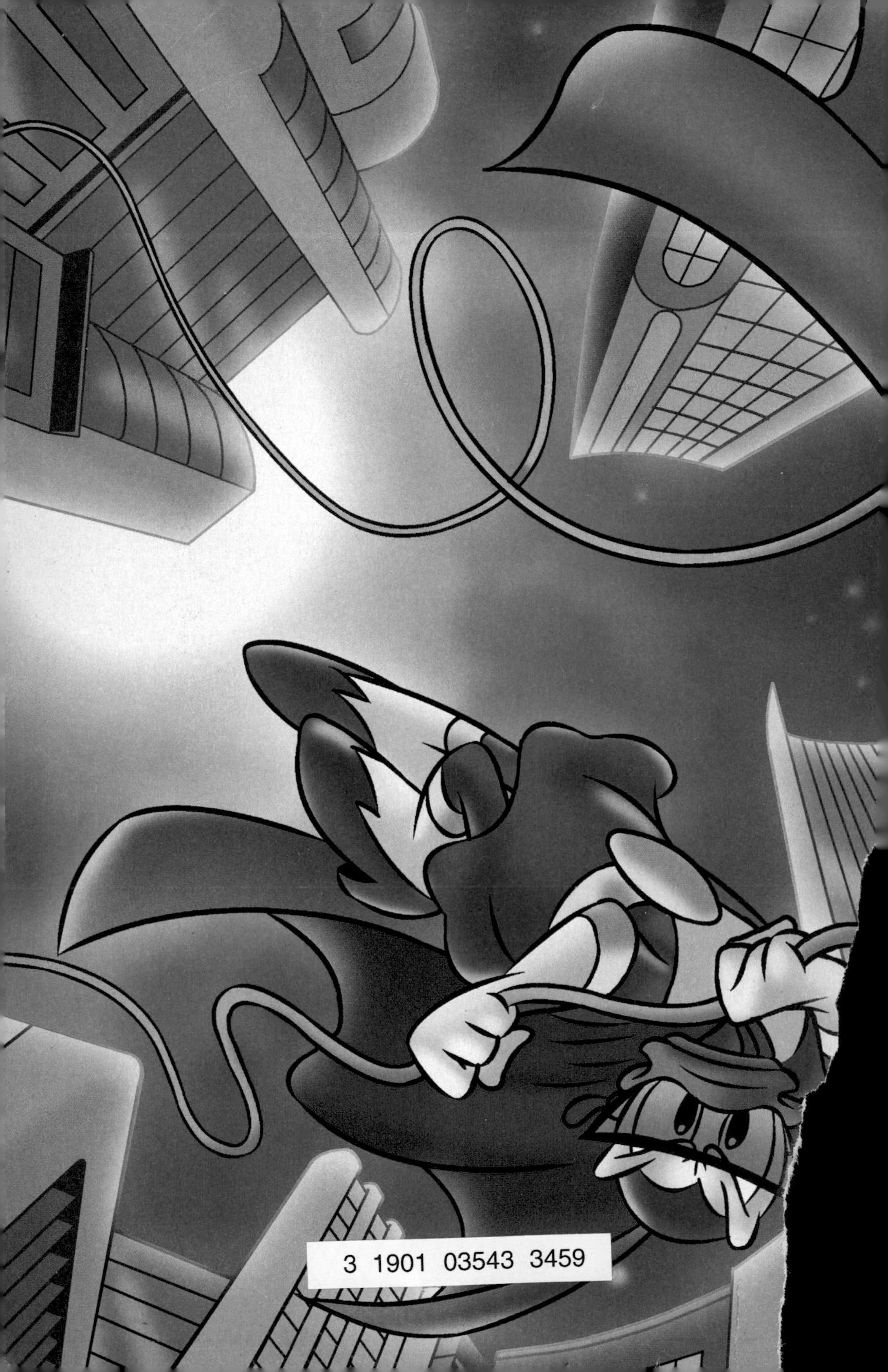